AN UNOFFICIAL GRAPHIC NOVEL
FOR MINECRAFTERS

REDSTONE JUNIOR HIGH

ZOMBIES ATE MY HOMEWORK

BOOK 1

CARA J. STEVENS

ART BY FRED BORCHERDT

SKY PONY PRESS
NEW YORK

Sky Pony Press books may be purchased in bulk at special discounts for sales promotion, corporate gifts, fund-raising, or educational purposes. Special editions can also be created to specifications. For details, contact the Special Sales Department, Sky Pony Press, 307 West 36th Street, 11th Floor, New York, NY 10018 or info@skyhorsepublishing.com.

Sky Pony® is a registered trademark of Skyhorse Publishing, Inc.®, a Delaware corporation.

Minecraft® is a registered trademark of Notch Development AB.
The Minecraft game is copyright © Mojang AB.

Visit our website at www.skyponypress.com.

10 9 8 7 6 5 4 3 2 1

Library of Congress Cataloging-in- Publication Data is available on file.

Cover design by Brian Peterson
Cover and interior art by Fred Borcherdt

Special thanks to TennisBrandon for his help with plot and character development.

Print ISBN: 978-1-51072-2323
Ebook ISBN: 978-1-51072-2330

Printed in China

Designer and Production Manager: Joshua Barnaby

REDSTONE JUNIOR HIGH

MEET THE

PIXEL: A girl with an unusual way with animals and other creatures

SKY: Pixel's first friend at Redstone Junior High

UMA: A mysterious, quiet girl who lurks in the shadows

CHARACTERS

ROB: A surprisingly friendly zombie

TINA AND THE VIOLETS: Pixel's sassy downstairs neighbor and her sidekicks

PRINCIPAL REDSTONE: The head of Redstone Junior High

INTRODUCTION

If you have played Minecraft, then you know all about Minecraft worlds. They're made of blocks you can mine, creatures you can interact with, and lands you can visit. On the outer edges of one world is an ordinary farm with ordinary animals, ordinary people, and one extraordinary girl.

The girl's name is Pixel and when our story begins, Pixel has no idea that she is destined for greatness, or even destined to be noticed by anyone other than her animal friends. The youngest of twelve brothers and sisters, Pixel has always kept to herself, preferring the company of animals and neutral mobs to other miners.

We join Pixel the day before she is set to embark on the biggest journey of her life. She is heading to the prestigious Redstone Junior High, a school for gifted students, where no hostile mob has dared enter for more than one hundred years. That is about to change.

CHAPTER 1

LEAVING HOME

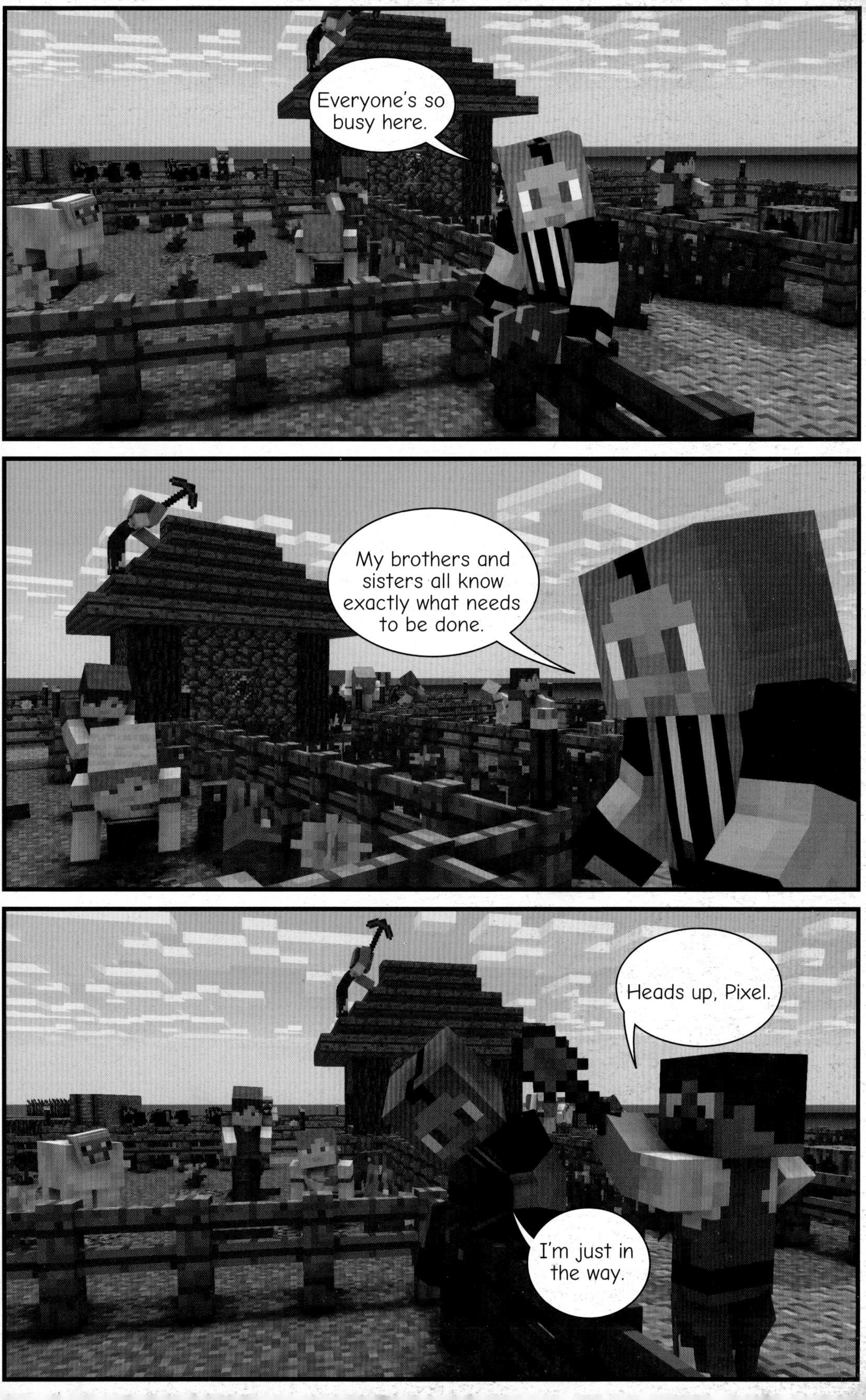
Everyone's so busy here.
My brothers and sisters all know exactly what needs to be done.
Heads up, Pixel.
I'm just in the way.

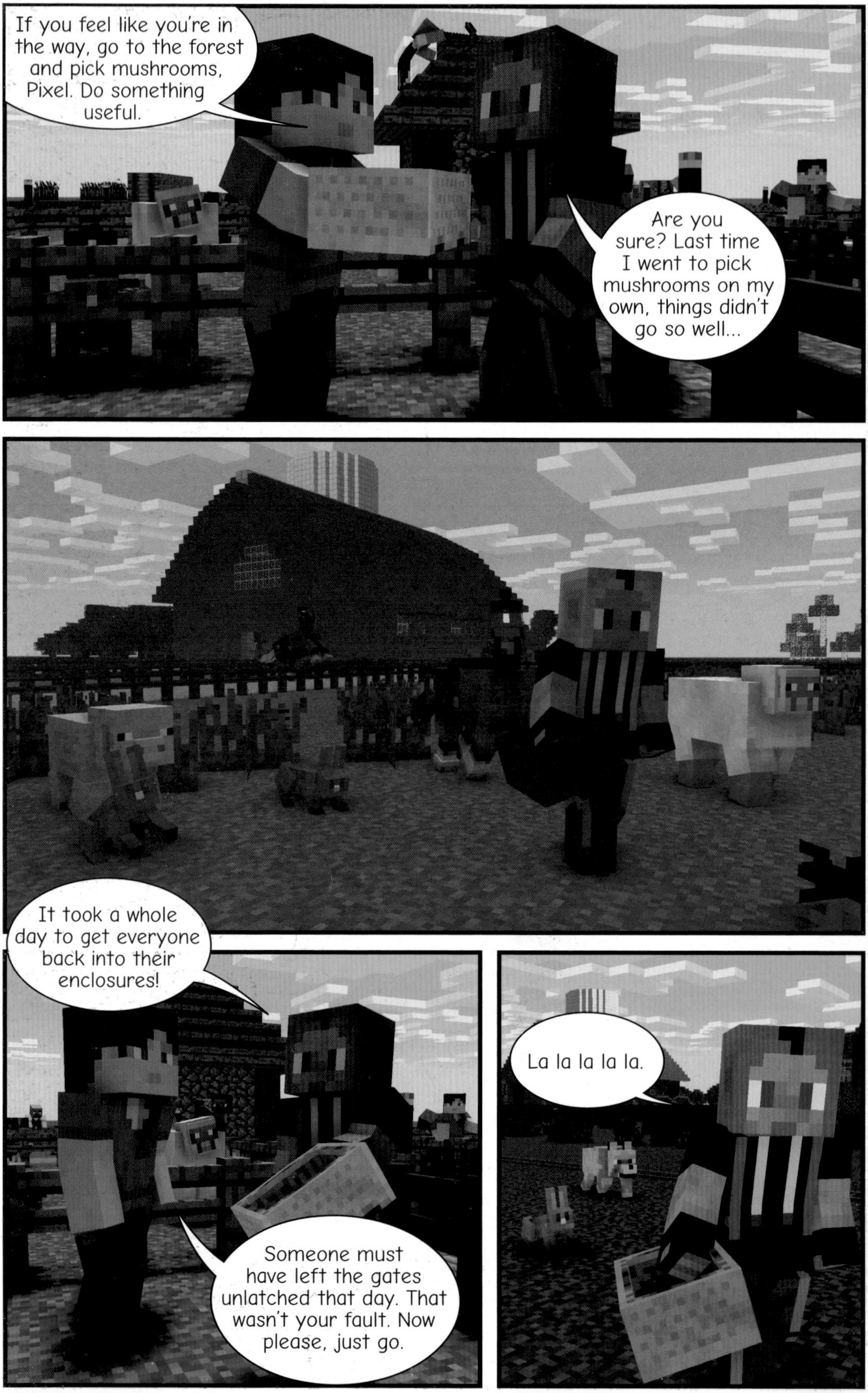
If you feel like you're in the way, go to the forest and pick mushrooms, Pixel. Do something useful.
Are you sure? Last time I went to pick mushrooms on my own, things didn't go so well...
It took a whole day to get everyone back into their enclosures!
Someone must have left the gates unlatched that day. That wasn't your fault. Now please, just go.
La la la la la.

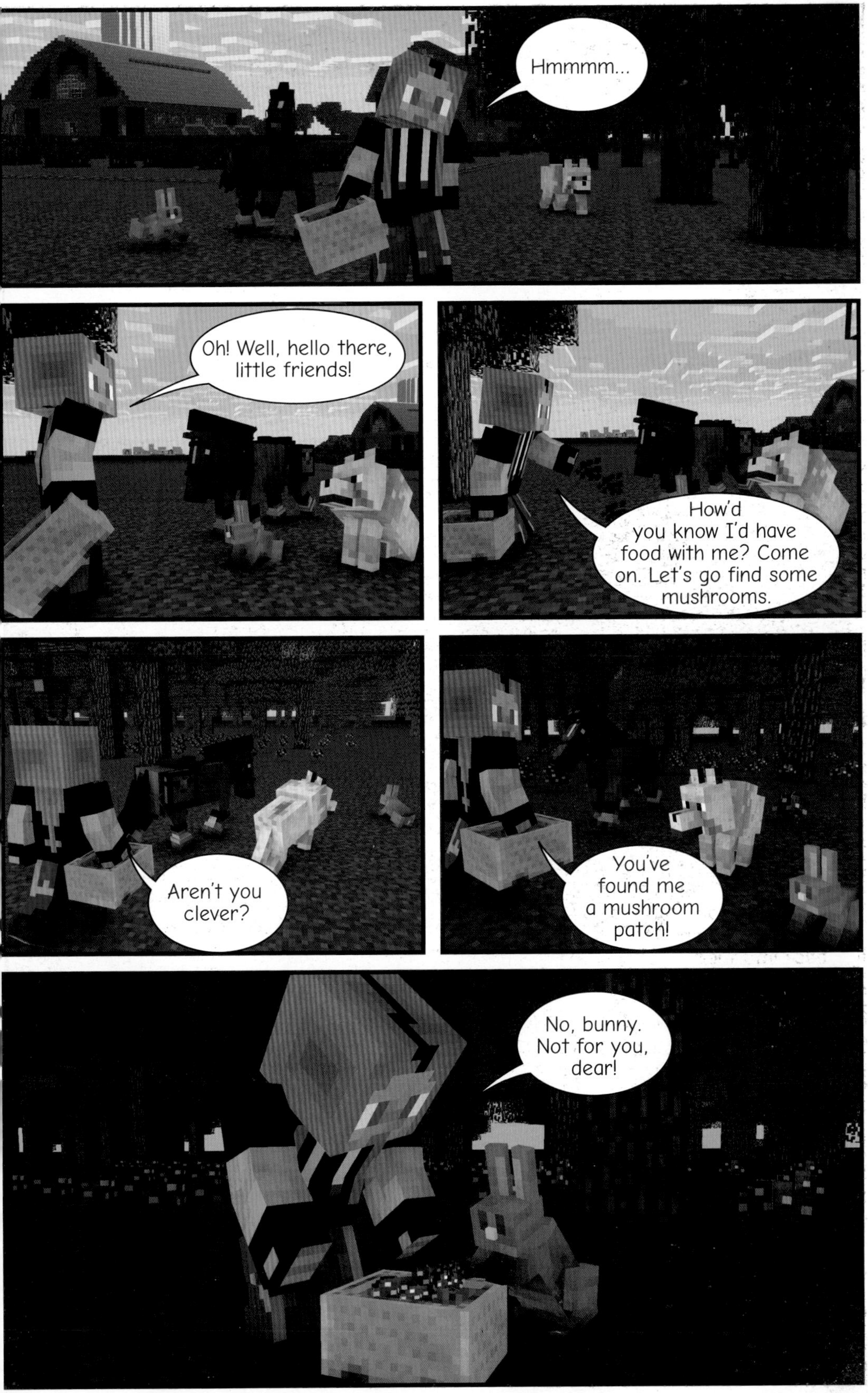
Hmmmm...
Oh! Well, hello there, little friends!
How'd you know I'd have food with me? Come on. Let's go find some mushrooms.
Aren't you clever?
You've found me a mushroom patch!
No, bunny. Not for you, dear!

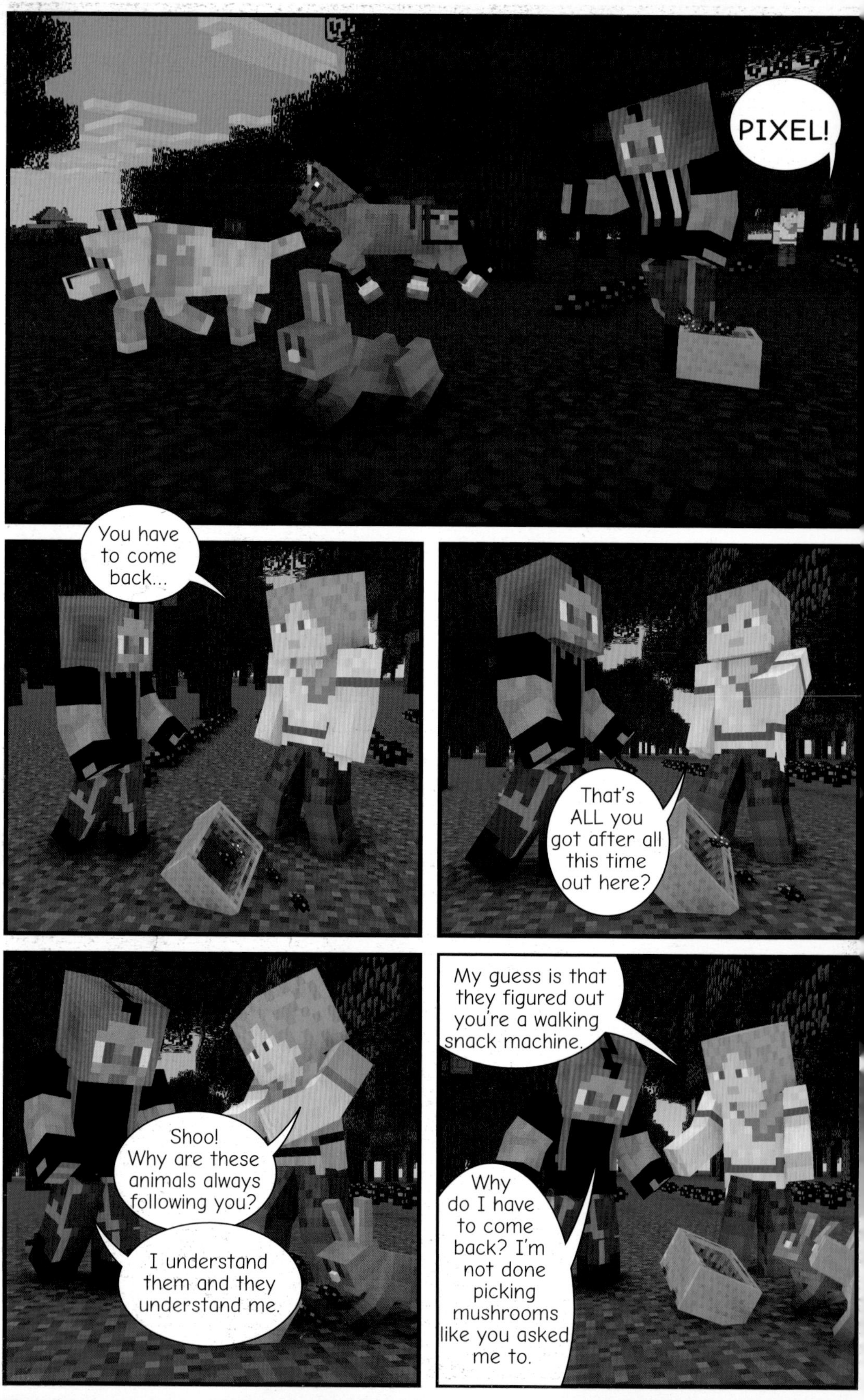
PIXEL!
You have to come back...
That's ALL you got after all this time out here?
Why do I have to come back? I'm not done picking mushrooms like you asked me to.
My guess is that they figured out you're a walking snack machine.
Shoo! Why are these animals always following you?
I understand them and they understand me.

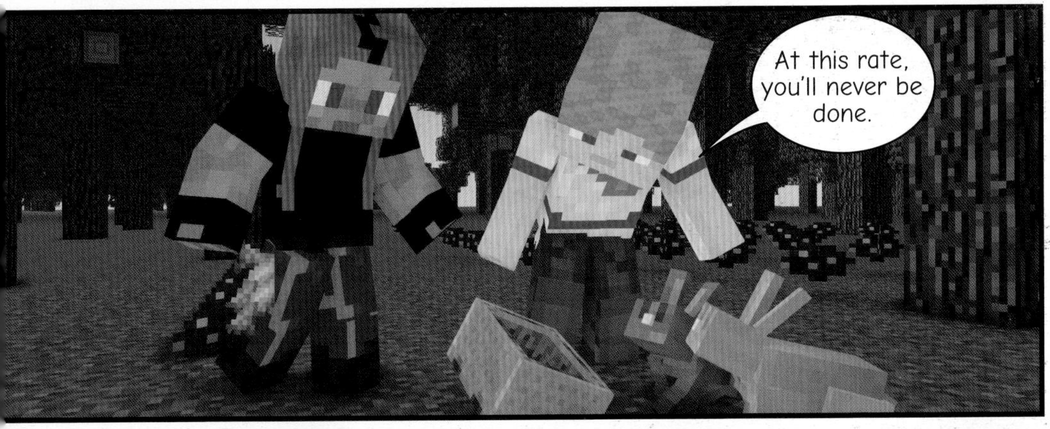
At this rate, you'll never be done.

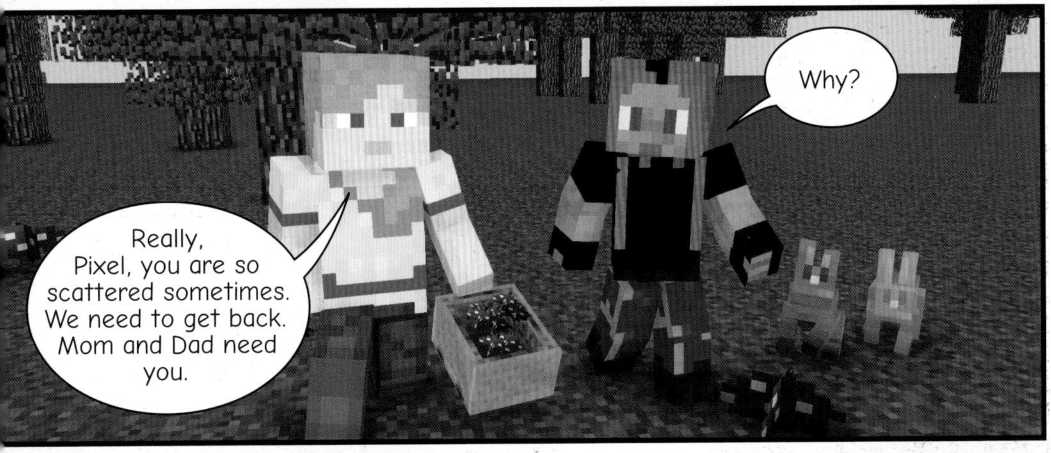
Why?
Really, Pixel, you are so scattered sometimes. We need to get back. Mom and Dad need you.

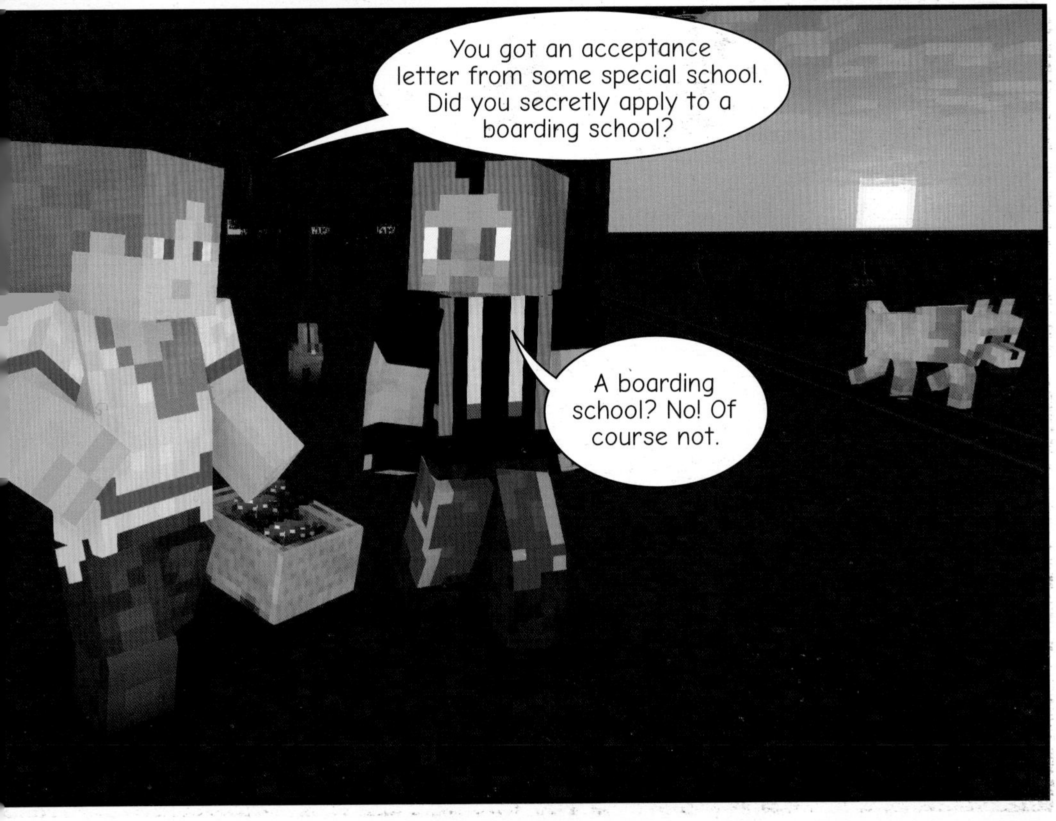
You got an acceptance letter from some special school. Did you secretly apply to a boarding school?
A boarding school? No! Of course not.

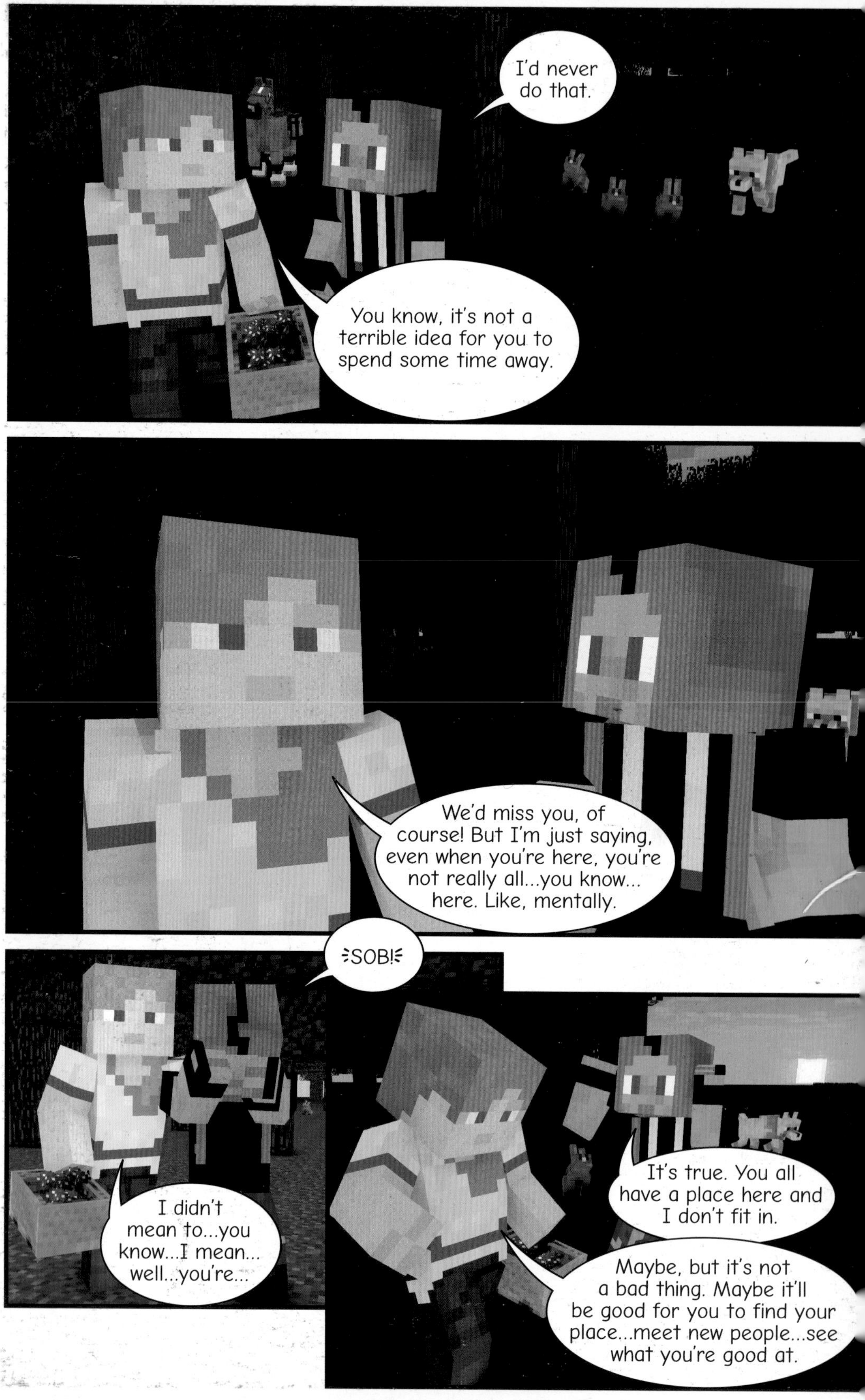
I'd never do that.
You know, it's not a terrible idea for you to spend some time away.
We'd miss you, of course! But I'm just saying, even when you're here, you're not really all...you know... here. Like, mentally.
SOB!
I didn't mean to...you know...I mean... well...you're...
It's true. You all have a place here and I don't fit in.
Maybe, but it's not a bad thing. Maybe it'll be good for you to find your place...meet new people...see what you're good at.

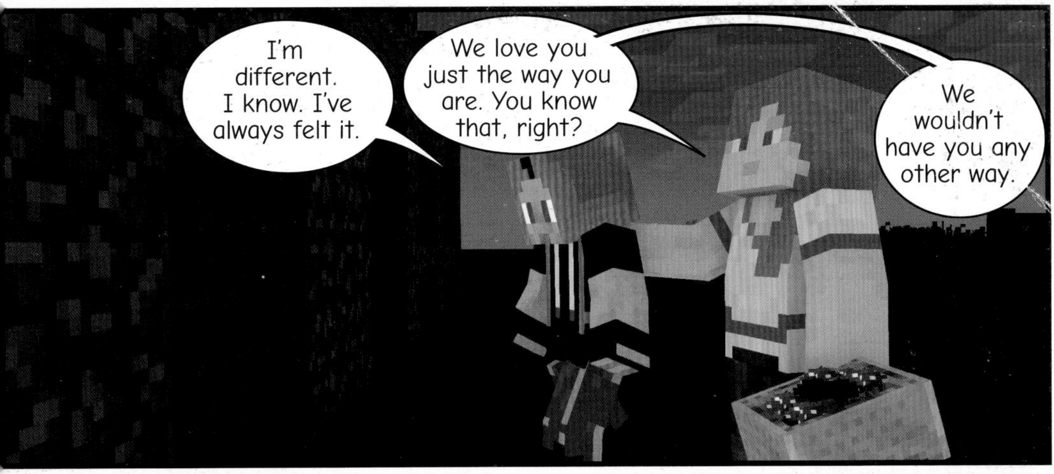
I'm different. I know. I've always felt it.
We love you just the way you are. You know that, right?
We wouldn't have you any other way.

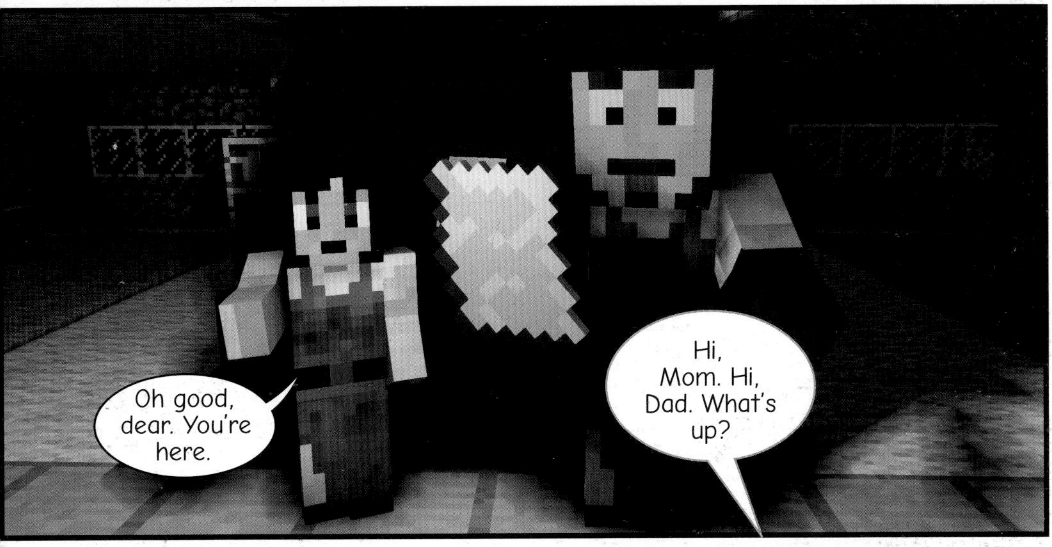
Hi, Mom. Hi, Dad. What's up?
Oh good, dear. You're here.

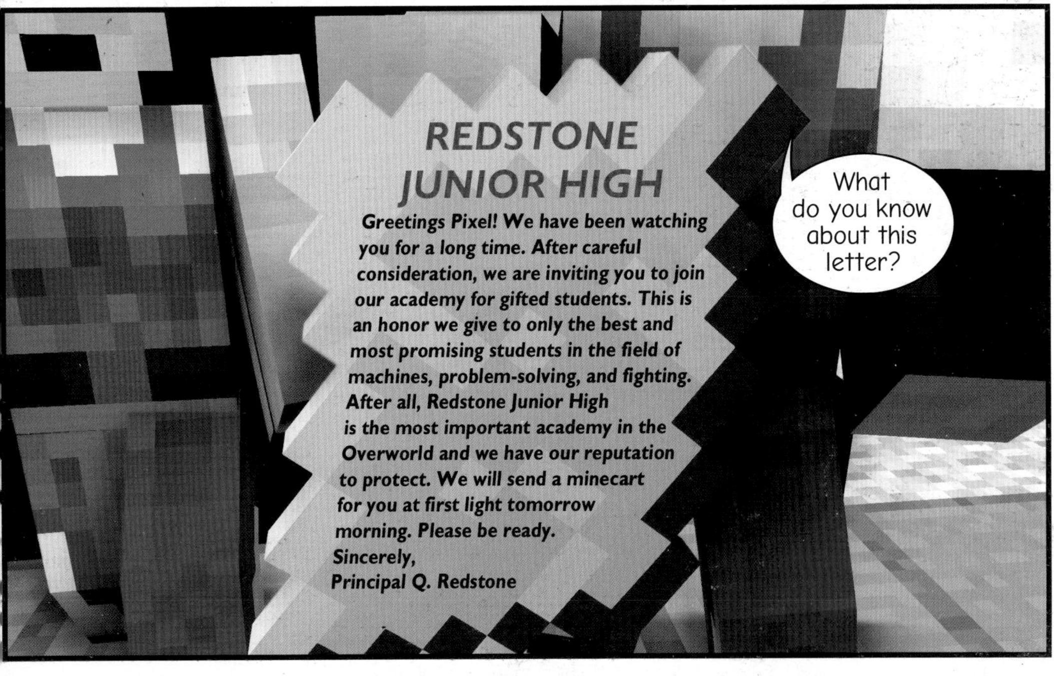
REDSTONE JUNIOR HIGH
Greetings Pixel! We have been watching you for a long time. After careful consideration, we are inviting you to join our academy for gifted students. This is an honor we give to only the best and most promising students in the field of machines, problem-solving, and fighting. After all, Redstone Junior High is the most important academy in the Overworld and we have our reputation to protect. We will send a minecart for you at first light tomorrow morning. Please be ready.
Sincerely,
Principal Q. Redstone
What do you know about this letter?

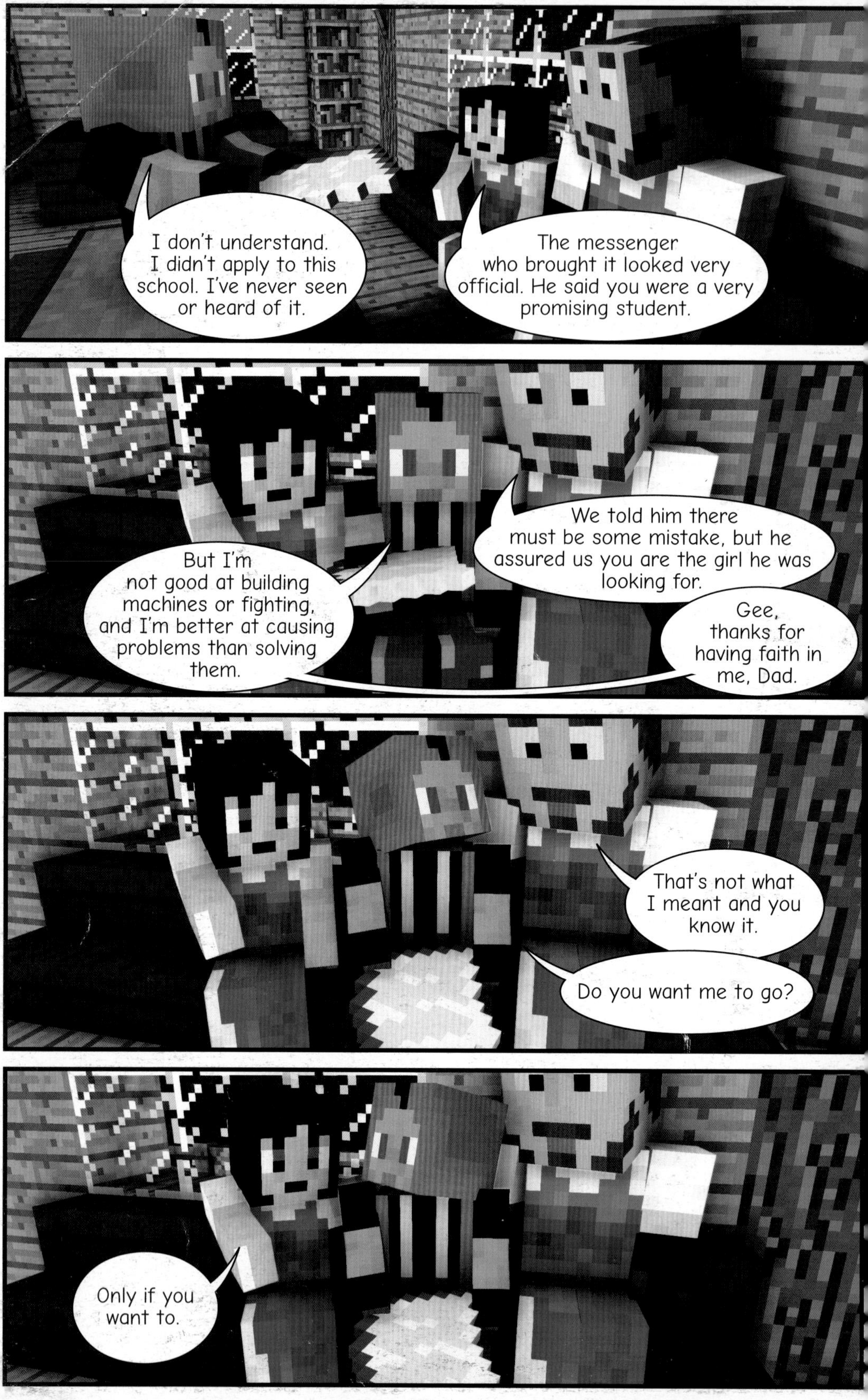
I don't understand. I didn't apply to this school. I've never seen or heard of it.
The messenger who brought it looked very official. He said you were a very promising student.
But I'm not good at building machines or fighting, and I'm better at causing problems than solving them.
We told him there must be some mistake, but he assured us you are the girl he was looking for.
Gee, thanks for having faith in me, Dad.
That's not what I meant and you know it.
Do you want me to go?
Only if you want to.

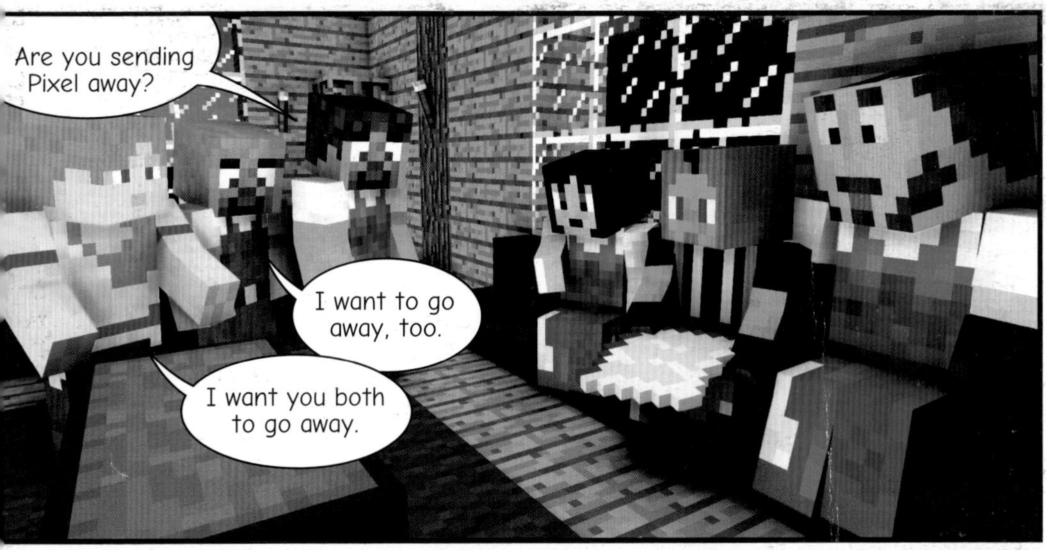
Are you sending Pixel away?
I want to go away, too.
I want you both to go away.

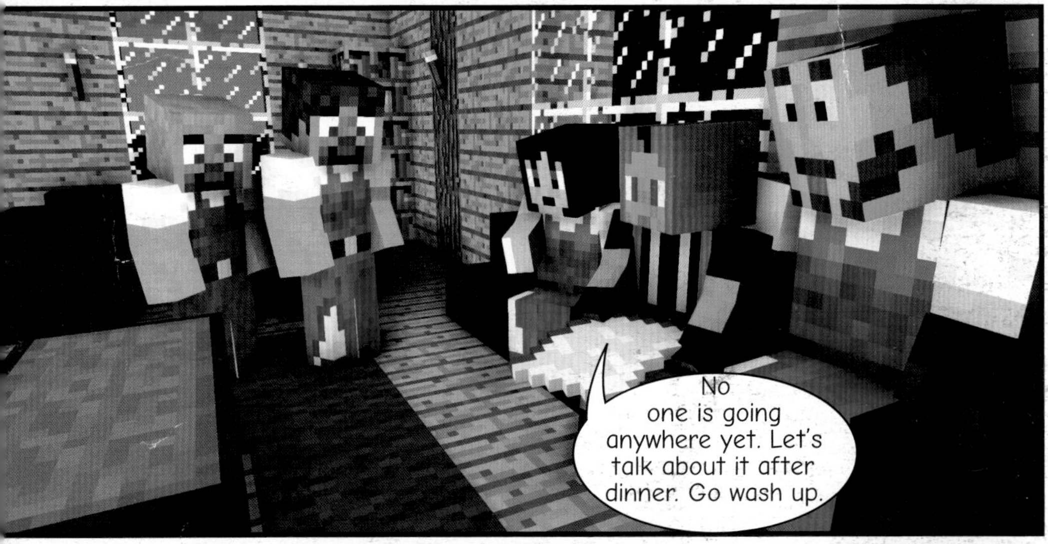
No one is going anywhere yet. Let's talk about it after dinner. Go wash up.

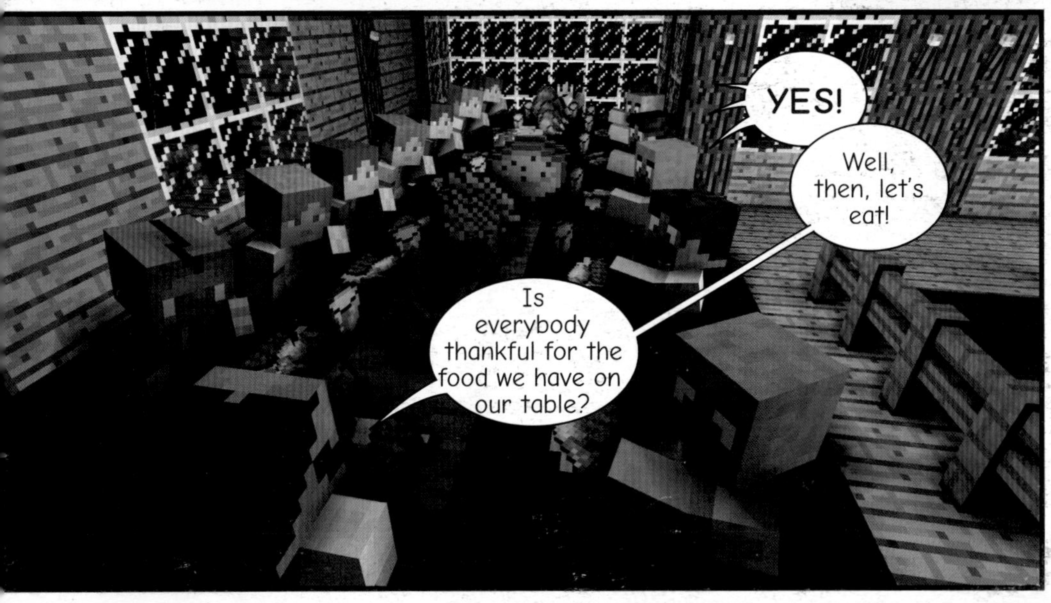
Is everybody thankful for the food we have on our table?
YES!
Well, then, let's eat!

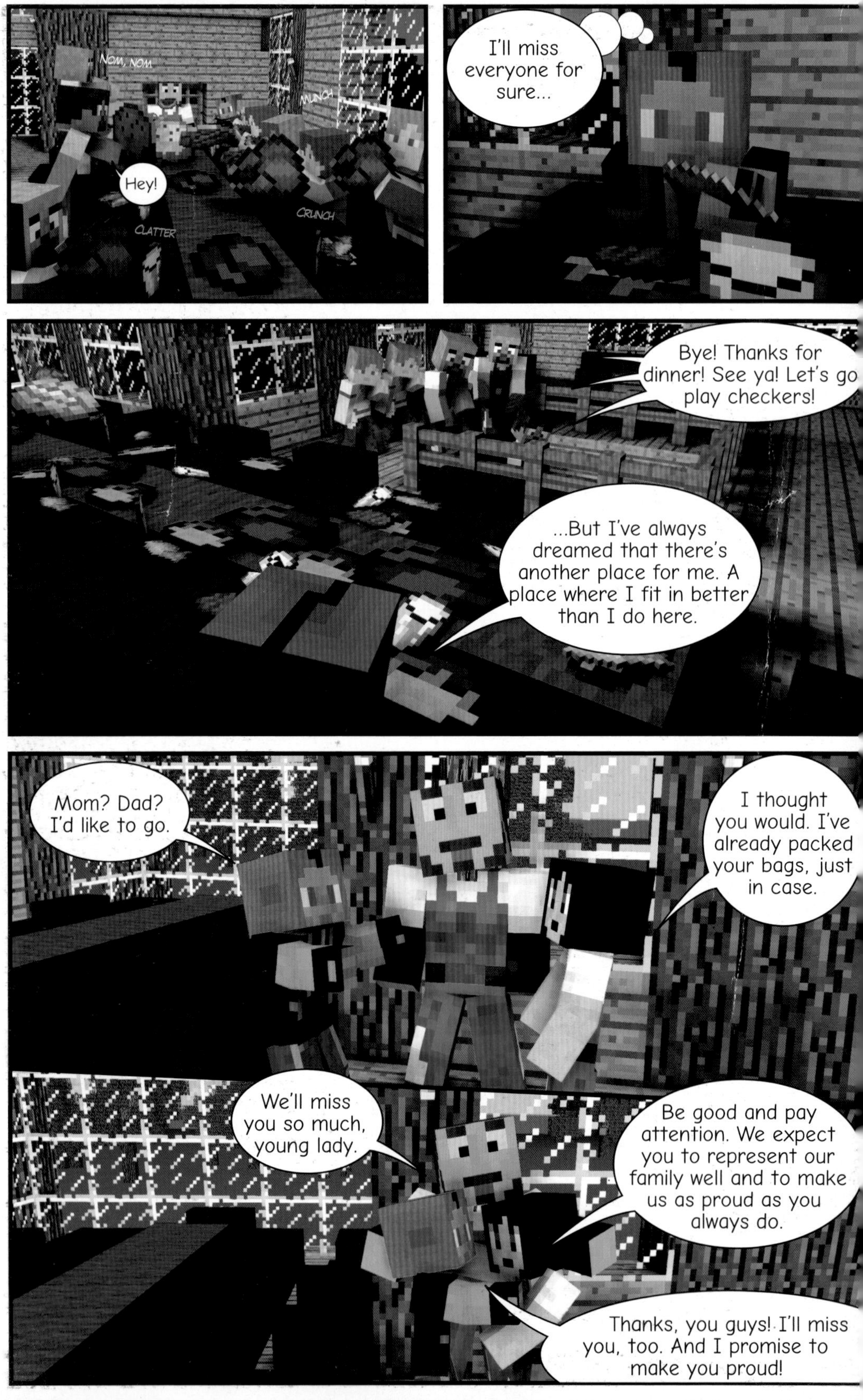

NOM, NOM
MUNCH
Hey!
CRUNCH
CLATTER
I'll miss everyone for sure...
Bye! Thanks for dinner! See ya! Let's go play checkers!
...But I've always dreamed that there's another place for me. A place where I fit in better than I do here.
Mom? Dad? I'd like to go.
I thought you would. I've already packed your bags, just in case.
We'll miss you so much, young lady.
Be good and pay attention. We expect you to represent our family well and to make us as proud as you always do.
Thanks, you guys! I'll miss you, too. And I promise to make you proud!

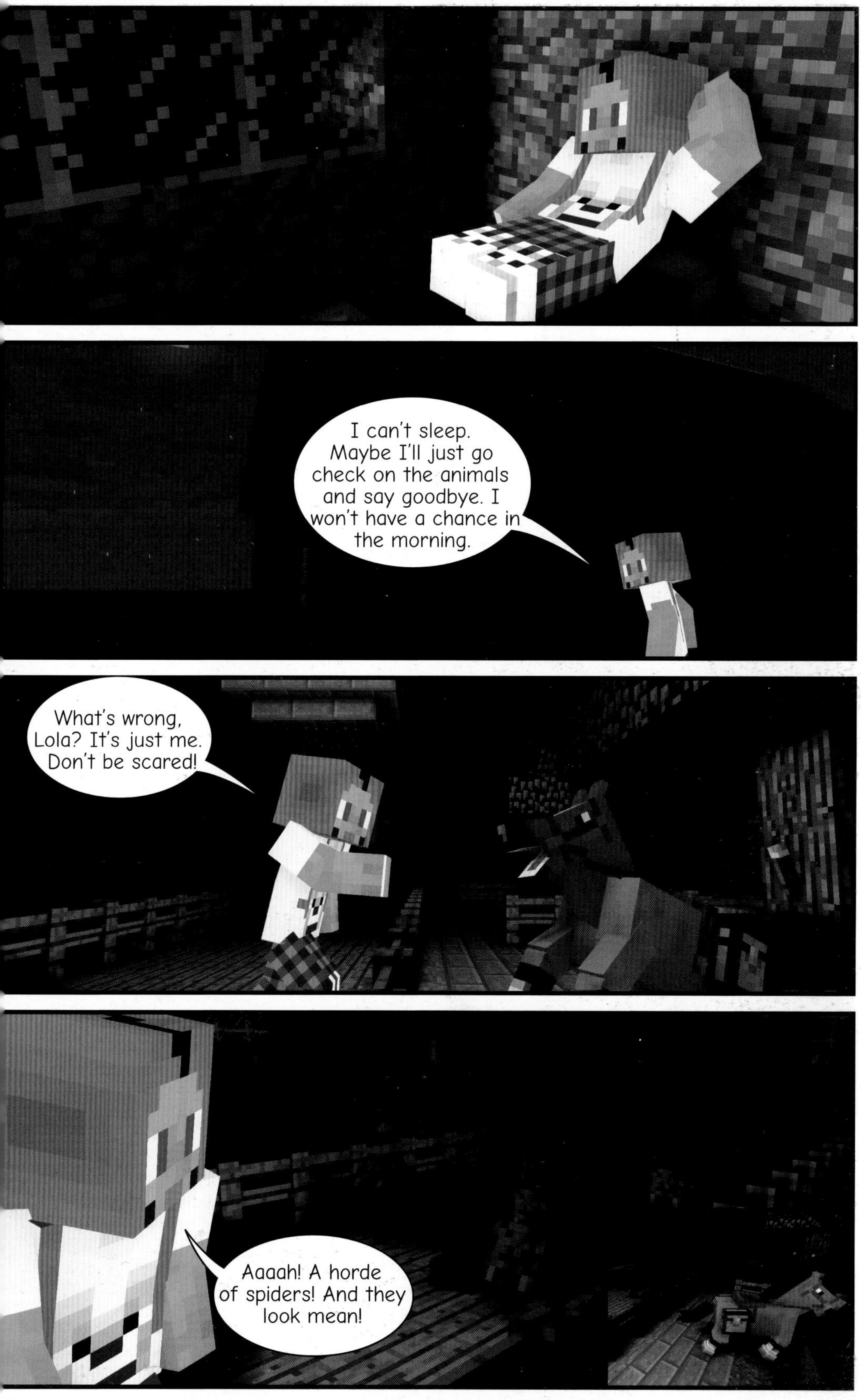
I can't sleep. Maybe I'll just go check on the animals and say goodbye. I won't have a chance in the morning.
What's wrong, Lola? It's just me. Don't be scared!
Aaaah! A horde of spiders! And they look mean!

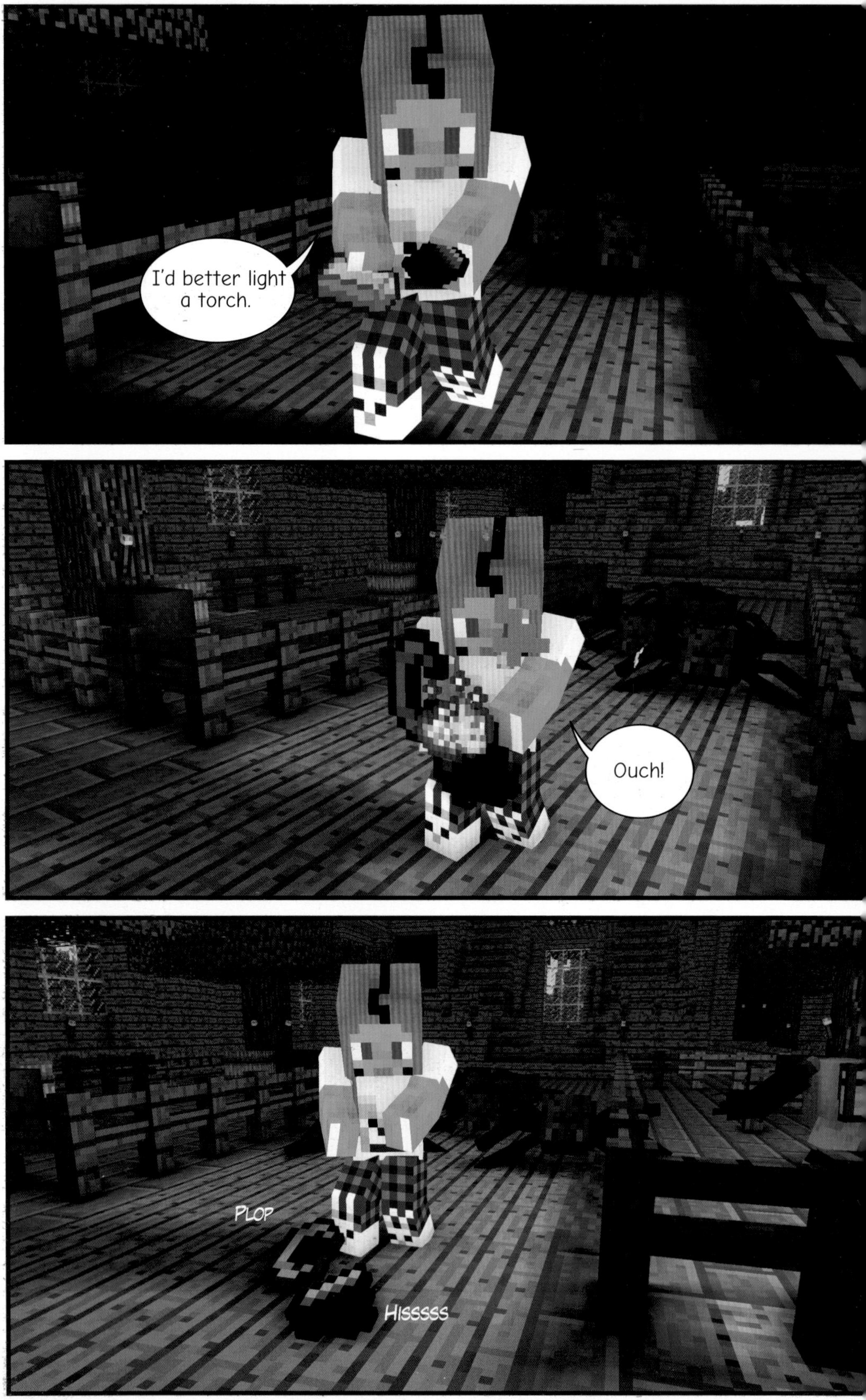
I'd better light a torch.
Ouch!
PLOP
HISSSSS

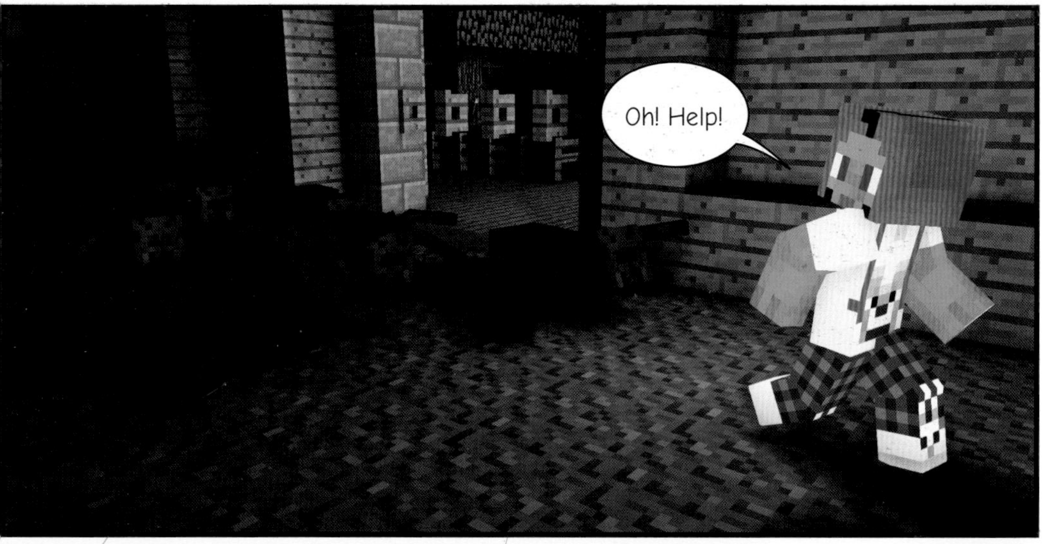
Oh! Help!
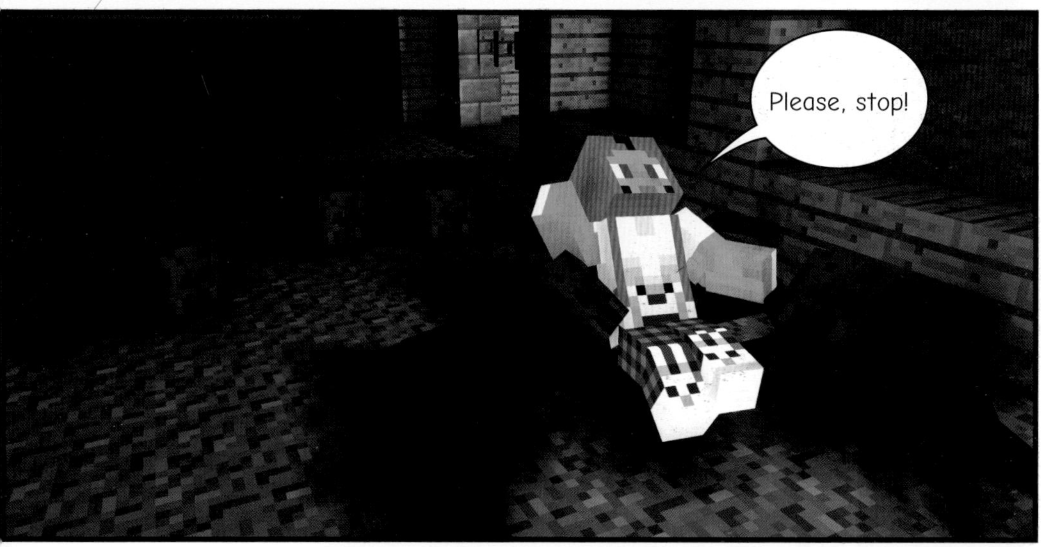
Please, stop!
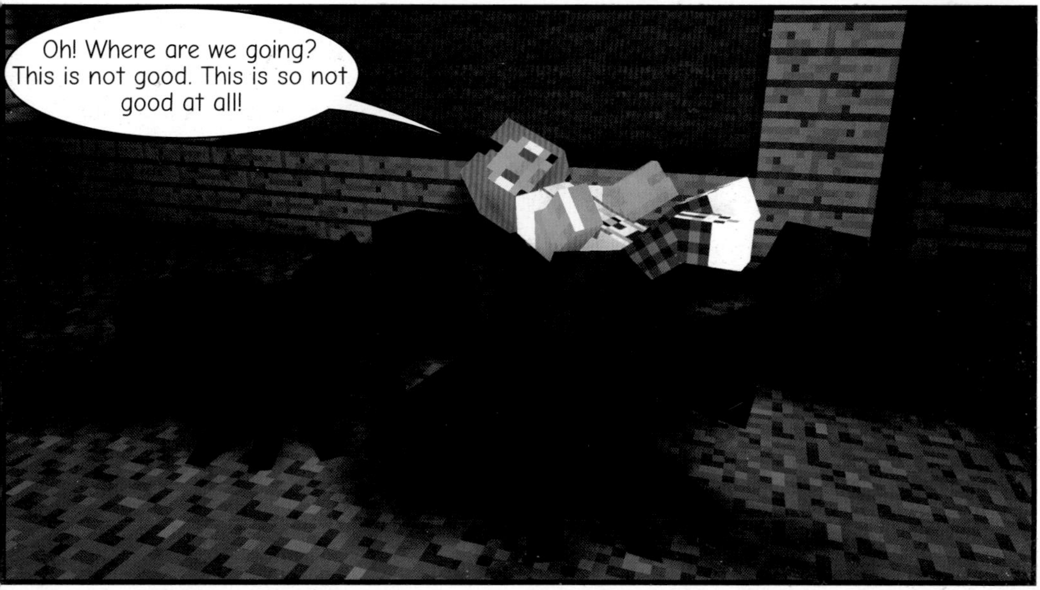
Oh! Where are we going? This is not good. This is so not good at all!

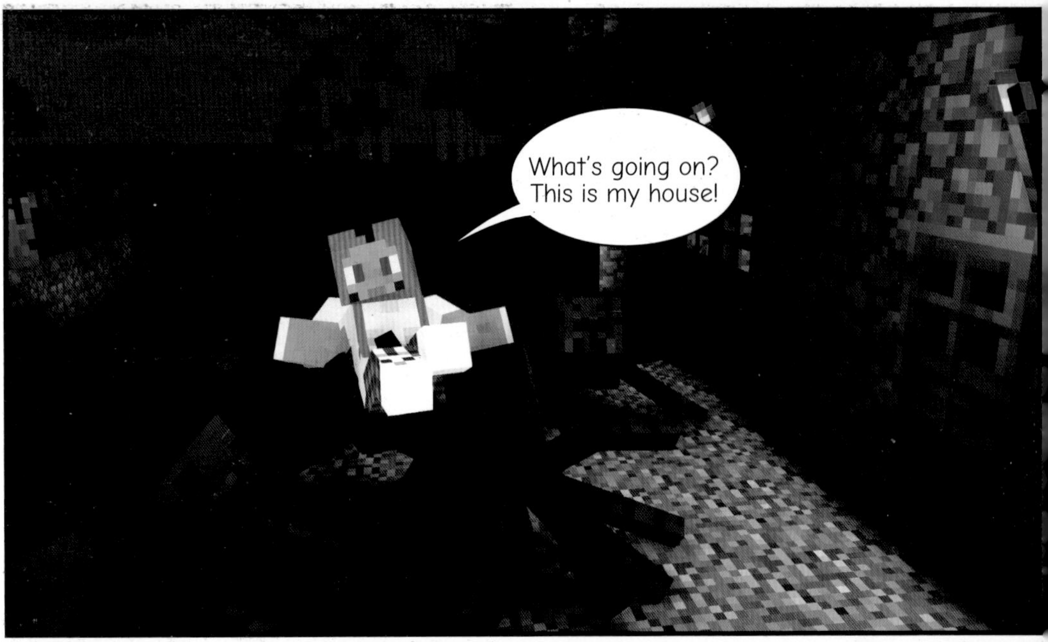
What's going on? This is my house!

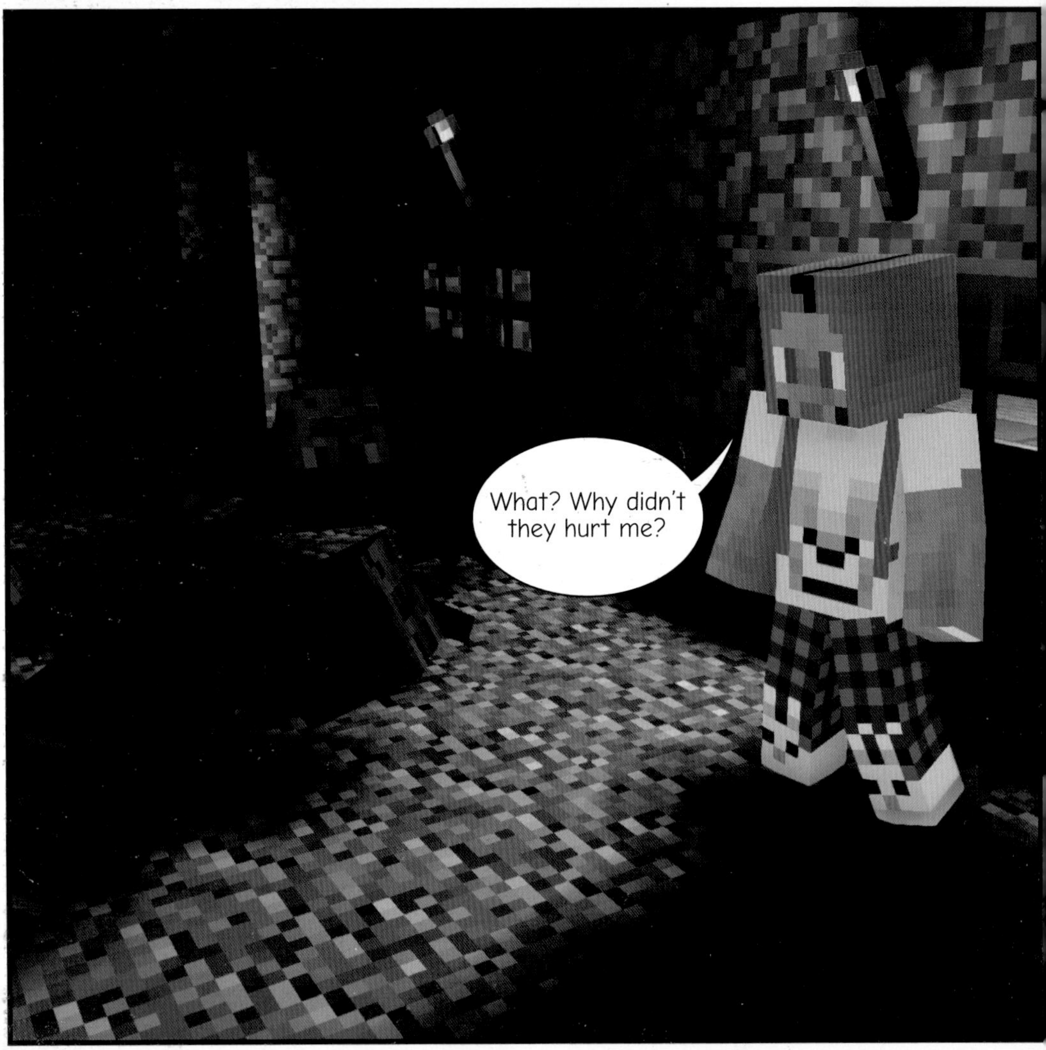
What? Why didn't they hurt me?

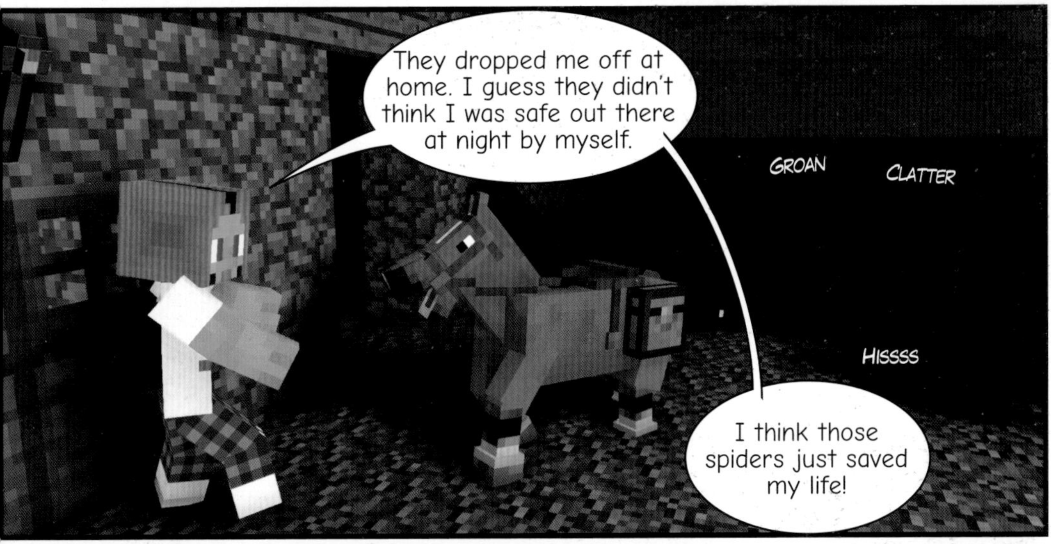
They dropped me off at home. I guess they didn't think I was safe out there at night by myself.
GROAN
CLATTER
HISSSS
I think those spiders just saved my life!

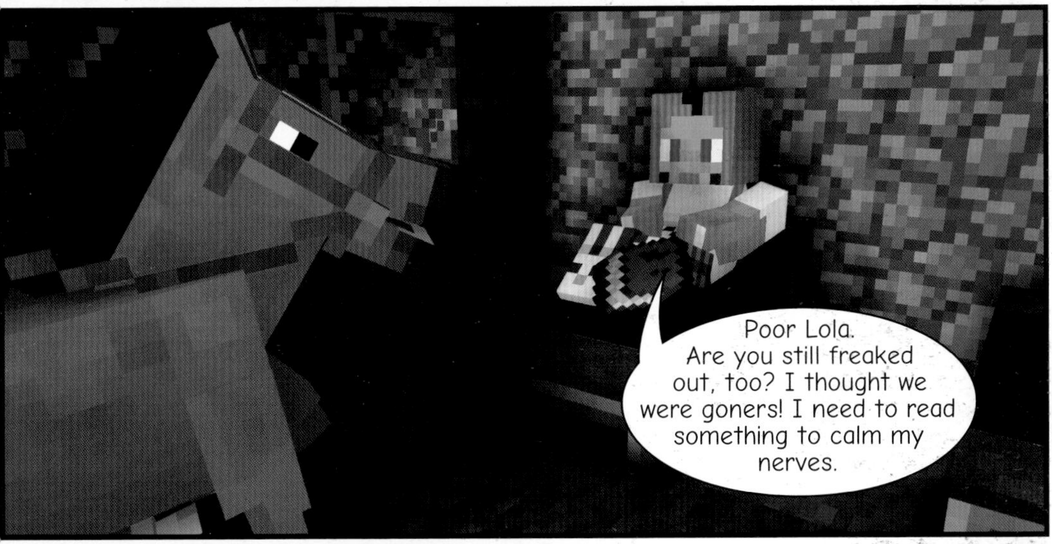
Poor Lola. Are you still freaked out, too? I thought we were goners! I need to read something to calm my nerves.

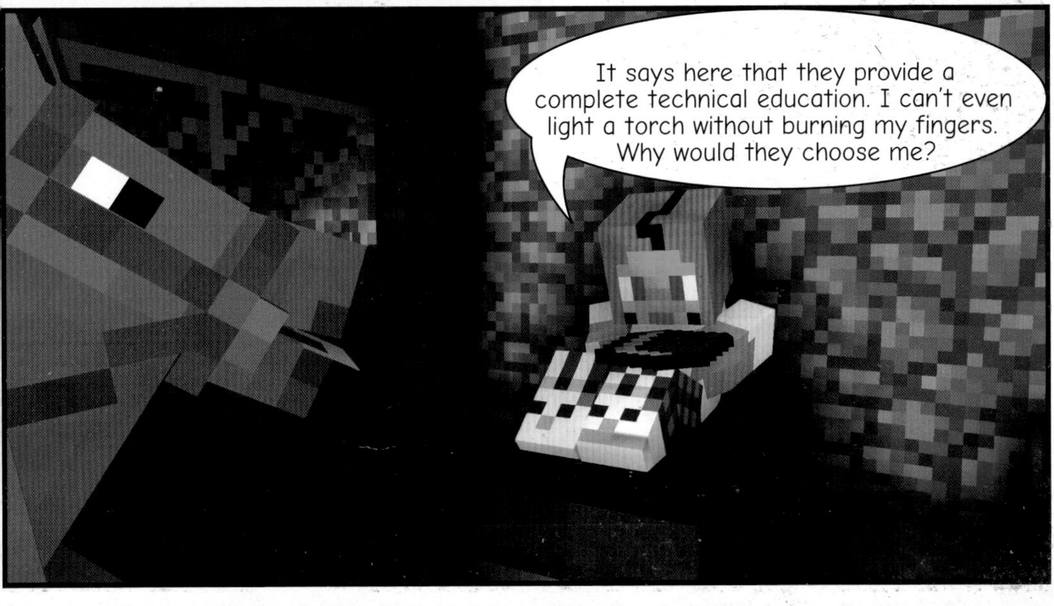
It says here that they provide a complete technical education. I can't even light a torch without burning my fingers. Why would they choose me?

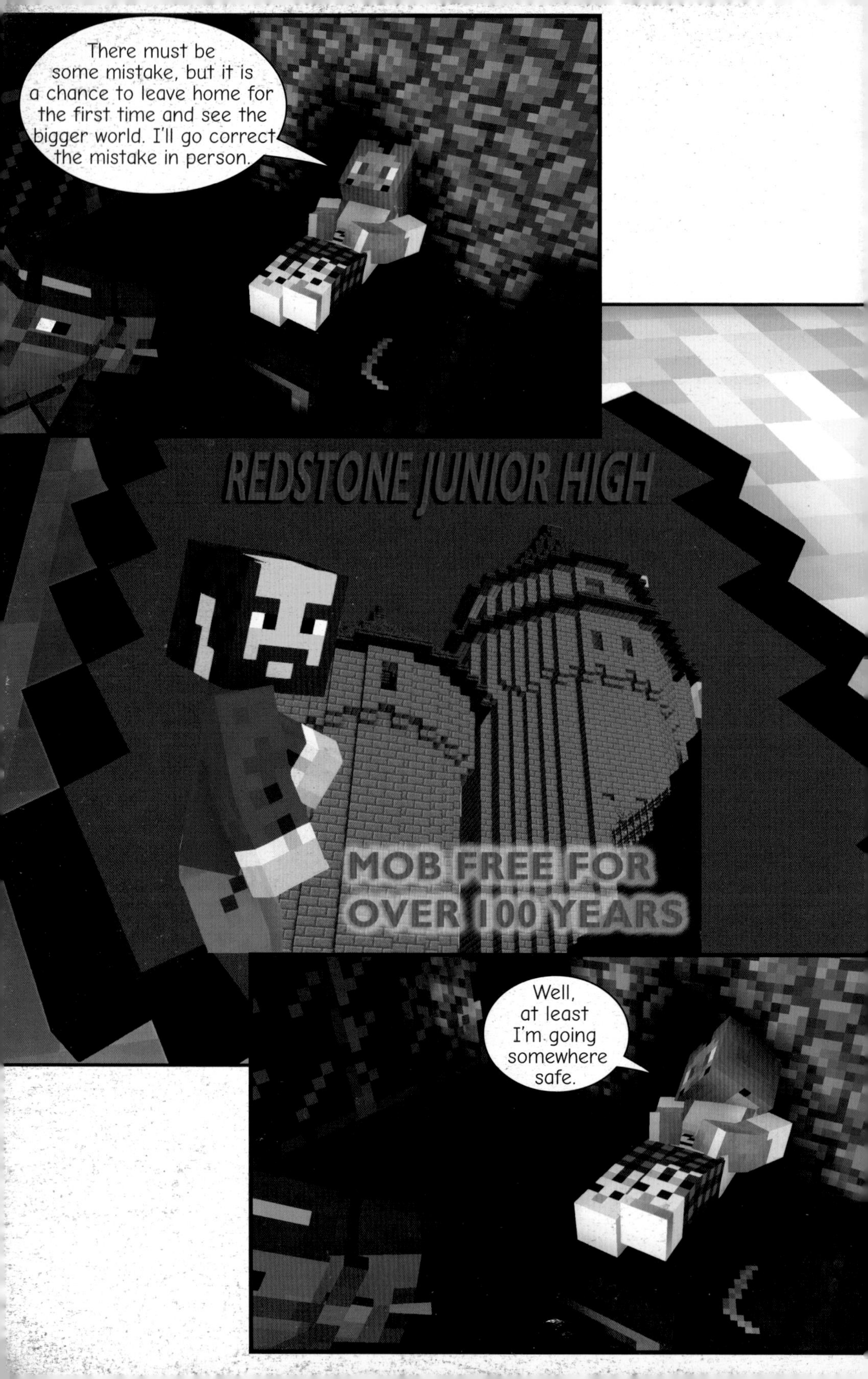
There must be some mistake, but it is a chance to leave home for the first time and see the bigger world. I'll go correct the mistake in person.
REDSTONE JUNIOR HIGH
MOB FREE FOR OVER 100 YEARS
Well, at least I'm going somewhere safe.

CHAPTER 2

NEW BEGINNINGS

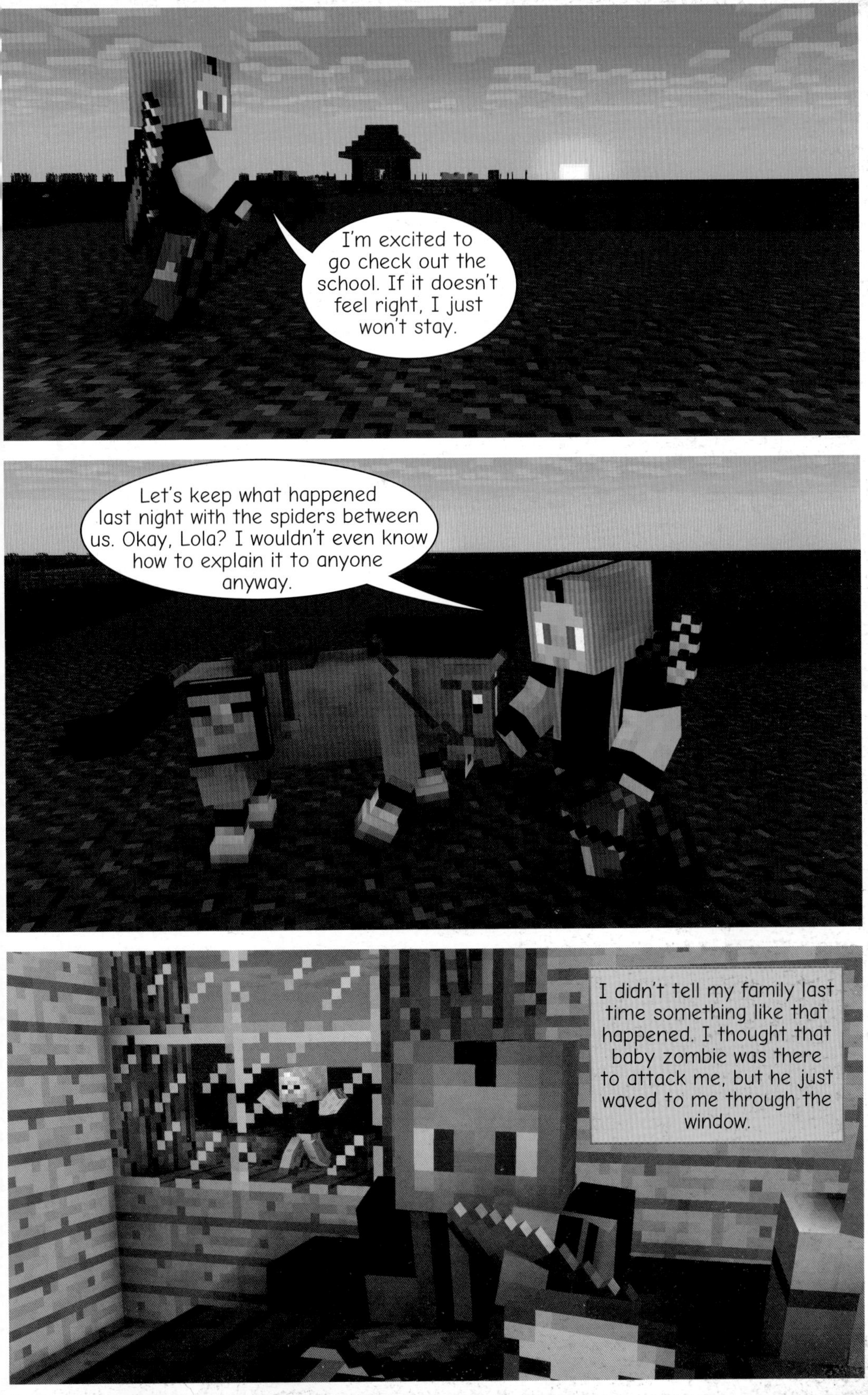
I'm excited to go check out the school. If it doesn't feel right, I just won't stay.
Let's keep what happened last night with the spiders between us. Okay, Lola? I wouldn't even know how to explain it to anyone anyway.
I didn't tell my family last time something like that happened. I thought that baby zombie was there to attack me, but he just waved to me through the window.

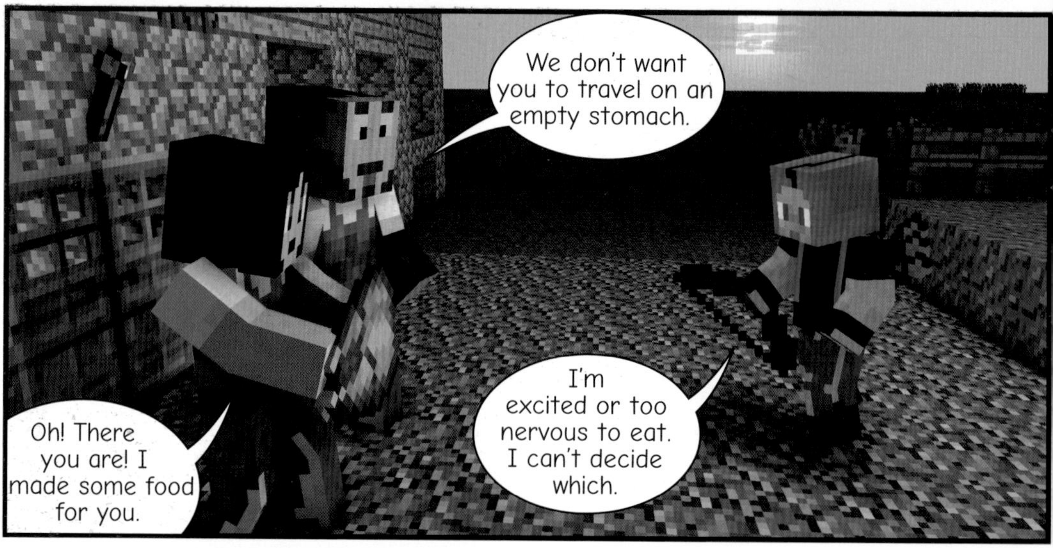
We don't want you to travel on an empty stomach.
Oh! There you are! I made some food for you.
I'm excited or too nervous to eat. I can't decide which.

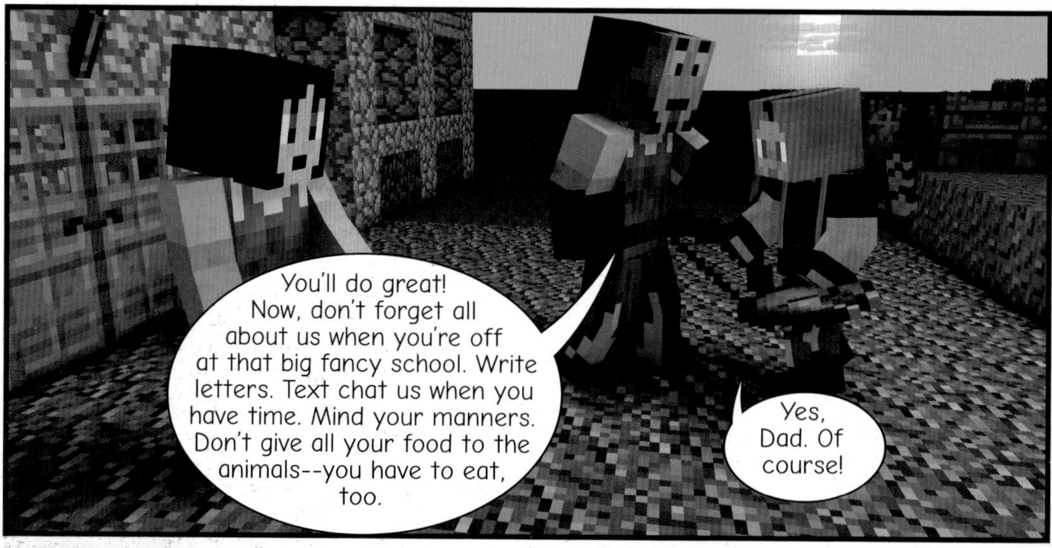
You'll do great! Now, don't forget all about us when you're off at that big fancy school. Write letters. Text chat us when you have time. Mind your manners. Don't give all your food to the animals--you have to eat, too.
Yes, Dad. Of course!

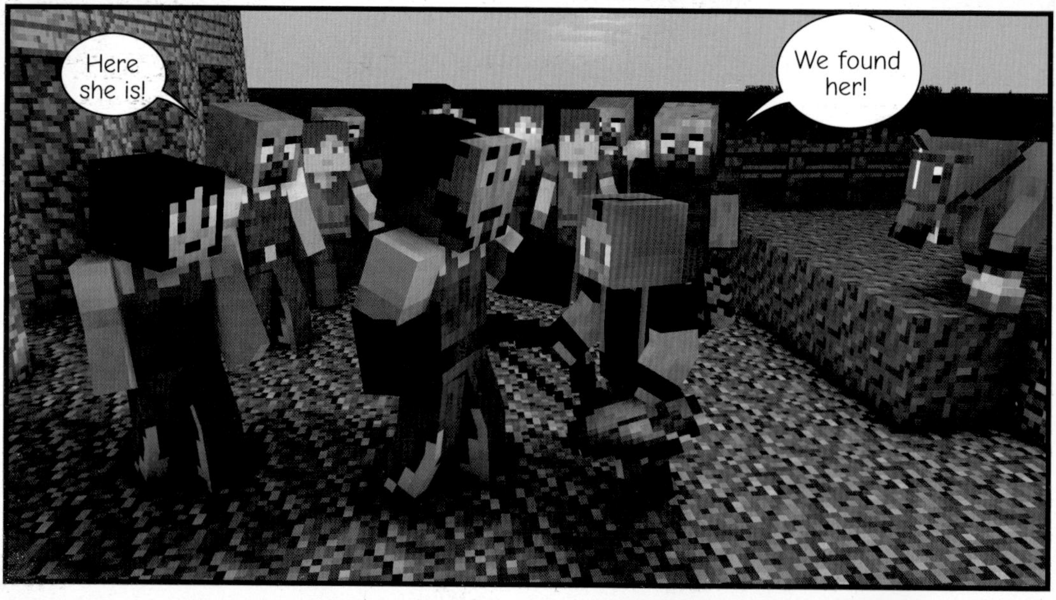
Here she is!
We found her!

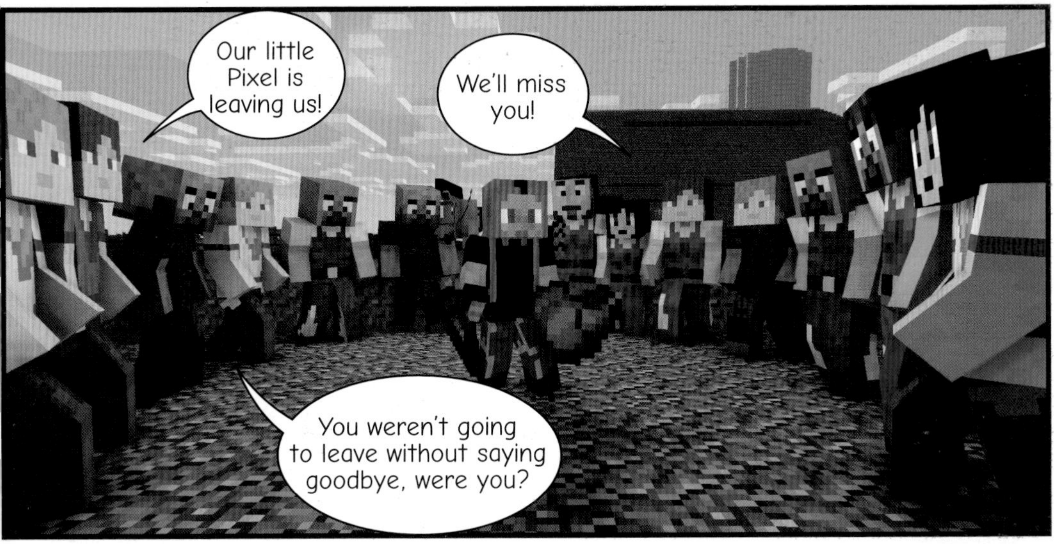
Our little Pixel is leaving us!
We'll miss you!
You weren't going to leave without saying goodbye, were you?

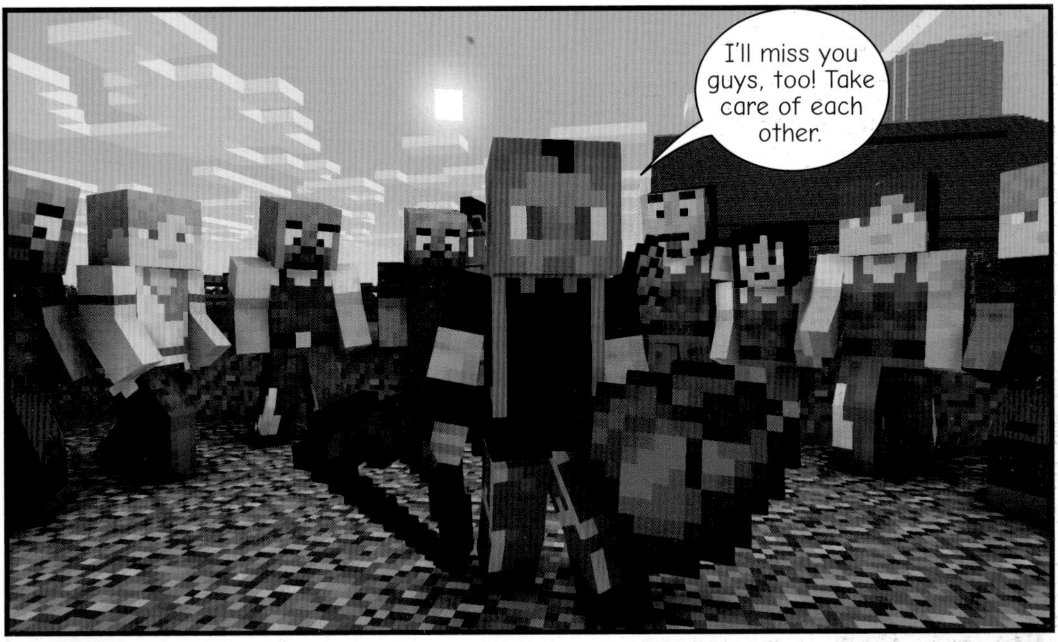
I'll miss you guys, too! Take care of each other.

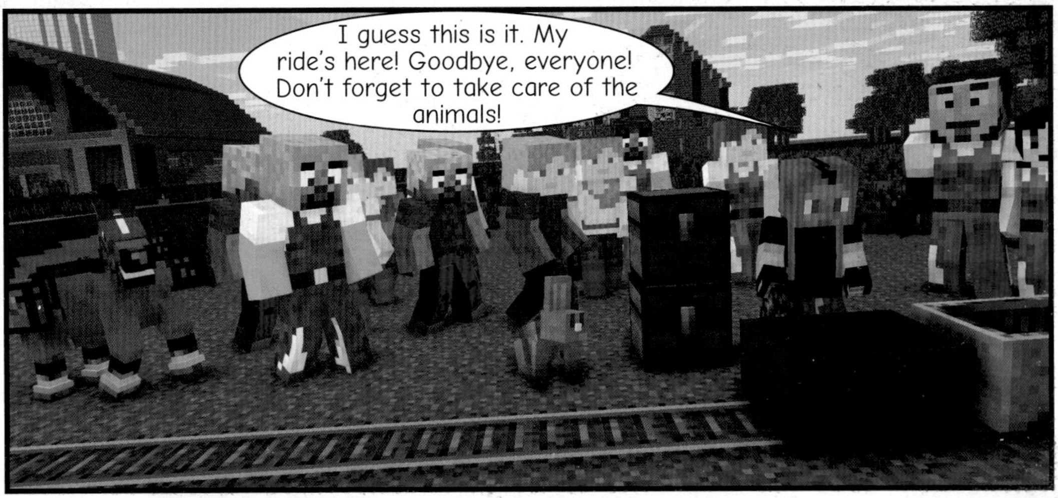
I guess this is it. My ride's here! Goodbye, everyone! Don't forget to take care of the animals!

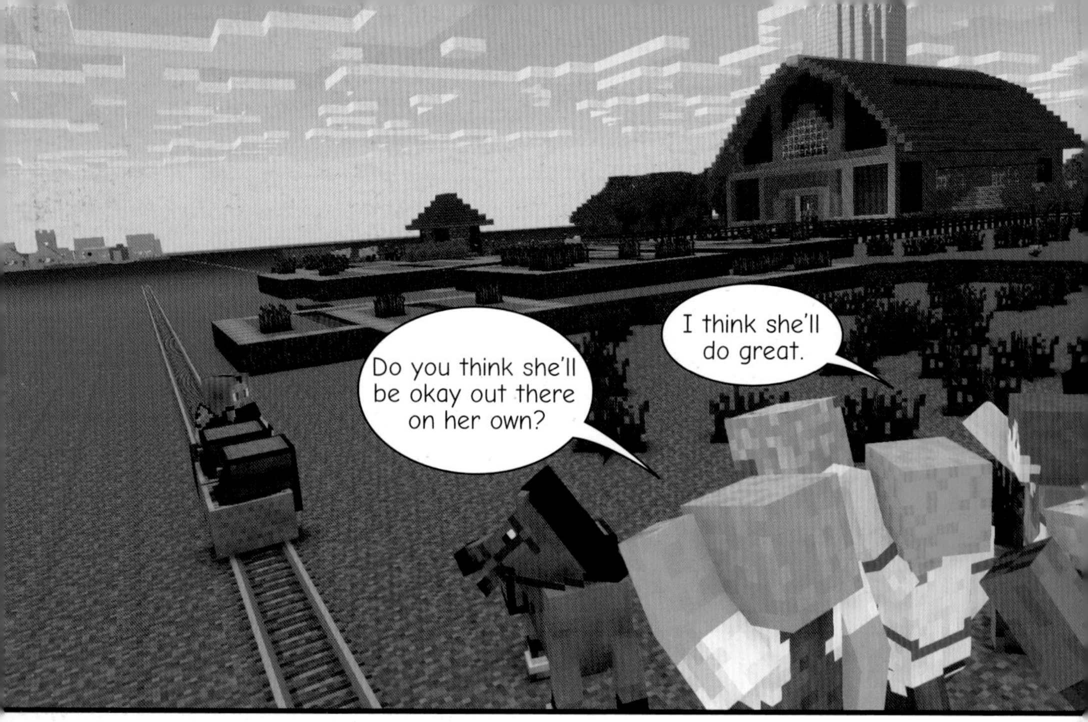
Do you think she'll be okay out there on her own?
I think she'll do great.

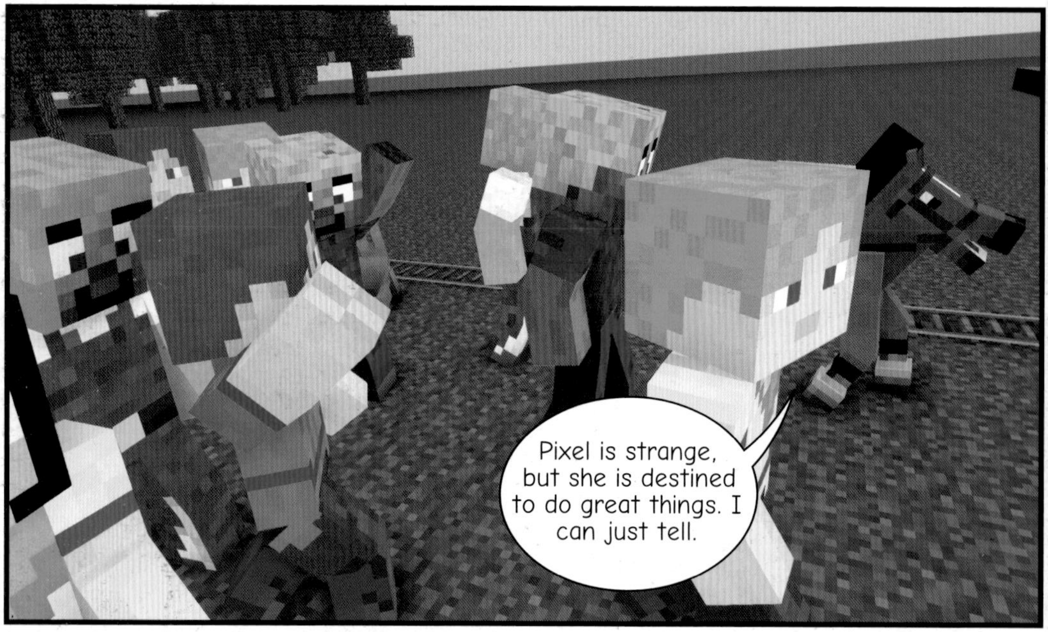
Pixel is strange, but she is destined to do great things. I can just tell.

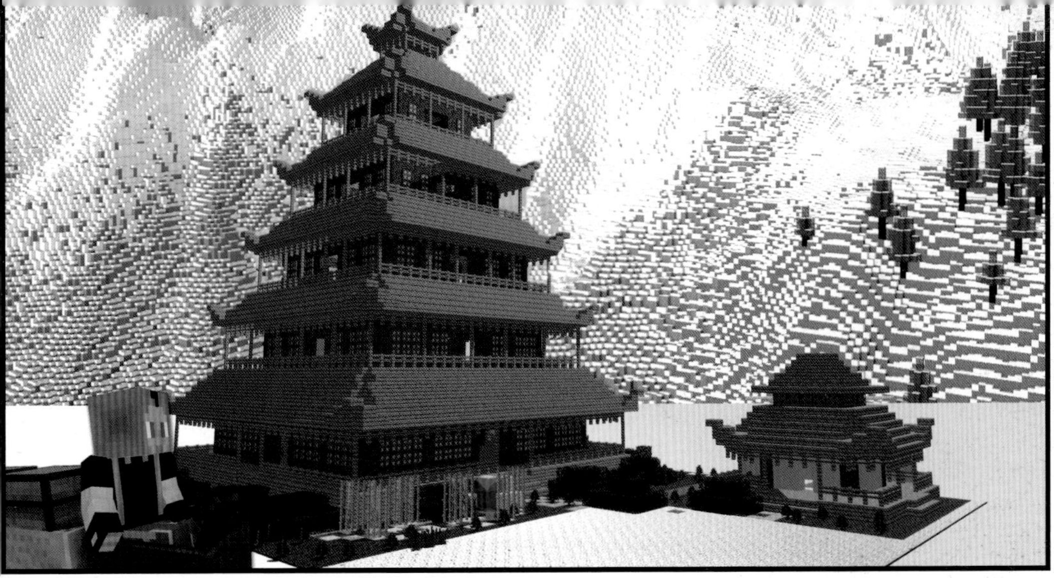

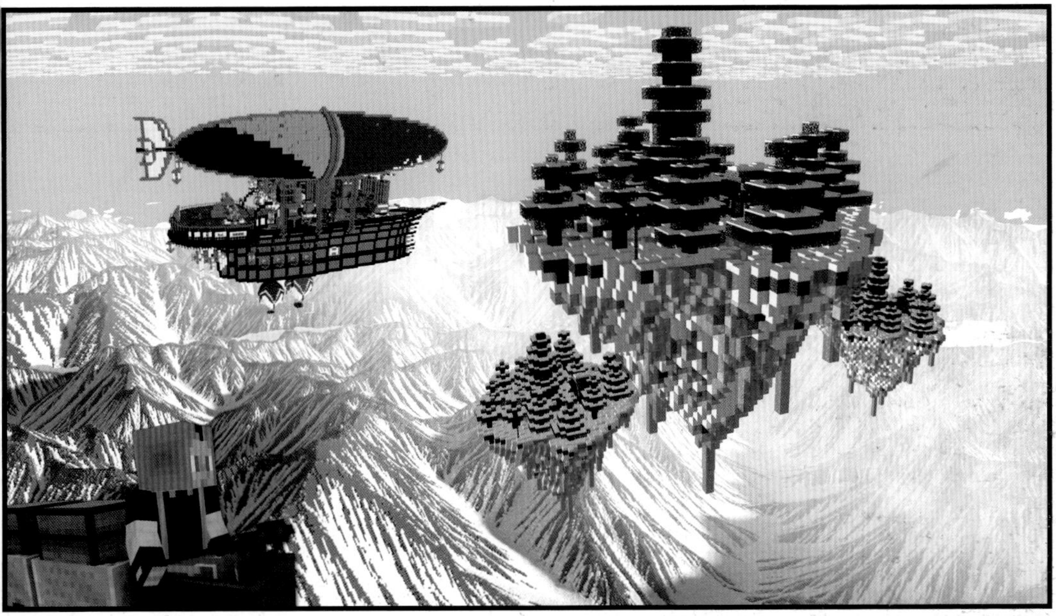

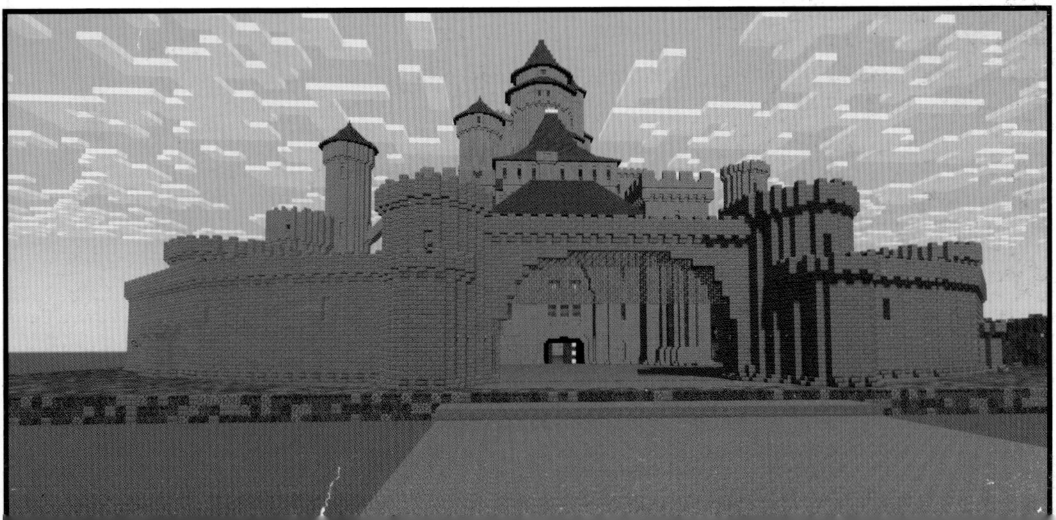

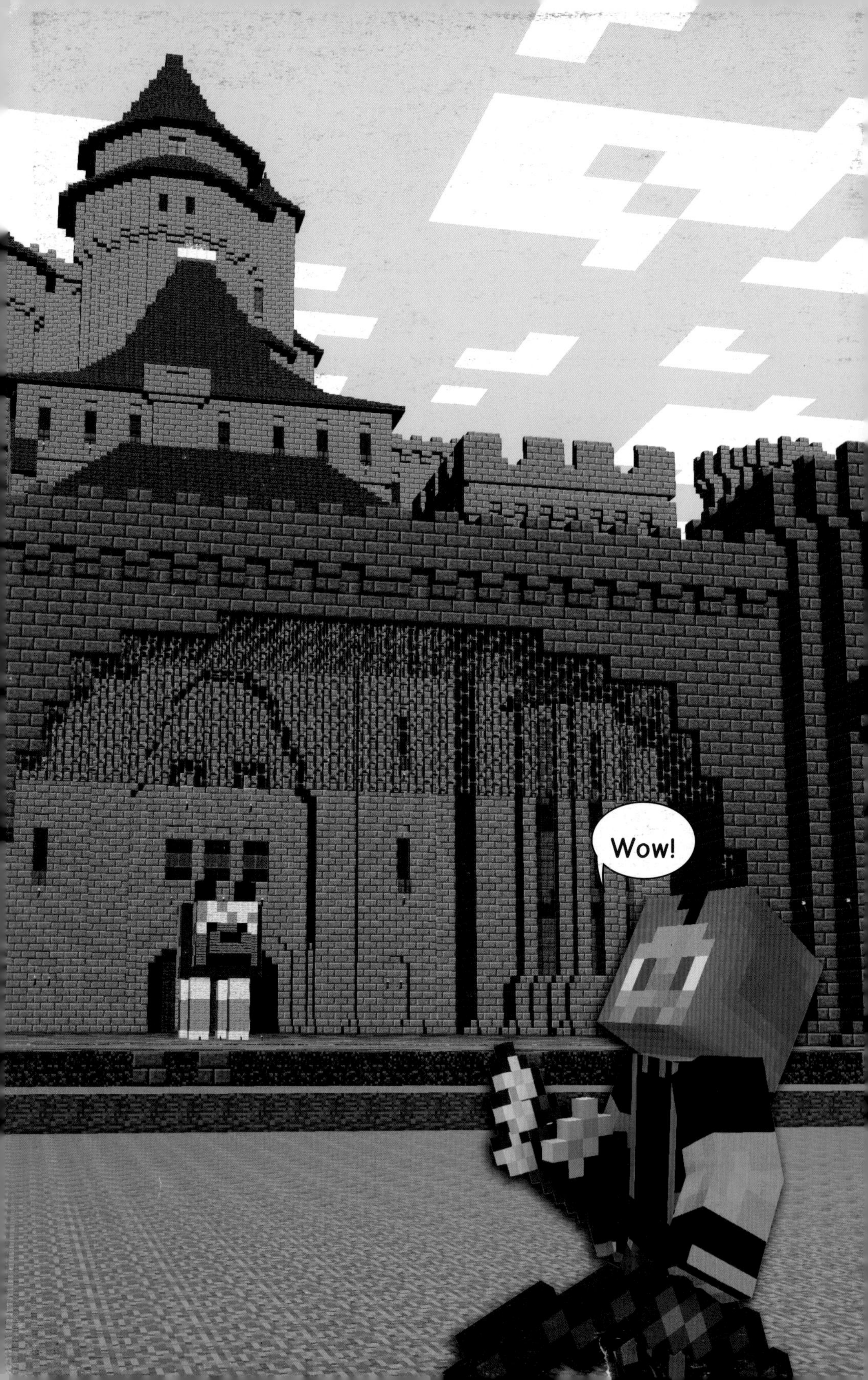
Wow!

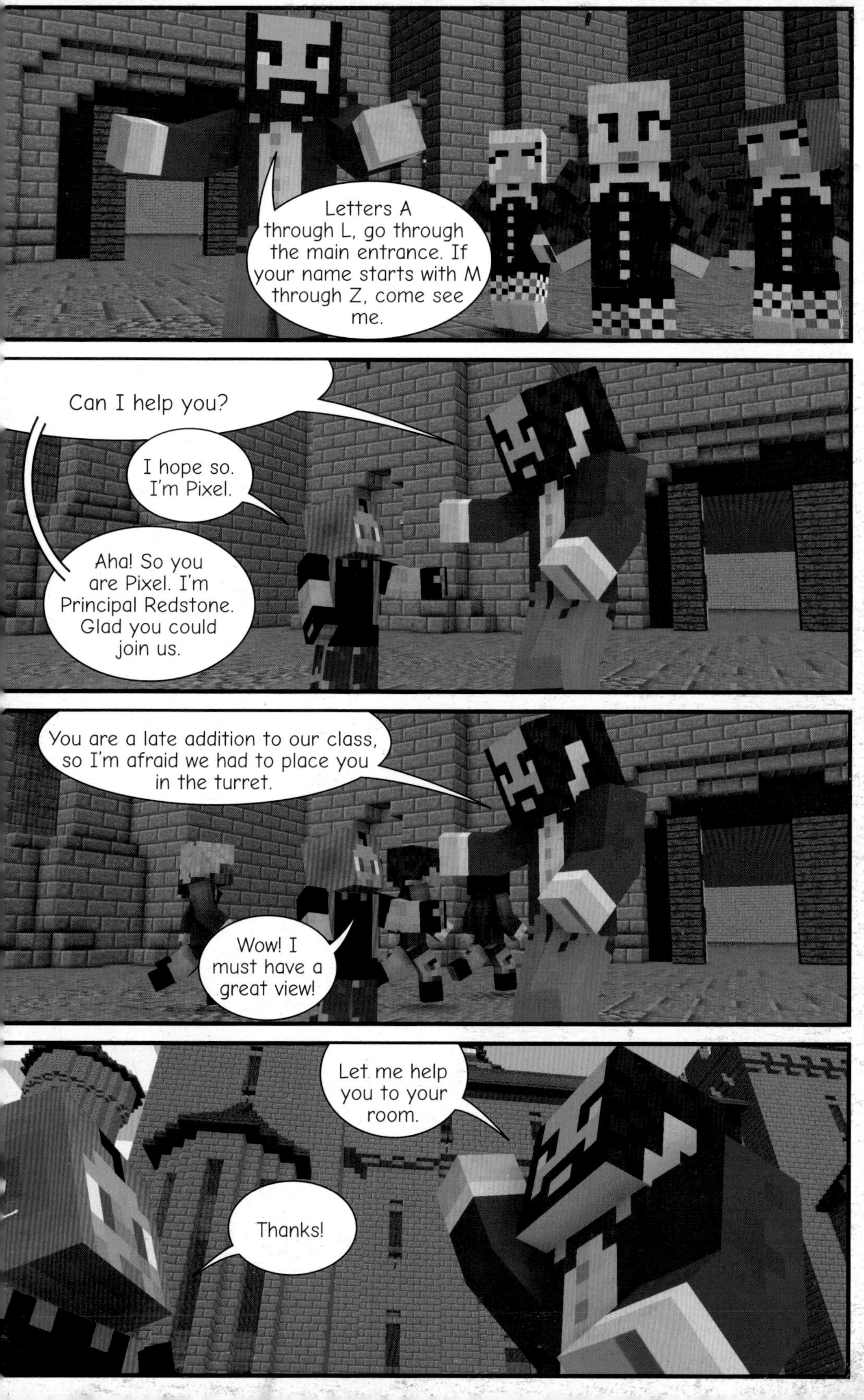
Letters A through L, go through the main entrance. If your name starts with M through Z, come see me.
Can I help you?
I hope so. I'm Pixel.
Aha! So you are Pixel. I'm Principal Redstone. Glad you could join us.
You are a late addition to our class, so I'm afraid we had to place you in the turret.
Wow! I must have a great view!
Let me help you to your room.
Thanks!

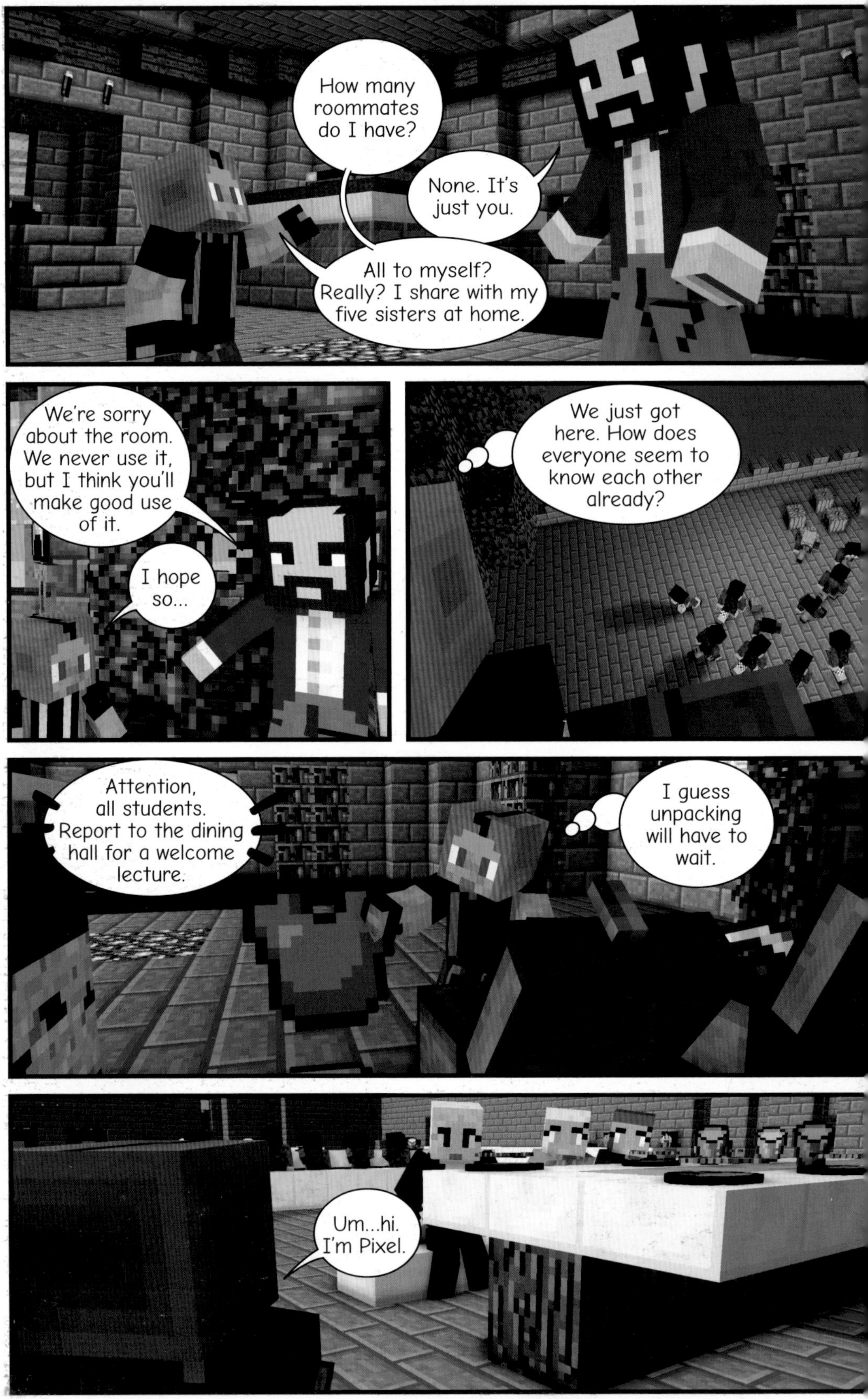
How many roommates do I have?
None. It's just you.
All to myself? Really? I share with my five sisters at home.
We're sorry about the room. We never use it, but I think you'll make good use of it.
I hope so...
We just got here. How does everyone seem to know each other already?
Attention, all students. Report to the dining hall for a welcome lecture.
I guess unpacking will have to wait.
Um...hi. I'm Pixel.

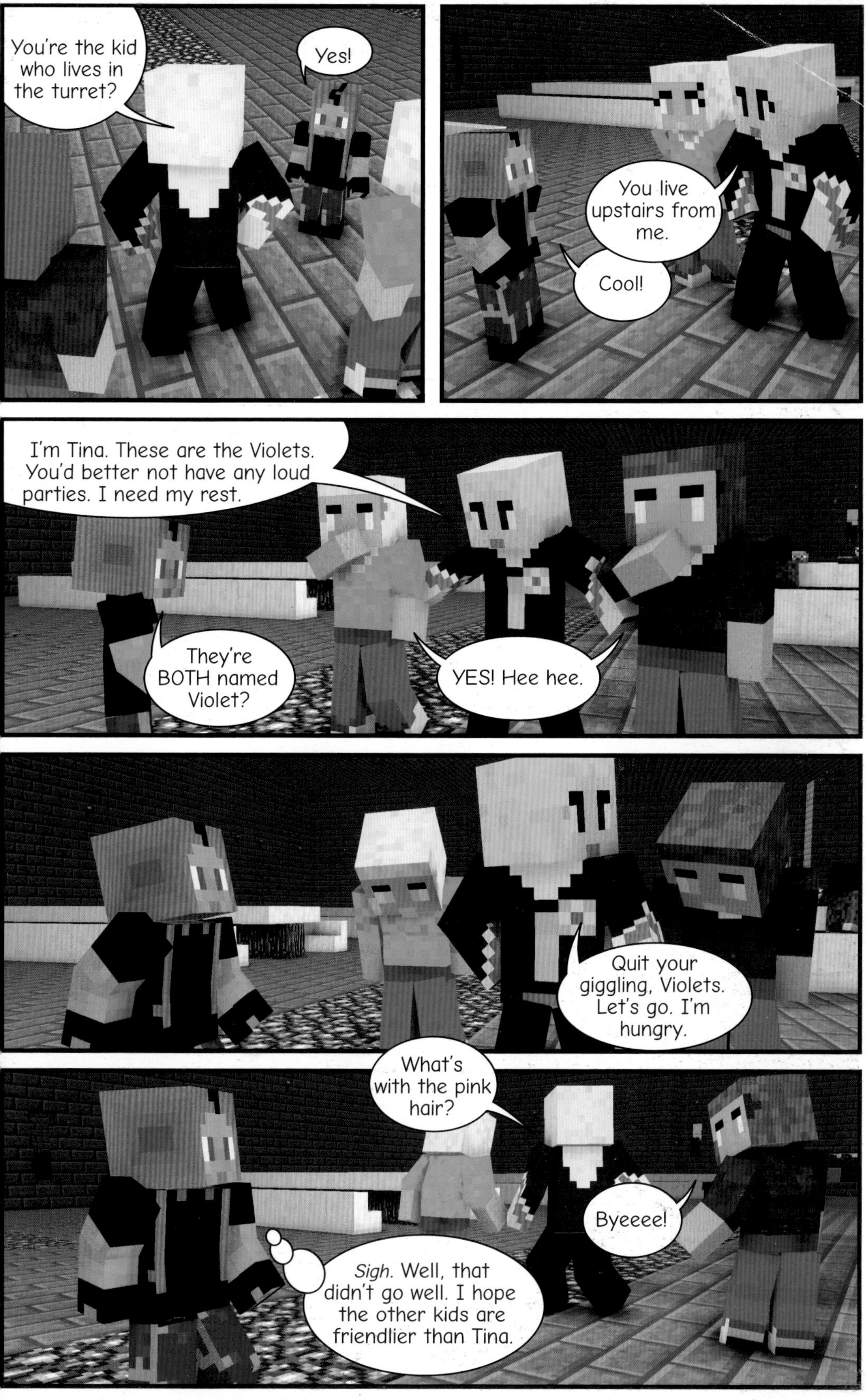
You're the kid who lives in the turret?
Yes!
You live upstairs from me.
Cool!
I'm Tina. These are the Violets. You'd better not have any loud parties. I need my rest.
They're BOTH named Violet?
YES! Hee hee.
Quit your giggling, Violets. Let's go. I'm hungry.
What's with the pink hair?
Byeeee!
Sigh. Well, that didn't go well. I hope the other kids are friendlier than Tina.

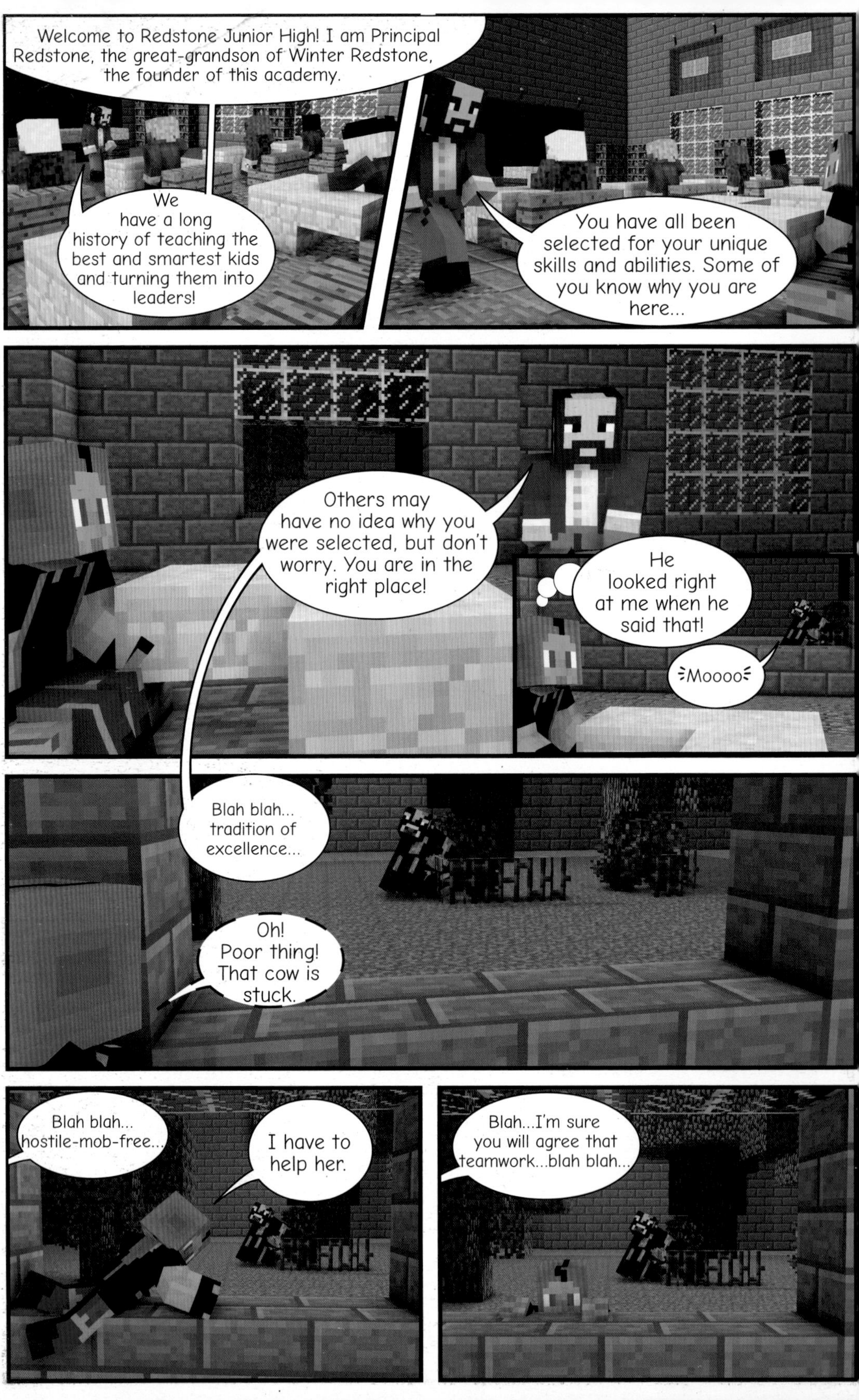
Welcome to Redstone Junior High! I am Principal Redstone, the great-grandson of Winter Redstone, the founder of this academy.
We have a long history of teaching the best and smartest kids and turning them into leaders!
You have all been selected for your unique skills and abilities. Some of you know why you are here...
Others may have no idea why you were selected, but don't worry. You are in the right place!
He looked right at me when he said that!
Moooo
Blah blah... tradition of excellence...
Oh! Poor thing! That cow is stuck.
Blah blah... hostile-mob-free...
I have to help her.
Blah...I'm sure you will agree that teamwork...blah blah...

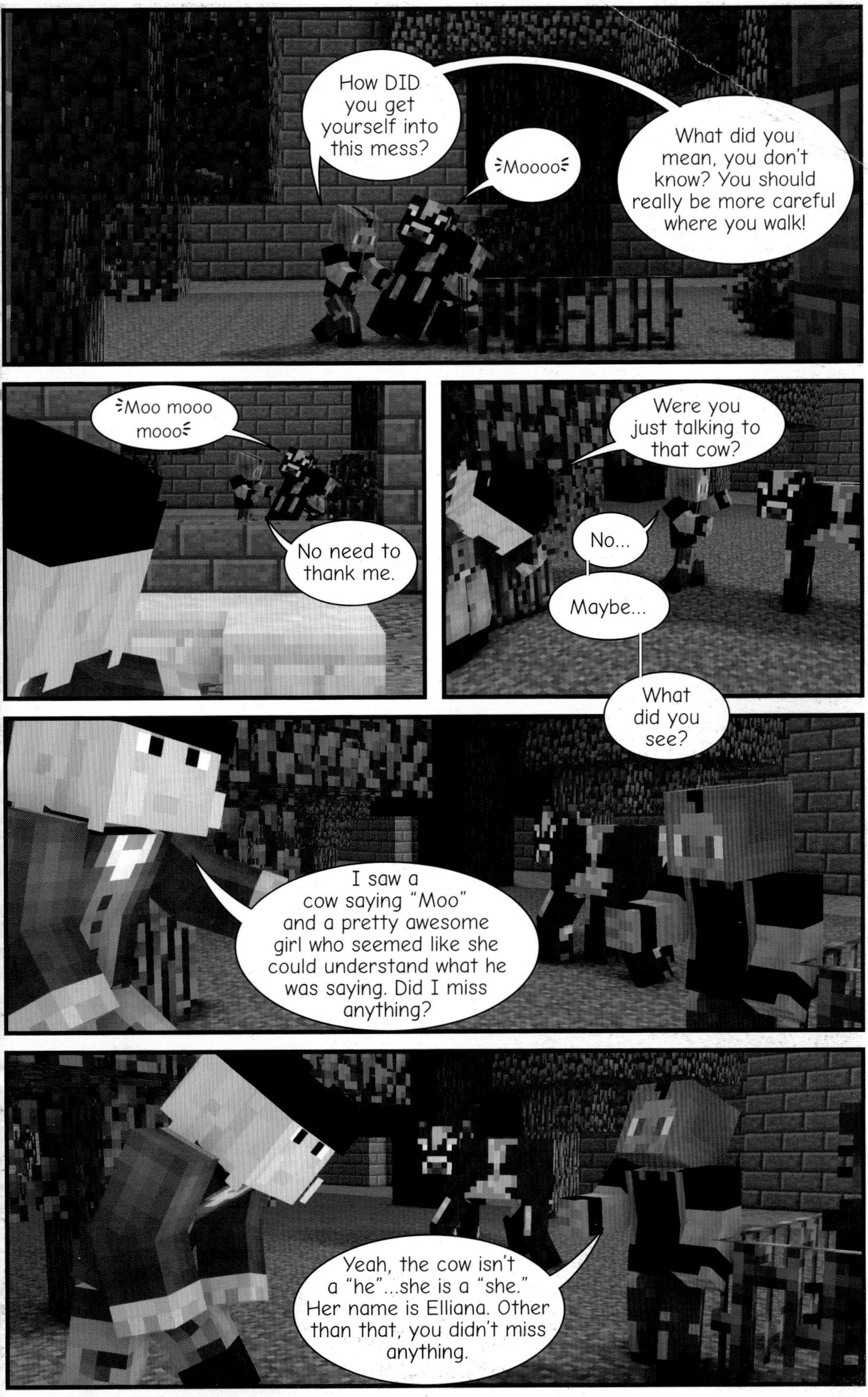
How DID you get yourself into this mess?
Moooo
What did you mean, you don't know? You should really be more careful where you walk!
Moo mooo mooo
No need to thank me.
Were you just talking to that cow?
No...
Maybe...
What did you see?
I saw a cow saying "Moo" and a pretty awesome girl who seemed like she could understand what he was saying. Did I miss anything?
Yeah, the cow isn't a "he"...she is a "she." Her name is Elliana. Other than that, you didn't miss anything.

It's not a big deal. I've been doing it all my life.

That's really cool. I can't speak to animals. I just make stuff.

Doesn't make it less cool.

Please don't tell anyone!

It'll be our secret.

What's this arrow for?

Ouch! Why did you do that?

Sorry. Hold still. It's tipped so we can sneak back in without Principal Redstone catching us.

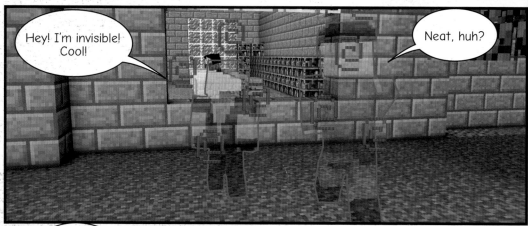

Hey! I'm invisible! Cool!

Neat, huh?

I'm Sky, by the way.

I'm Pixel. Nice to meet you.

You're the first person I've met here who is actually nice.

Same here. But I've only met three people so far.

Now you've met four.

CHAPTER 3

HUNGRY

ZOMBIES

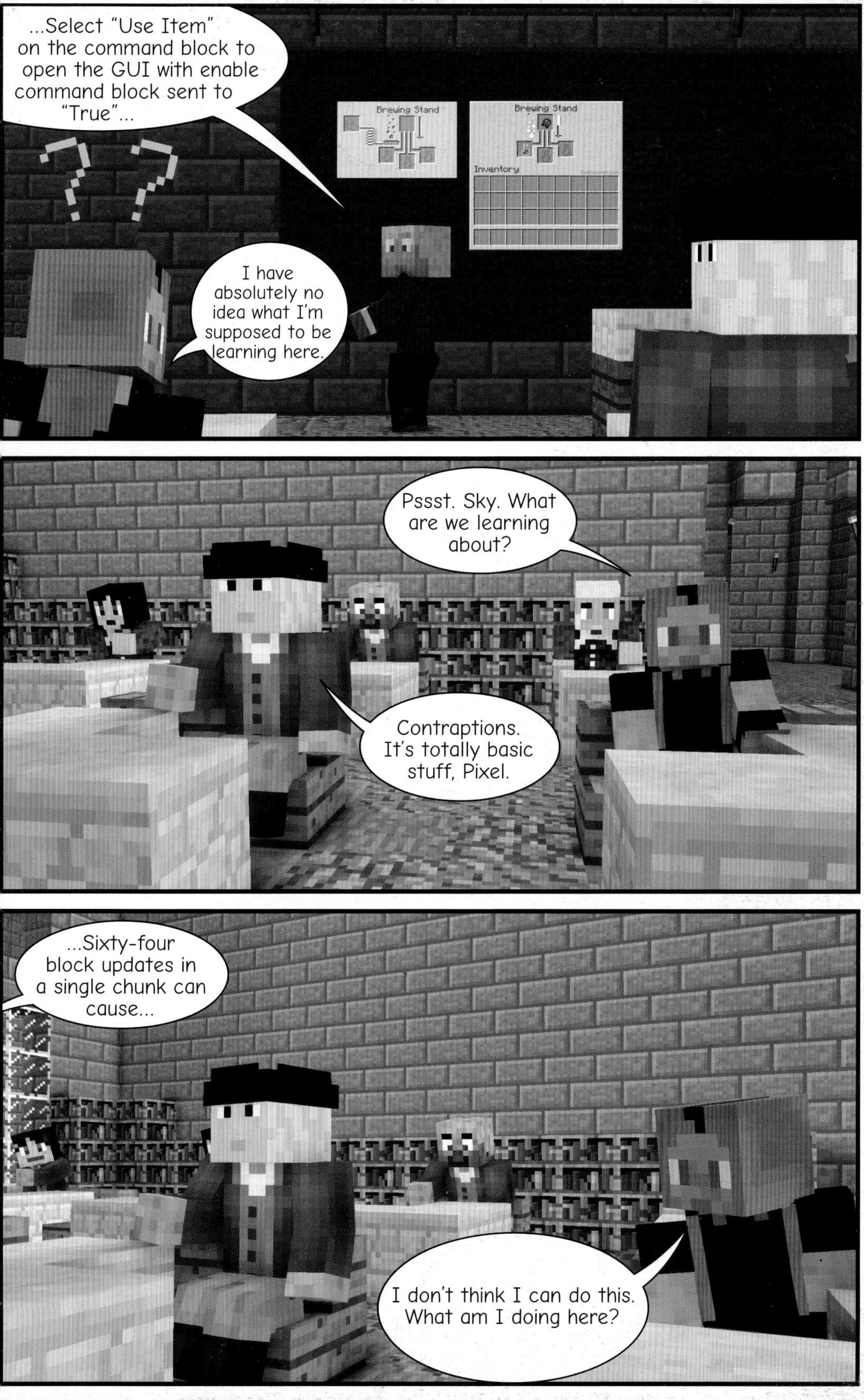
...Select "Use Item" on the command block to open the GUI with enable command block sent to "True"...
Brewing Stand
Brewing Stand
Inventory
I have absolutely no idea what I'm supposed to be learning here.
Pssst. Sky. What are we learning about?
Contraptions. It's totally basic stuff, Pixel.
...Sixty-four block updates in a single chunk can cause...
I don't think I can do this. What am I doing here?

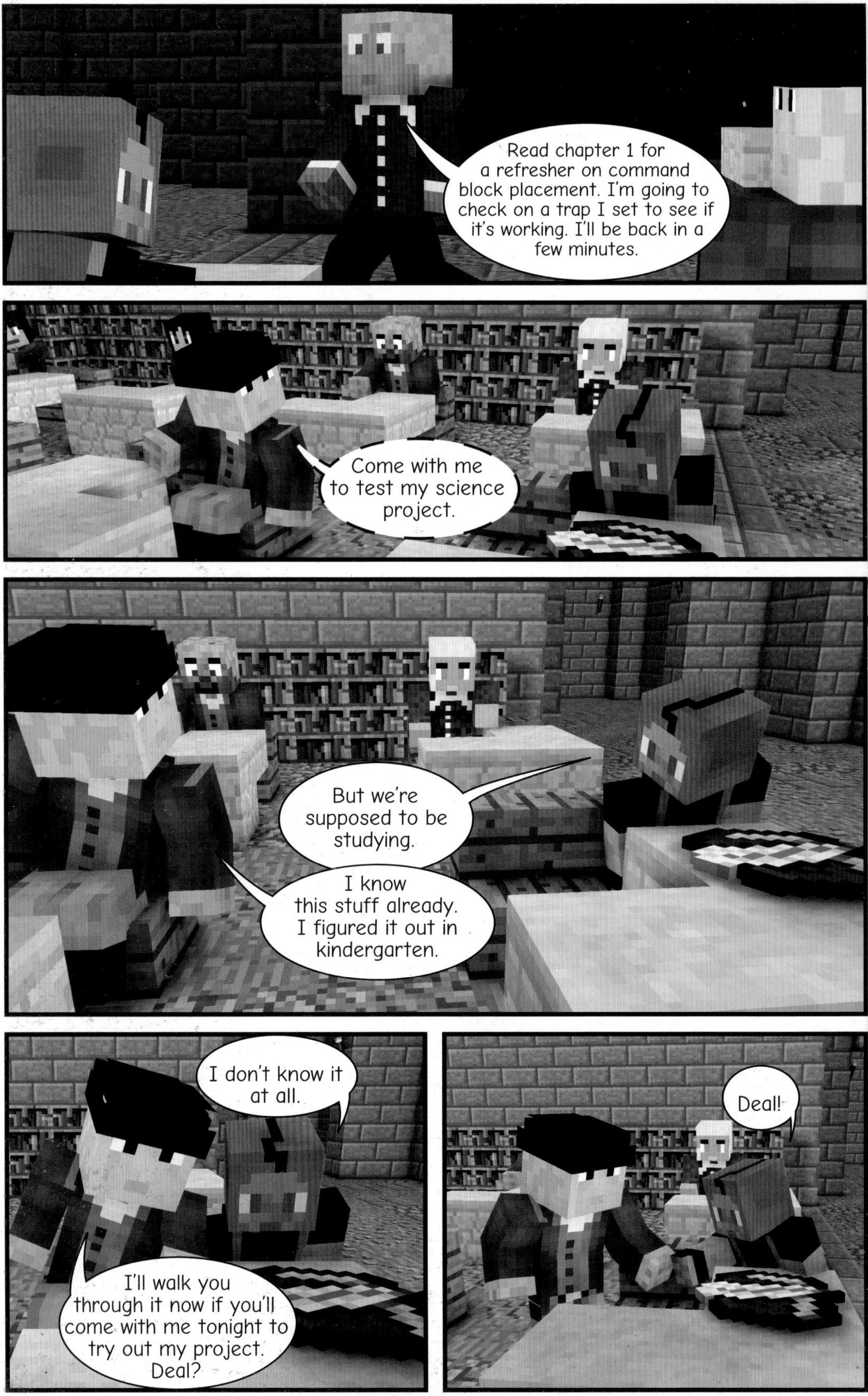
Read chapter 1 for a refresher on command block placement. I'm going to check on a trap I set to see if it's working. I'll be back in a few minutes.
Come with me to test my science project.
But we're supposed to be studying.
I know this stuff already. I figured it out in kindergarten.
I don't know it at all.
I'll walk you through it now if you'll come with me tonight to try out my project. Deal?
Deal!

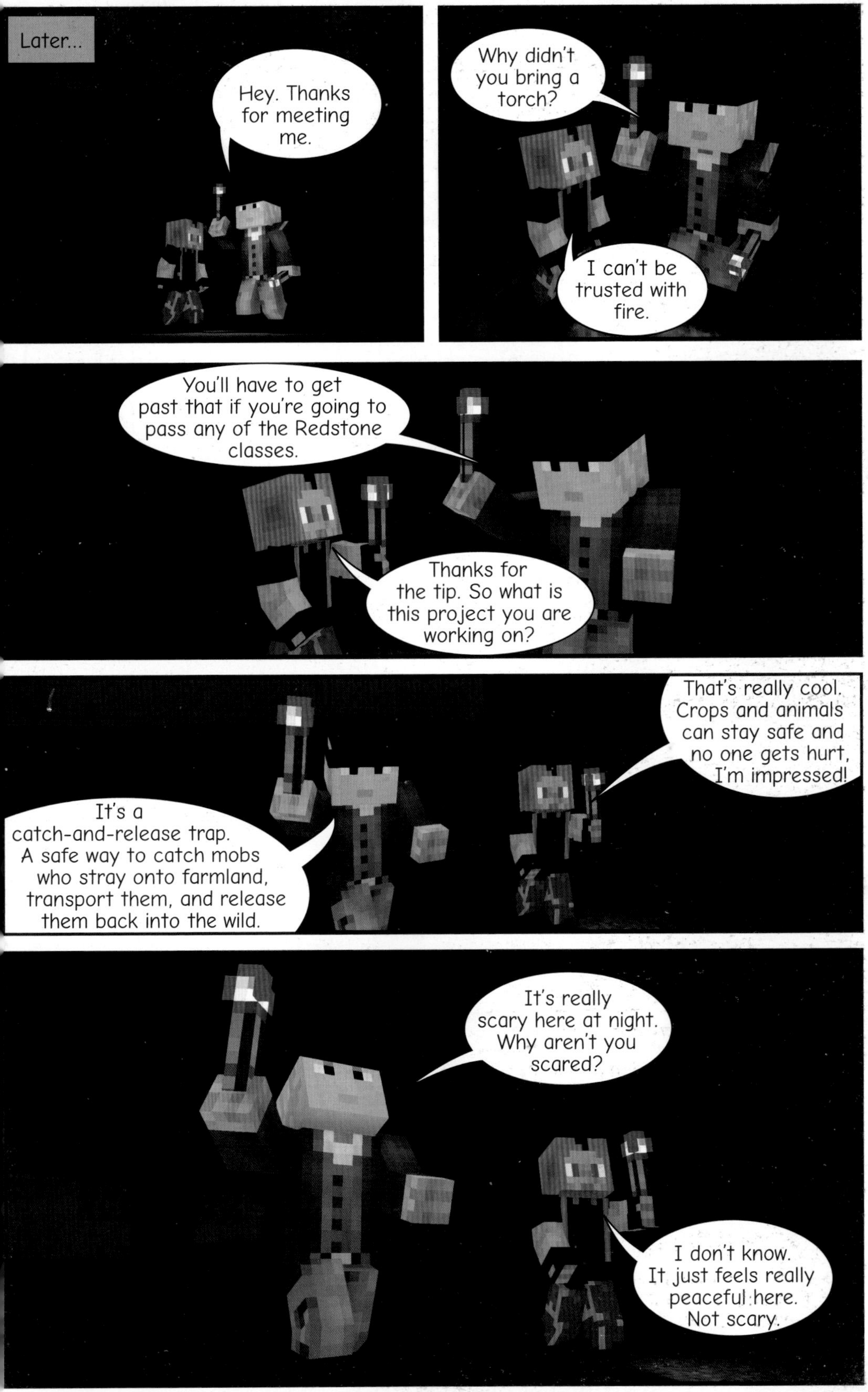
Later...
Hey. Thanks for meeting me.
Why didn't you bring a torch?
I can't be trusted with fire.
You'll have to get past that if you're going to pass any of the Redstone classes.
Thanks for the tip. So what is this project you are working on?
It's a catch-and-release trap. A safe way to catch mobs who stray onto farmland, transport them, and release them back into the wild.
That's really cool. Crops and animals can stay safe and no one gets hurt, I'm impressed!
It's really scary here at night. Why aren't you scared?
I don't know. It just feels really peaceful here. Not scary.

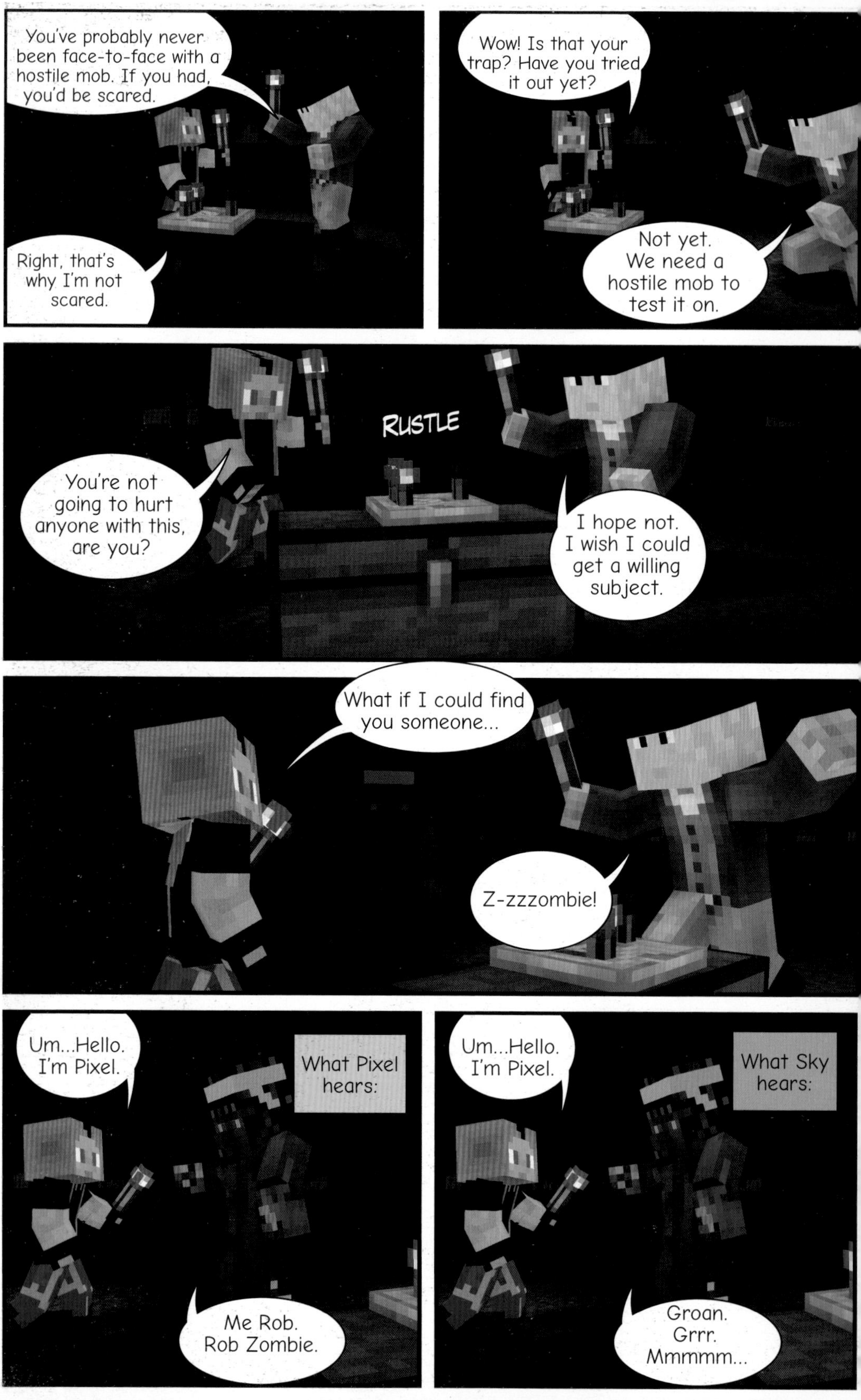
You've probably never been face-to-face with a hostile mob. If you had, you'd be scared.
Right, that's why I'm not scared.
Wow! Is that your trap? Have you tried it out yet?
Not yet. We need a hostile mob to test it on.
RUSTLE
You're not going to hurt anyone with this, are you?
I hope not. I wish I could get a willing subject.
What if I could find you someone...
Z-zzzombie!
Um...Hello. I'm Pixel.
What Pixel hears:
Me Rob. Rob Zombie.
Um...Hello. I'm Pixel.
What Sky hears:
Groan. Grrr. Mmmmm...

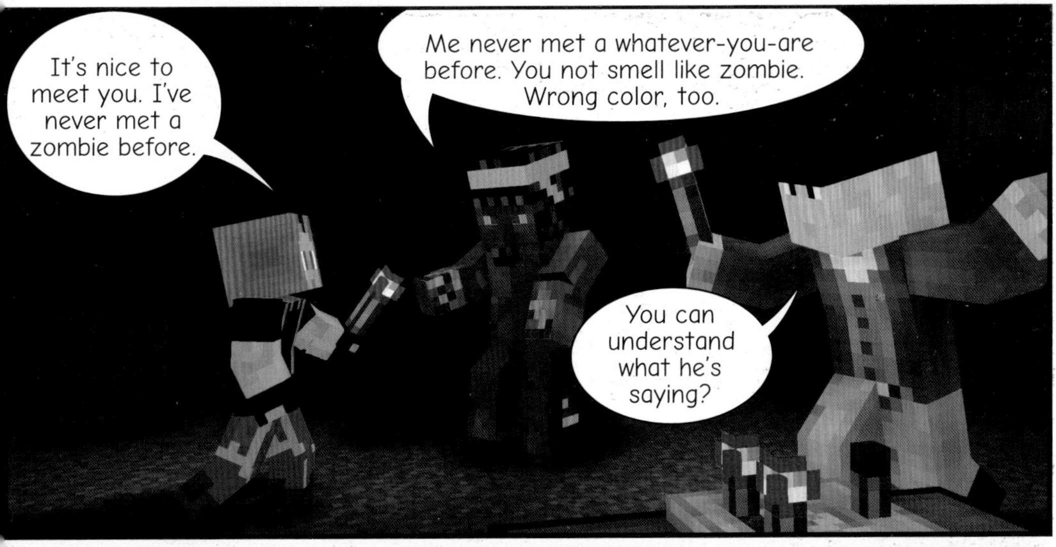
It's nice to meet you. I've never met a zombie before.
Me never met a whatever-you-are before. You not smell like zombie. Wrong color, too.
You can understand what he's saying?

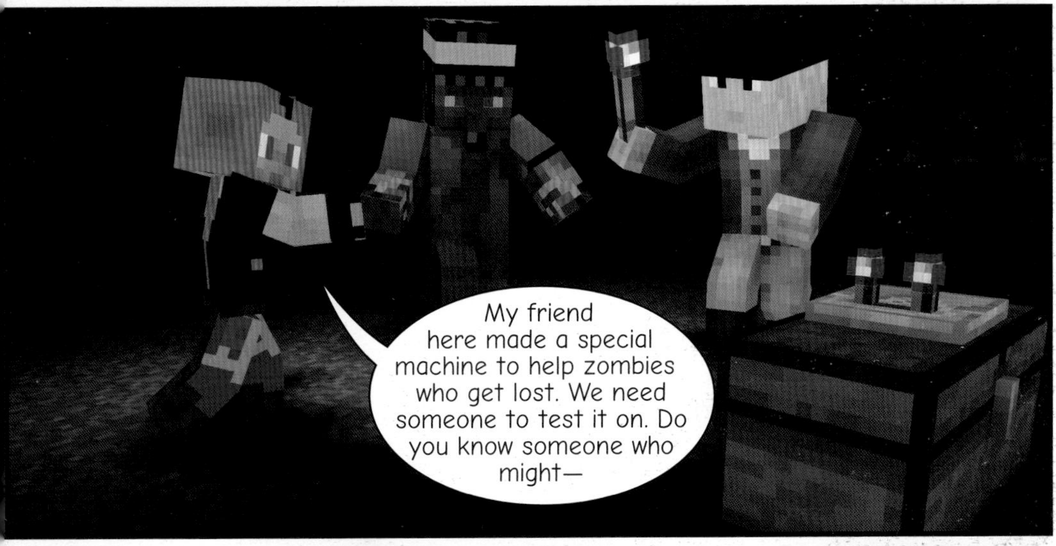
My friend here made a special machine to help zombies who get lost. We need someone to test it on. Do you know someone who might—

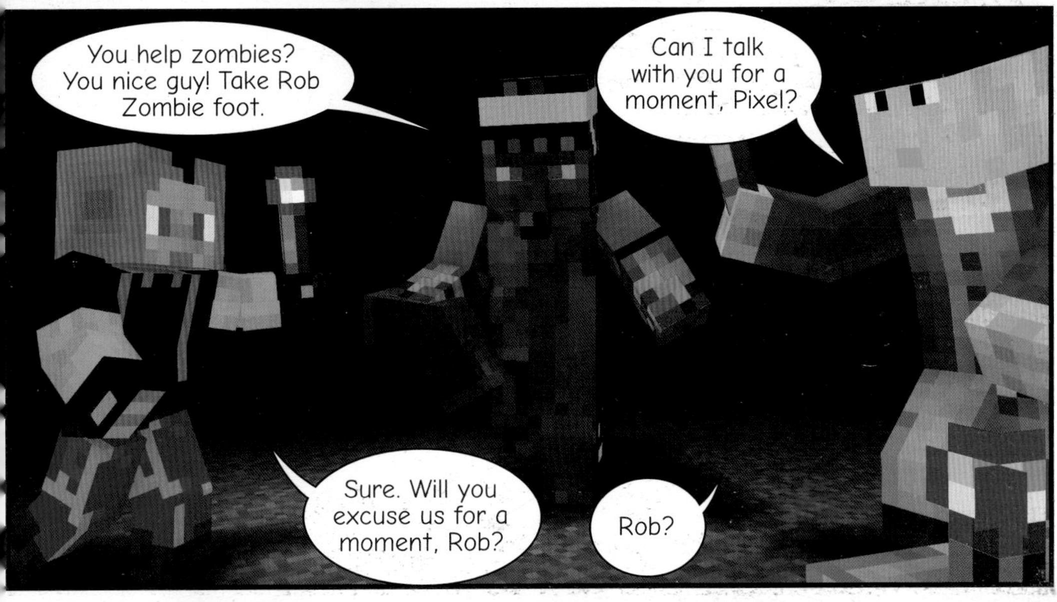
You help zombies? You nice guy! Take Rob Zombie foot.
Can I talk with you for a moment, Pixel?
Sure. Will you excuse us for a moment, Rob?
Rob?

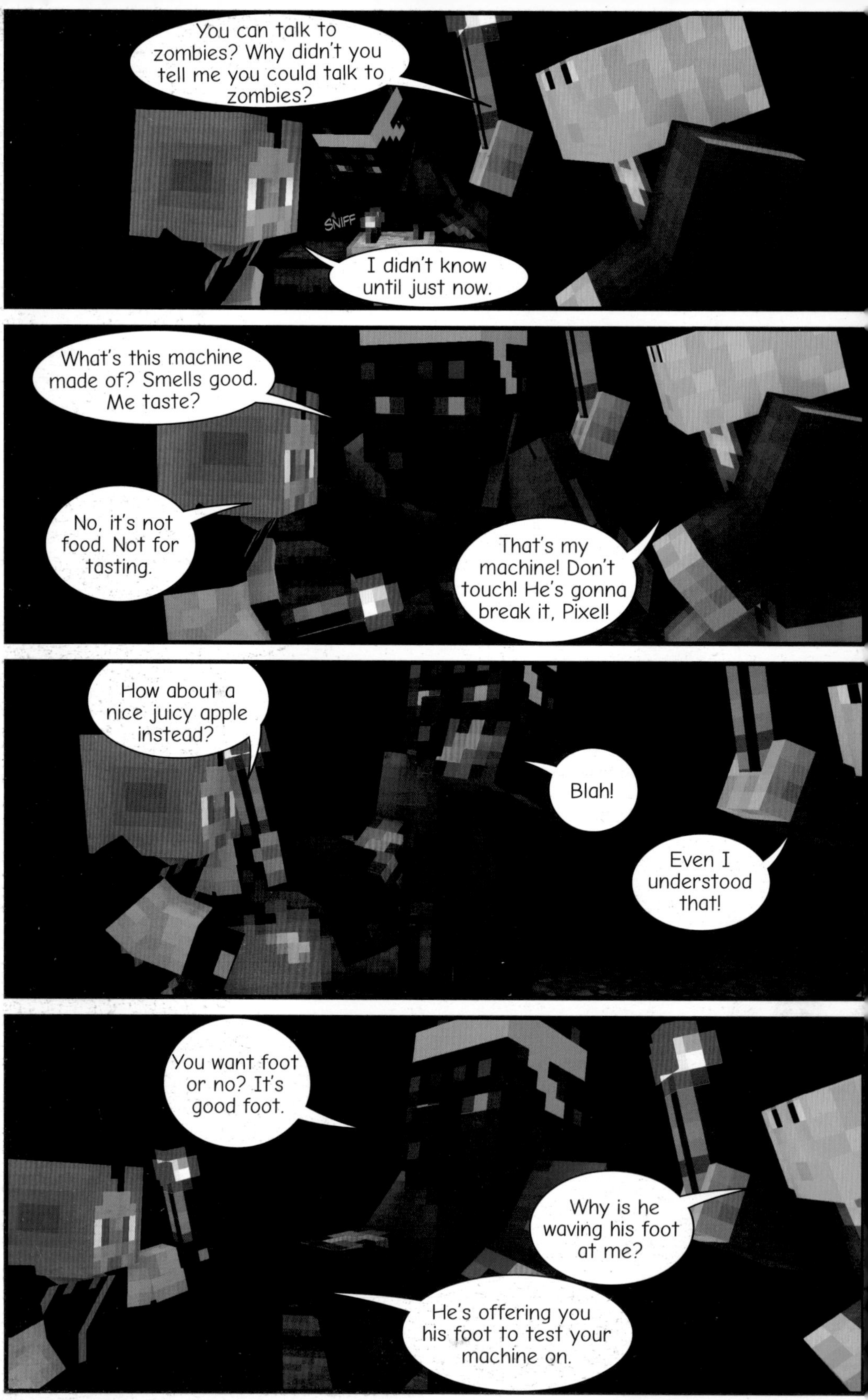
You can talk to zombies? Why didn't you tell me you could talk to zombies?
SNIFF
I didn't know until just now.
What's this machine made of? Smells good. Me taste?
No, it's not food. Not for tasting.
That's my machine! Don't touch! He's gonna break it, Pixel!
How about a nice juicy apple instead?
Blah!
Even I understood that!
You want foot or no? It's good foot.
Why is he waving his foot at me?
He's offering you his foot to test your machine on.

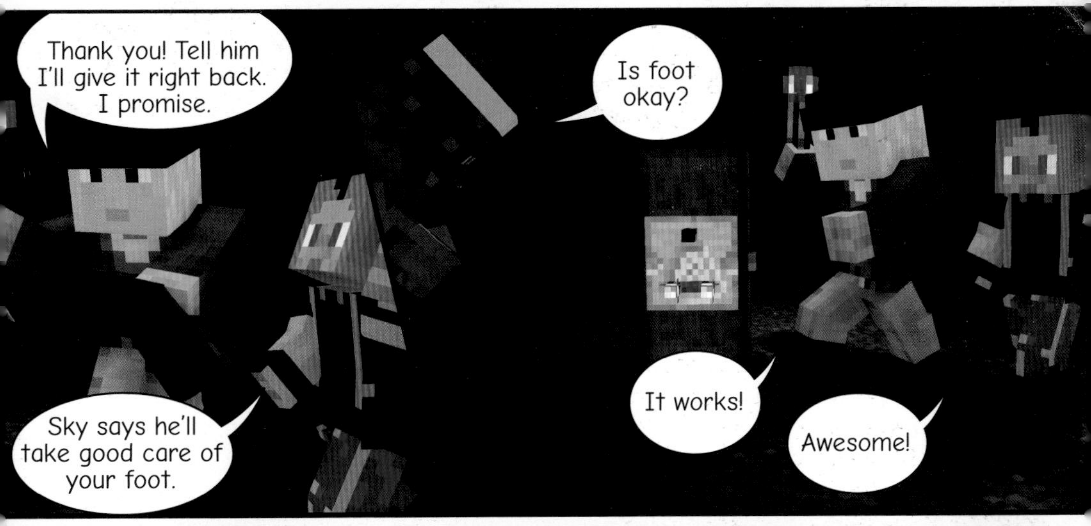
Thank you! Tell him I'll give it right back. I promise.
Is foot okay?
Sky says he'll take good care of your foot.
It works!
Awesome!

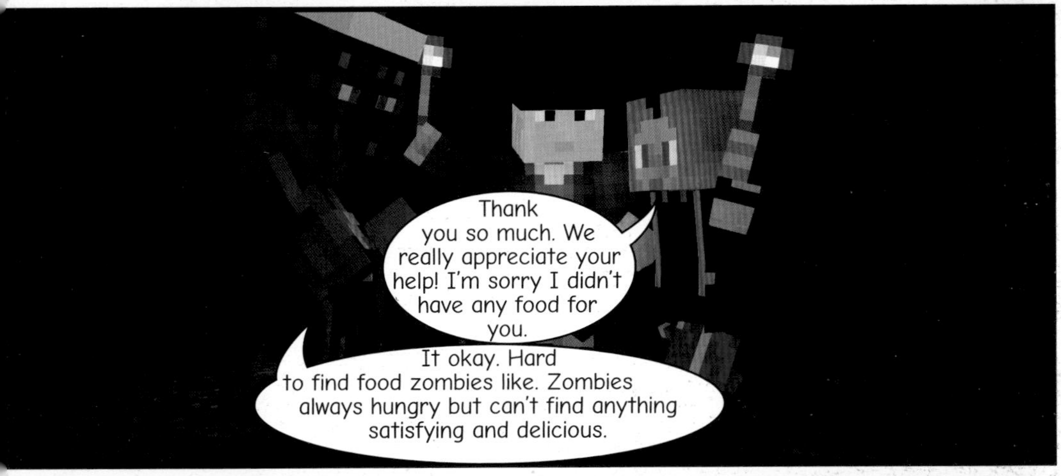
Thank you so much. We really appreciate your help! I'm sorry I didn't have any food for you.
It okay. Hard to find food zombies like. Zombies always hungry but can't find anything satisfying and delicious.

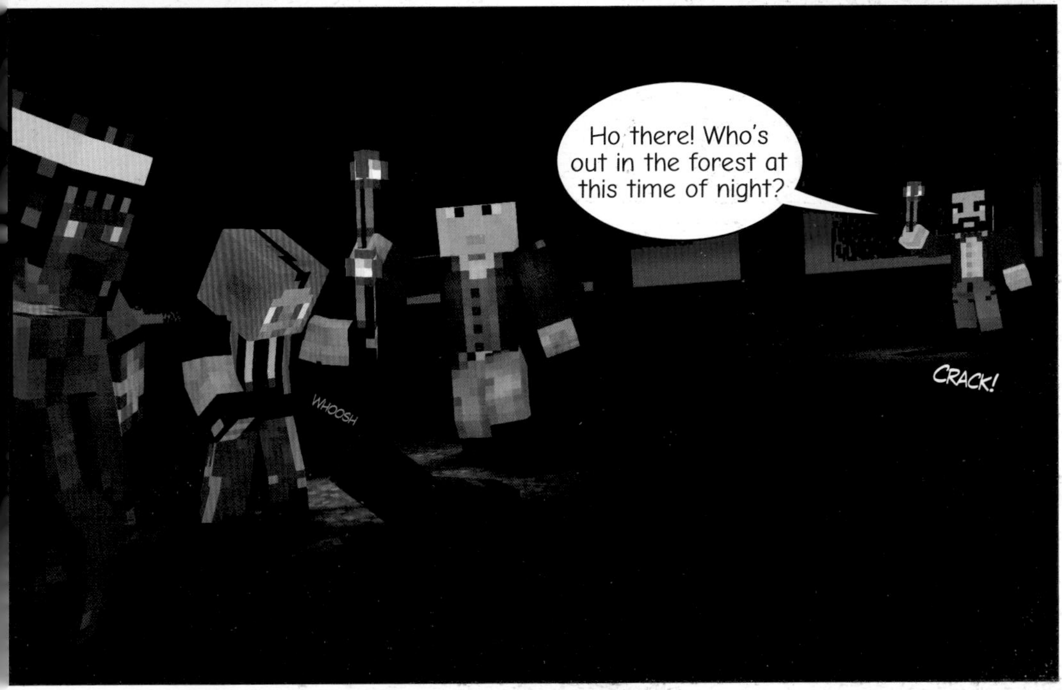
Ho there! Who's out in the forest at this time of night?
WHOOSH
CRACK!

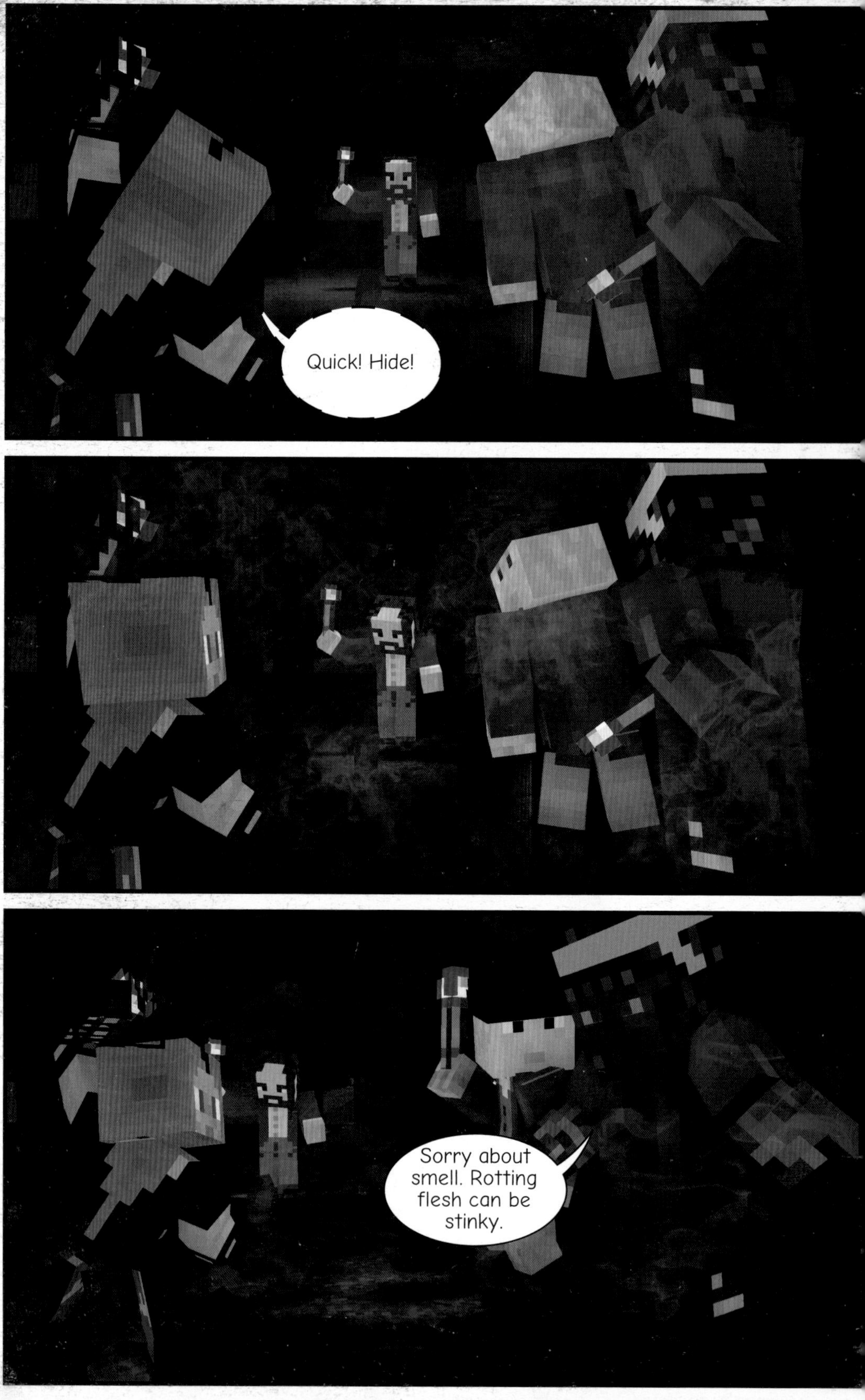
Quick! Hide!
Sorry about smell. Rotting flesh can be stinky.

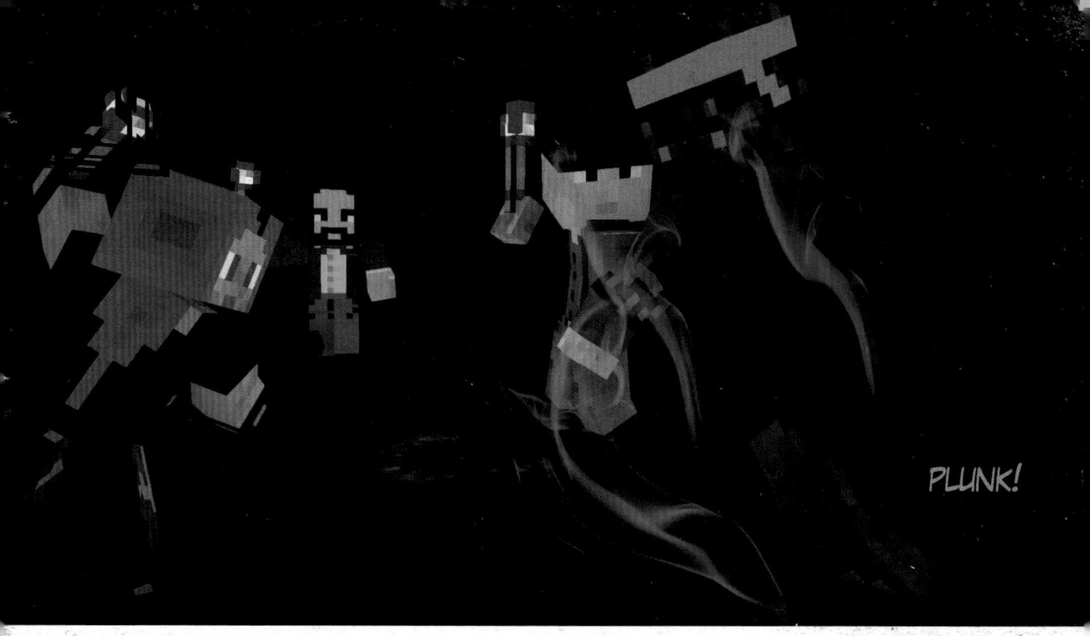
PLUNK!

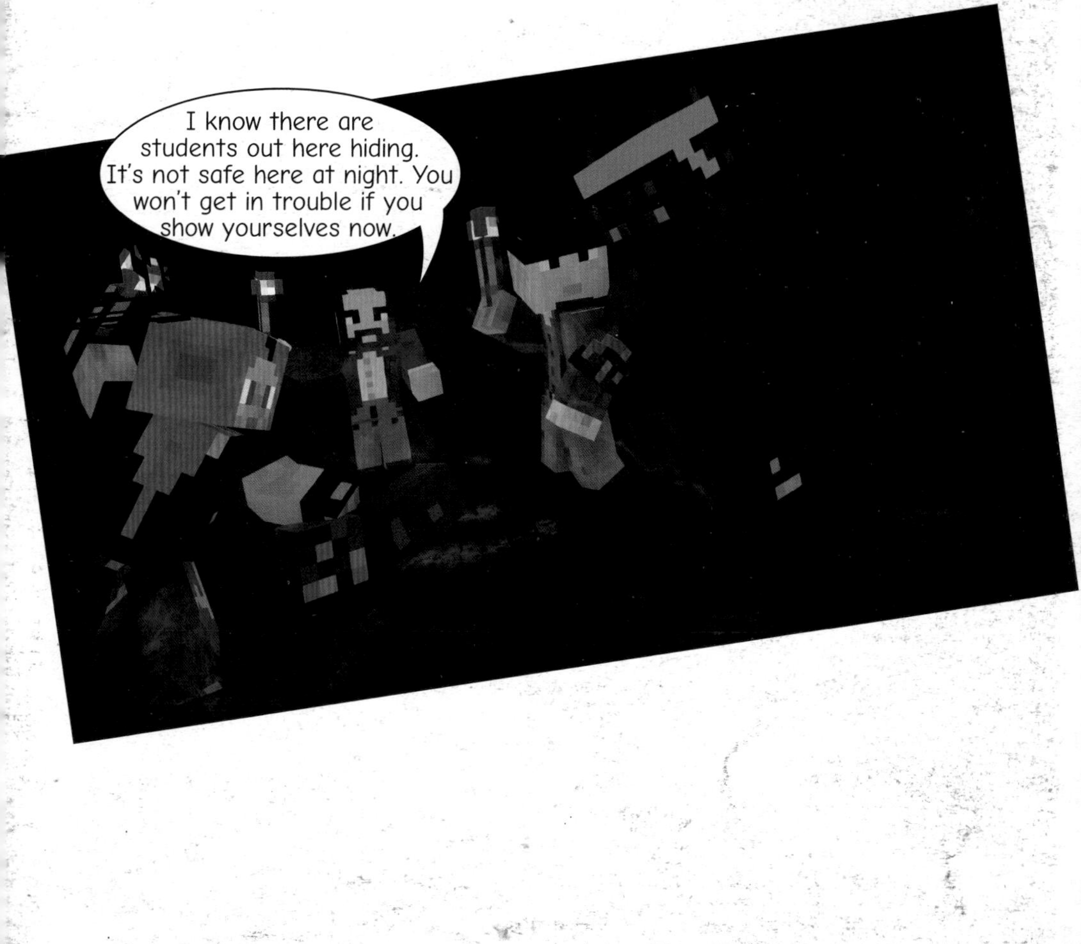
I know there are students out here hiding. It's not safe here at night. You won't get in trouble if you show yourselves now.

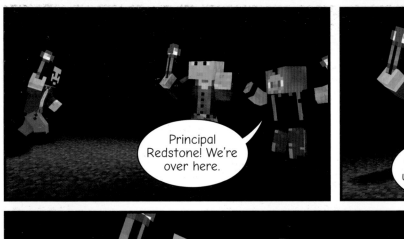

Principal Redstone! We're over here.

Well, that doesn't usually work. Good.

I see it's my new friend Pixel. Hello there. And who is this?

I'm Sky Torrance, sir.

Ah, the mechanical genius. Of course. Pleasure to meet you. I'm sure you both have an excellent reason for being in the woods in the dark of night and just forgot to get permission, right?

Um...

It's my fault, sir. I needed to test my latest invention before submitting it to the teacher. It's a safe mob relocation system.

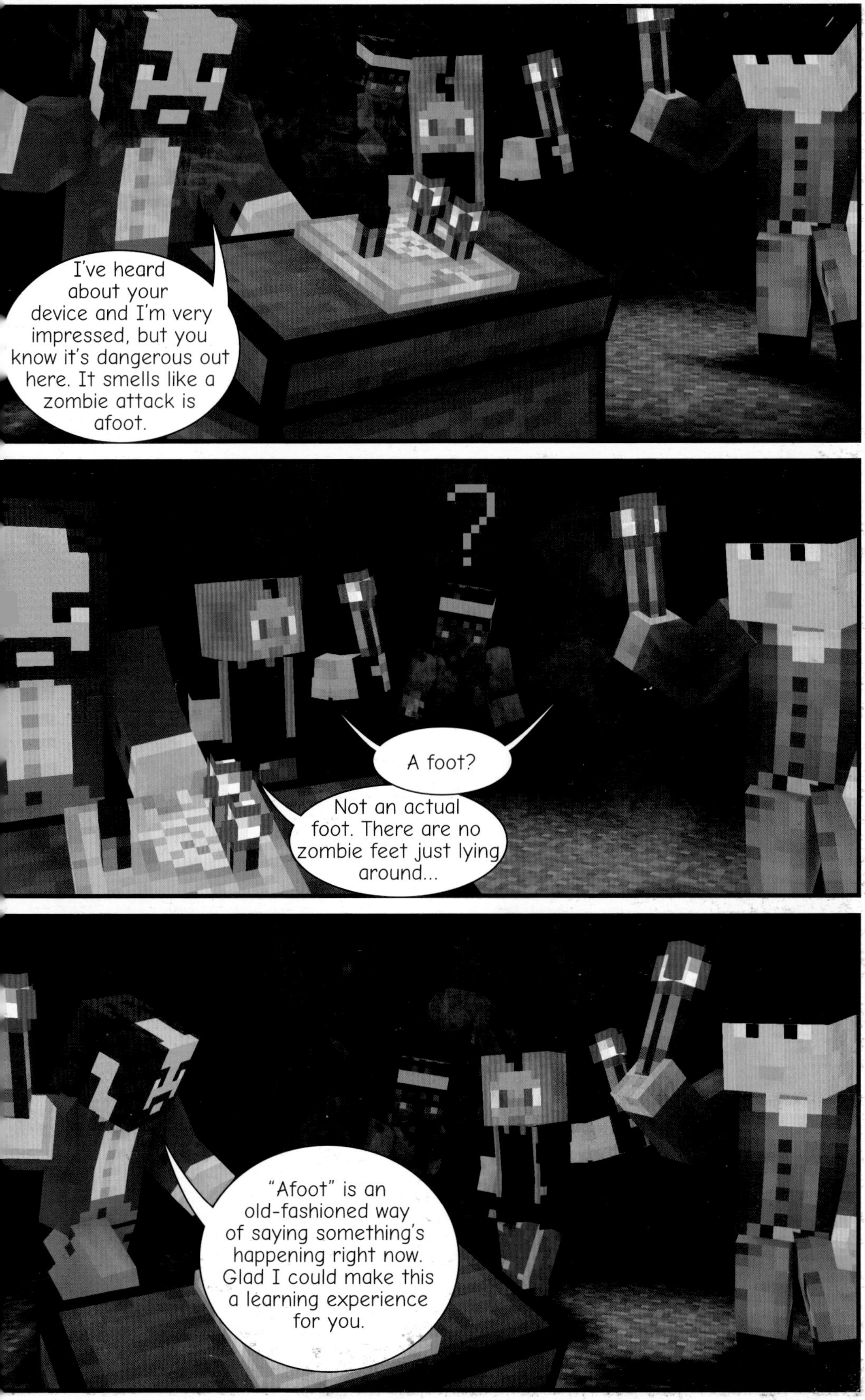
I've heard about your device and I'm very impressed, but you know it's dangerous out here. It smells like a zombie attack is afoot.
A foot?
Not an actual foot. There are no zombie feet just lying around...
"Afoot" is an old-fashioned way of saying something's happening right now. Glad I could make this a learning experience for you.

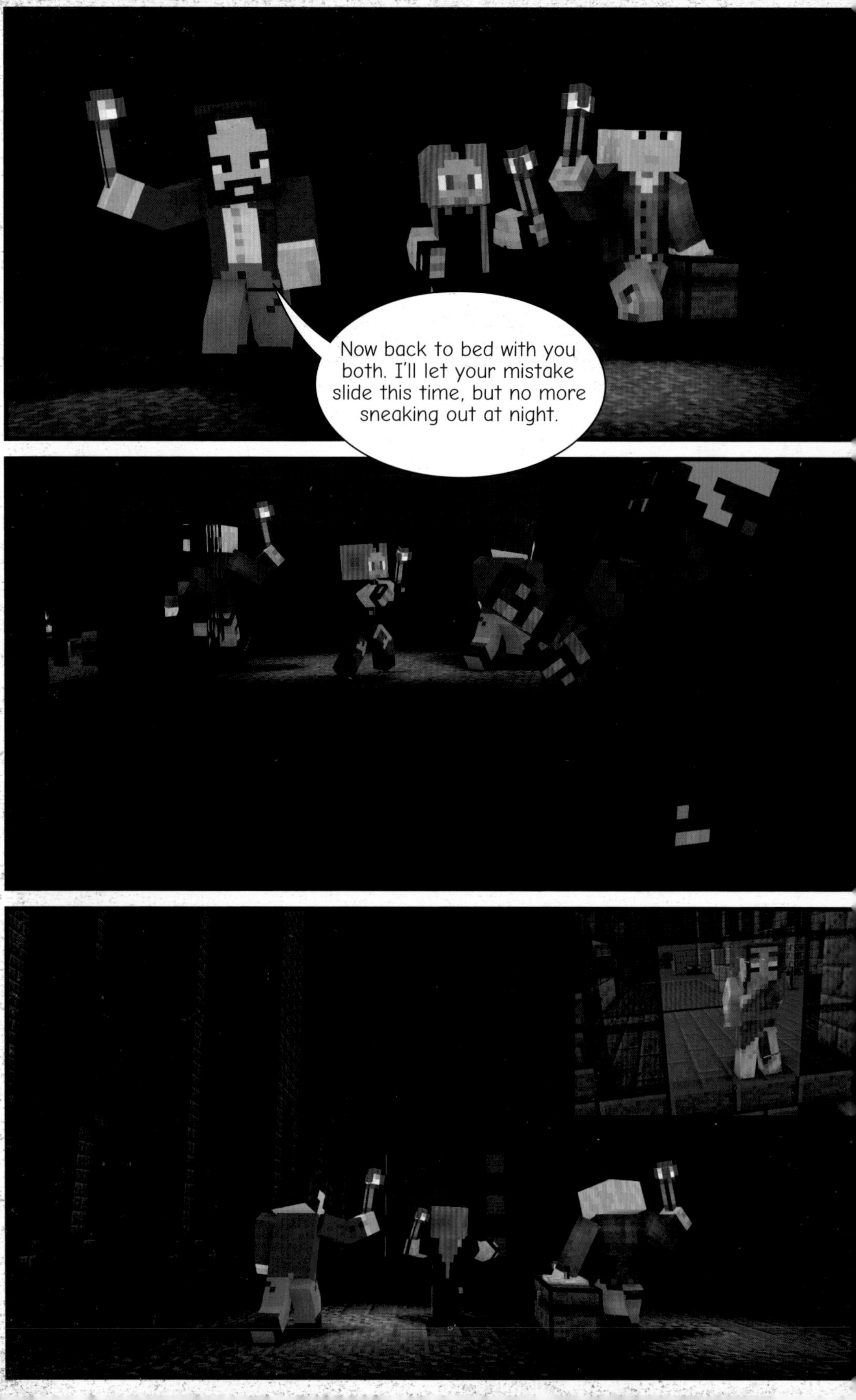
Now back to bed with you both. I'll let your mistake slide this time, but no more sneaking out at night.

CHAPTER 4

SATURDAY IS COMING

BEWARE OF SATURDAY

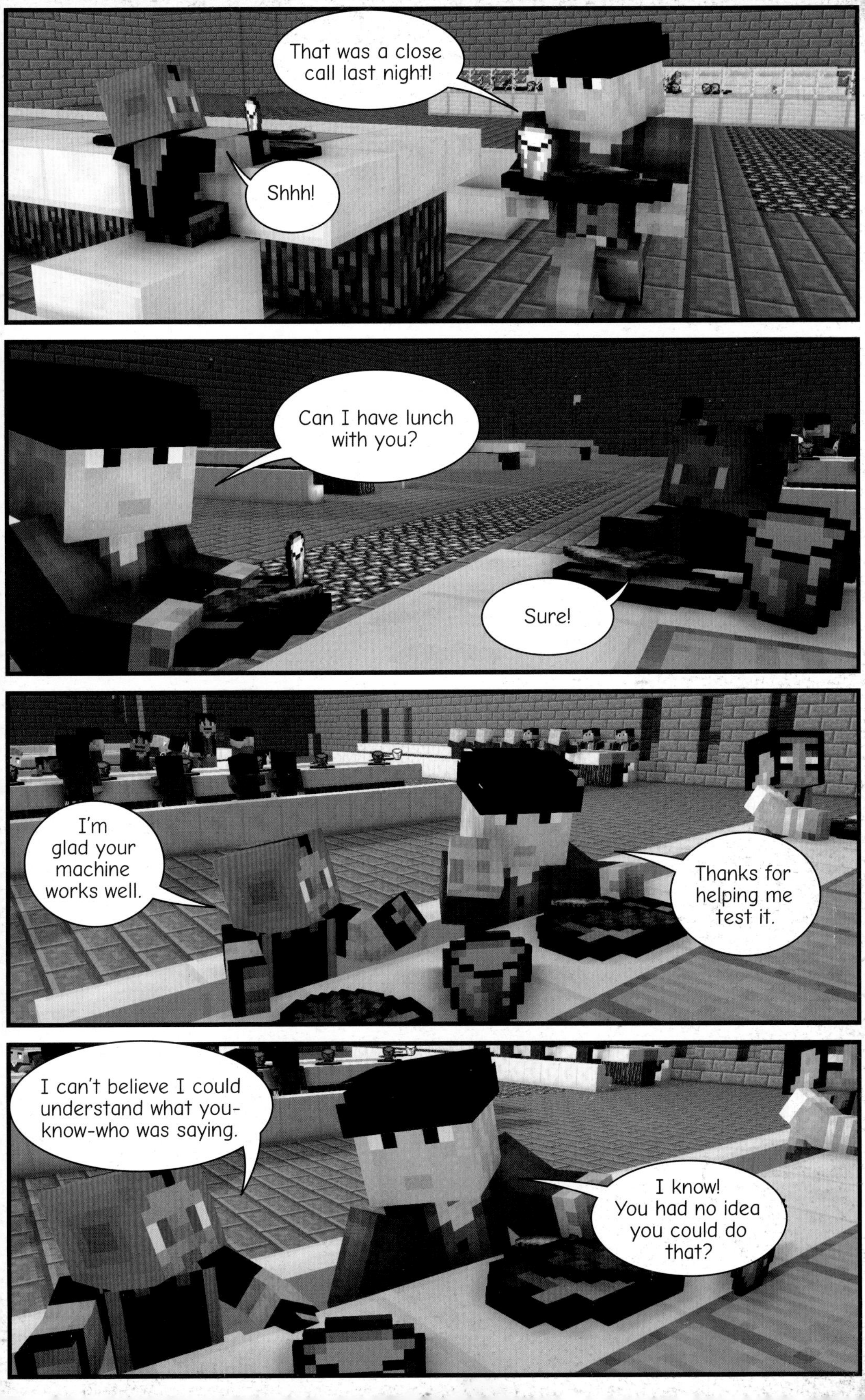
That was a close call last night!
Shhh!
Can I have lunch with you?
Sure!
I'm glad your machine works well.
Thanks for helping me test it.
I can't believe I could understand what you-know-who was saying.
I know! You had no idea you could do that?

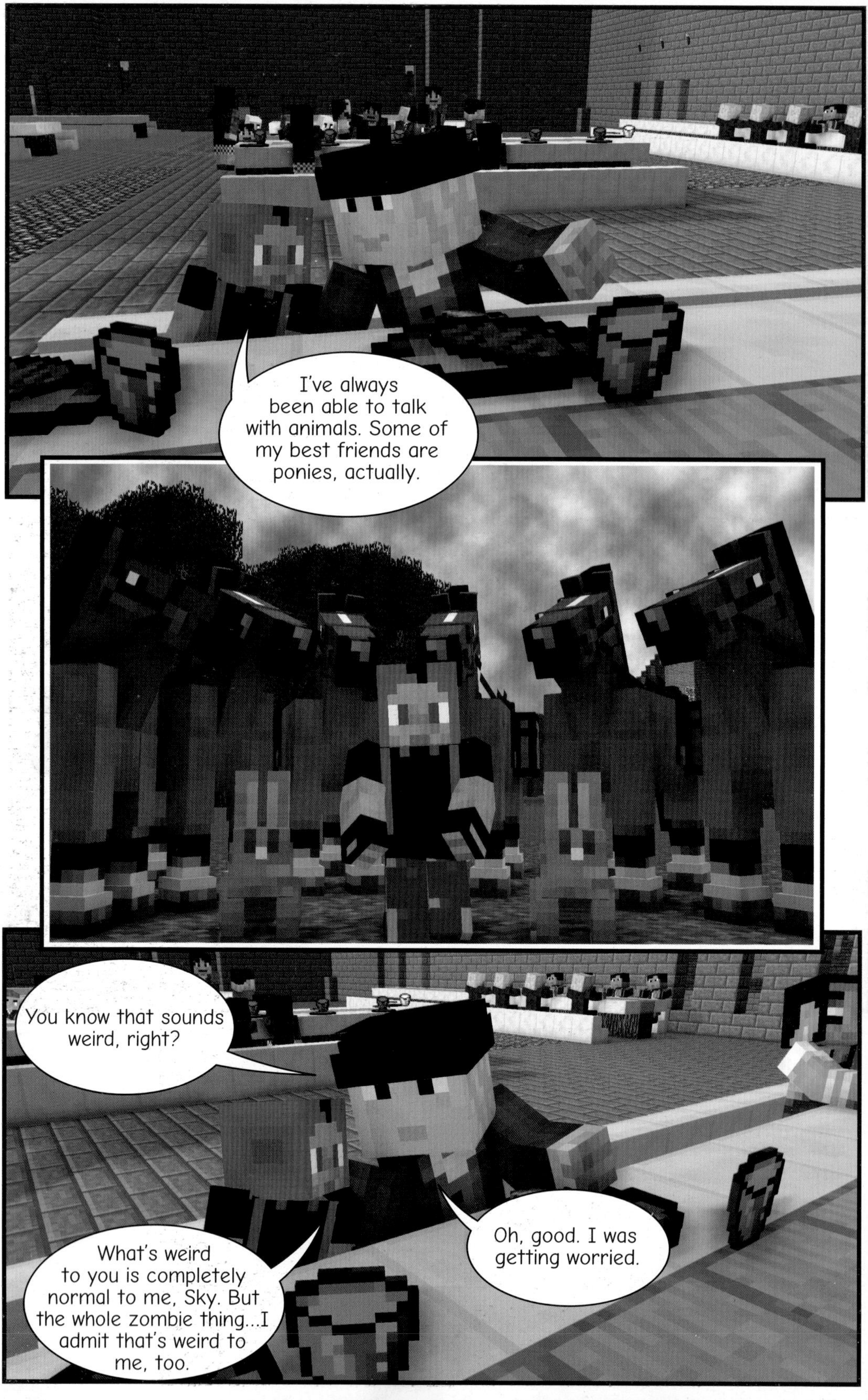
I've always been able to talk with animals. Some of my best friends are ponies, actually.
You know that sounds weird, right?
What's weird to you is completely normal to me, Sky. But the whole zombie thing...I admit that's weird to me, too.
Oh, good. I was getting worried.

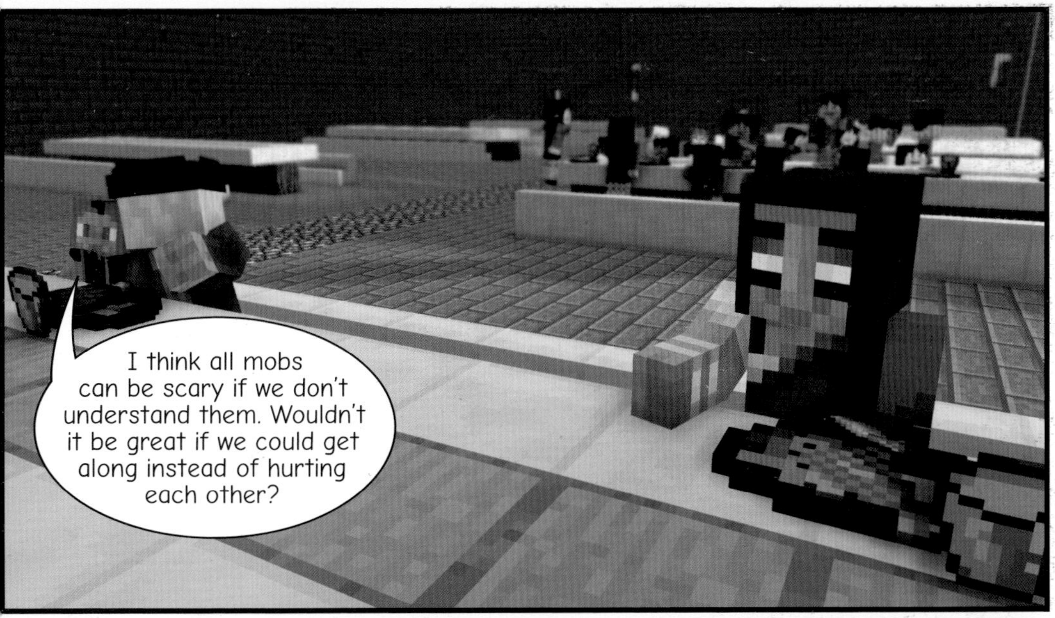

I think all mobs can be scary if we don't understand them. Wouldn't it be great if we could get along instead of hurting each other?

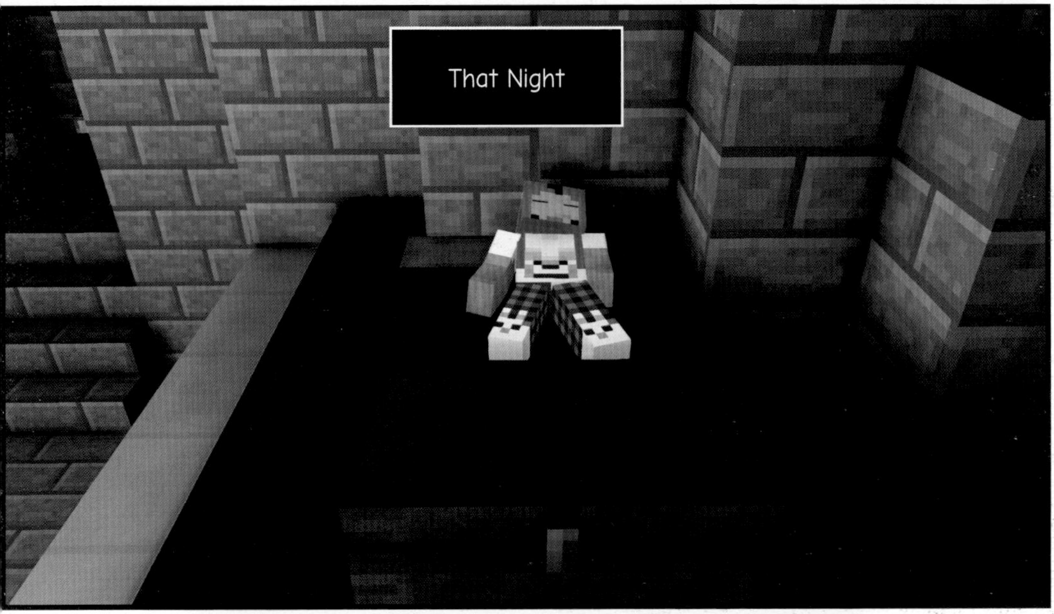

That Night

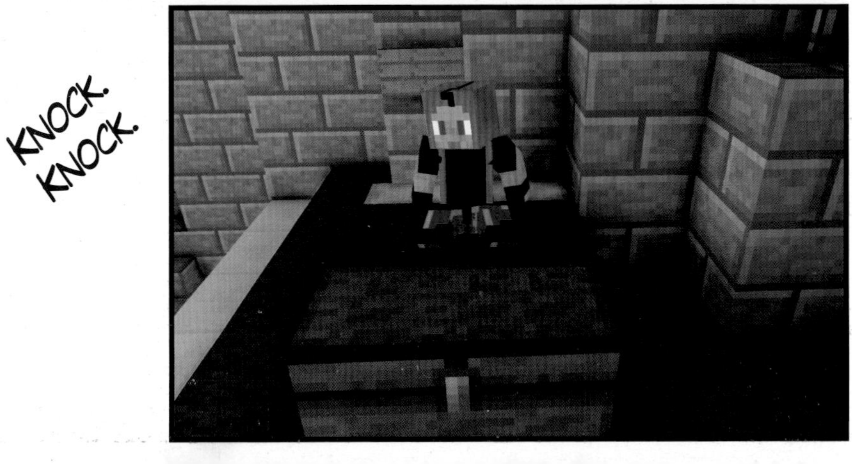

KNOCK. KNOCK.

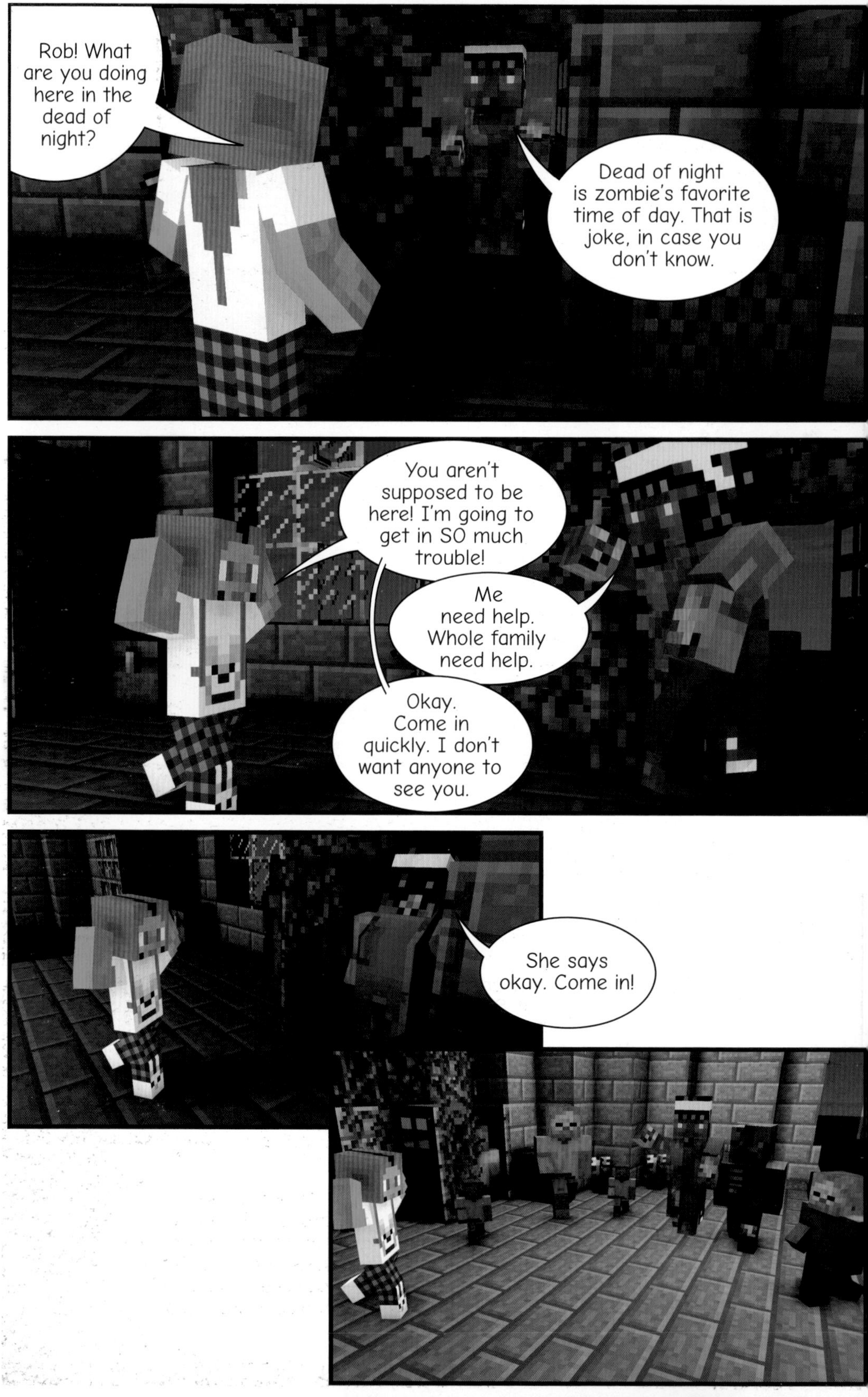
Rob! What are you doing here in the dead of night?
Dead of night is zombie's favorite time of day. That is joke, in case you don't know.
You aren't supposed to be here! I'm going to get in SO much trouble!
Me need help. Whole family need help.
Okay. Come in quickly. I don't want anyone to see you.
She says okay. Come in!

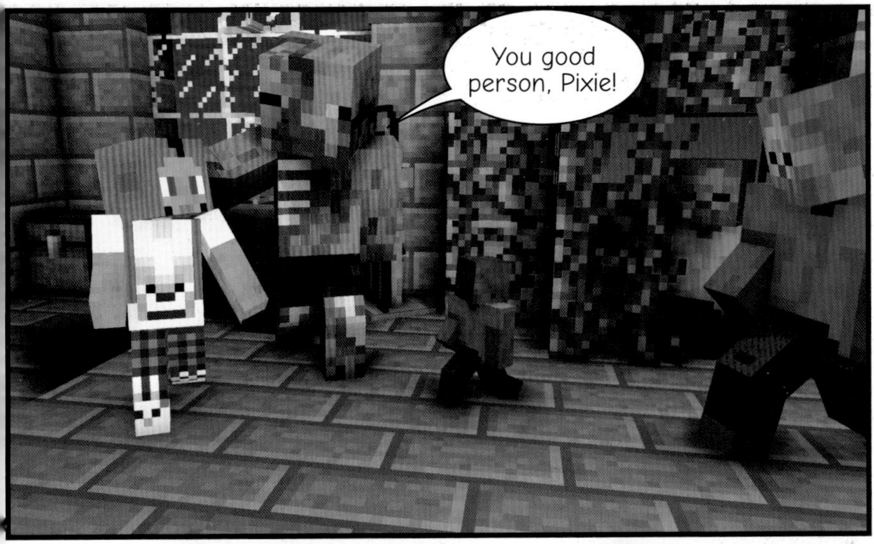
You good person, Pixie!

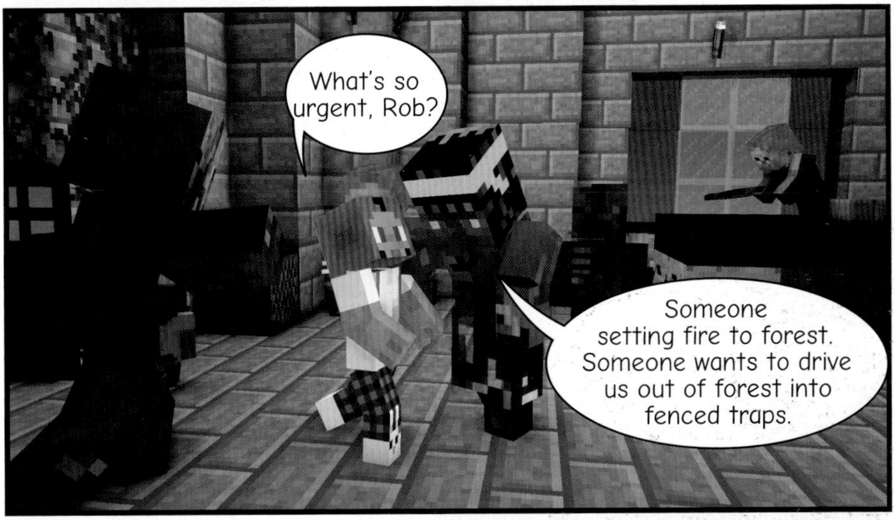
What's so urgent, Rob?
Someone setting fire to forest. Someone wants to drive us out of forest into fenced traps.

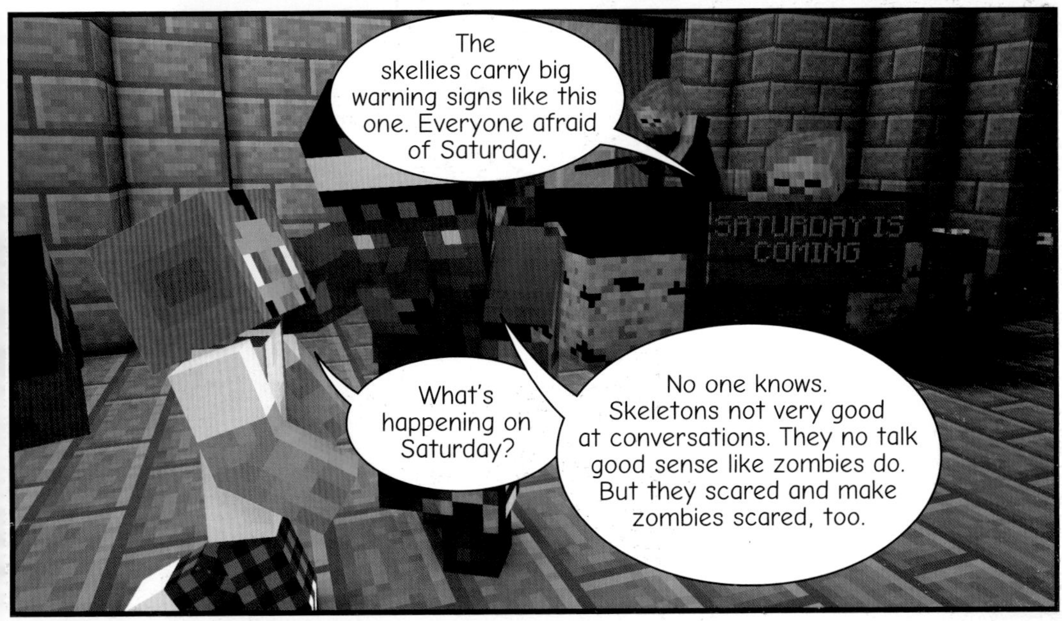
The skellies carry big warning signs like this one. Everyone afraid of Saturday.
SATURDAY IS COMING
What's happening on Saturday?
No one knows. Skeletons not very good at conversations. They no talk good sense like zombies do. But they scared and make zombies scared, too.

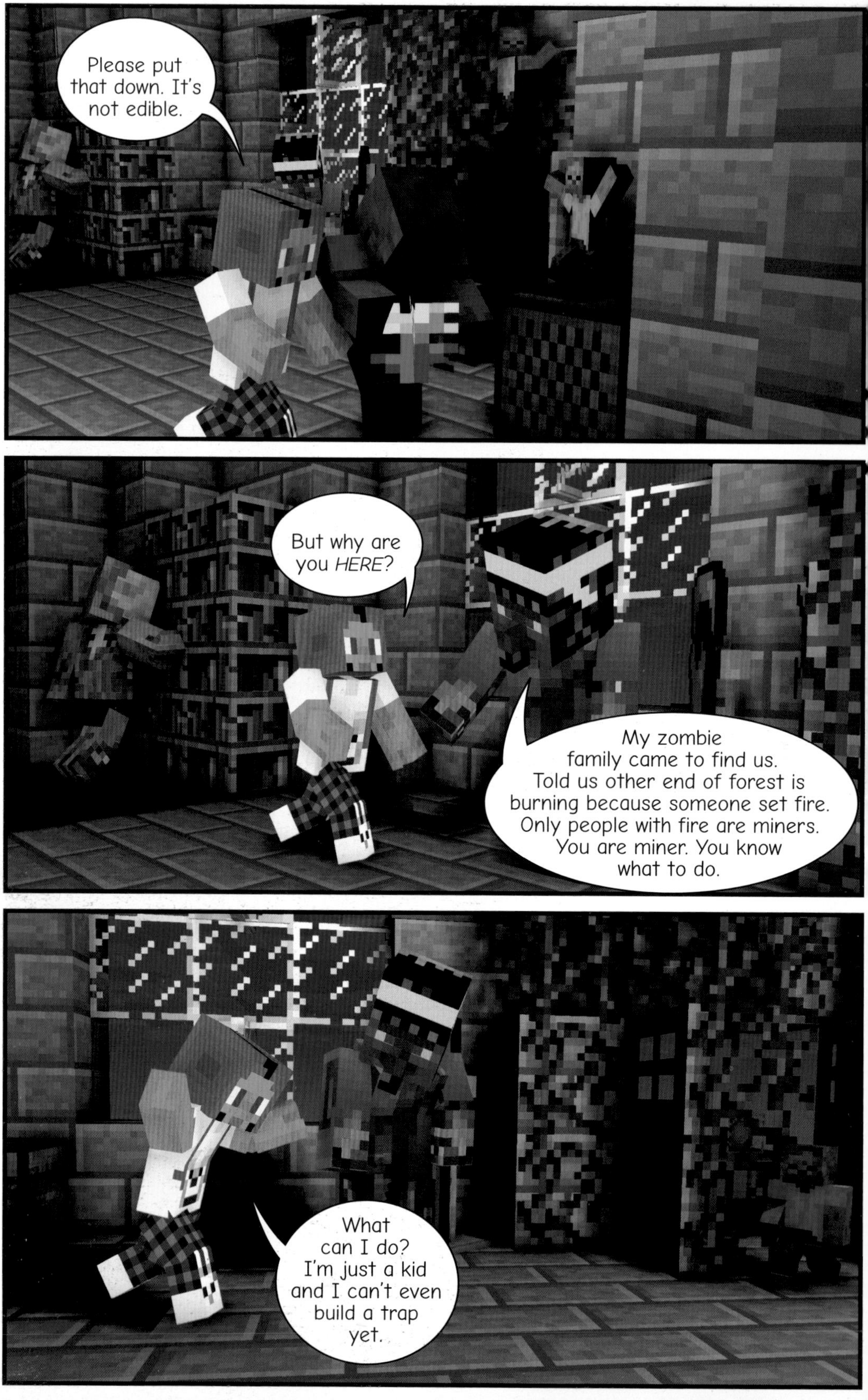
Please put that down. It's not edible.
But why are you *HERE*?
My zombie family came to find us. Told us other end of forest is burning because someone set fire. Only people with fire are miners. You are miner. You know what to do.
What can I do? I'm just a kid and I can't even build a trap yet.

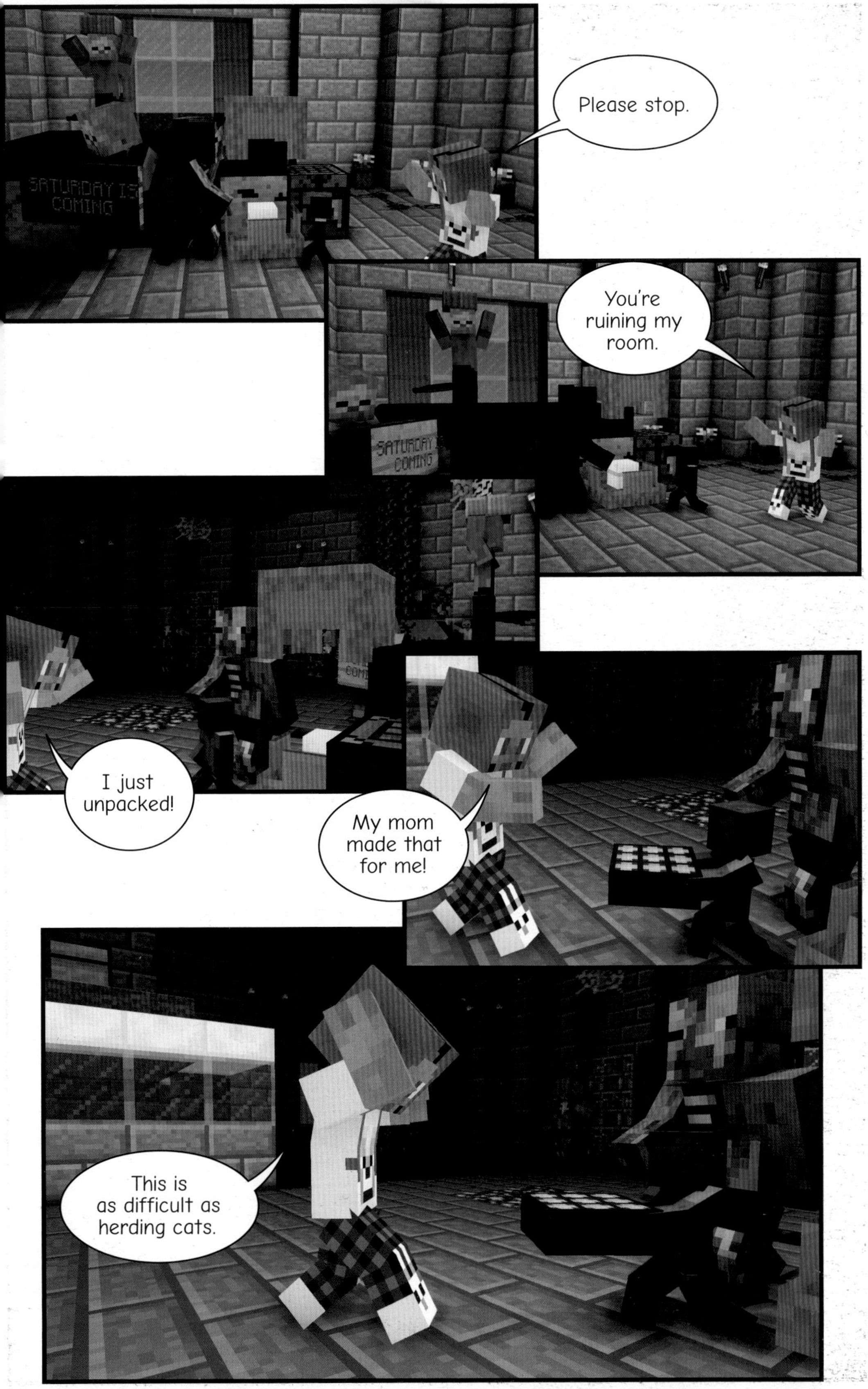
SATURDAY IS COMING
Please stop.
SATURDAY IS COMING
You're ruining my room.
I just unpacked!
My mom made that for me!
This is as difficult as herding cats.

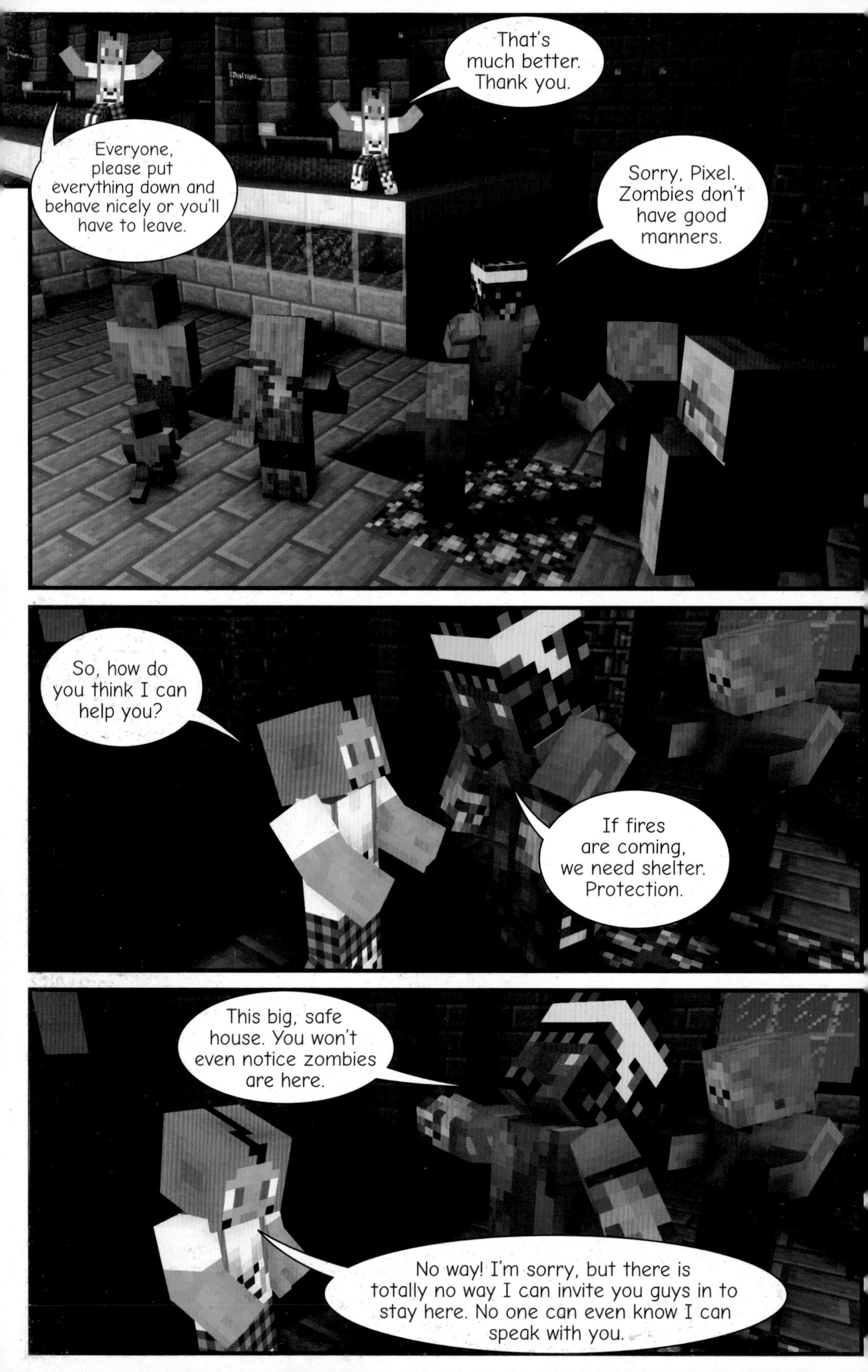
Everyone, please put everything down and behave nicely or you'll have to leave.
That's much better. Thank you.
Sorry, Pixel. Zombies don't have good manners.
So, how do you think I can help you?
If fires are coming, we need shelter. Protection.
This big, safe house. You won't even notice zombies are here.
No way! I'm sorry, but there is totally no way I can invite you guys in to stay here. No one can even know I can speak with you.

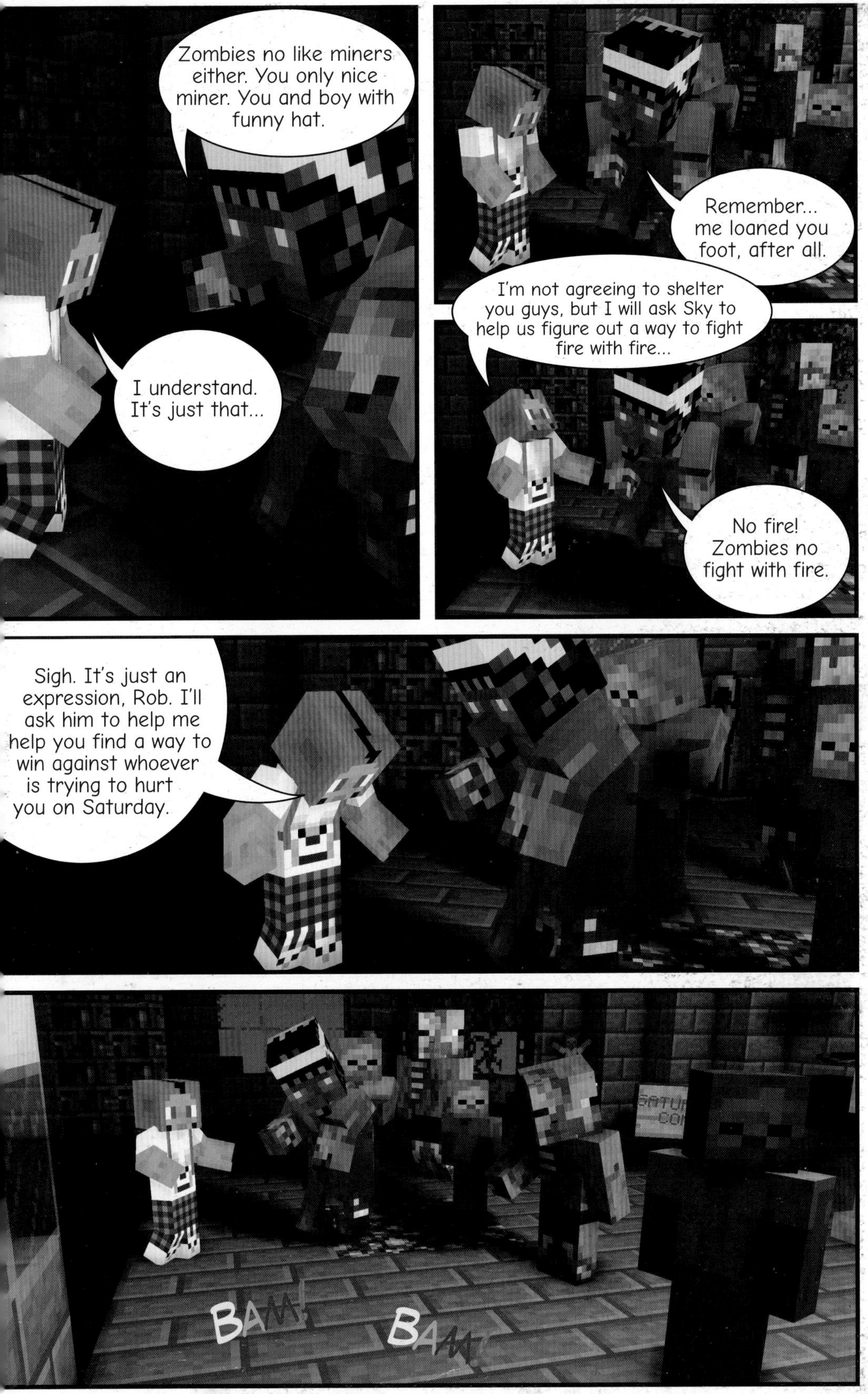
Zombies no like miners either. You only nice miner. You and boy with funny hat.
I understand. It's just that...
Remember... me loaned you foot, after all.
I'm not agreeing to shelter you guys, but I will ask Sky to help us figure out a way to fight fire with fire...
No fire! Zombies no fight with fire.
Sigh. It's just an expression, Rob. I'll ask him to help me help you find a way to win against whoever is trying to hurt you on Saturday.
BAM!
BAM!

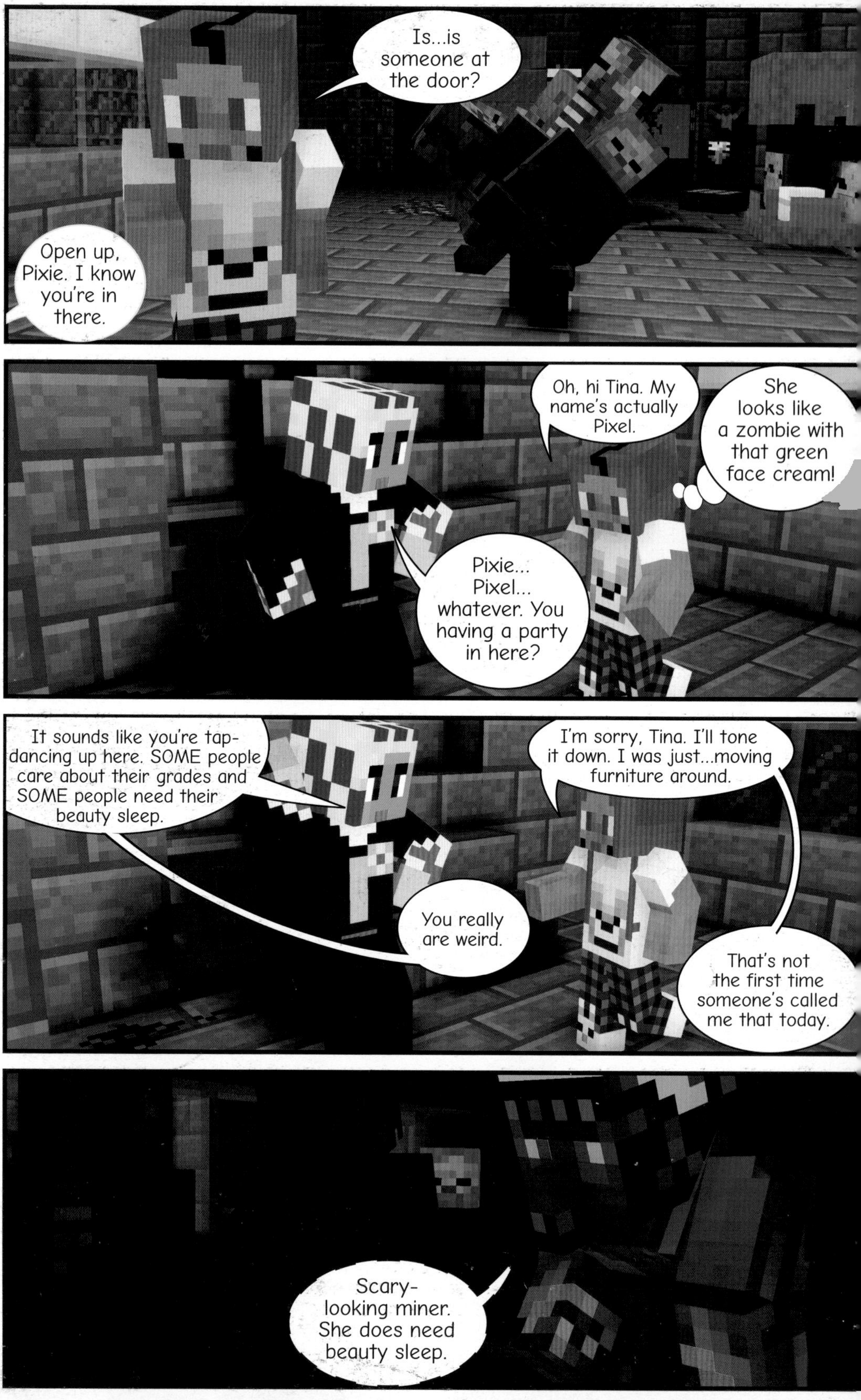
Is...is someone at the door?
Open up, Pixie. I know you're in there.
Oh, hi Tina. My name's actually Pixel.
She looks like a zombie with that green face cream!
Pixie... Pixel... whatever. You having a party in here?
It sounds like you're tap-dancing up here. SOME people care about their grades and SOME people need their beauty sleep.
I'm sorry, Tina. I'll tone it down. I was just...moving furniture around.
You really are weird.
That's not the first time someone's called me that today.
Scary-looking miner. She does need beauty sleep.

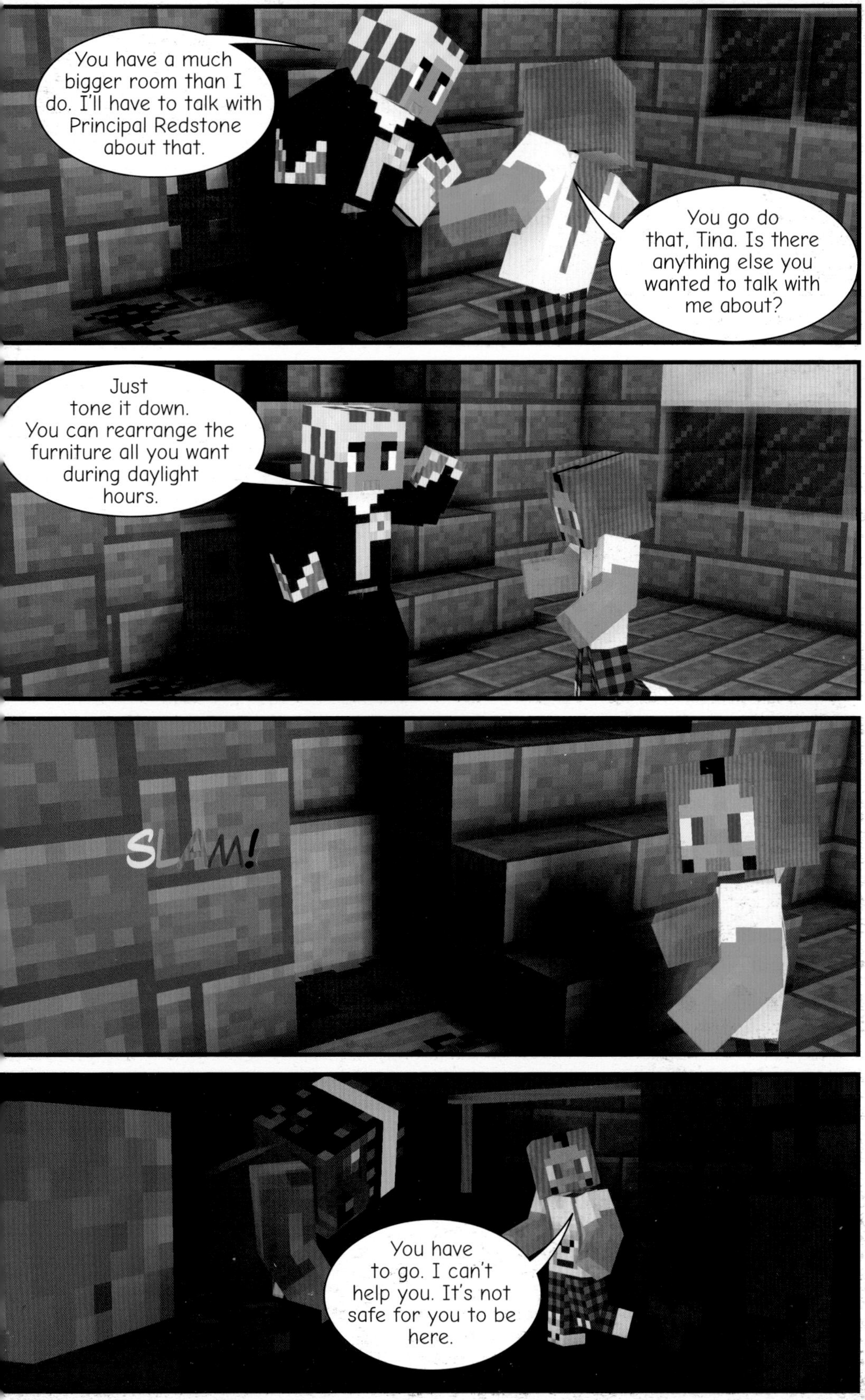
You have a much bigger room than I do. I'll have to talk with Principal Redstone about that.
You go do that, Tina. Is there anything else you wanted to talk with me about?
Just tone it down. You can rearrange the furniture all you want during daylight hours.
SLAM!
You have to go. I can't help you. It's not safe for you to be here.

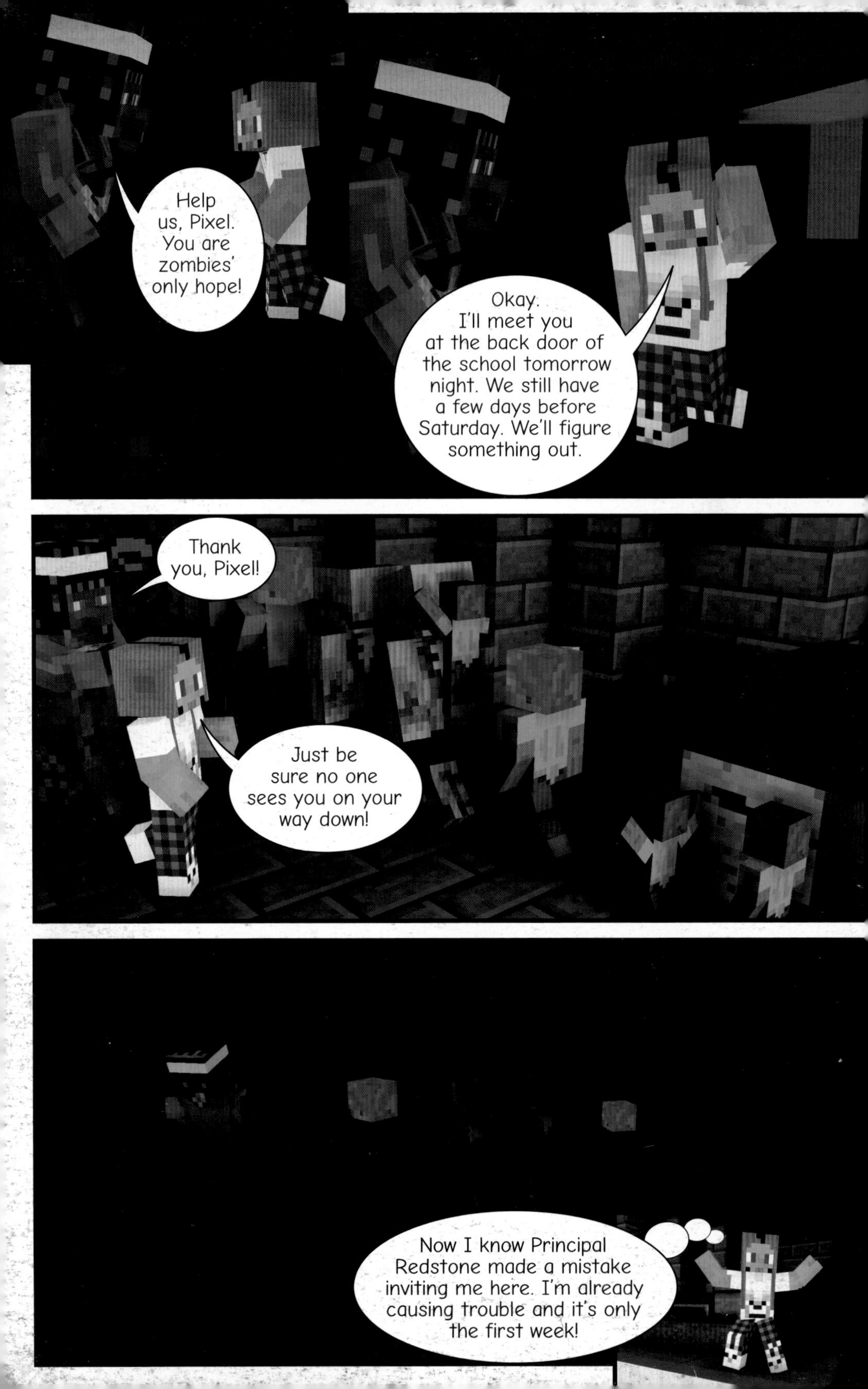
Help us, Pixel. You are zombies' only hope!
Okay. I'll meet you at the back door of the school tomorrow night. We still have a few days before Saturday. We'll figure something out.
Thank you, Pixel!
Just be sure no one sees you on your way down!
Now I know Principal Redstone made a mistake inviting me here. I'm already causing trouble and it's only the first week!

CHAPTER 5

STINKY NIGHT

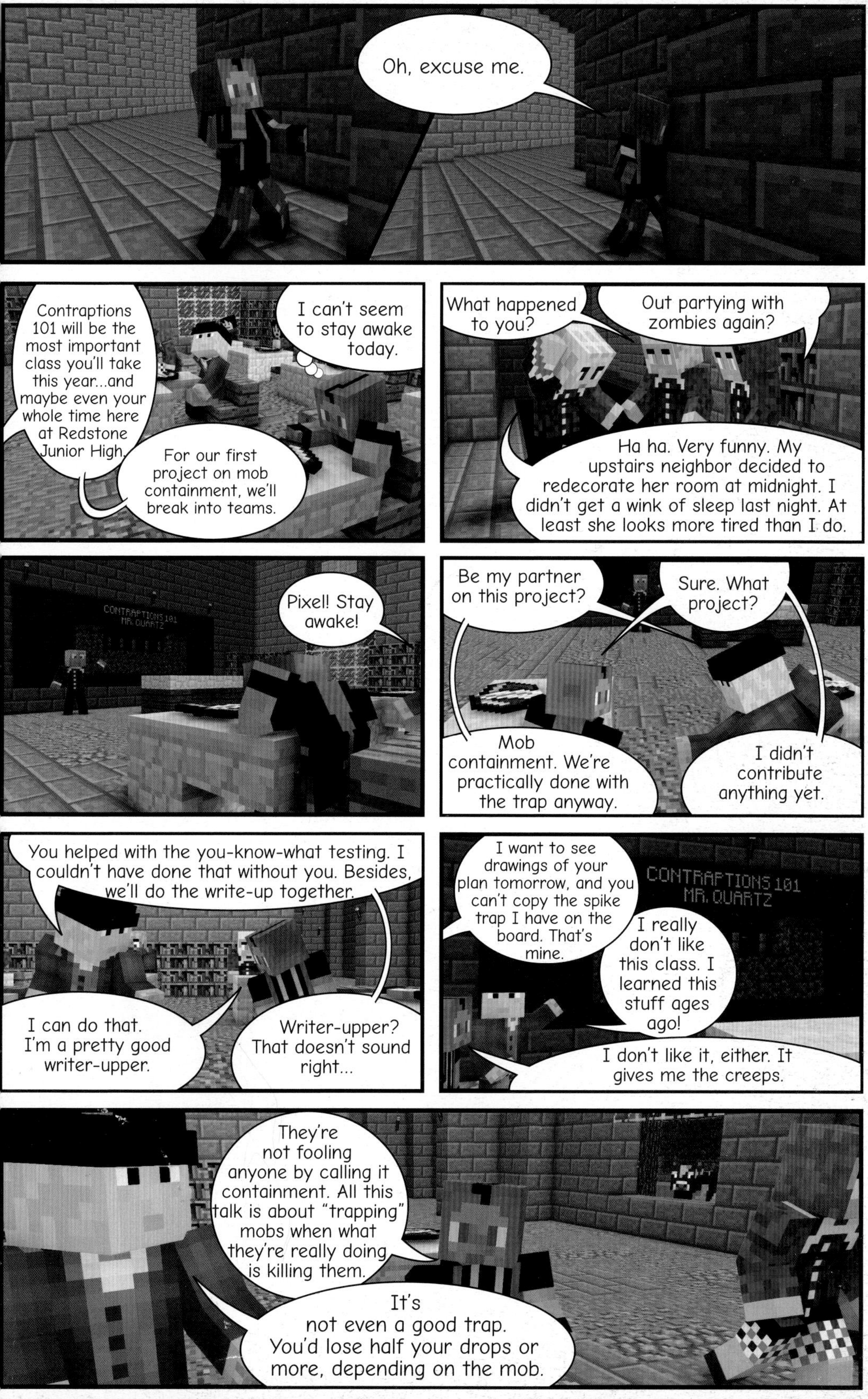
Oh, excuse me.
Contraptions 101 will be the most important class you'll take this year...and maybe even your whole time here at Redstone Junior High.
I can't seem to stay awake today.
For our first project on mob containment, we'll break into teams.
What happened to you?
Out partying with zombies again?
Ha ha. Very funny. My upstairs neighbor decided to redecorate her room at midnight. I didn't get a wink of sleep last night. At least she looks more tired than I do.
CONTRAPTIONS 101
MR. QUARTZ
Pixel! Stay awake!
Be my partner on this project?
Sure. What project?
Mob containment. We're practically done with the trap anyway.
I didn't contribute anything yet.
You helped with the you-know-what testing. I couldn't have done that without you. Besides, we'll do the write-up together.
I can do that. I'm a pretty good writer-upper.
Writer-upper? That doesn't sound right...
I want to see drawings of your plan tomorrow, and you can't copy the spike trap I have on the board. That's mine.
CONTRAPTIONS 101
MR. QUARTZ
I really don't like this class. I learned this stuff ages ago!
I don't like it, either. It gives me the creeps.
They're not fooling anyone by calling it containment. All this talk is about "trapping" mobs when what they're really doing is killing them.
It's not even a good trap. You'd lose half your drops or more, depending on the mob.

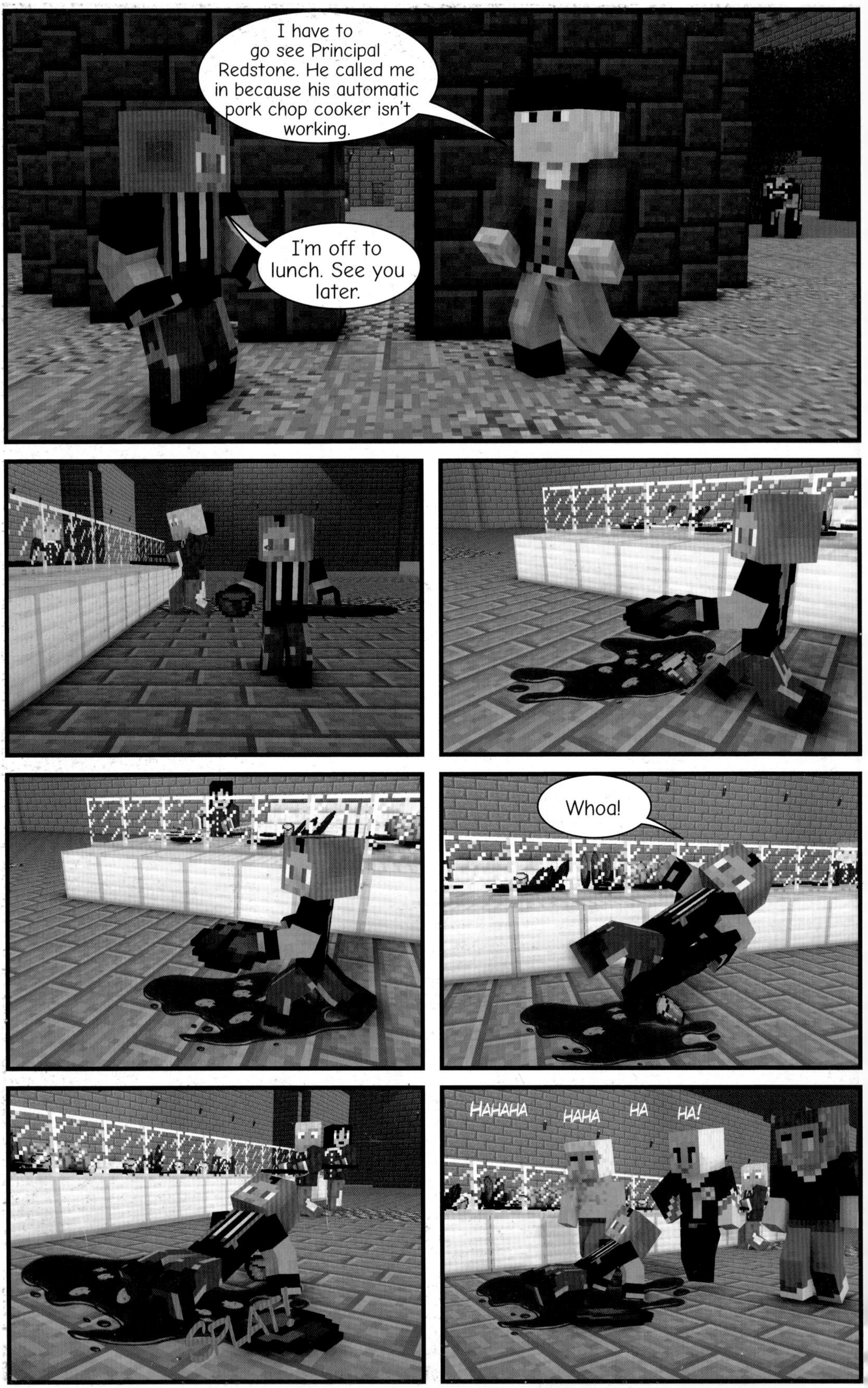

I have to go see Principal Redstone. He called me in because his automatic pork chop cooker isn't working.
I'm off to lunch. See you later.
Whoa!
SPLAT!
HAHAHA
HAHA
HA
HA!

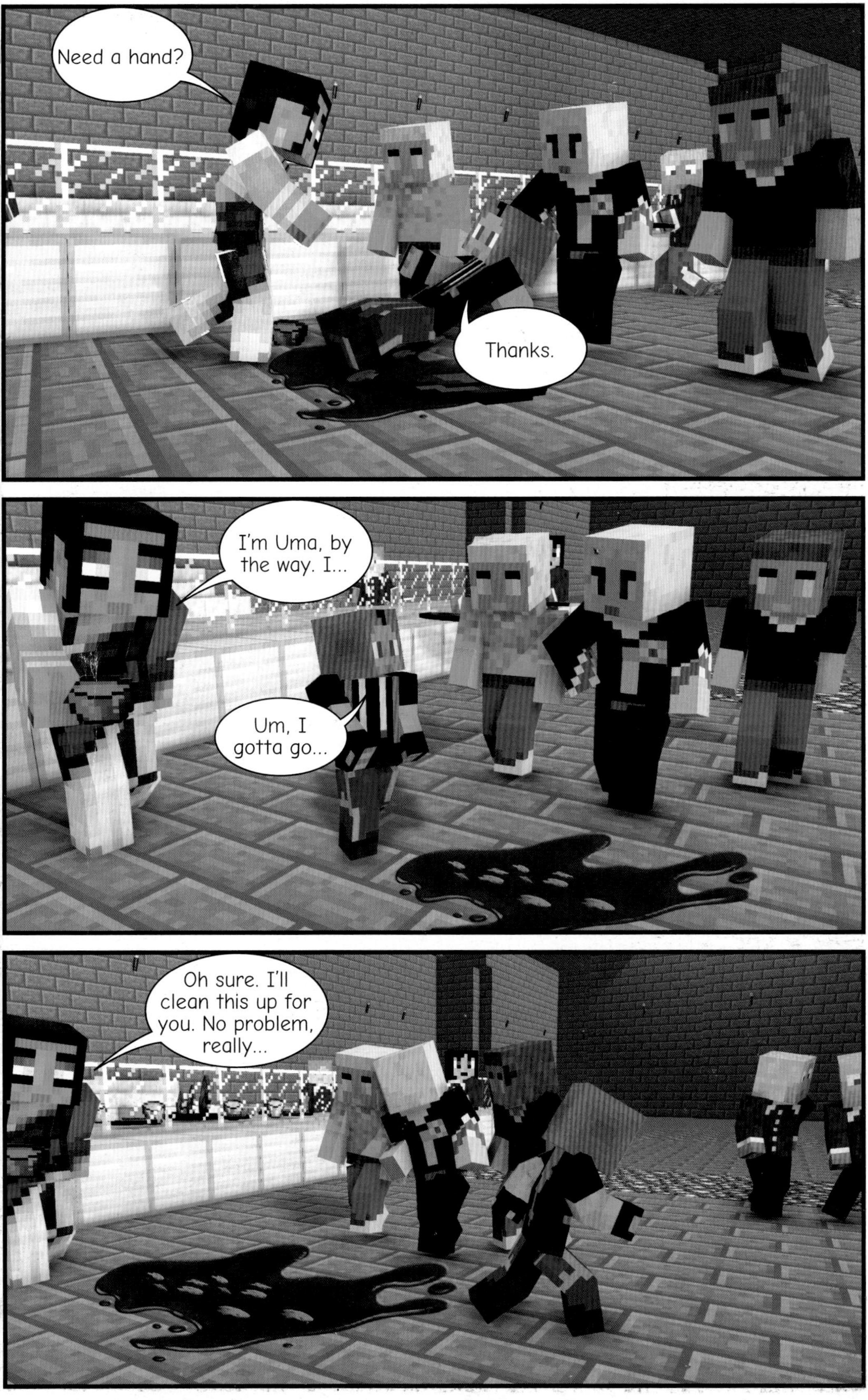
Need a hand?
Thanks.
I'm Uma, by the way. I...
Um, I gotta go...
Oh sure. I'll clean this up for you. No problem, really...

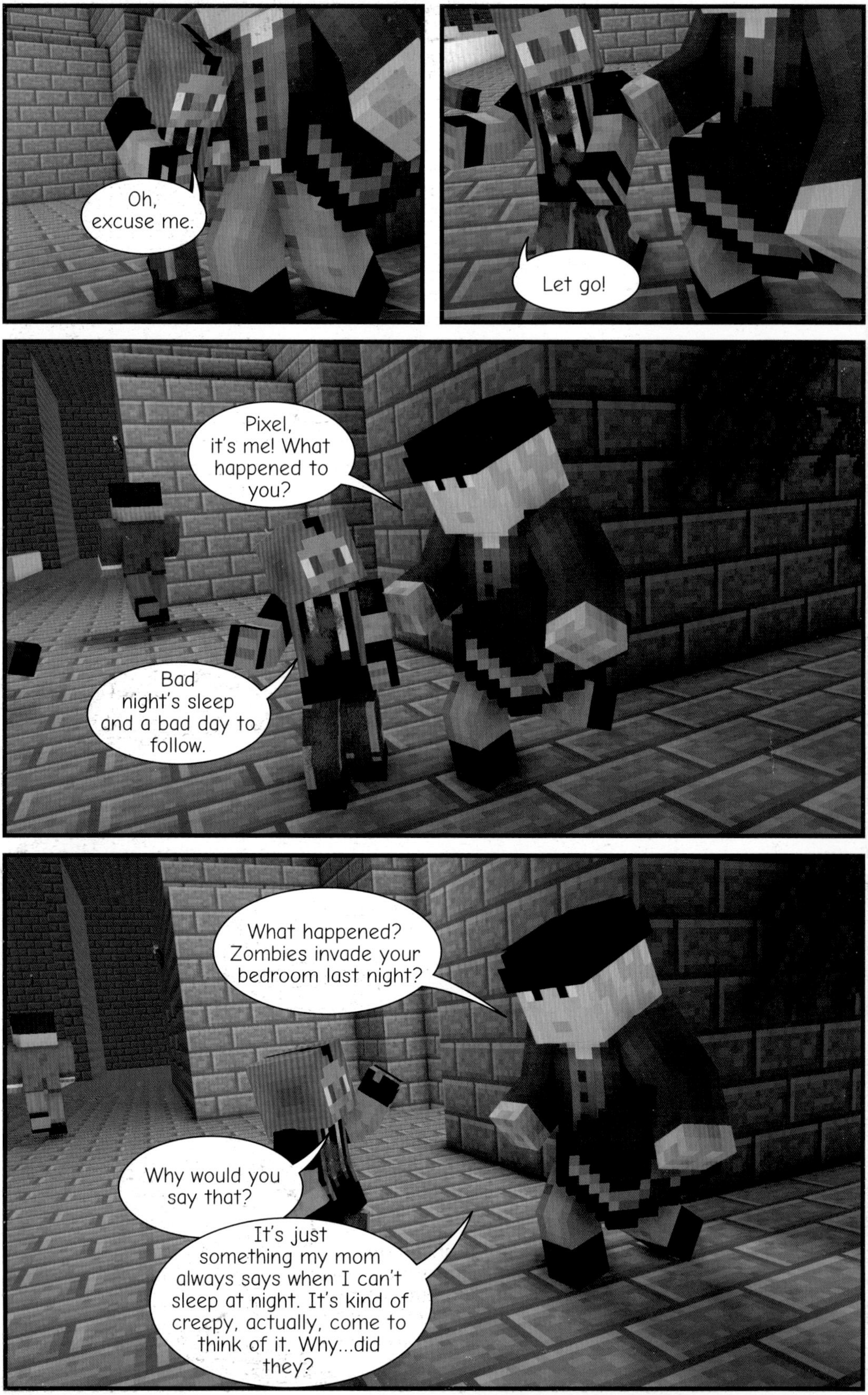
Oh, excuse me.
Let go!
Pixel, it's me! What happened to you?
Bad night's sleep and a bad day to follow.
What happened? Zombies invade your bedroom last night?
Why would you say that?
It's just something my mom always says when I can't sleep at night. It's kind of creepy, actually, come to think of it. Why...did they?

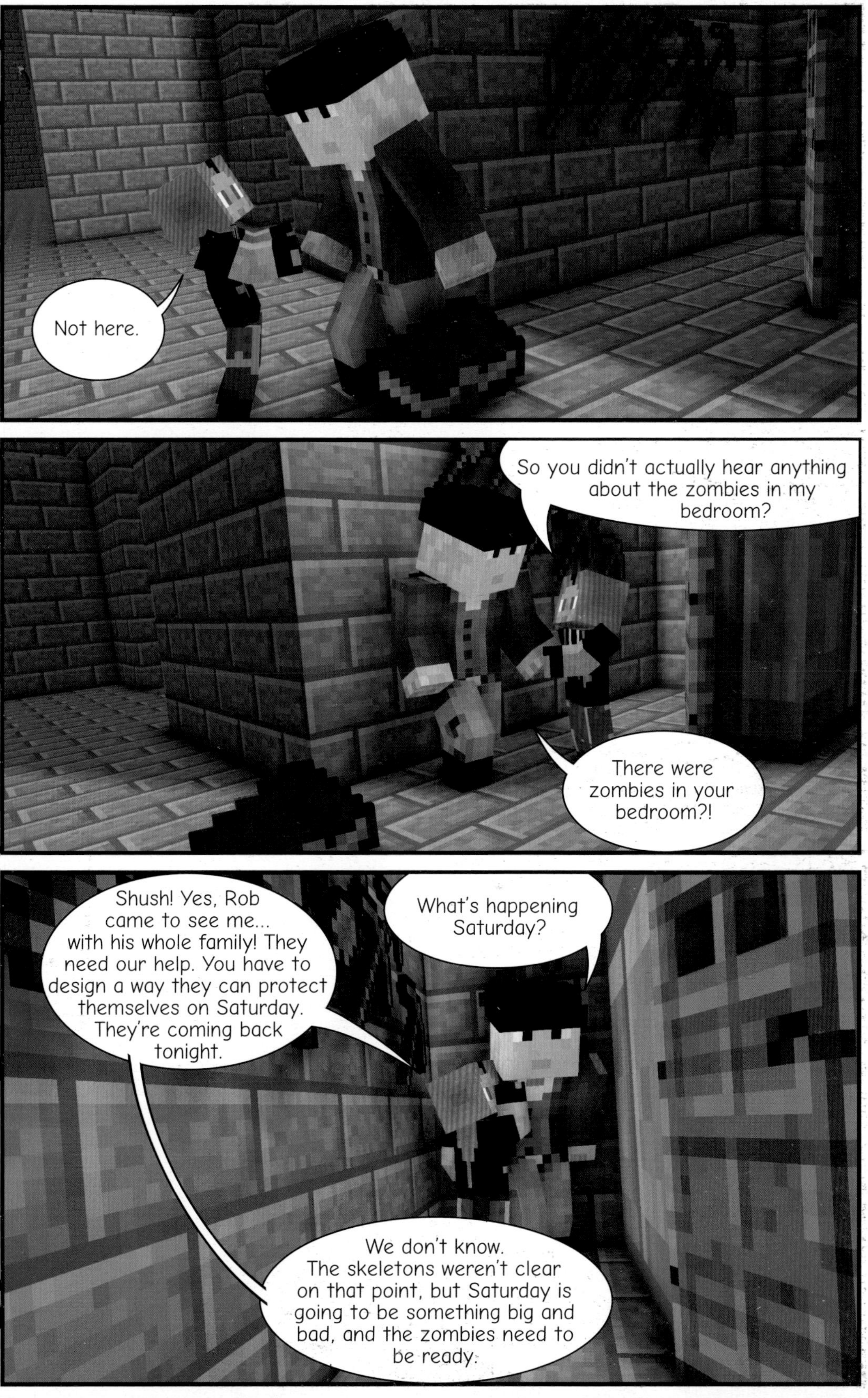
Not here.
So you didn't actually hear anything about the zombies in my bedroom?
There were zombies in your bedroom?!
Shush! Yes, Rob came to see me... with his whole family! They need our help. You have to design a way they can protect themselves on Saturday. They're coming back tonight.
What's happening Saturday?
We don't know. The skeletons weren't clear on that point, but Saturday is going to be something big and bad, and the zombies need to be ready.

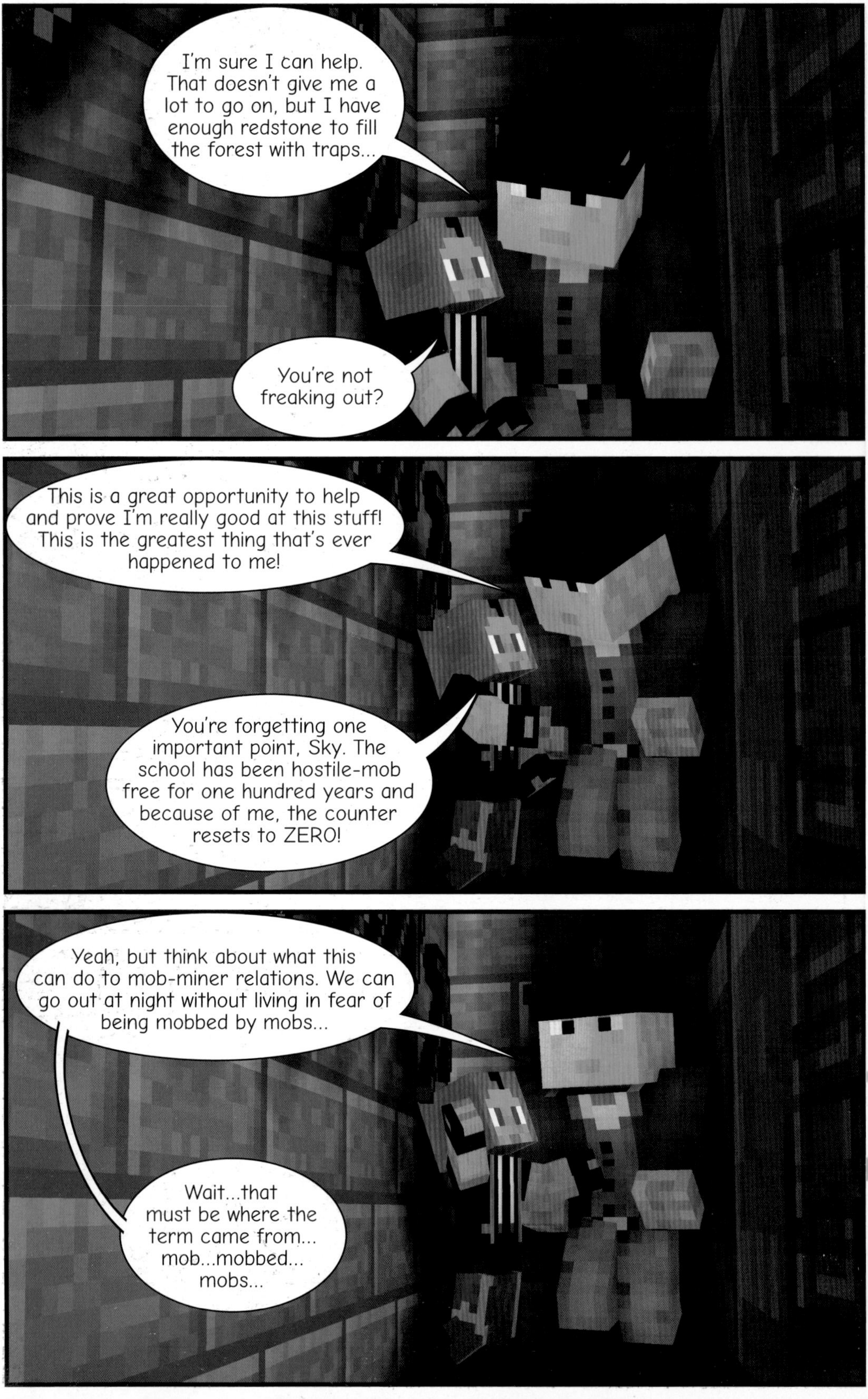

I'm sure I can help. That doesn't give me a lot to go on, but I have enough redstone to fill the forest with traps...
You're not freaking out?
This is a great opportunity to help and prove I'm really good at this stuff! This is the greatest thing that's ever happened to me!
You're forgetting one important point, Sky. The school has been hostile-mob free for one hundred years and because of me, the counter resets to ZERO!
Yeah, but think about what this can do to mob-miner relations. We can go out at night without living in fear of being mobbed by mobs...
Wait...that must be where the term came from... mob...mobbed... mobs...

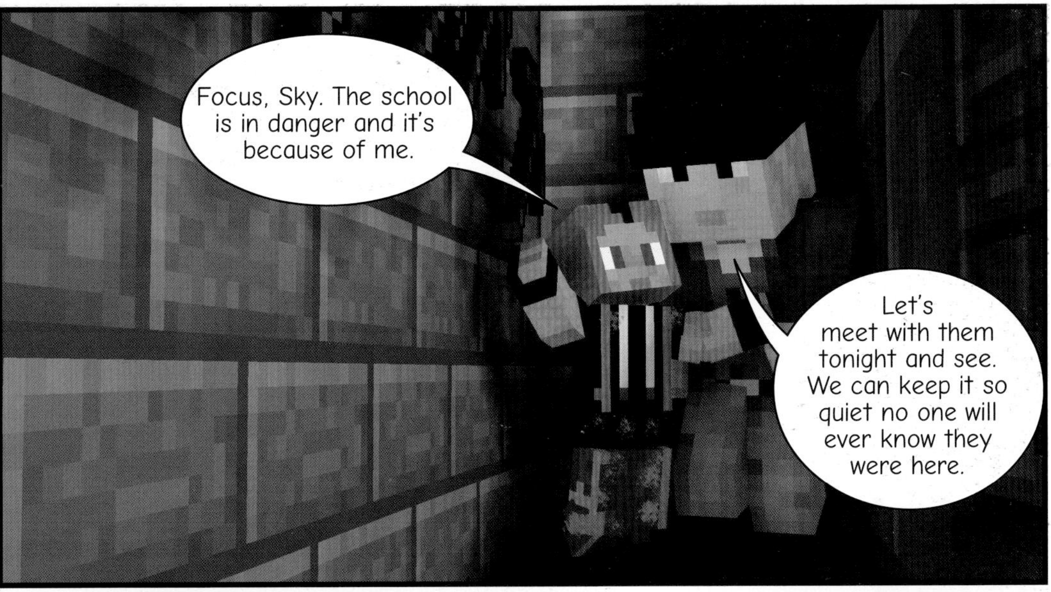
Focus, Sky. The school is in danger and it's because of me.
Let's meet with them tonight and see. We can keep it so quiet no one will ever know they were here.

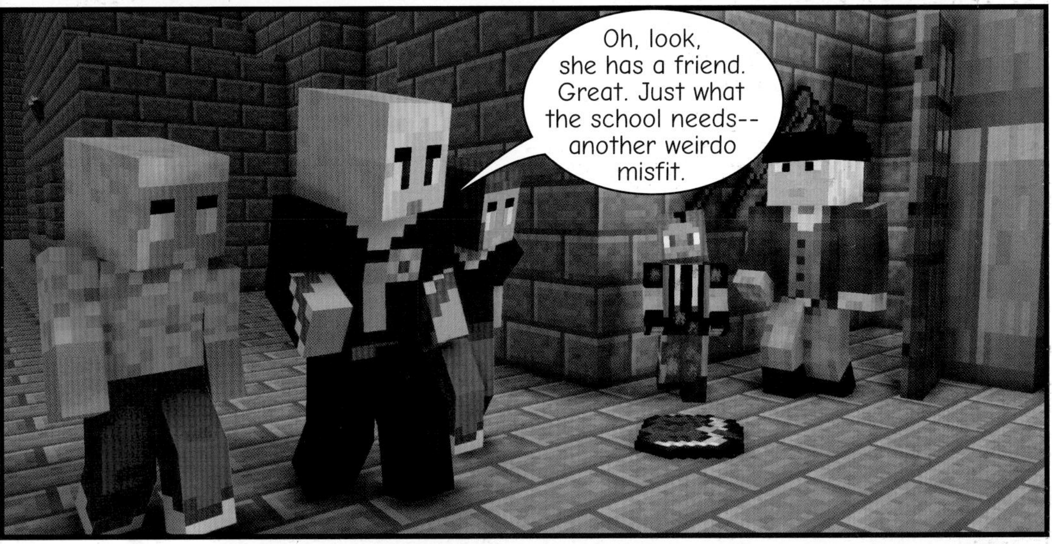
Oh, look, she has a friend. Great. Just what the school needs--another weirdo misfit.

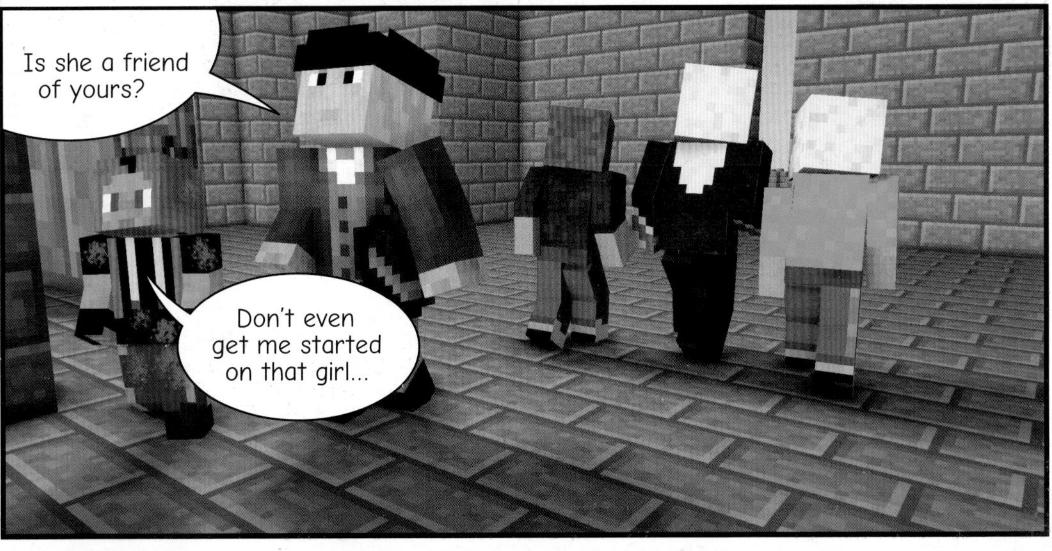
Is she a friend of yours?
Don't even get me started on that girl...

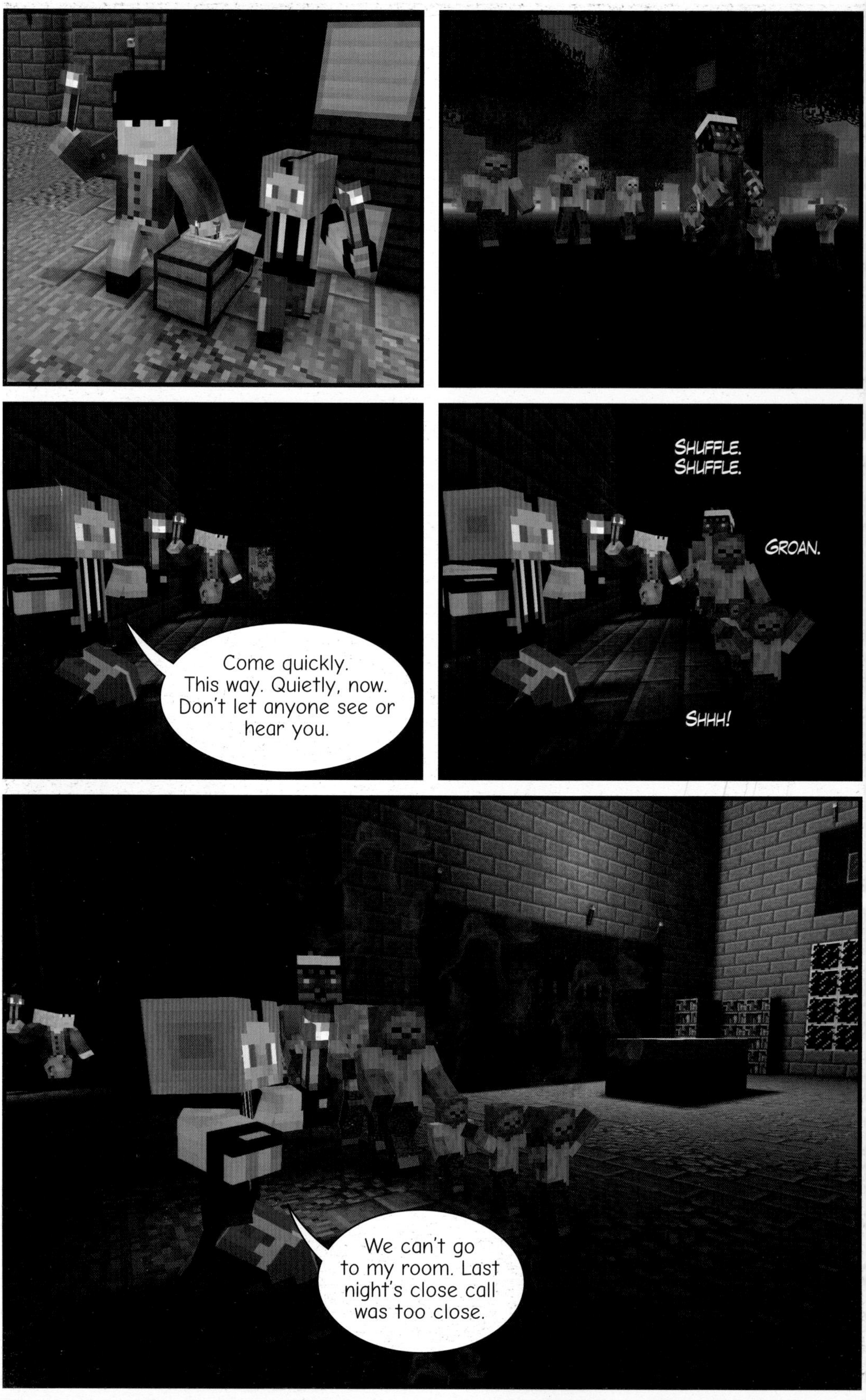

Come quickly. This way. Quietly, now. Don't let anyone see or hear you.
SHUFFLE. SHUFFLE.
GROAN.
SHHH!
We can't go to my room. Last night's close call was too close.

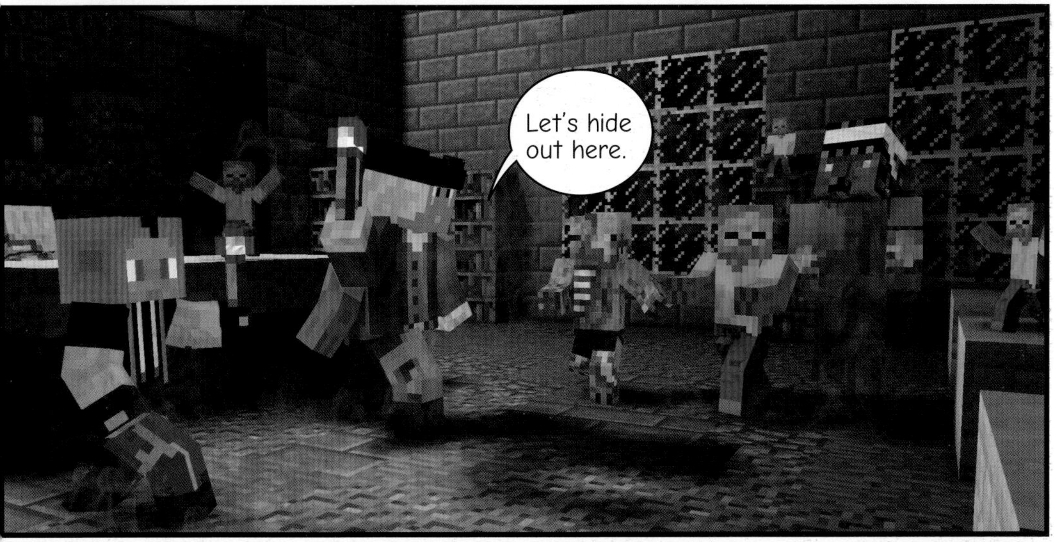
Let's hide out here.

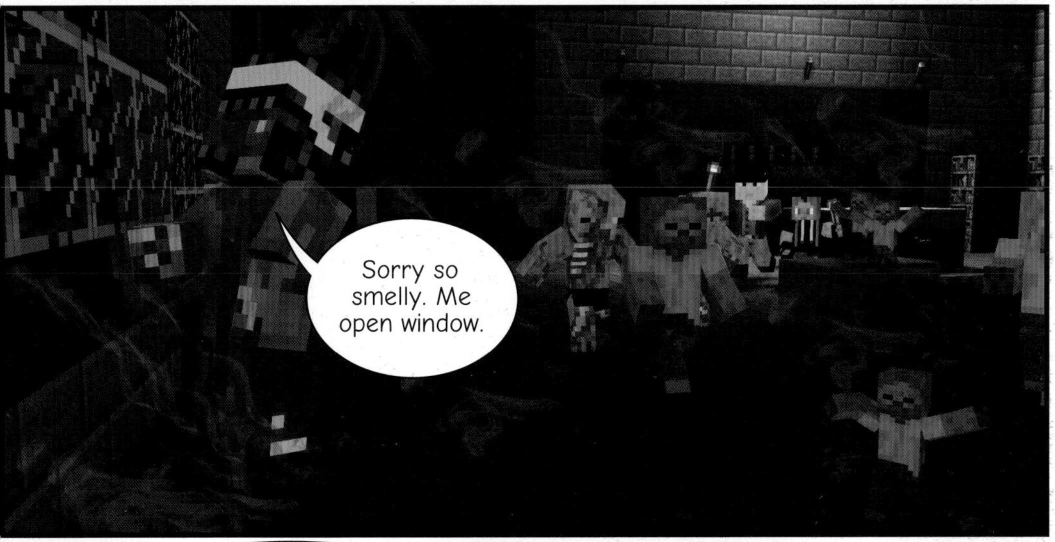
Sorry so smelly. Me open window.

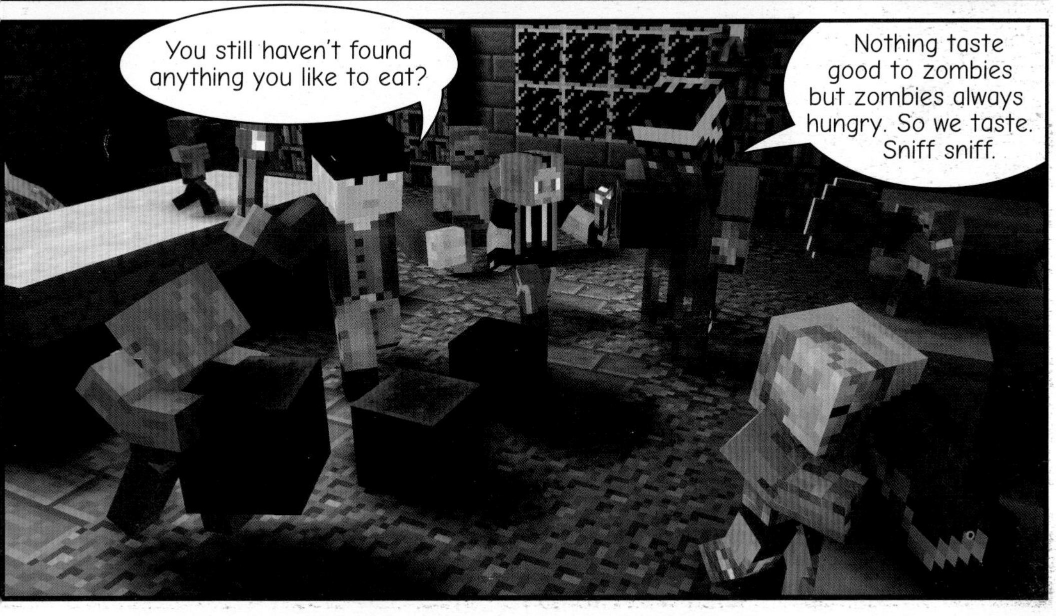
You still haven't found anything you like to eat?
Nothing taste good to zombies but zombies always hungry. So we taste. Sniff sniff.

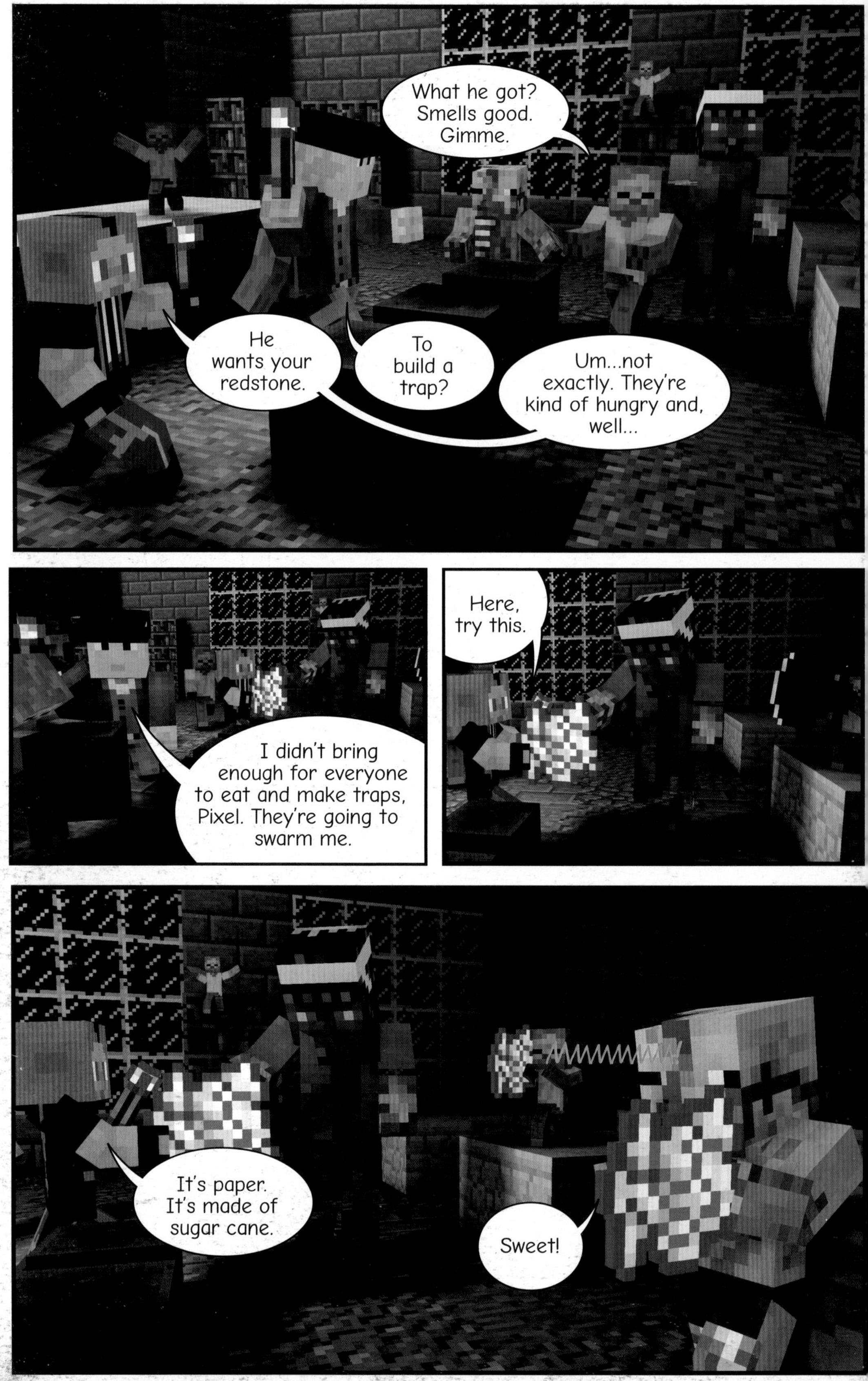
What he got? Smells good. Gimme.
He wants your redstone.
To build a trap?
Um...not exactly. They're kind of hungry and, well...
I didn't bring enough for everyone to eat and make traps, Pixel. They're going to swarm me.
Here, try this.
It's paper. It's made of sugar cane.
Sweet!

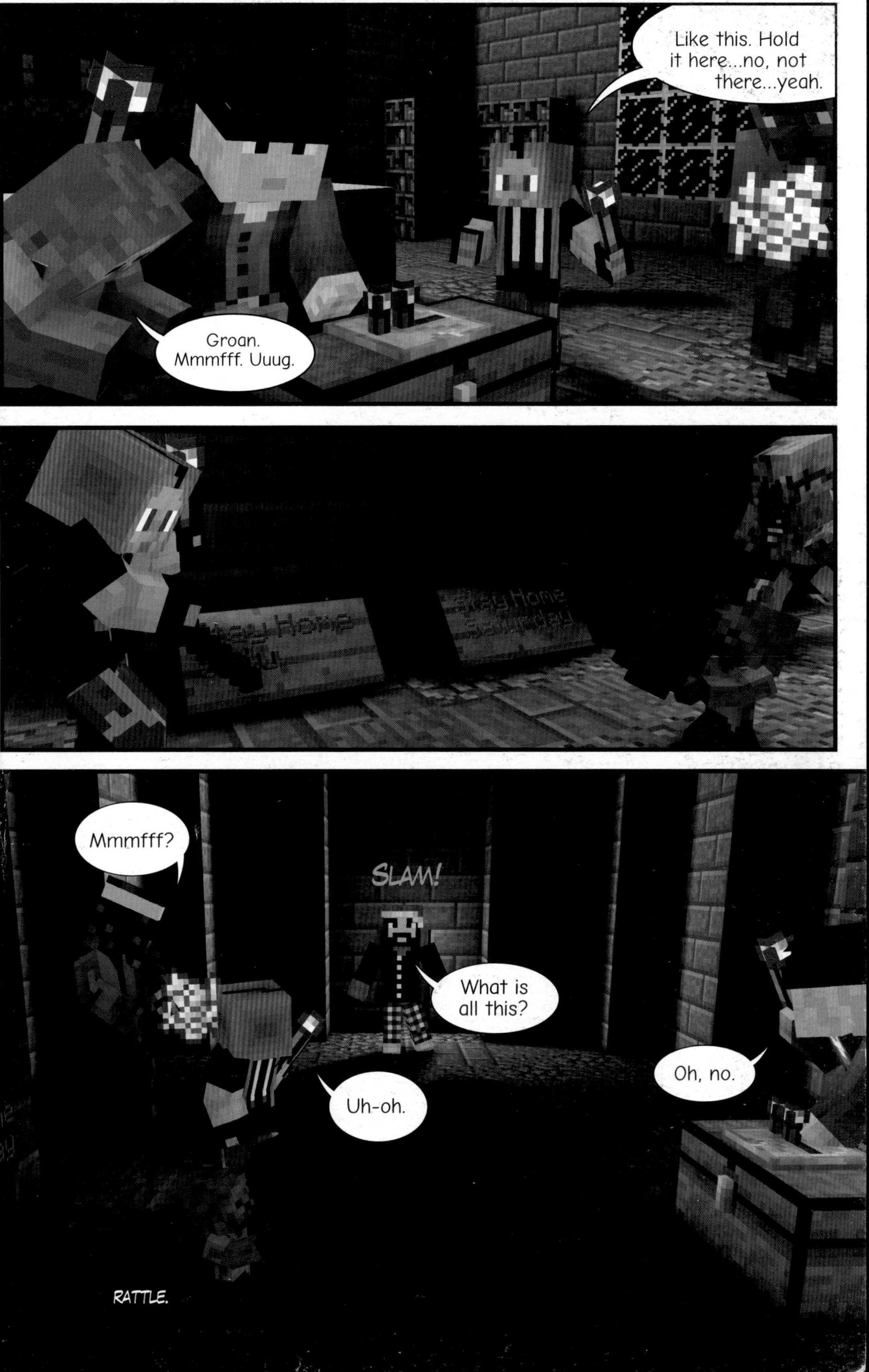
Like this. Hold it here...no, not there...yeah.
Groan. Mmmfff. Uuug.
Mmmfff?
SLAM!
What is all this?
Oh, no.
Uh-oh.
RATTLE.

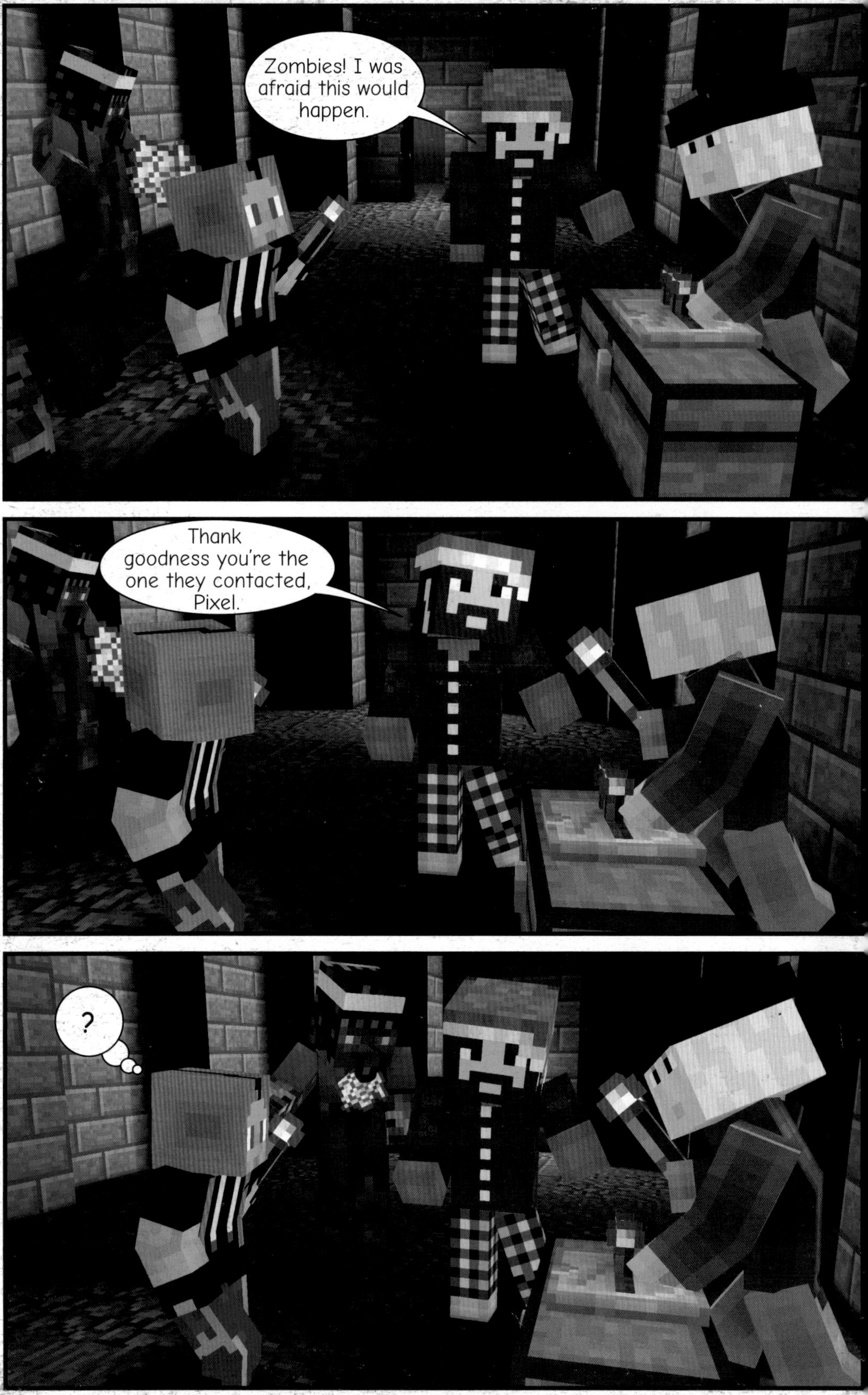
Zombies! I was afraid this would happen.
Thank goodness you're the one they contacted, Pixel.
?

CHAPTER 6

SECRETS
REVEALED

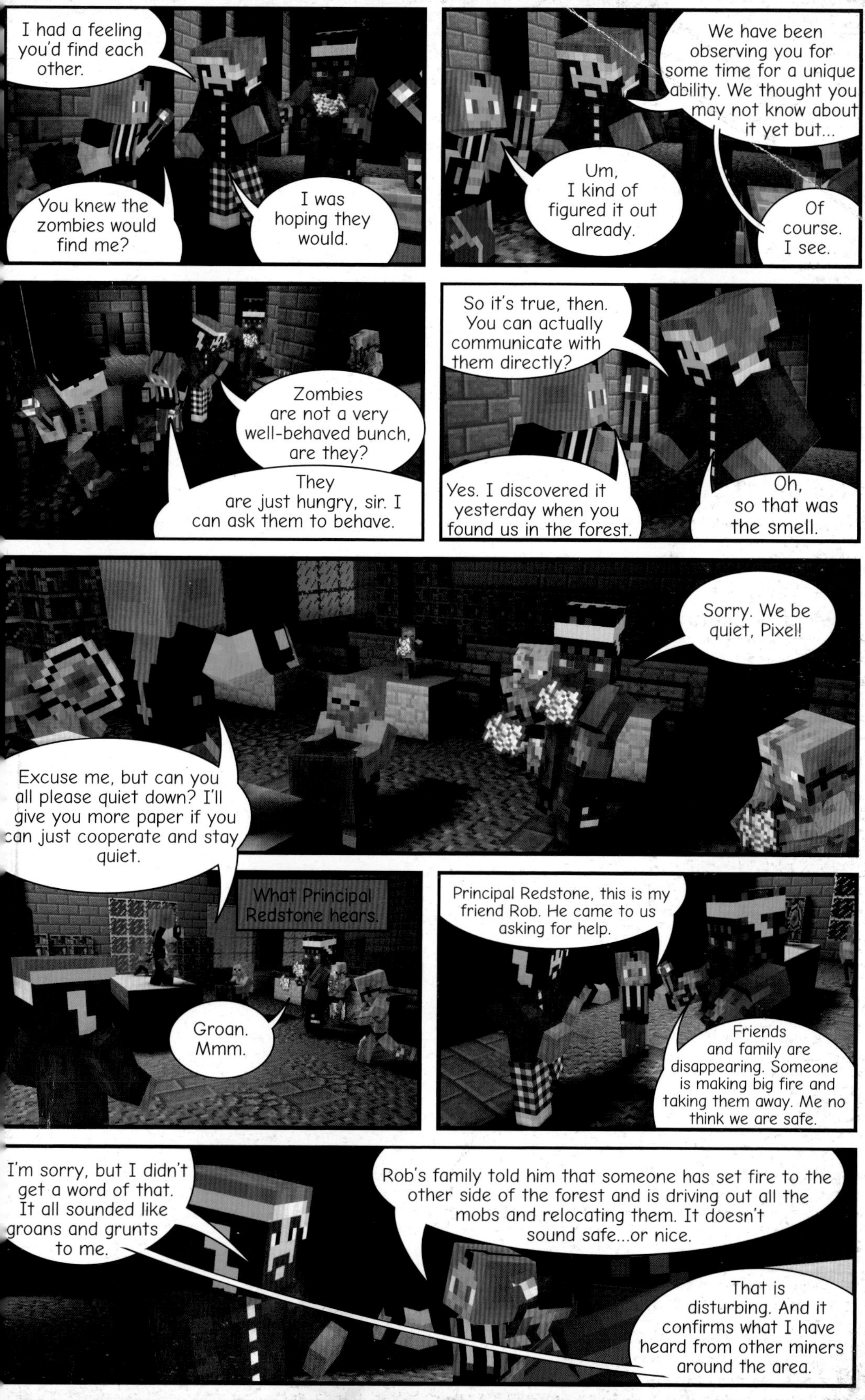
I had a feeling you'd find each other.
You knew the zombies would find me?
I was hoping they would.
We have been observing you for some time for a unique ability. We thought you may not know about it yet but...
Um, I kind of figured it out already.
Of course. I see.
Zombies are not a very well-behaved bunch, are they?
They are just hungry, sir. I can ask them to behave.
So it's true, then. You can actually communicate with them directly?
Yes. I discovered it yesterday when you found us in the forest.
Oh, so that was the smell.
Sorry. We be quiet, Pixel!
Excuse me, but can you all please quiet down? I'll give you more paper if you can just cooperate and stay quiet.
What Principal Redstone hears.
Groan. Mmm.
Principal Redstone, this is my friend Rob. He came to us asking for help.
Friends and family are disappearing. Someone is making big fire and taking them away. Me no think we are safe.
I'm sorry, but I didn't get a word of that. It all sounded like groans and grunts to me.
Rob's family told him that someone has set fire to the other side of the forest and is driving out all the mobs and relocating them. It doesn't sound safe...or nice.
That is disturbing. And it confirms what I have heard from other miners around the area.

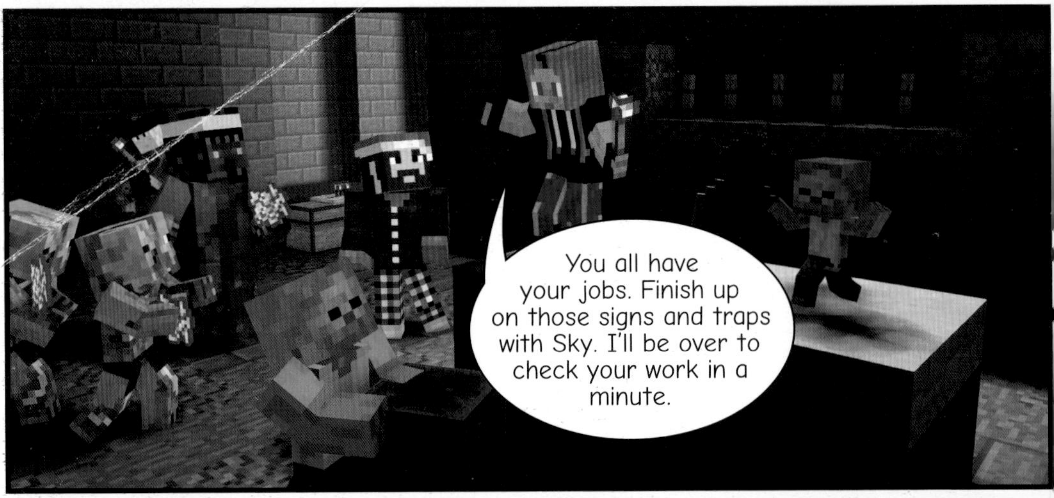
You all have your jobs. Finish up on those signs and traps with Sky. I'll be over to check your work in a minute.

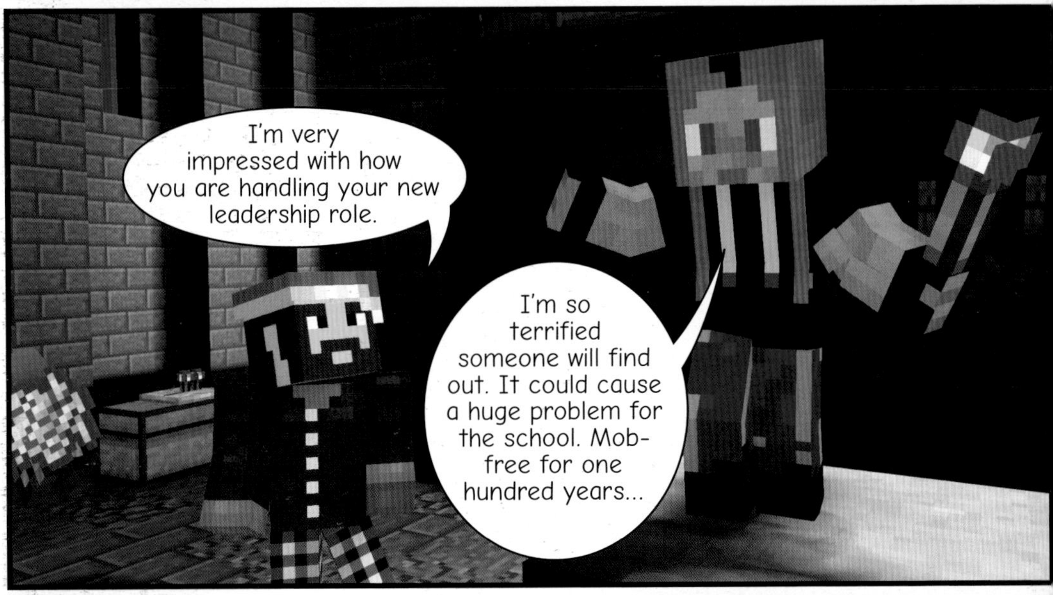
I'm very impressed with how you are handling your new leadership role.
I'm so terrified someone will find out. It could cause a huge problem for the school. Mob-free for one hundred years...

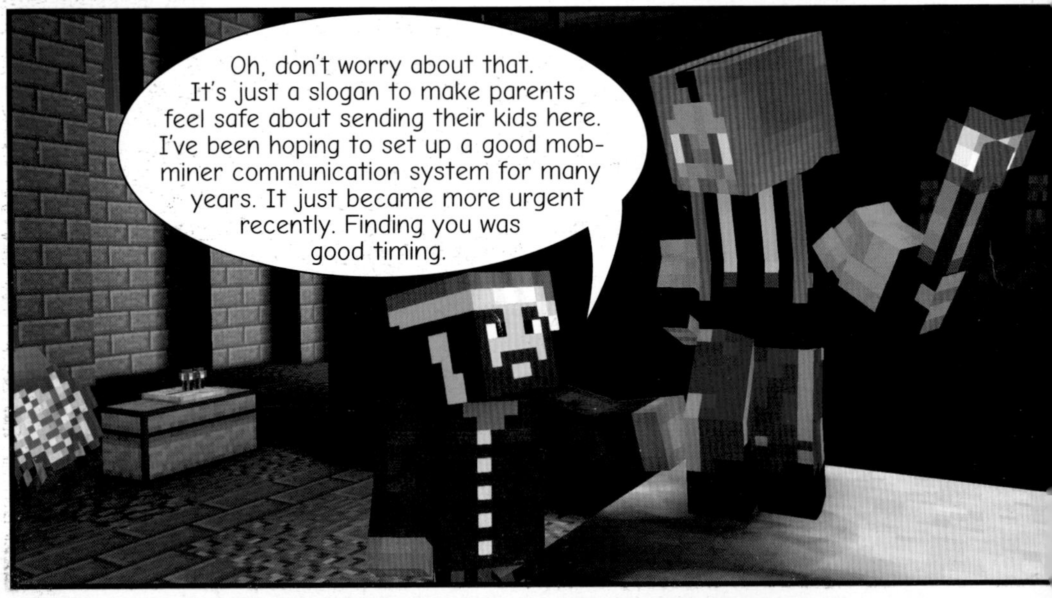
Oh, don't worry about that. It's just a slogan to make parents feel safe about sending their kids here. I've been hoping to set up a good mob-miner communication system for many years. It just became more urgent recently. Finding you was good timing.

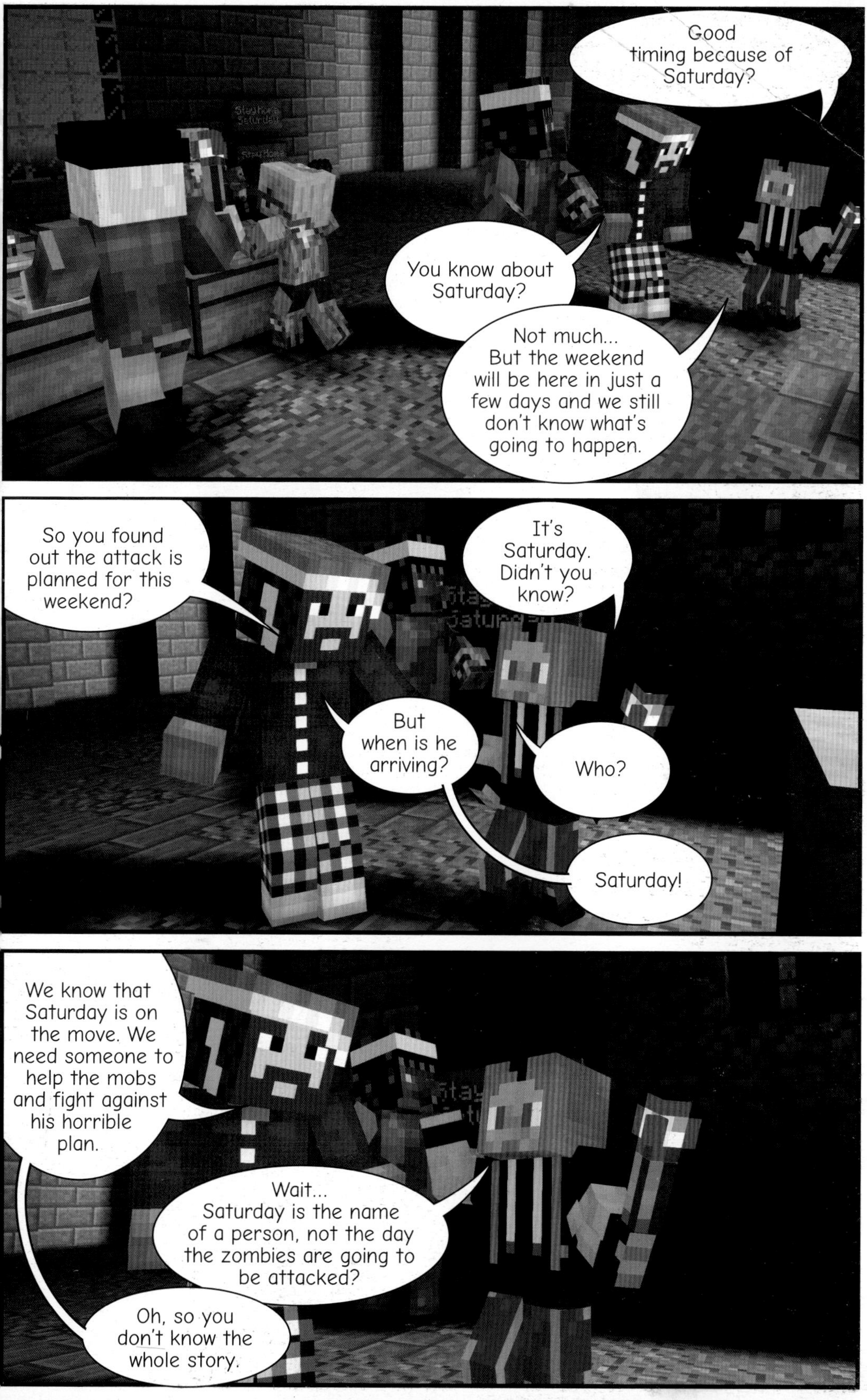
Good timing because of Saturday?
You know about Saturday?
Not much... But the weekend will be here in just a few days and we still don't know what's going to happen.
So you found out the attack is planned for this weekend?
It's Saturday. Didn't you know?
But when is he arriving?
Who?
Saturday!
We know that Saturday is on the move. We need someone to help the mobs and fight against his horrible plan.
Wait... Saturday is the name of a person, not the day the zombies are going to be attacked?
Oh, so you don't know the whole story.

Saturday is a member of the SAMD, the Society for Advanced Mob Domestication. They pretend to be good guys, but make no mistake...they are not. They want to kill the mobs and use them for their drops. I've heard their real slogan is, "The only good z-o-m-b-i-e is a dead z-o-m-b-i-e."

That's horrible. Wait, why did you spell out the word zombie? They can't understand you.

Sorry. I forgot. And yes, it is horrible!

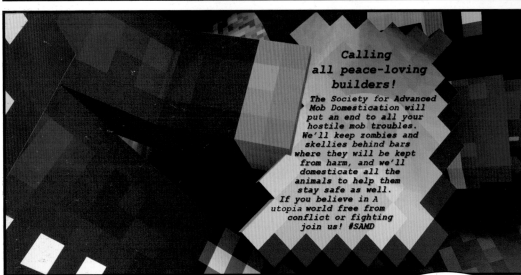

Calling all peace-loving builders!

The Society for Advanced Mob Domestication will put an end to all your hostile mob troubles. We'll keep zombies and skellies behind bars where they will be kept from harm, and we'll domesticate all the animals to help them stay safe as well. If you believe in A utopia world free from conflict or fighting join us! #SAMD

Here Rob. Take some fliers for you and some for your family. Only eat the blank paper. Paper with writing is important. We need it, okay?

Rob understand perfectly. Eat blank paper only. Gotcha, boss.

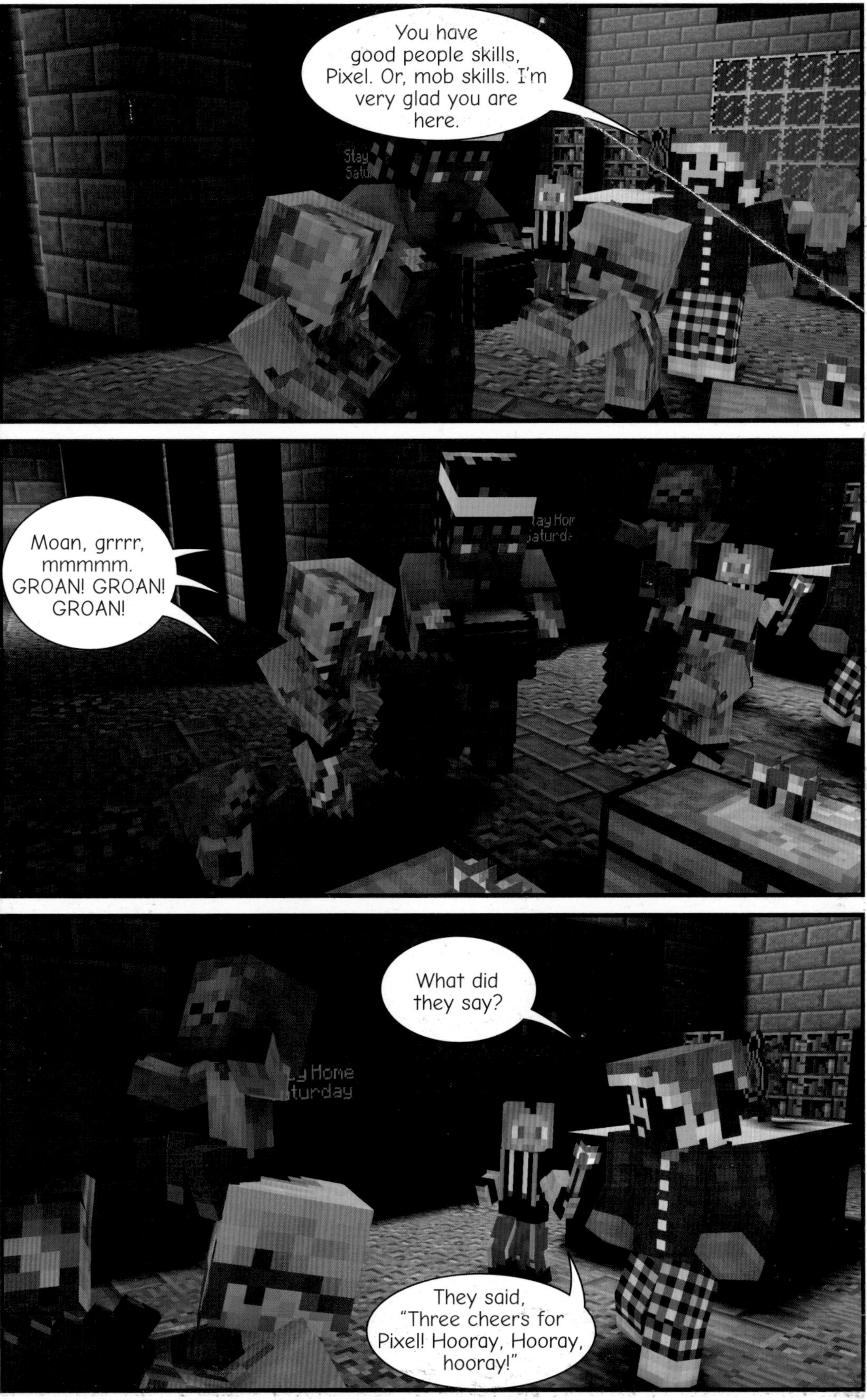
You have good people skills, Pixel. Or, mob skills. I'm very glad you are here.
Moan, grrrr, mmmmm. GROAN! GROAN! GROAN!
What did they say?
They said, "Three cheers for Pixel! Hooray, Hooray, hooray!"

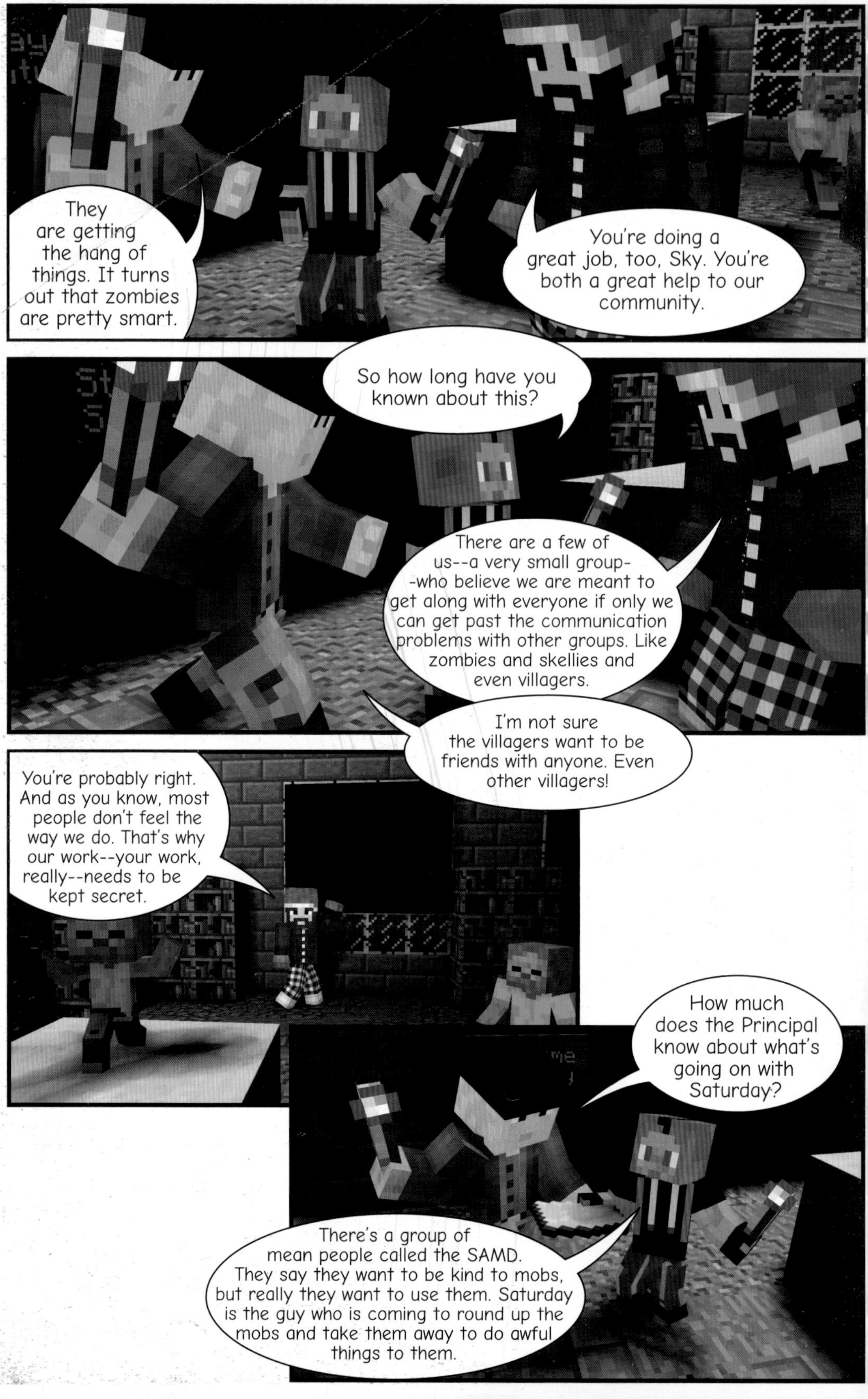
They are getting the hang of things. It turns out that zombies are pretty smart.
You're doing a great job, too, Sky. You're both a great help to our community.
So how long have you known about this?
There are a few of us--a very small group--who believe we are meant to get along with everyone if only we can get past the communication problems with other groups. Like zombies and skellies and even villagers.
I'm not sure the villagers want to be friends with anyone. Even other villagers!
You're probably right. And as you know, most people don't feel the way we do. That's why our work--your work, really--needs to be kept secret.
How much does the Principal know about what's going on with Saturday?
There's a group of mean people called the SAMD. They say they want to be kind to mobs, but really they want to use them. Saturday is the guy who is coming to round up the mobs and take them away to do awful things to them.

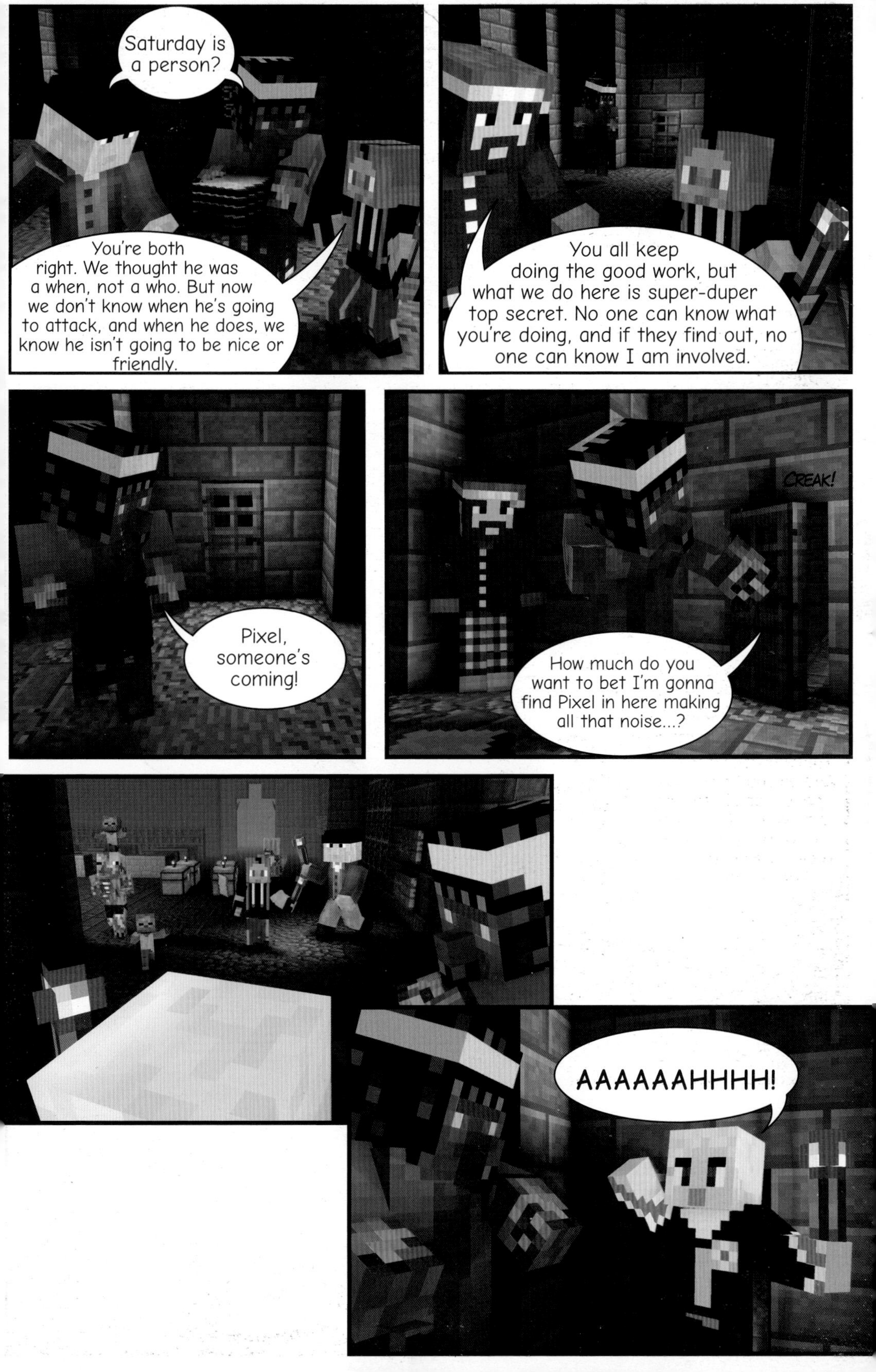
Saturday is a person?
You're both right. We thought he was a when, not a who. But now we don't know when he's going to attack, and when he does, we know he isn't going to be nice or friendly.
You all keep doing the good work, but what we do here is super-duper top secret. No one can know what you're doing, and if they find out, no one can know I am involved.
Pixel, someone's coming!
CREAK!
How much do you want to bet I'm gonna find Pixel in here making all that noise...?
AAAAAAHHHH!

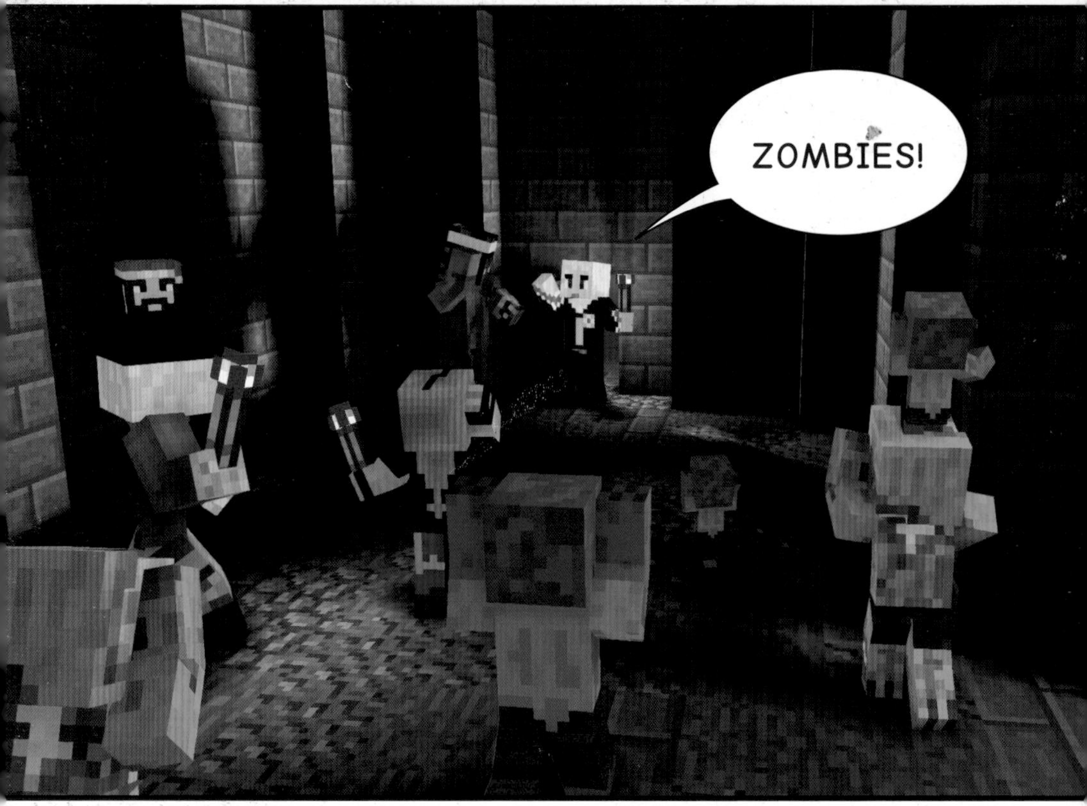
ZOMBIES!

EEEEeeeeEEeeEe!

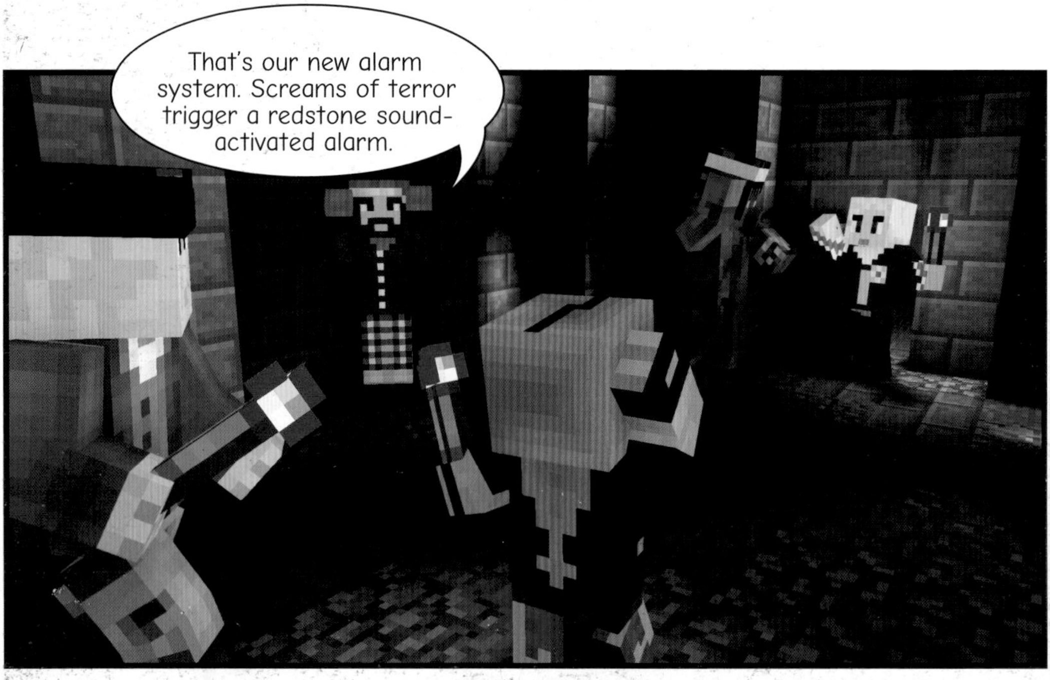
That's our new alarm system. Screams of terror trigger a redstone sound-activated alarm.

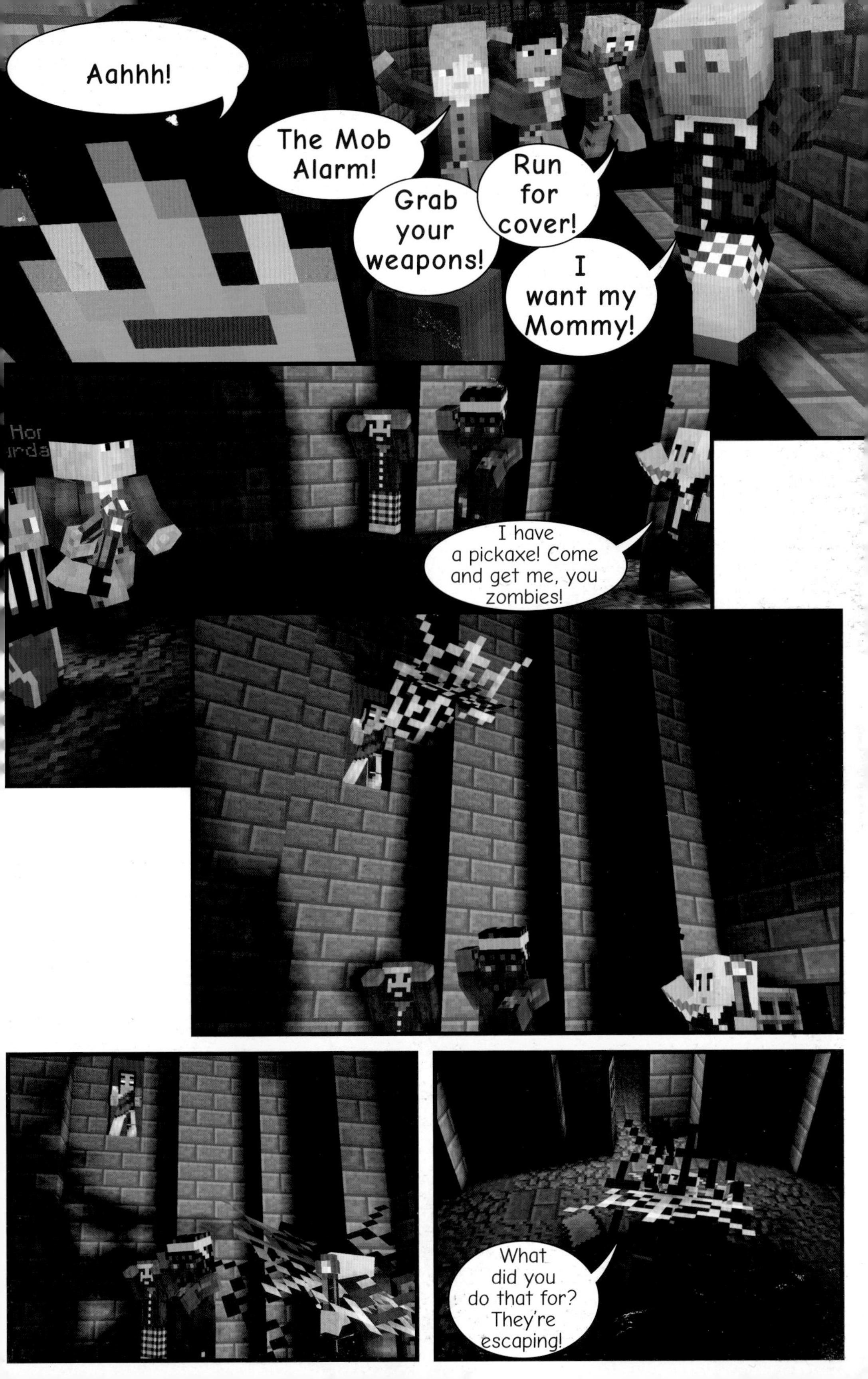
Aahhh!
The Mob Alarm!
Run for cover!
Grab your weapons!
I want my Mommy!
I have a pickaxe! Come and get me, you zombies!
What did you do that for? They're escaping!

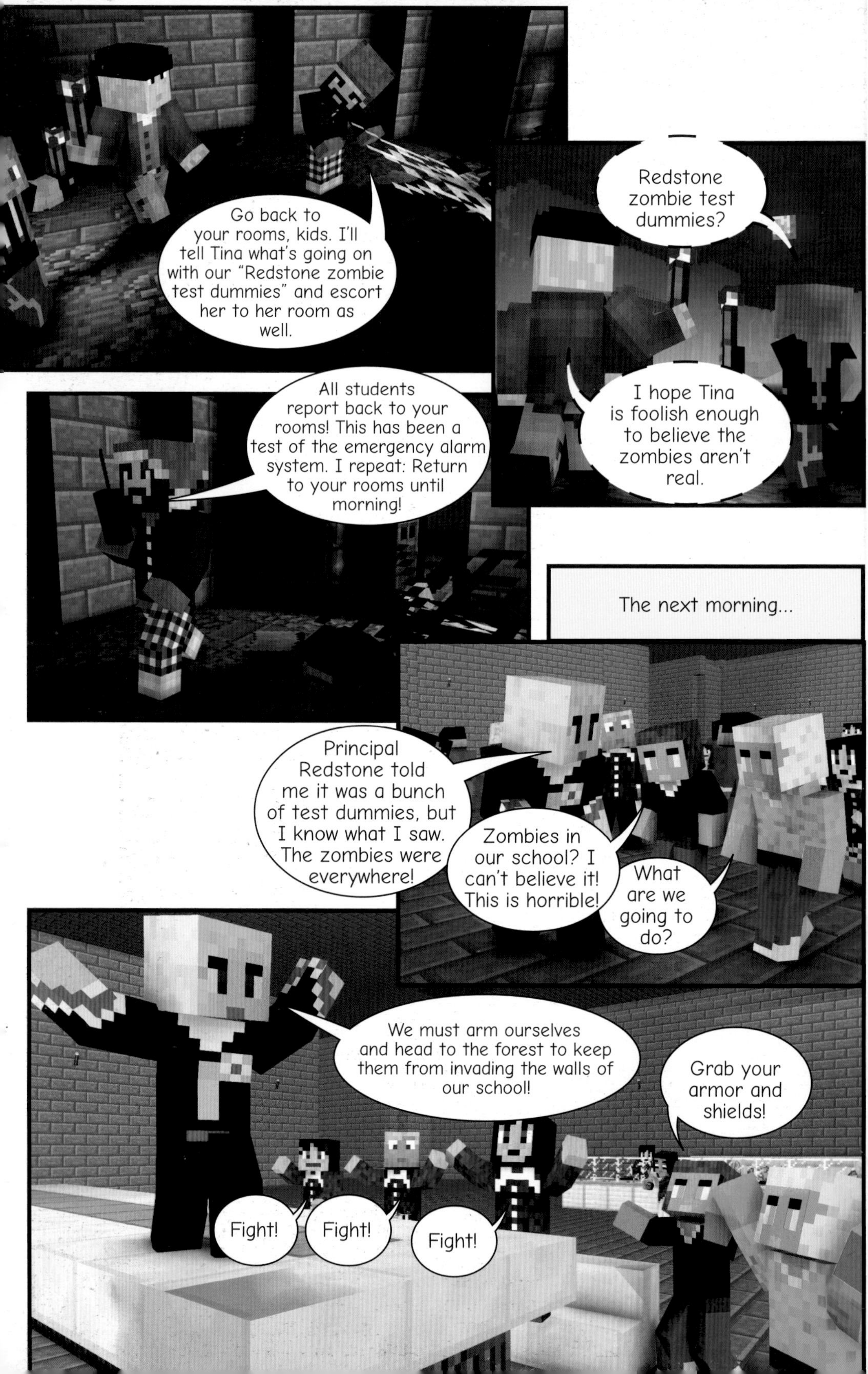

Go back to your rooms, kids. I'll tell Tina what's going on with our "Redstone zombie test dummies" and escort her to her room as well.
Redstone zombie test dummies?
I hope Tina is foolish enough to believe the zombies aren't real.
All students report back to your rooms! This has been a test of the emergency alarm system. I repeat: Return to your rooms until morning!
The next morning...
Principal Redstone told me it was a bunch of test dummies, but I know what I saw. The zombies were everywhere!
Zombies in our school? I can't believe it! This is horrible!
What are we going to do?
We must arm ourselves and head to the forest to keep them from invading the walls of our school!
Grab your armor and shields!
Fight!
Fight!
Fight!

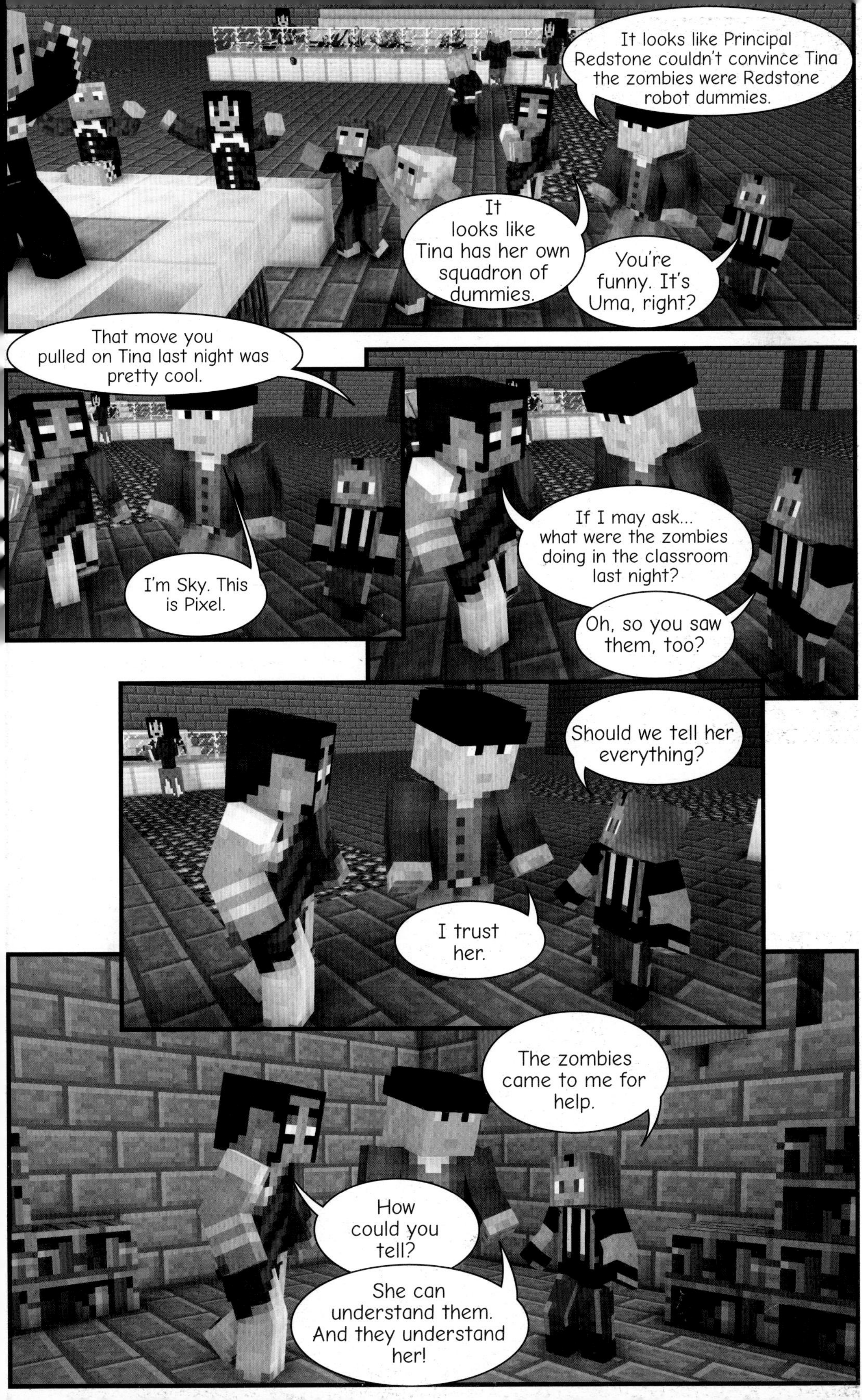
It looks like Principal Redstone couldn't convince Tina the zombies were Redstone robot dummies.
It looks like Tina has her own squadron of dummies.
You're funny. It's Uma, right?
That move you pulled on Tina last night was pretty cool.
I'm Sky. This is Pixel.
If I may ask... what were the zombies doing in the classroom last night?
Oh, so you saw them, too?
Should we tell her everything?
I trust her.
The zombies came to me for help.
How could you tell?
She can understand them. And they understand her!

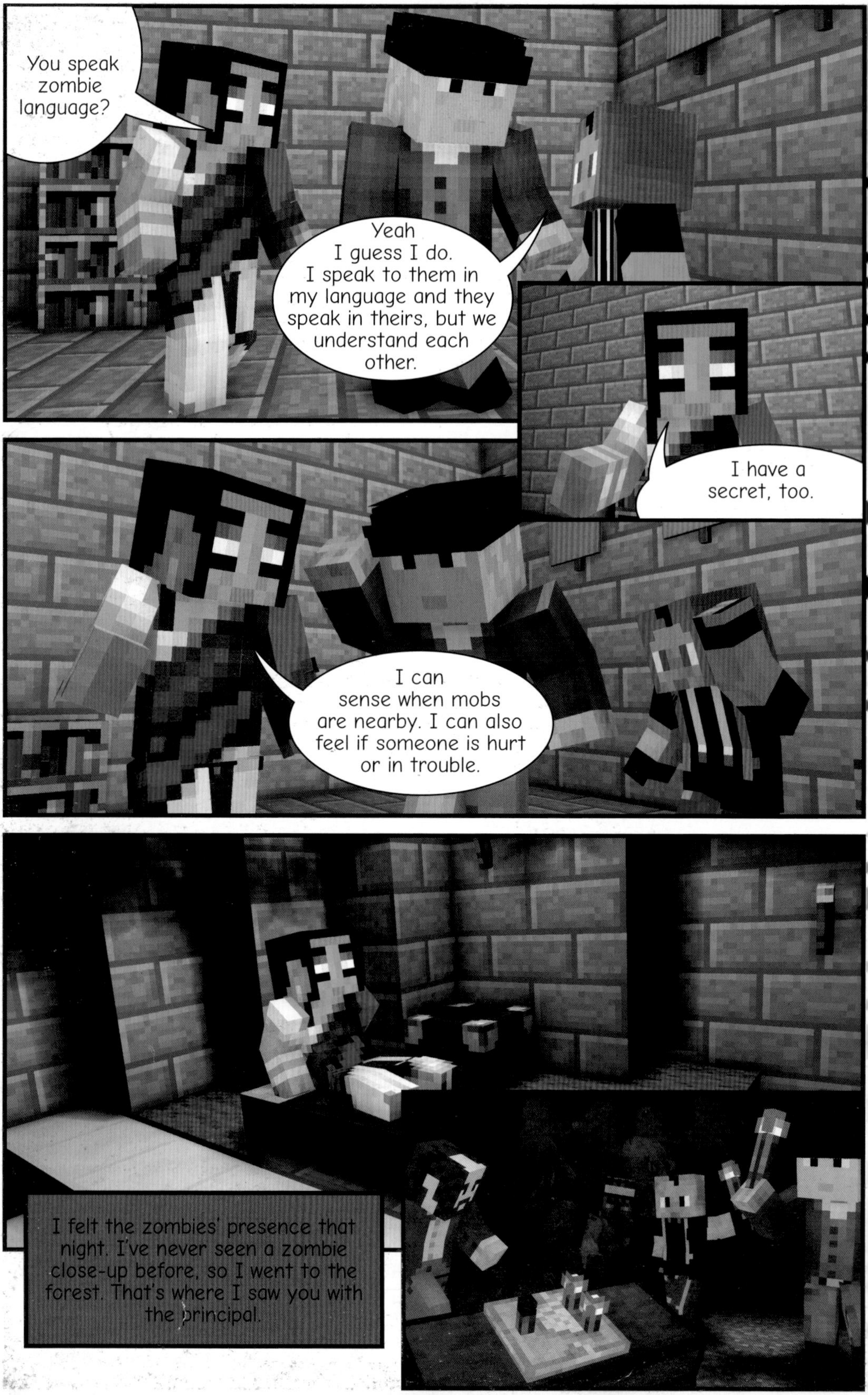
You speak zombie language?
Yeah I guess I do. I speak to them in my language and they speak in theirs, but we understand each other.
I have a secret, too.
I can sense when mobs are nearby. I can also feel if someone is hurt or in trouble.
I felt the zombies' presence that night. I've never seen a zombie close-up before, so I went to the forest. That's where I saw you with the principal.

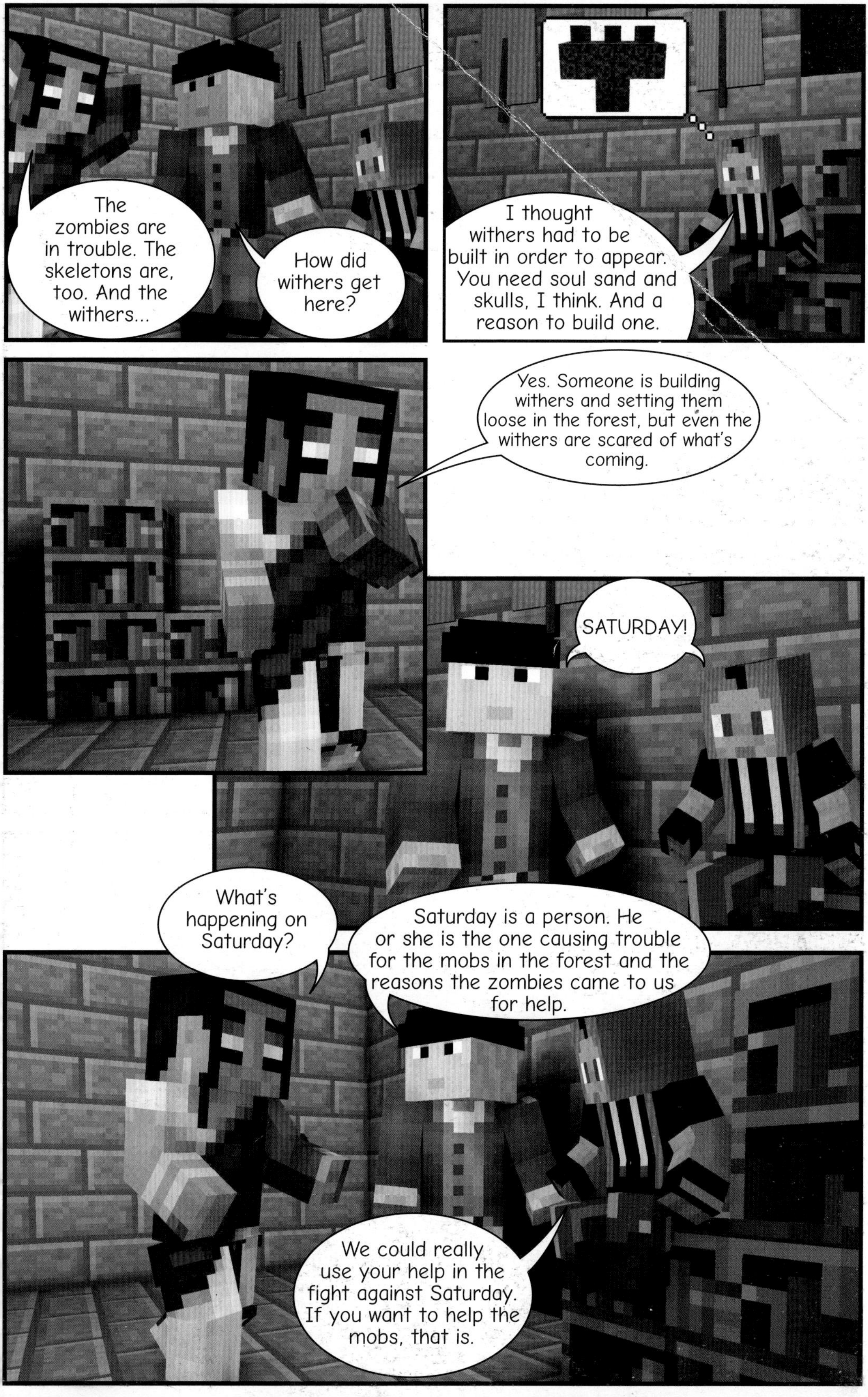
The zombies are in trouble. The skeletons are, too. And the withers...
How did withers get here?
I thought withers had to be built in order to appear. You need soul sand and skulls, I think. And a reason to build one.
Yes. Someone is building withers and setting them loose in the forest, but even the withers are scared of what's coming.
SATURDAY!
What's happening on Saturday?
Saturday is a person. He or she is the one causing trouble for the mobs in the forest and the reasons the zombies came to us for help.
We could really use your help in the fight against Saturday. If you want to help the mobs, that is.

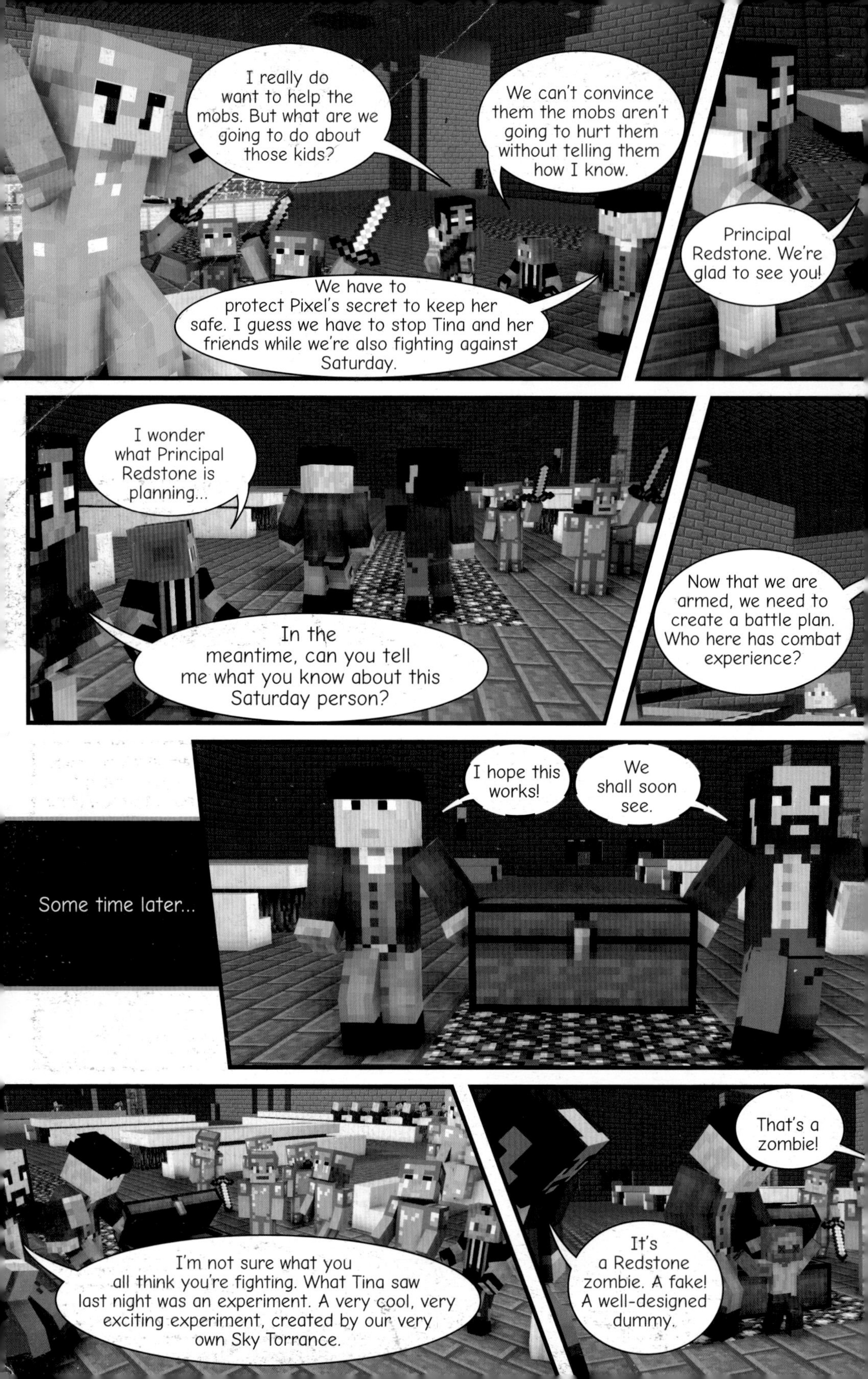
I really do want to help the mobs. But what are we going to do about those kids?
We can't convince them the mobs aren't going to hurt them without telling them how I know.
We have to protect Pixel's secret to keep her safe. I guess we have to stop Tina and her friends while we're also fighting against Saturday.
Principal Redstone. We're glad to see you!
I wonder what Principal Redstone is planning...
In the meantime, can you tell me what you know about this Saturday person?
Now that we are armed, we need to create a battle plan. Who here has combat experience?
Some time later...
I hope this works!
We shall soon see.
I'm not sure what you all think you're fighting. What Tina saw last night was an experiment. A very cool, very exciting experiment, created by our very own Sky Torrance.
That's a zombie!
It's a Redstone zombie. A fake! A well-designed dummy.

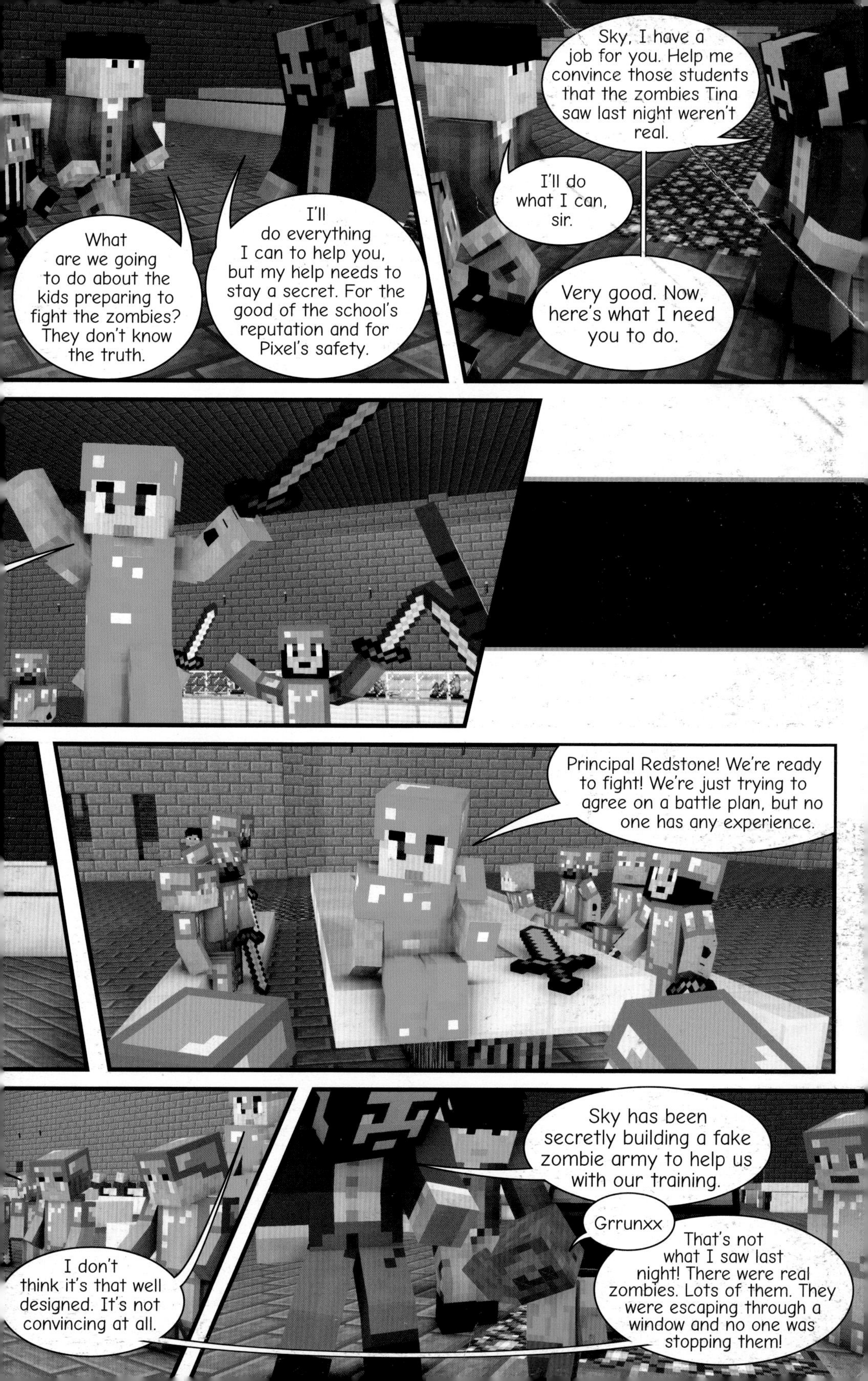
What are we going to do about the kids preparing to fight the zombies? They don't know the truth.
I'll do everything I can to help you, but my help needs to stay a secret. For the good of the school's reputation and for Pixel's safety.
Sky, I have a job for you. Help me convince those students that the zombies Tina saw last night weren't real.
I'll do what I can, sir.
Very good. Now, here's what I need you to do.
Principal Redstone! We're ready to fight! We're just trying to agree on a battle plan, but no one has any experience.
Sky has been secretly building a fake zombie army to help us with our training.
Grrunxx
I don't think it's that well designed. It's not convincing at all.
That's not what I saw last night! There were real zombies. Lots of them. They were escaping through a window and no one was stopping them!

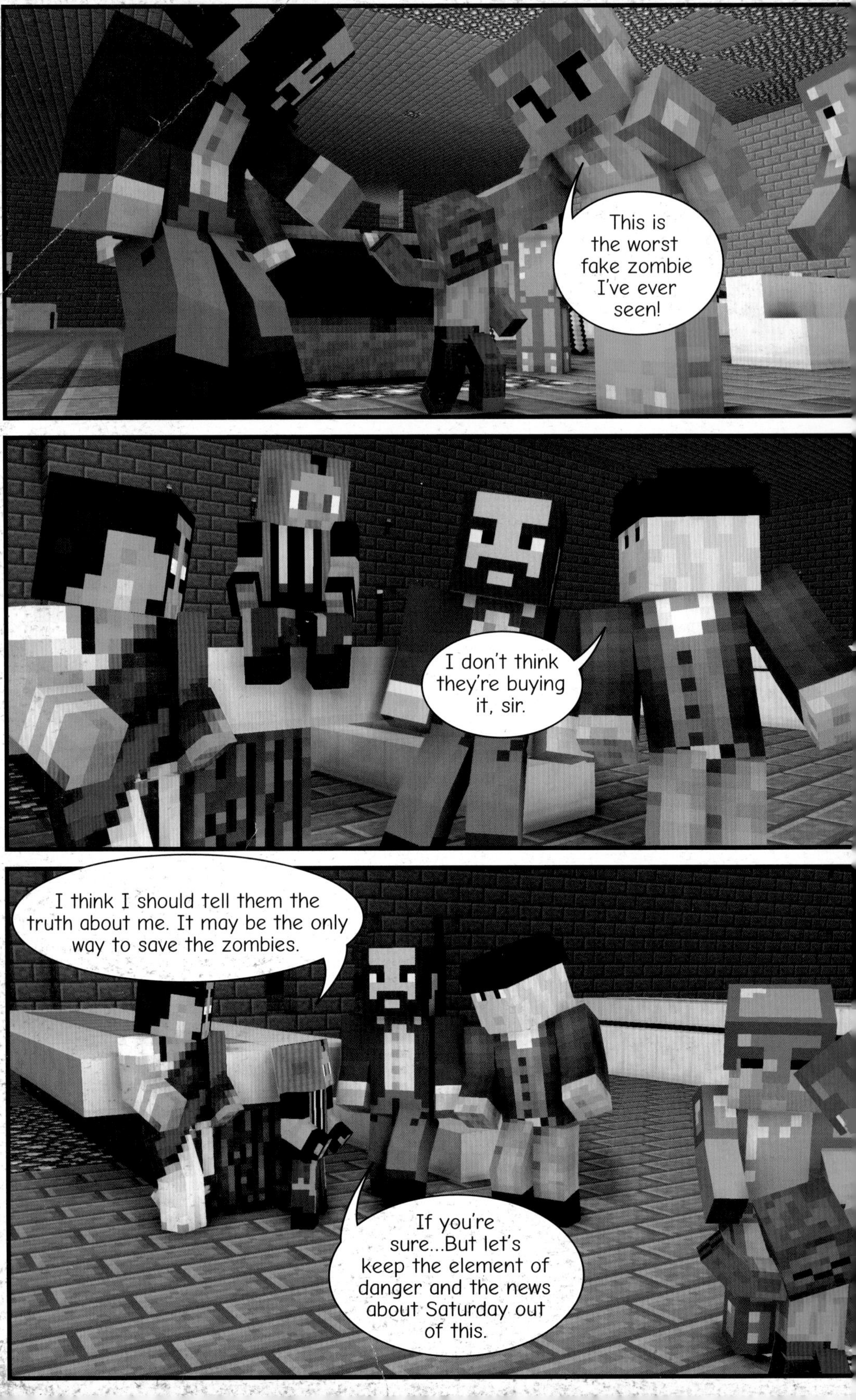
This is the worst fake zombie I've ever seen!
I don't think they're buying it, sir.
I think I should tell them the truth about me. It may be the only way to save the zombies.
If you're sure...But let's keep the element of danger and the news about Saturday out of this.

CHAPTER 7

CONTRAPTIONS 101
MR. QUARTZ

me to the ZSA
tudent Alliance

THE ZOMBIE
STUDENT
ALLIANCE

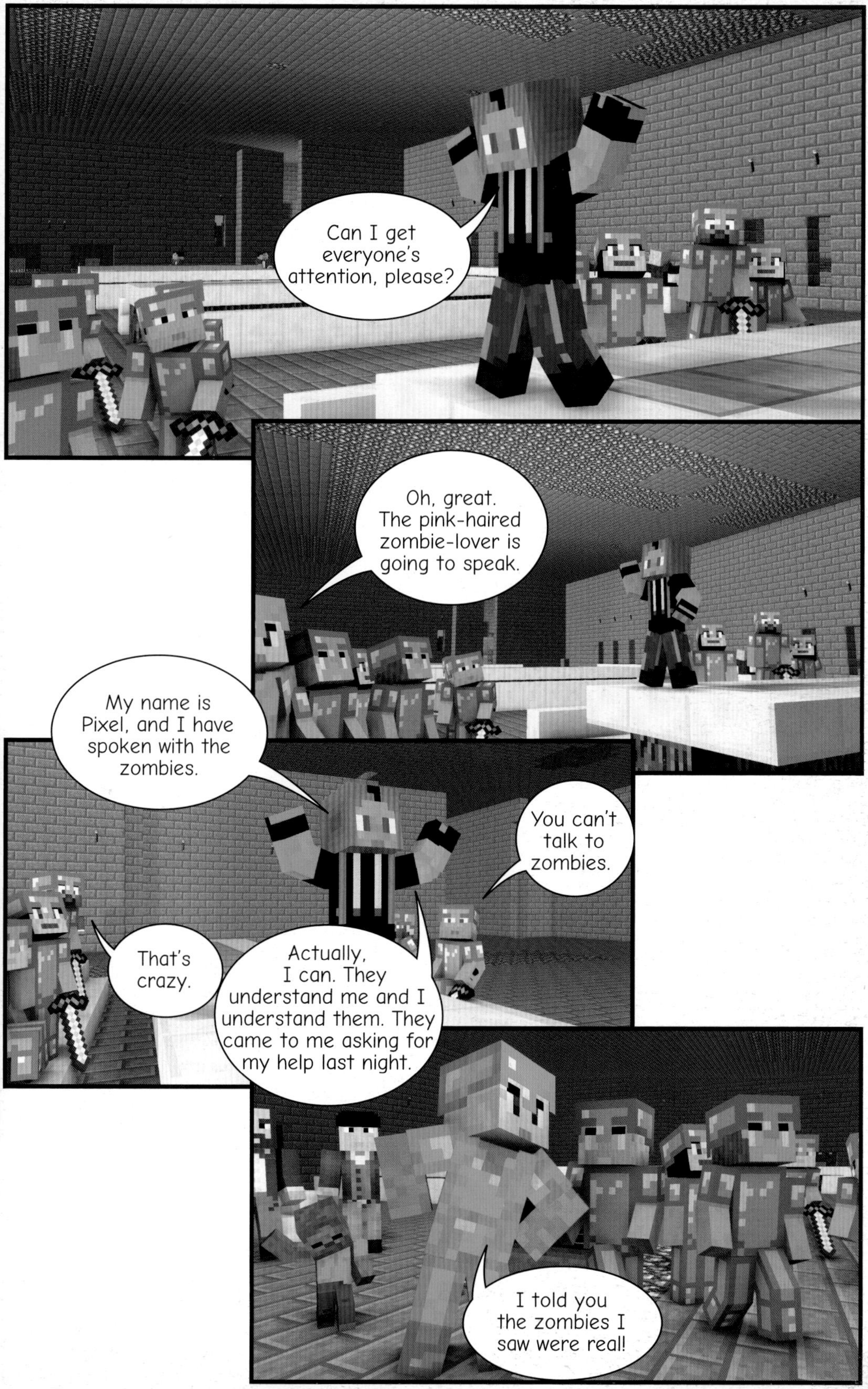
Can I get everyone's attention, please?
Oh, great. The pink-haired zombie-lover is going to speak.
My name is Pixel, and I have spoken with the zombies.
You can't talk to zombies.
That's crazy.
Actually, I can. They understand me and I understand them. They came to me asking for my help last night.
I told you the zombies I saw were real!

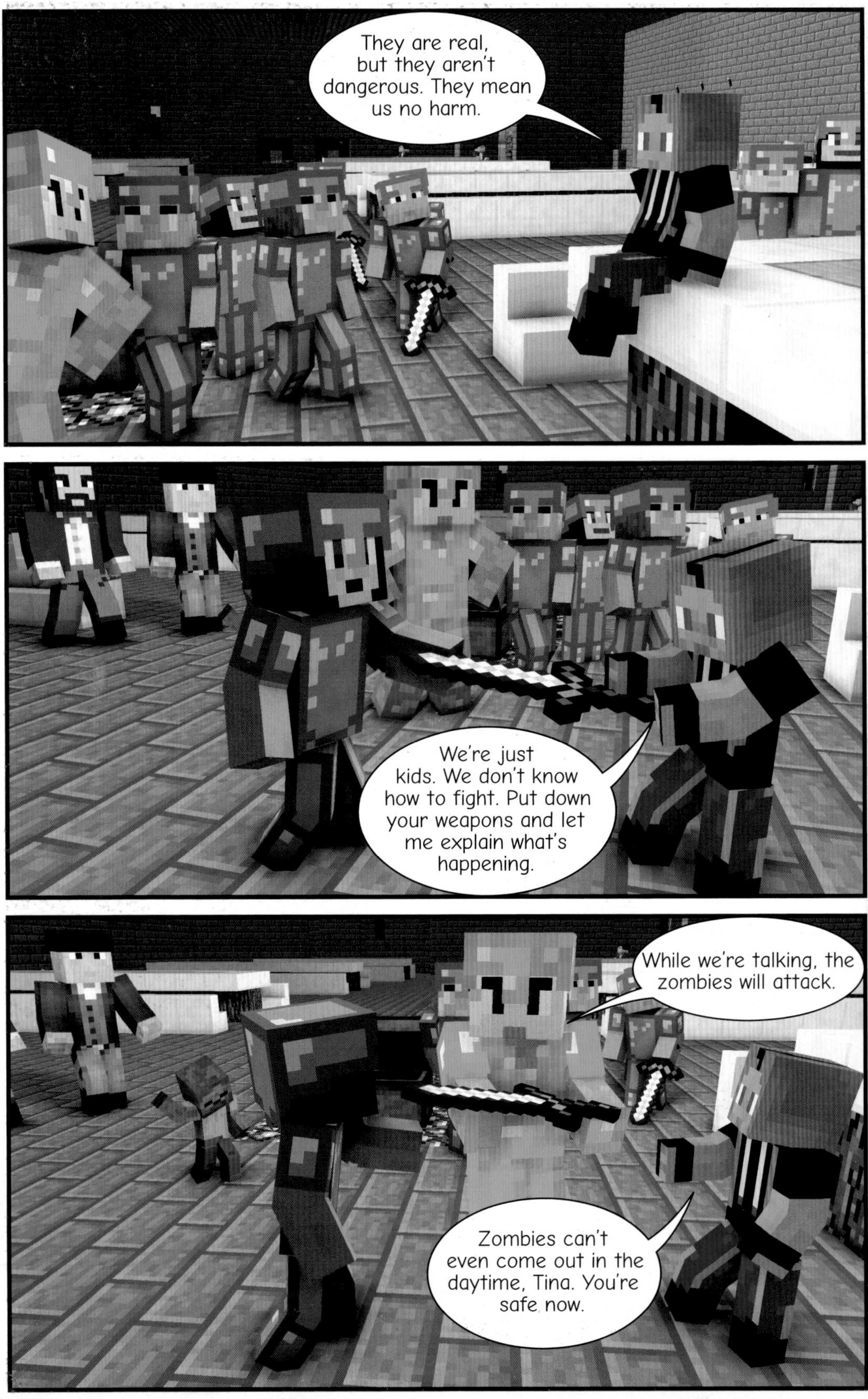
They are real, but they aren't dangerous. They mean us no harm.
We're just kids. We don't know how to fight. Put down your weapons and let me explain what's happening.
While we're talking, the zombies will attack.
Zombies can't even come out in the daytime, Tina. You're safe now.

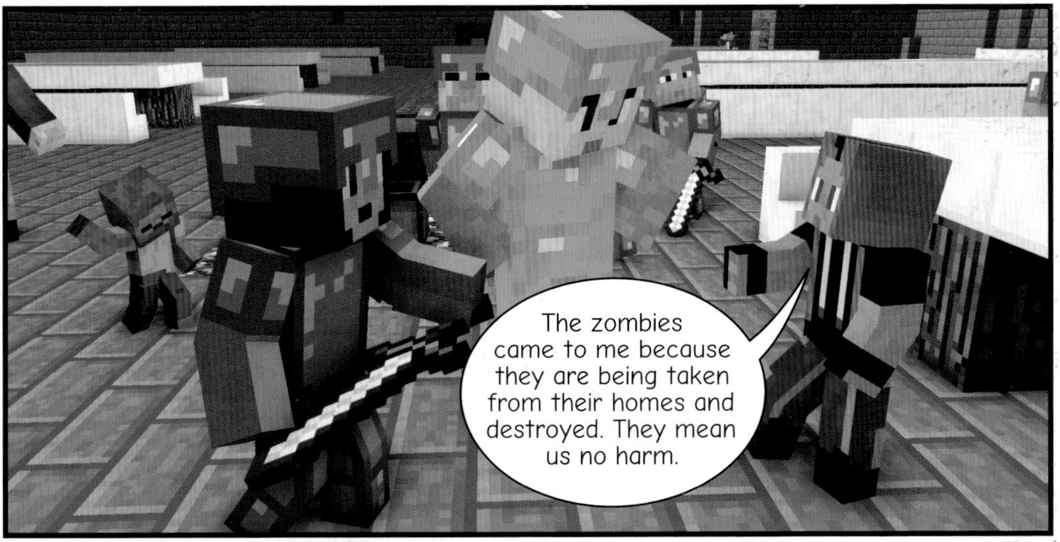
The zombies came to me because they are being taken from their homes and destroyed. They mean us no harm.

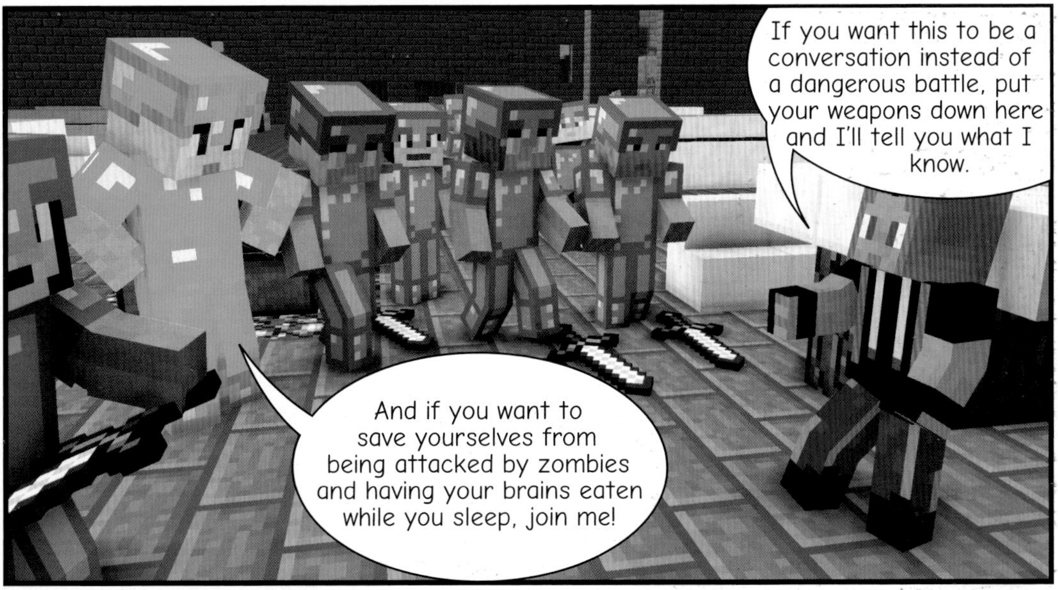
If you want this to be a conversation instead of a dangerous battle, put your weapons down here and I'll tell you what I know.
And if you want to save yourselves from being attacked by zombies and having your brains eaten while you sleep, join me!

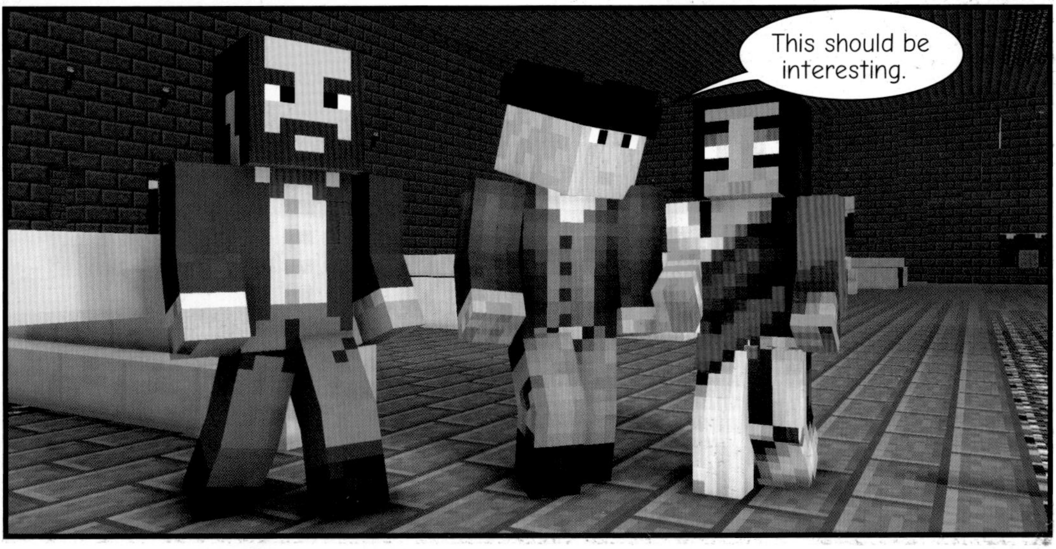
This should be interesting.

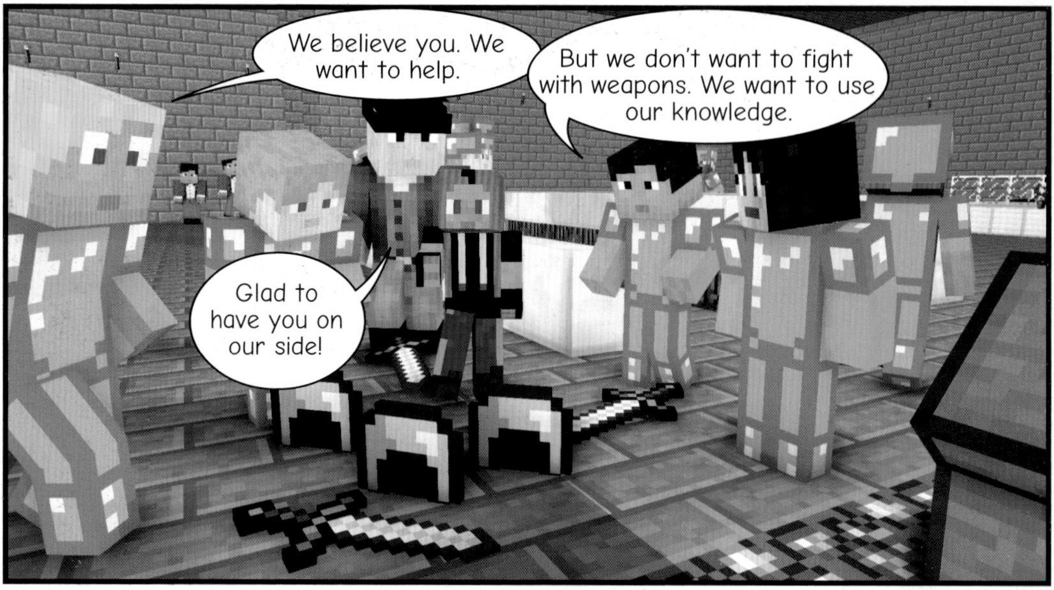
We believe you. We want to help.
But we don't want to fight with weapons. We want to use our knowledge.
Glad to have you on our side!

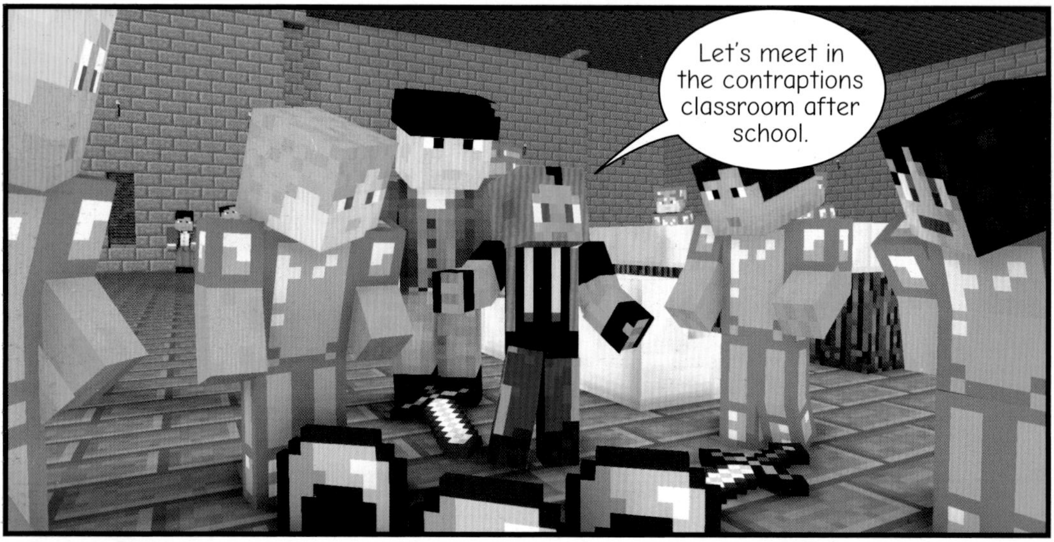
Let's meet in the contraptions classroom after school.

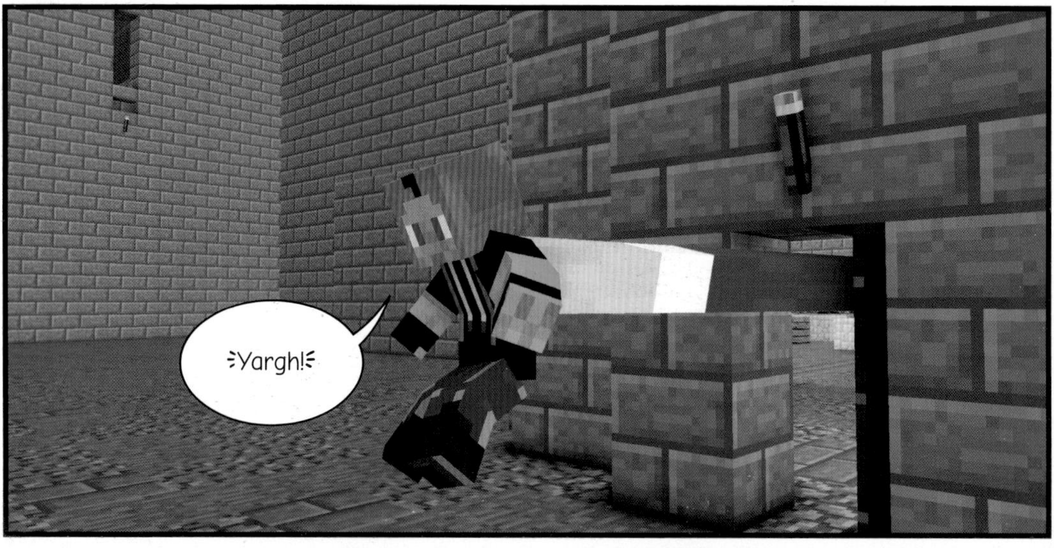
Yargh!

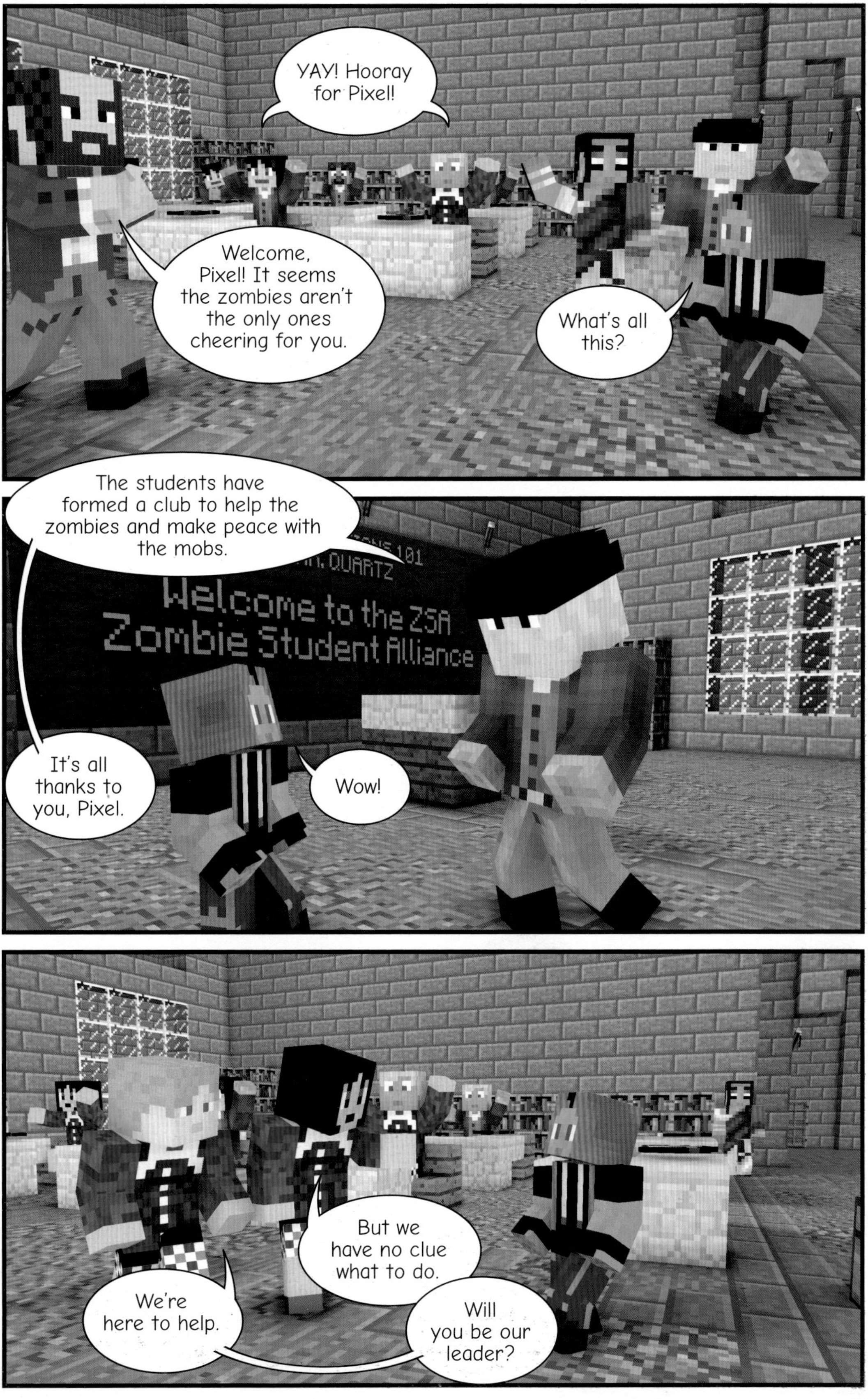
YAY! Hooray for Pixel!
Welcome, Pixel! It seems the zombies aren't the only ones cheering for you.
What's all this?
The students have formed a club to help the zombies and make peace with the mobs.
Welcome to the ZSA
Zombie Student Alliance
It's all thanks to you, Pixel.
Wow!
But we have no clue what to do.
We're here to help.
Will you be our leader?

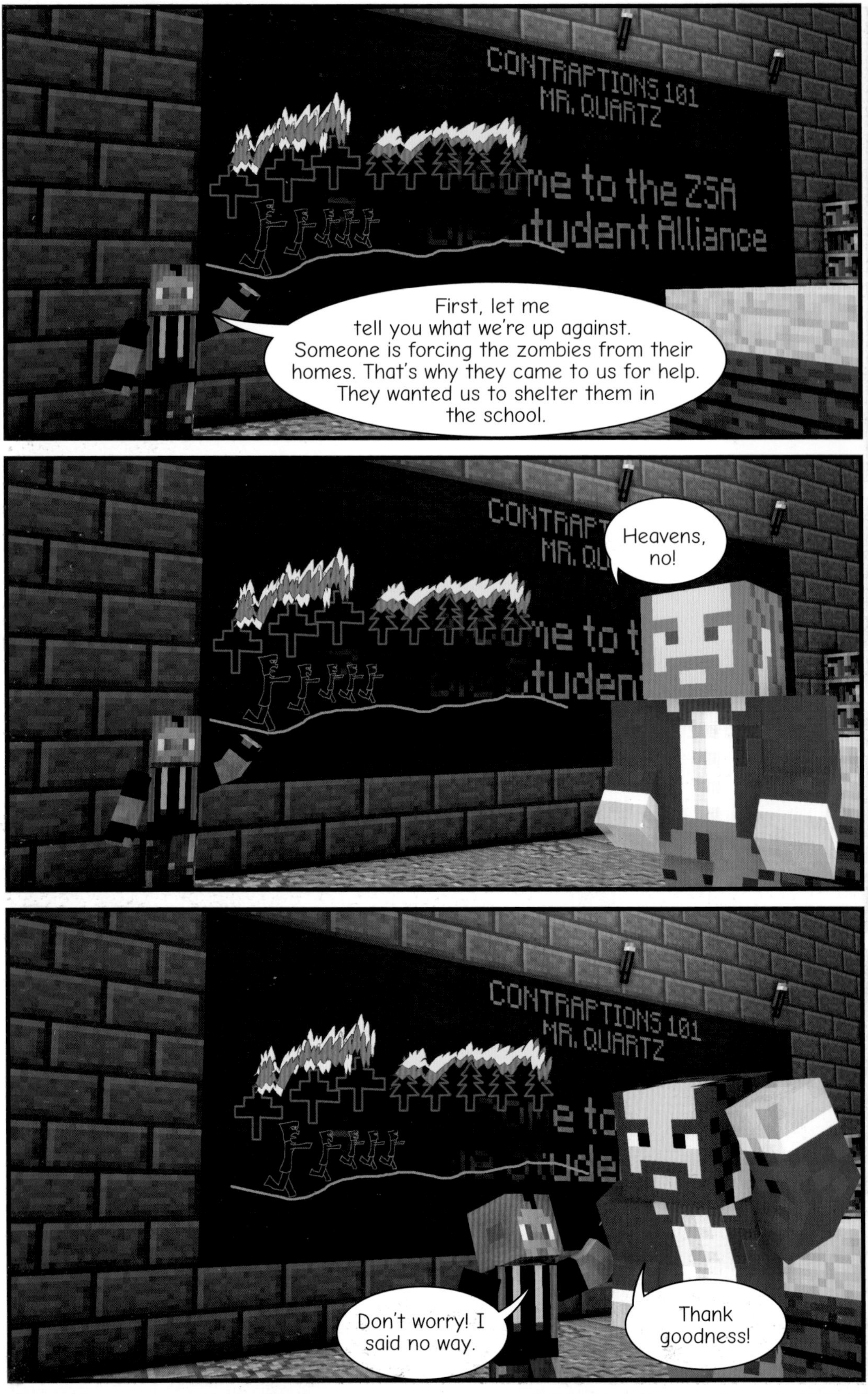
CONTRAPTIONS 101
MR. QUARTZ
First, let me tell you what we're up against. Someone is forcing the zombies from their homes. That's why they came to us for help. They wanted us to shelter them in the school.
Heavens, no!
CONTRAPTIONS 101
MR. QUARTZ
Don't worry! I said no way.
Thank goodness!

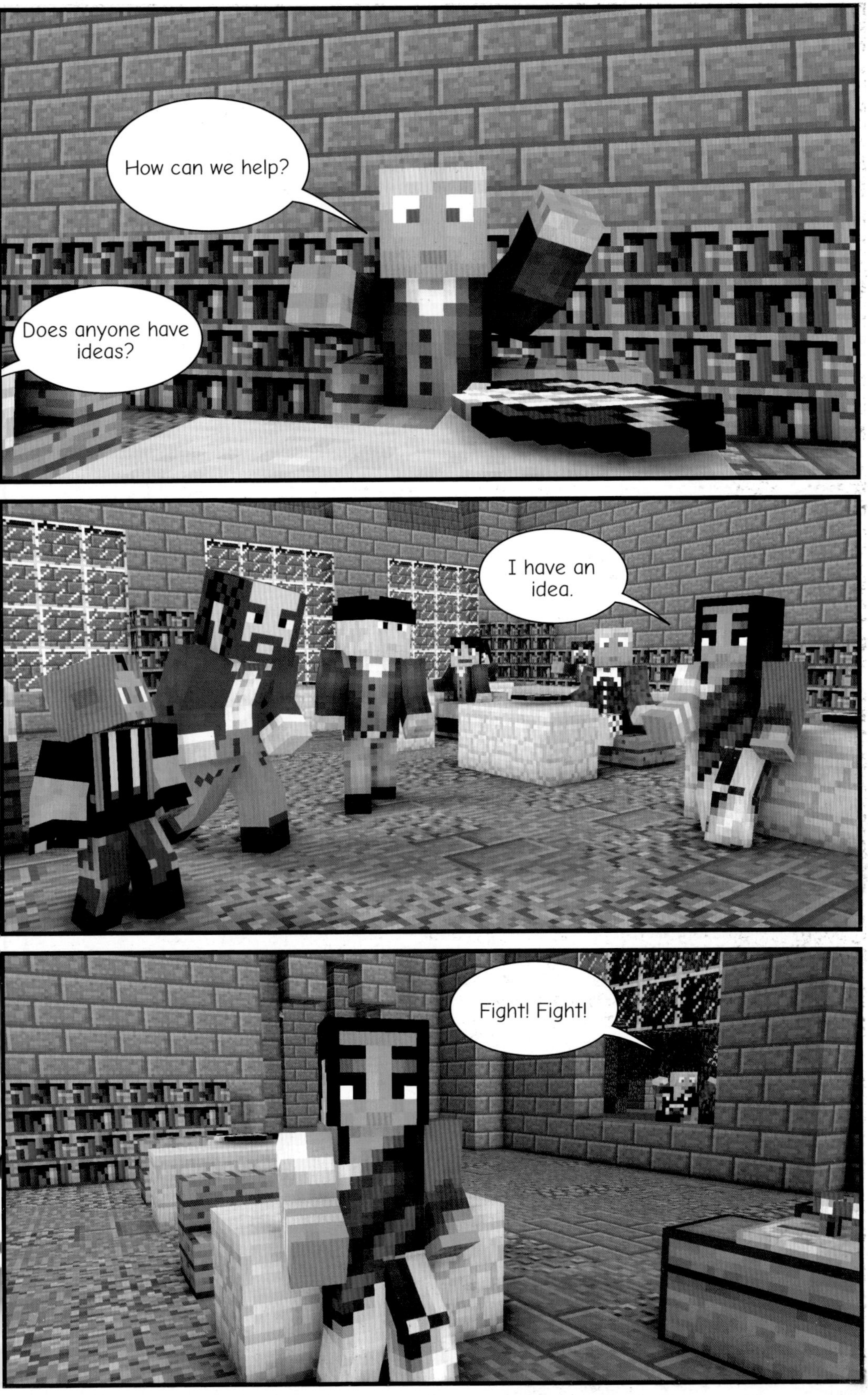
How can we help?
Does anyone have ideas?
I have an idea.
Fight! Fight!

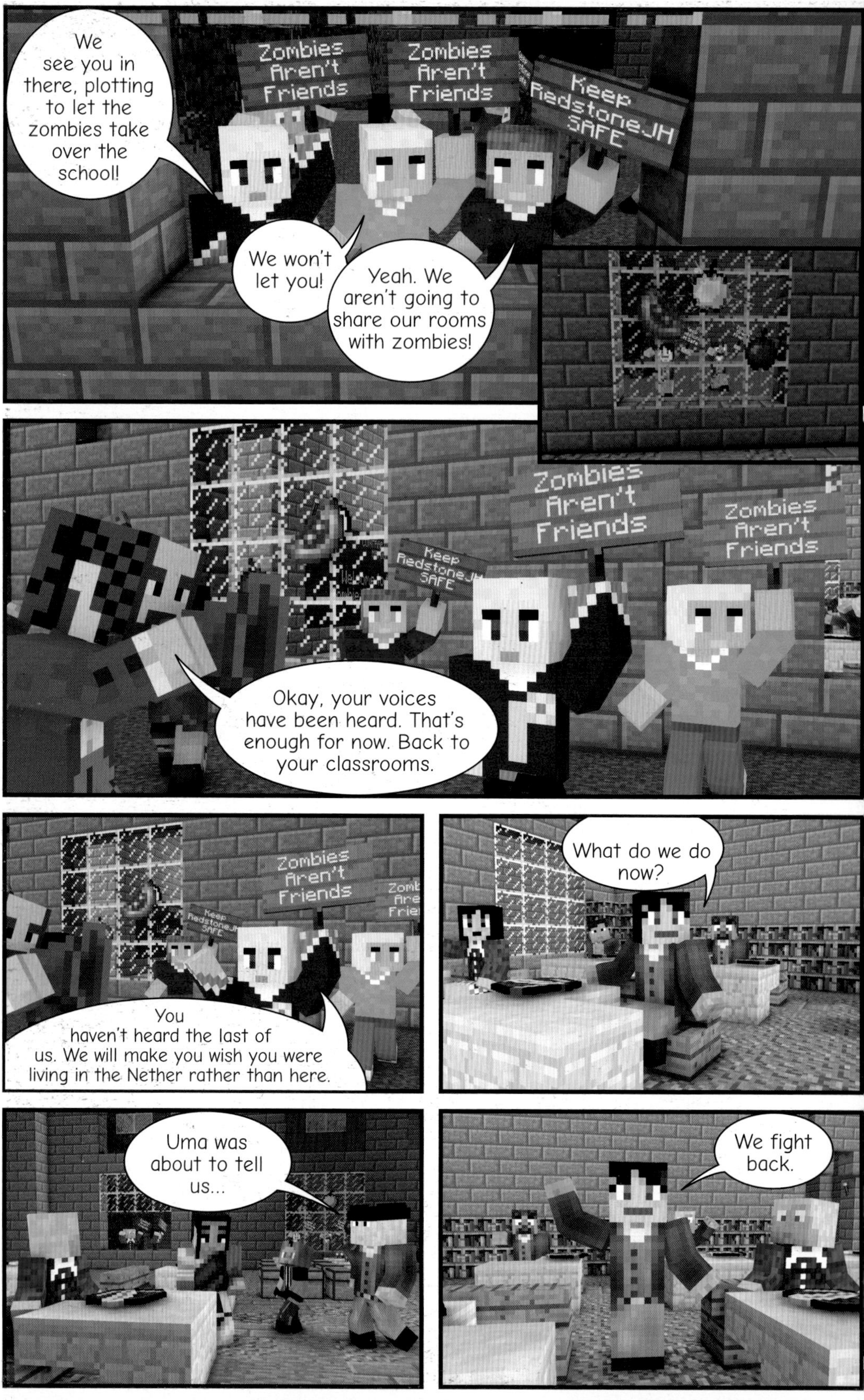

We see you in there, plotting to let the zombies take over the school!
Zombies Aren't Friends
Zombies Aren't Friends
Keep RedstoneJH SAFE
We won't let you!
Yeah. We aren't going to share our rooms with zombies!
Zombies Aren't Friends
Zombies Aren't Friends
Keep RedstoneJH SAFE
Okay, your voices have been heard. That's enough for now. Back to your classrooms.
Zombies Aren't Friends
Keep RedstoneJH SAFE
You haven't heard the last of us. We will make you wish you were living in the Nether rather than here.
What do we do now?
Uma was about to tell us...
We fight back.

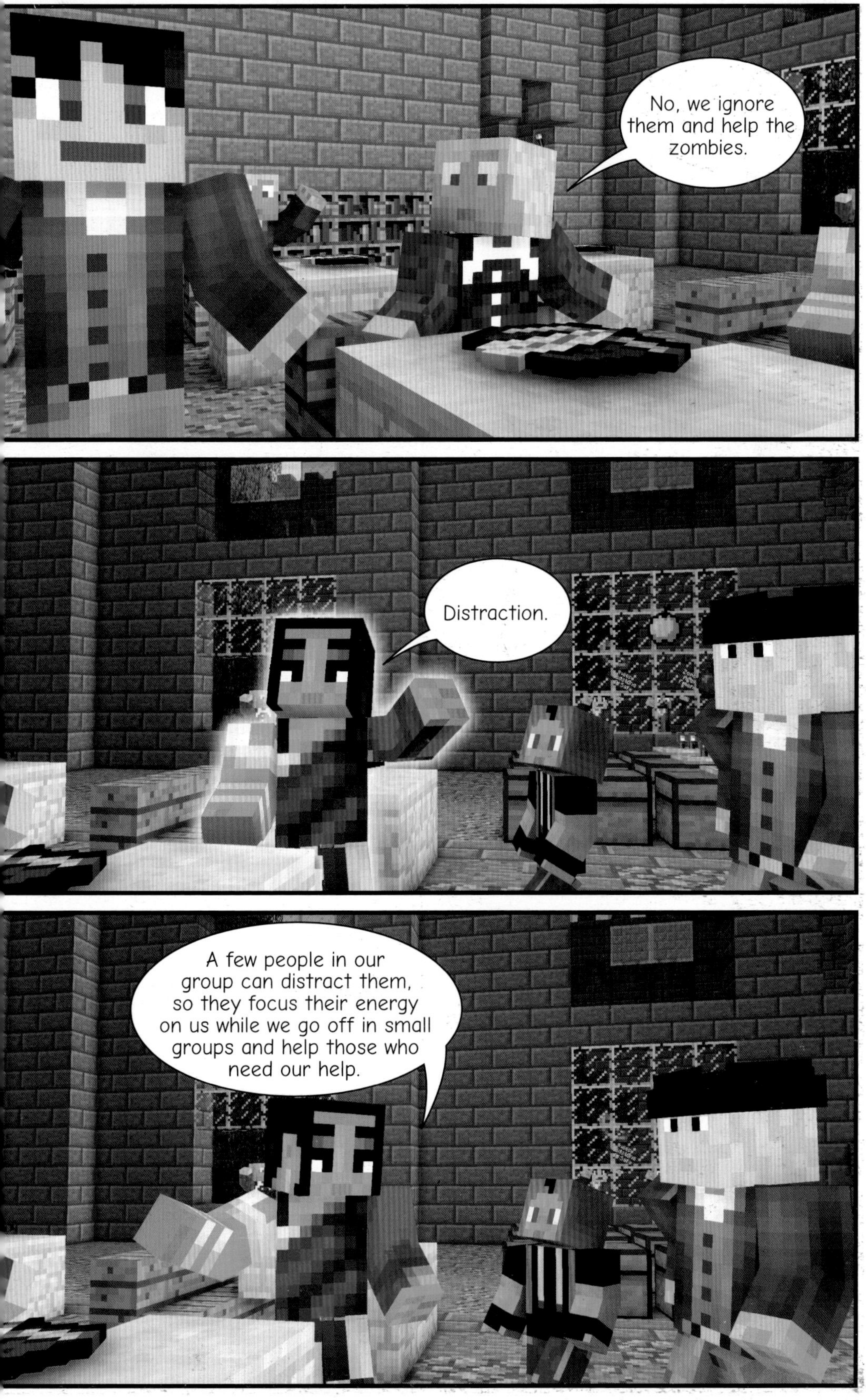
No, we ignore them and help the zombies.
Distraction.
A few people in our group can distract them, so they focus their energy on us while we go off in small groups and help those who need our help.

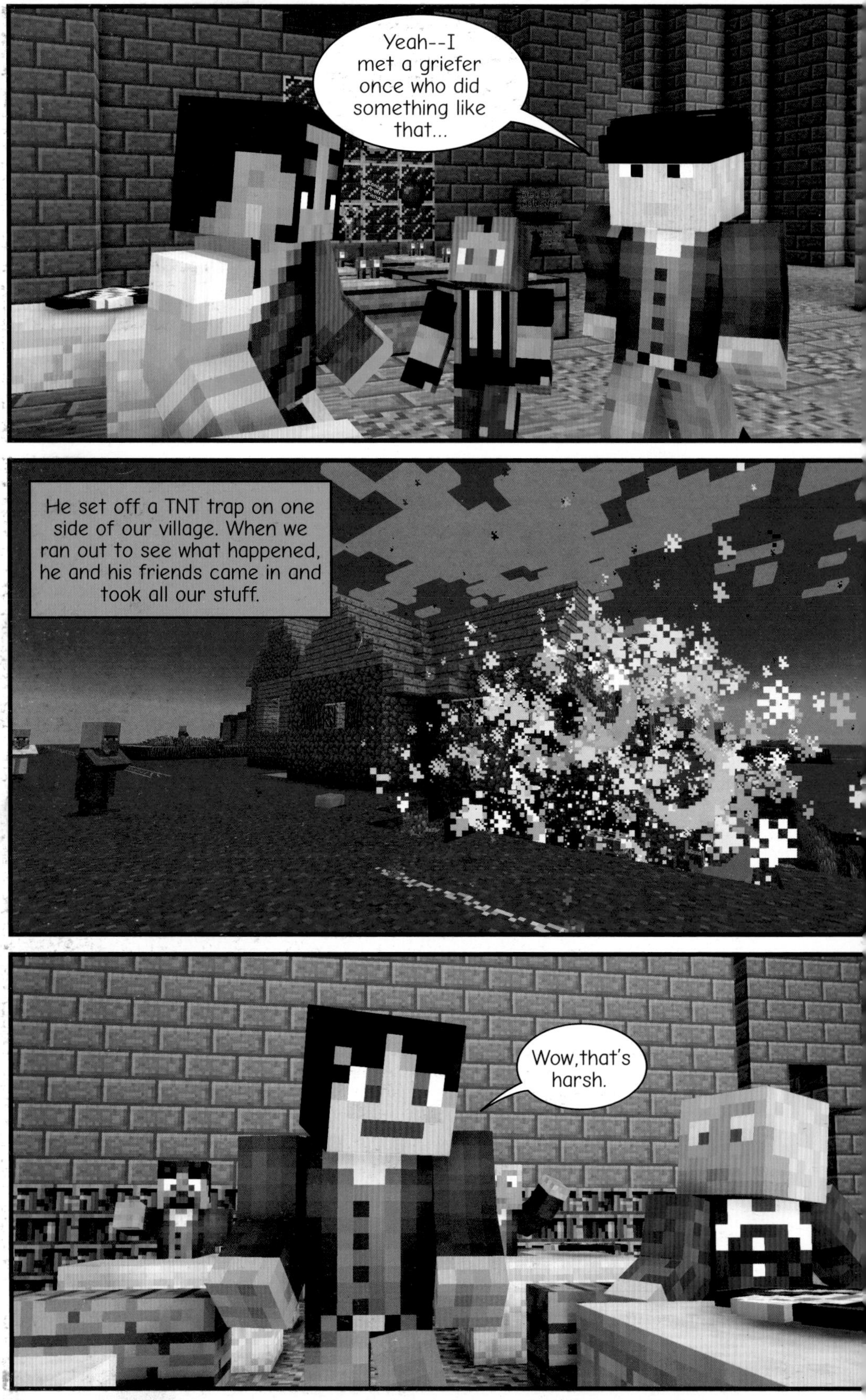
Yeah--I met a griefer once who did something like that...
He set off a TNT trap on one side of our village. When we ran out to see what happened, he and his friends came in and took all our stuff.
Wow,that's harsh.

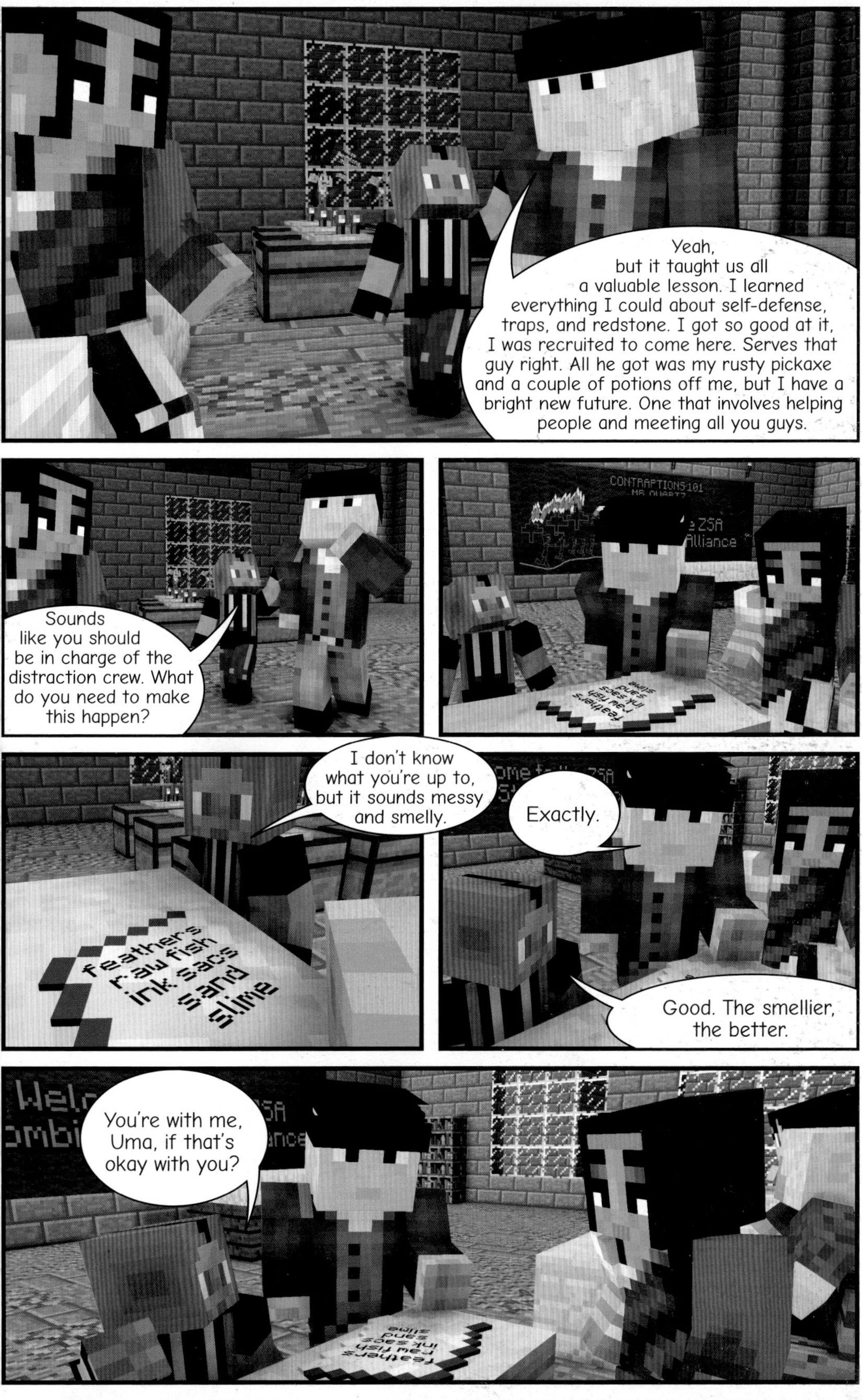

Yeah, but it taught us all a valuable lesson. I learned everything I could about self-defense, traps, and redstone. I got so good at it, I was recruited to come here. Serves that guy right. All he got was my rusty pickaxe and a couple of potions off me, but I have a bright new future. One that involves helping people and meeting all you guys.
Sounds like you should be in charge of the distraction crew. What do you need to make this happen?
CONTRAPTIONS 101
I don't know what you're up to, but it sounds messy and smelly.
feathers raw fish ink sacs sand slime
Exactly.
Good. The smellier, the better.
You're with me, Uma, if that's okay with you?

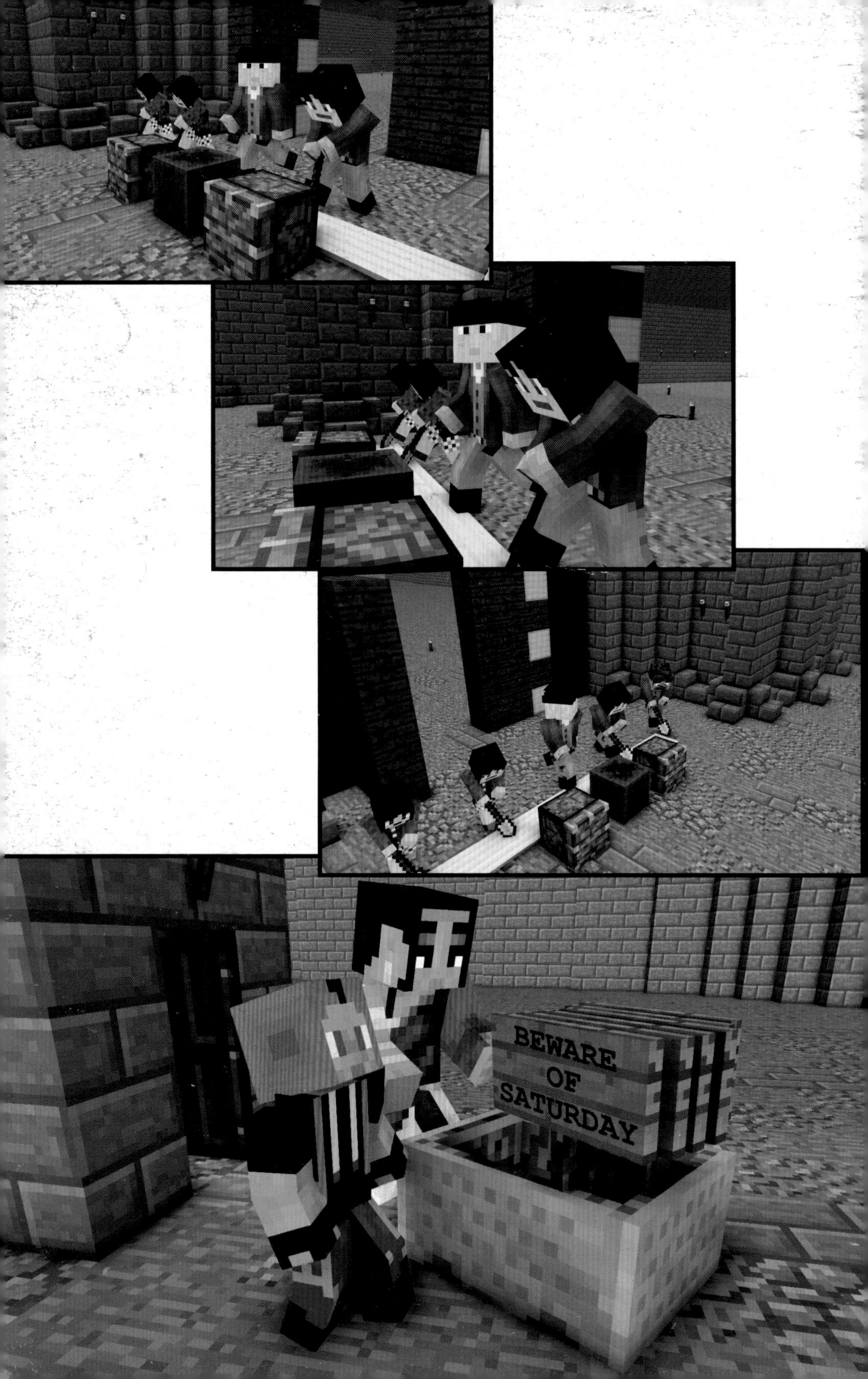
BEWARE
OF
SATURDAY

CHAPTER 8

SLIMED AND FEATHERED

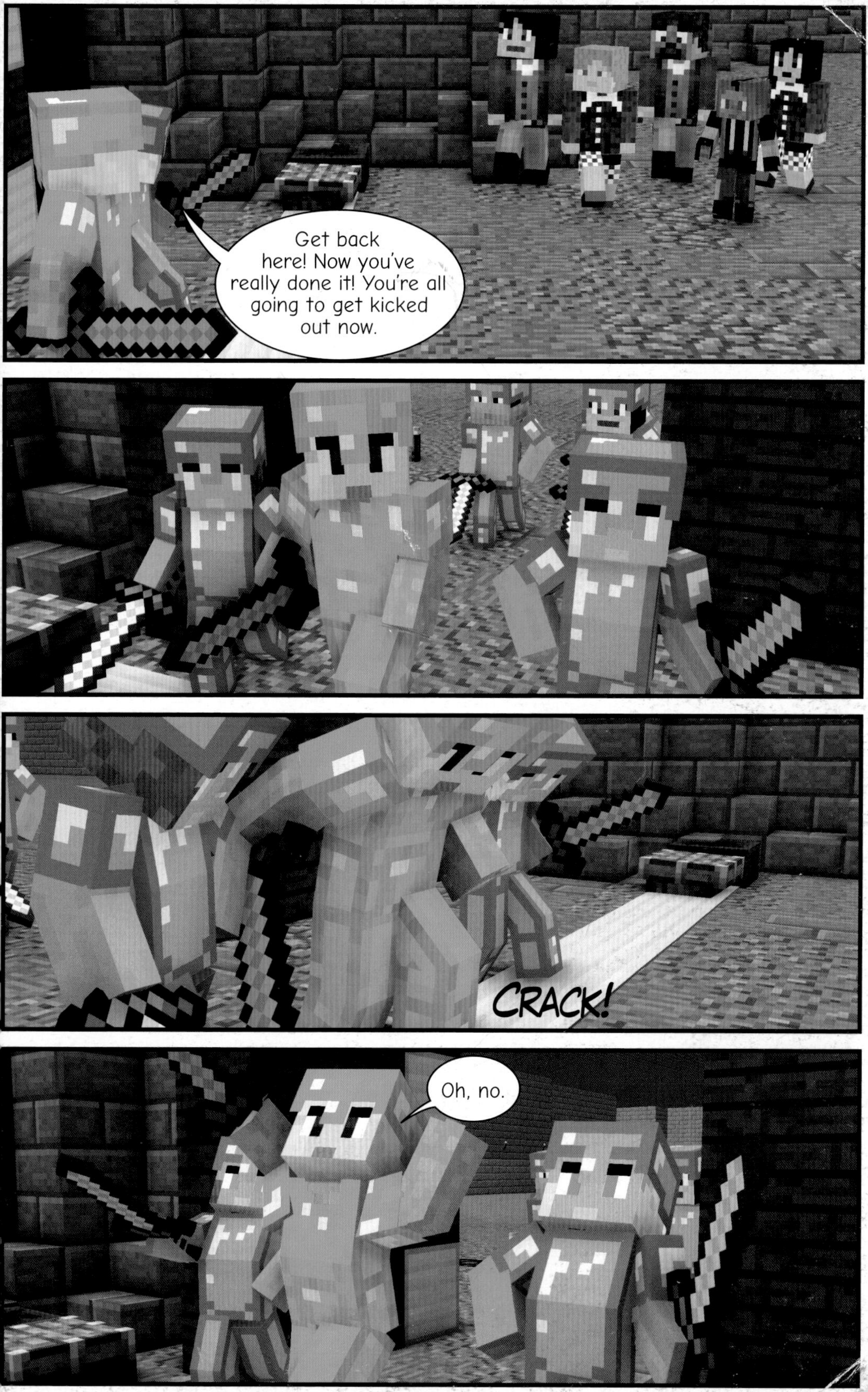
Get back here! Now you've really done it! You're all going to get kicked out now.
CRACK!
Oh, no.

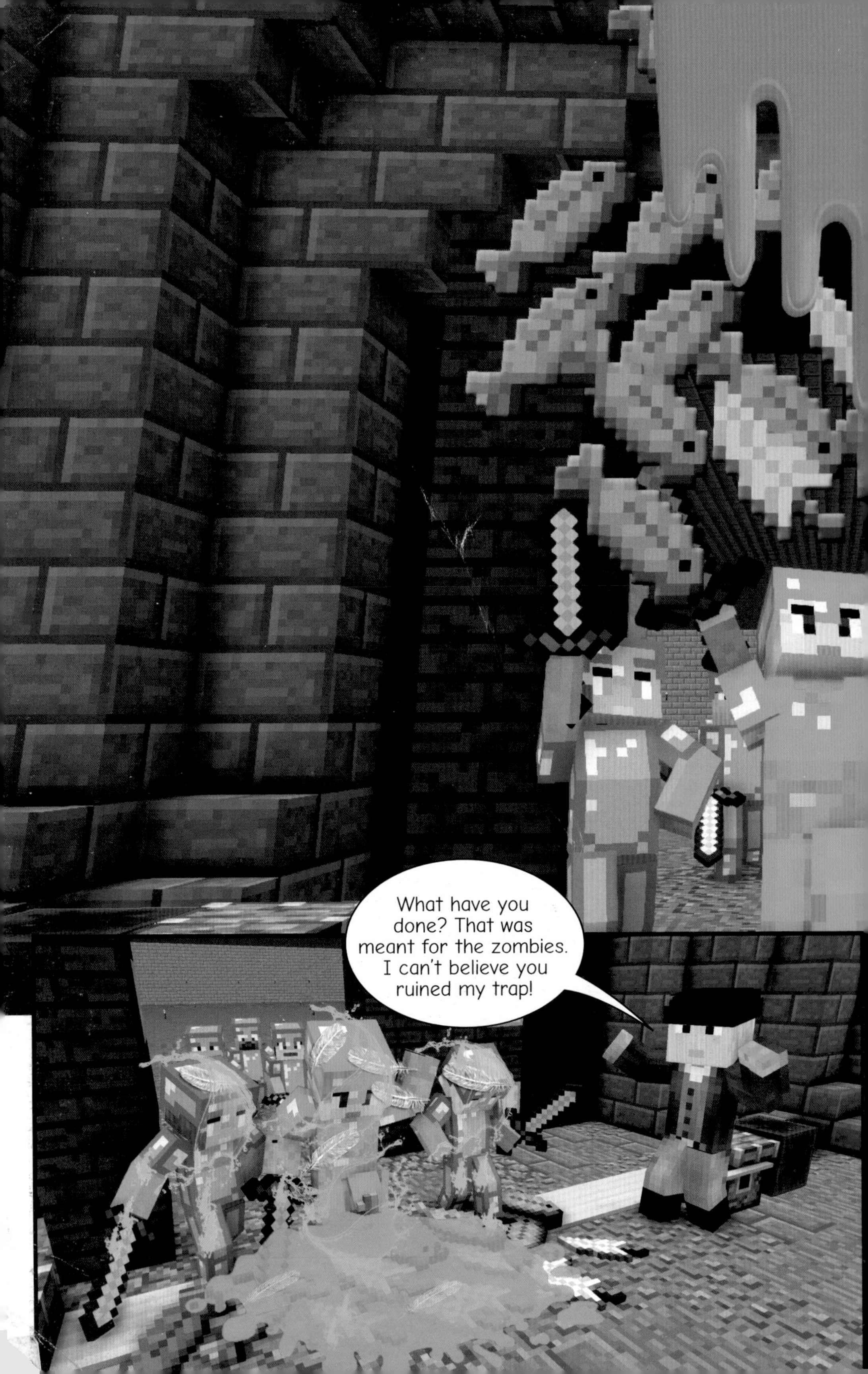
What have you done? That was meant for the zombies. I can't believe you ruined my trap!

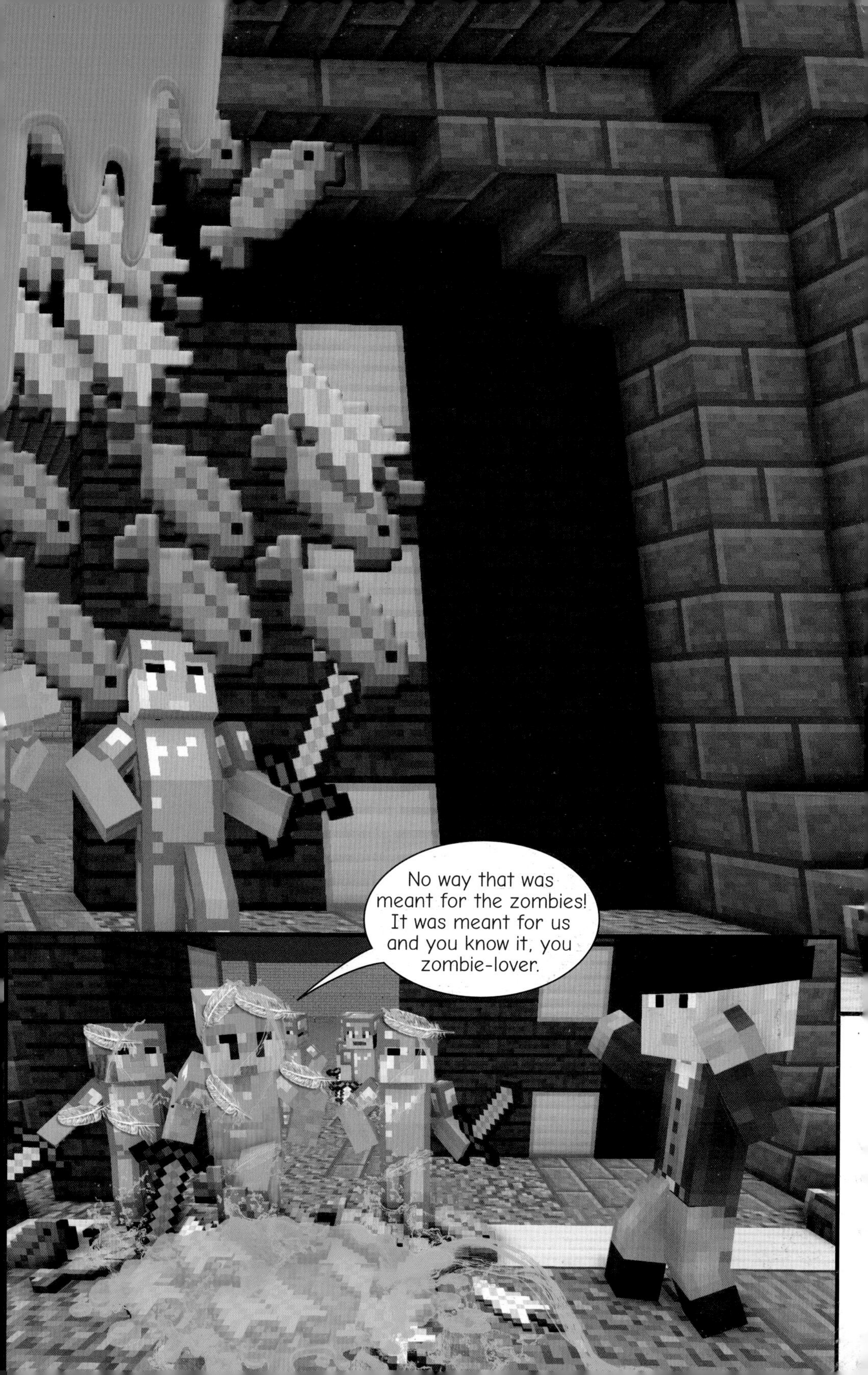
No way that was meant for the zombies! It was meant for us and you know it, you zombie-lover.

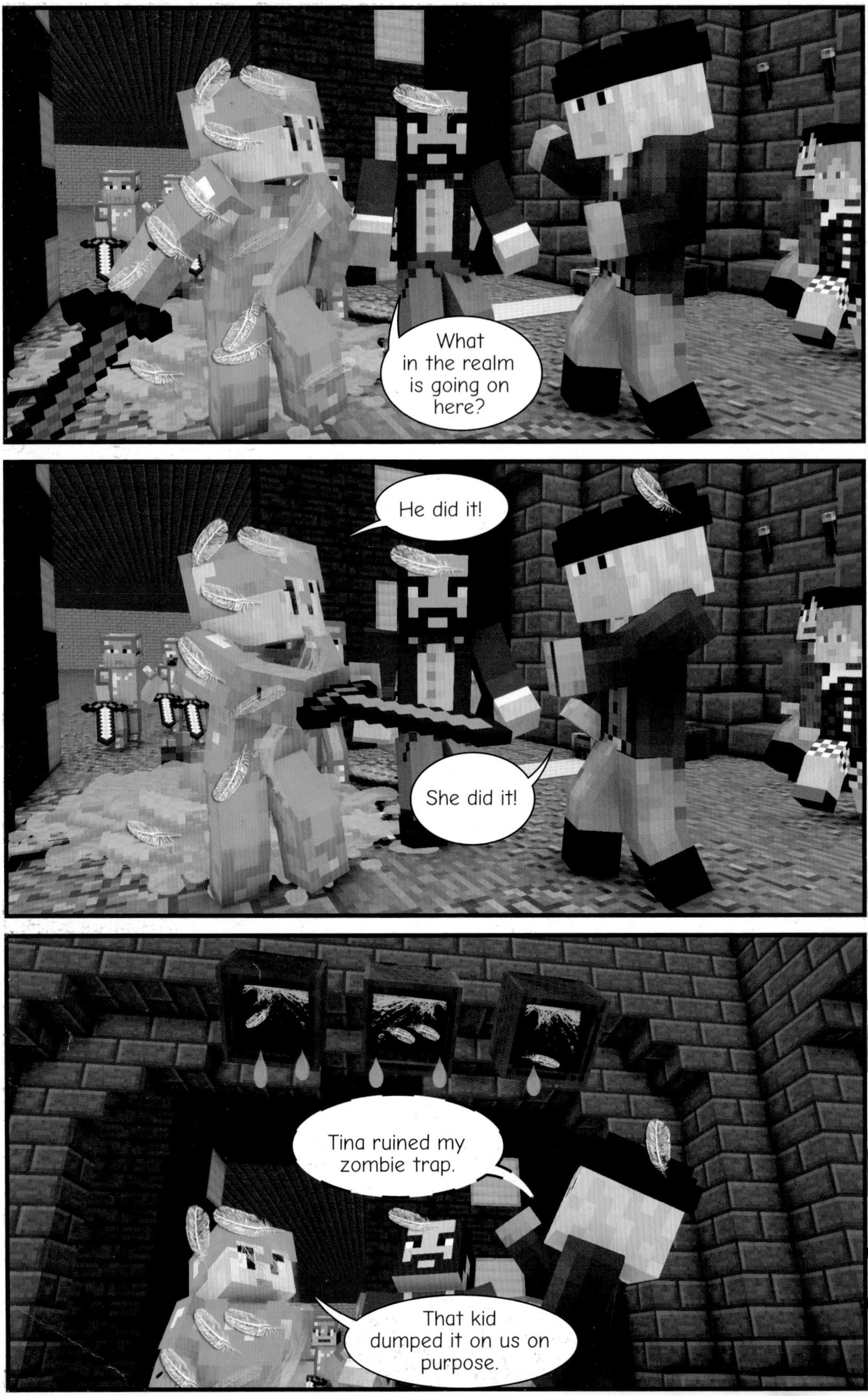
What in the realm is going on here?
He did it!
She did it!
Tina ruined my zombie trap.
That kid dumped it on us on purpose.

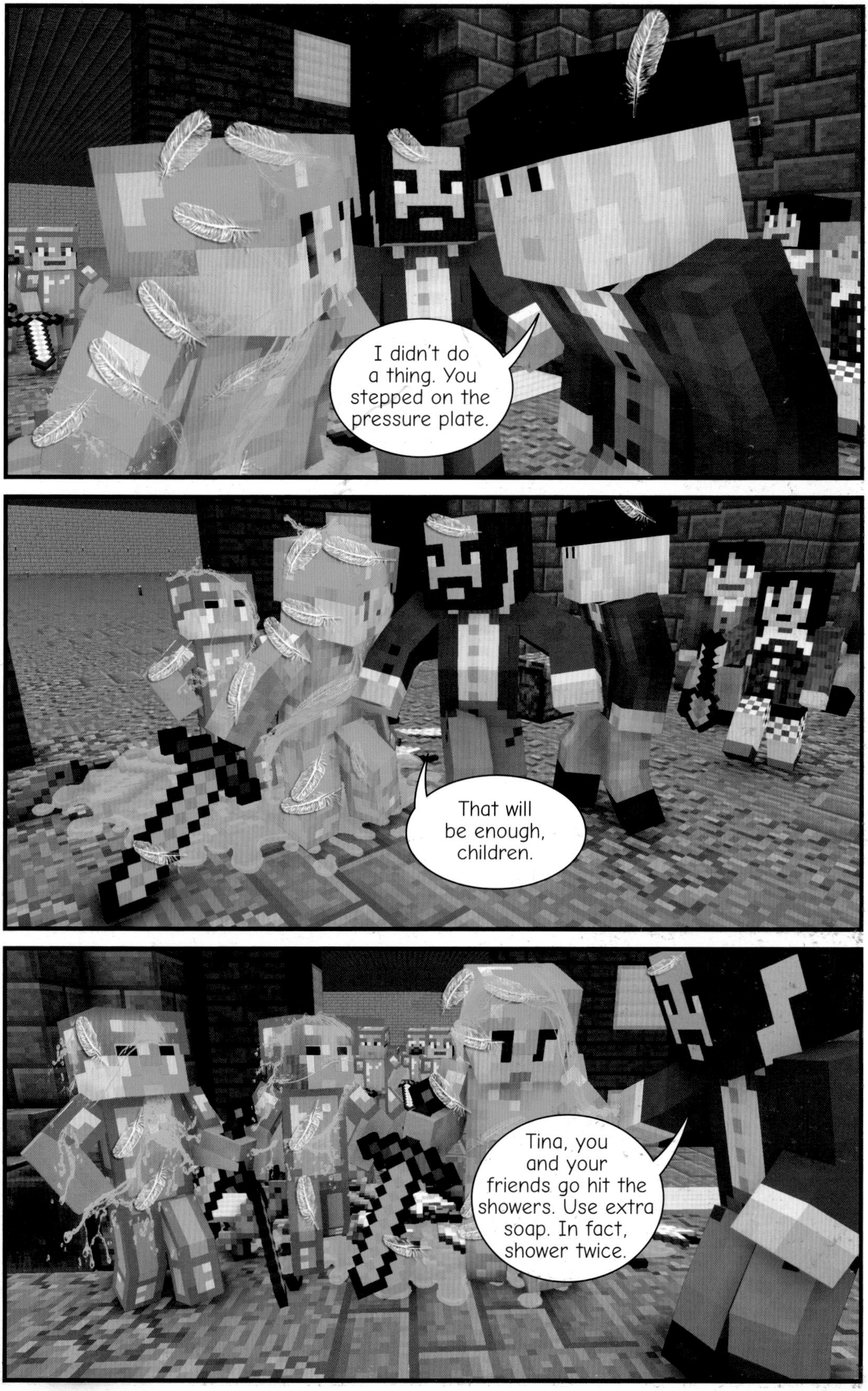
I didn't do a thing. You stepped on the pressure plate.
That will be enough, children.
Tina, you and your friends go hit the showers. Use extra soap. In fact, shower twice.

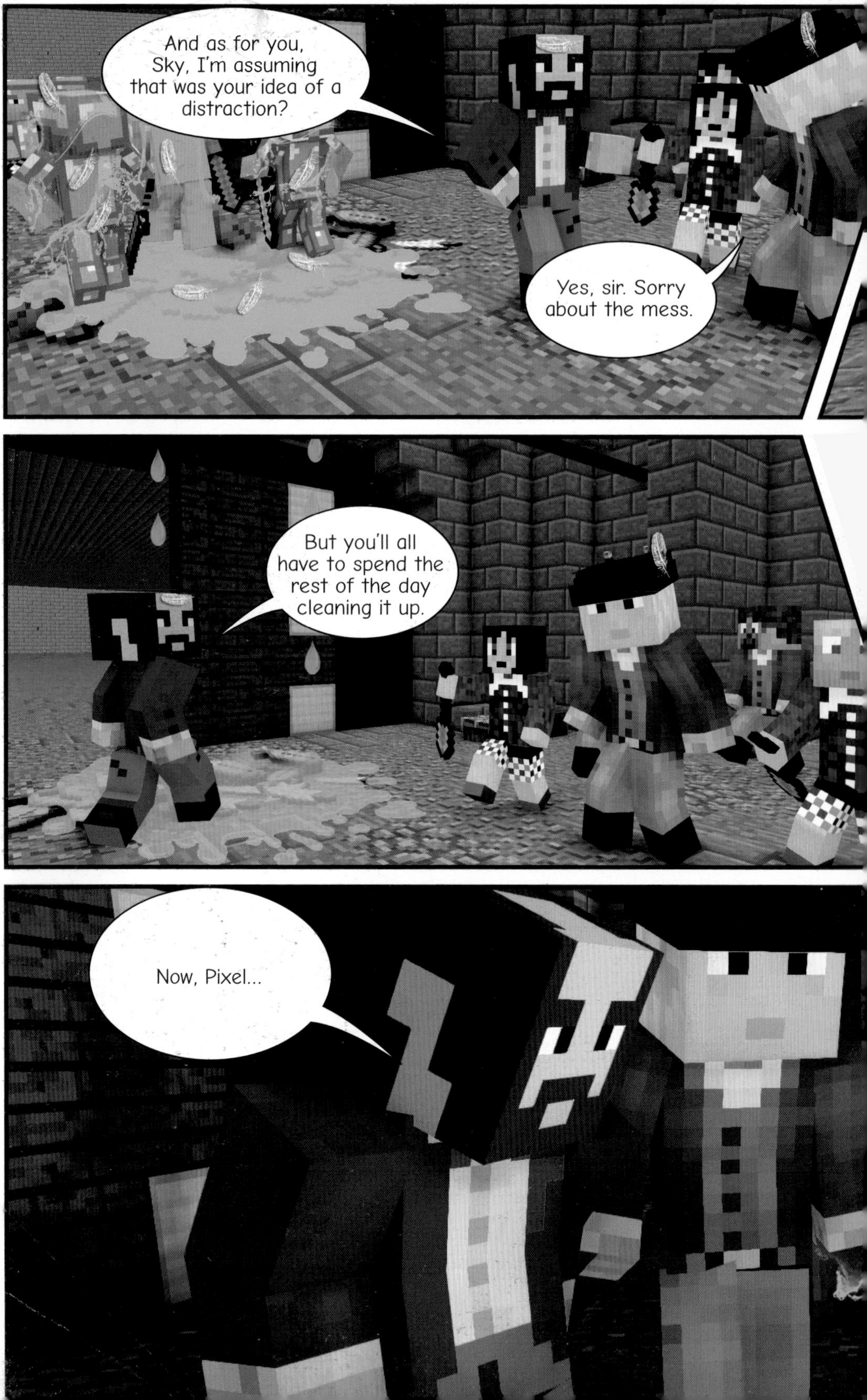
And as for you, Sky, I'm assuming that was your idea of a distraction?
Yes, sir. Sorry about the mess.
But you'll all have to spend the rest of the day cleaning it up.
Now, Pixel...

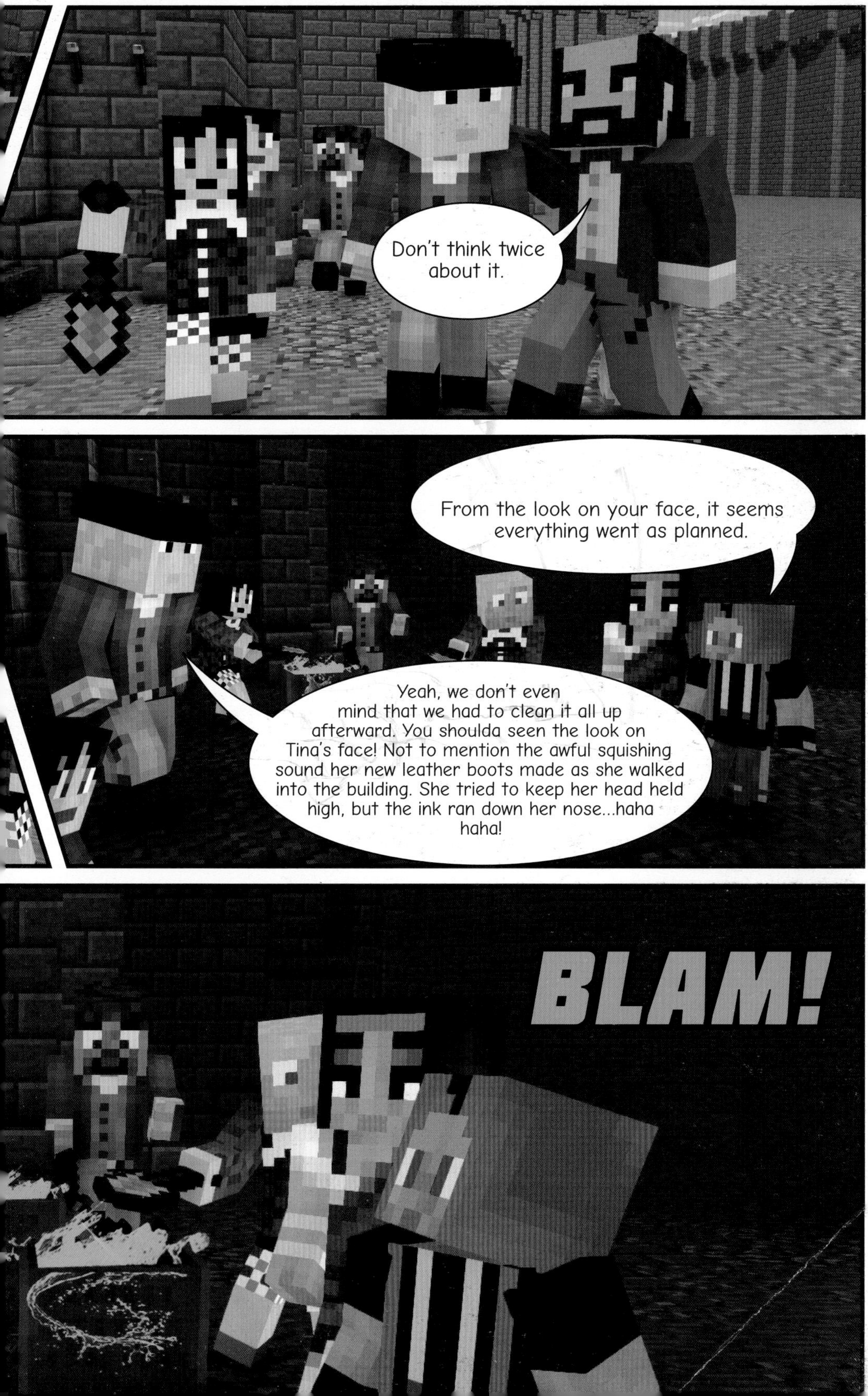
Don't think twice about it.
From the look on your face, it seems everything went as planned.
Yeah, we don't even mind that we had to clean it all up afterward. You shoulda seen the look on Tina's face! Not to mention the awful squishing sound her new leather boots made as she walked into the building. She tried to keep her head held high, but the ink ran down her nose...haha haha!
BLAM!

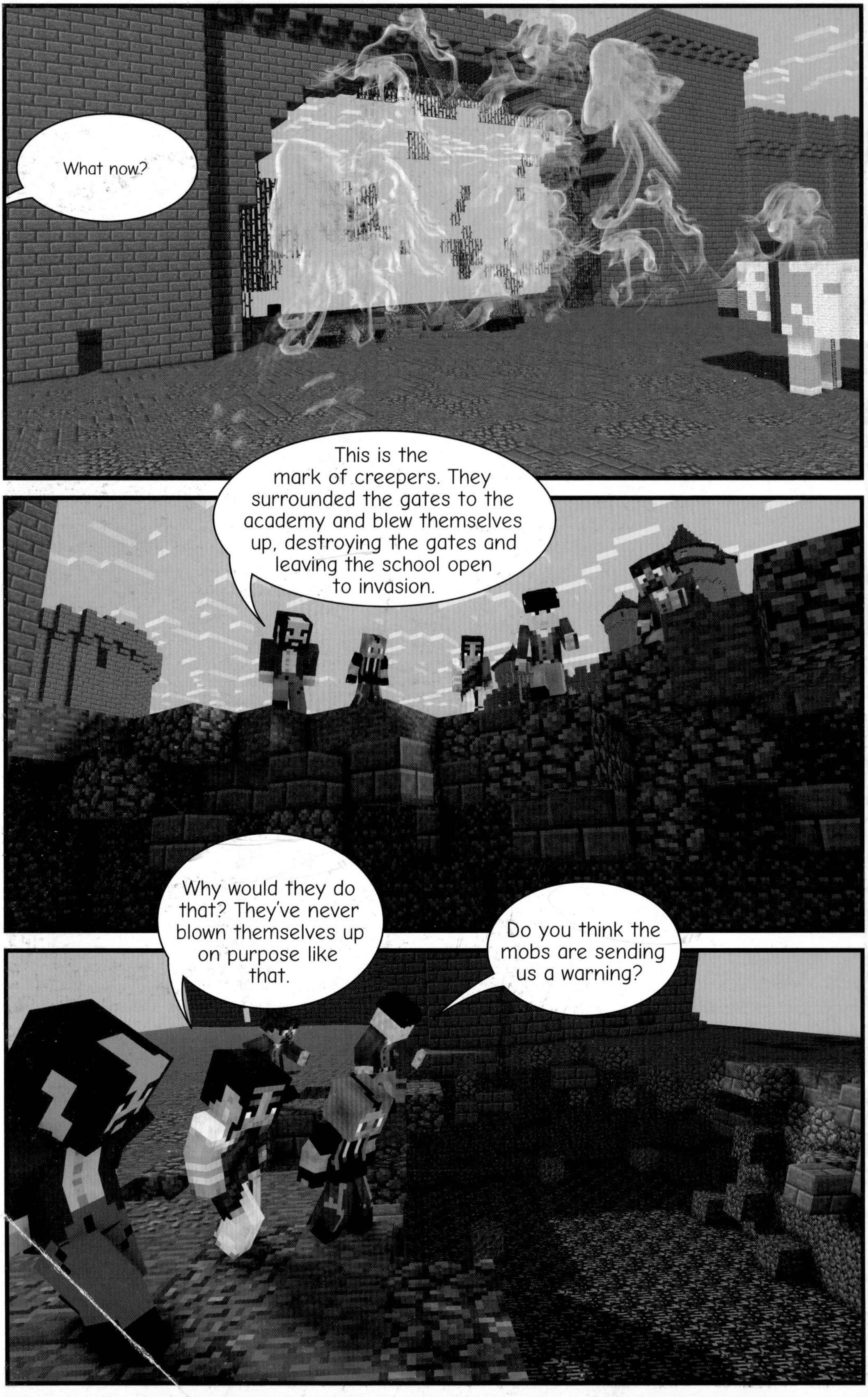

What now?
This is the mark of creepers. They surrounded the gates to the academy and blew themselves up, destroying the gates and leaving the school open to invasion.
Why would they do that? They've never blown themselves up on purpose like that.
Do you think the mobs are sending us a warning?

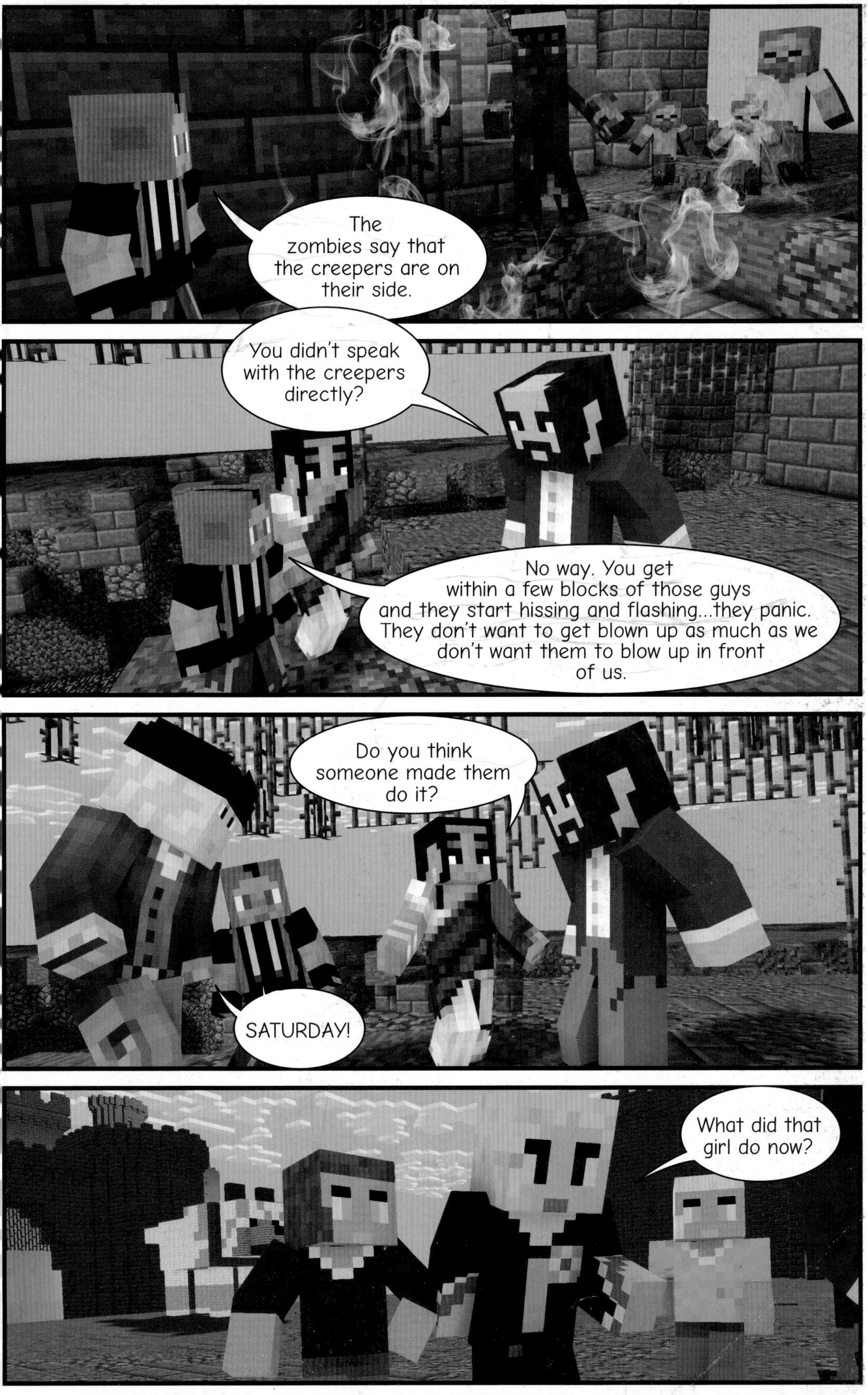

The zombies say that the creepers are on their side.
You didn't speak with the creepers directly?
No way. You get within a few blocks of those guys and they start hissing and flashing...they panic. They don't want to get blown up as much as we don't want them to blow up in front of us.
Do you think someone made them do it?
SATURDAY!
What did that girl do now?

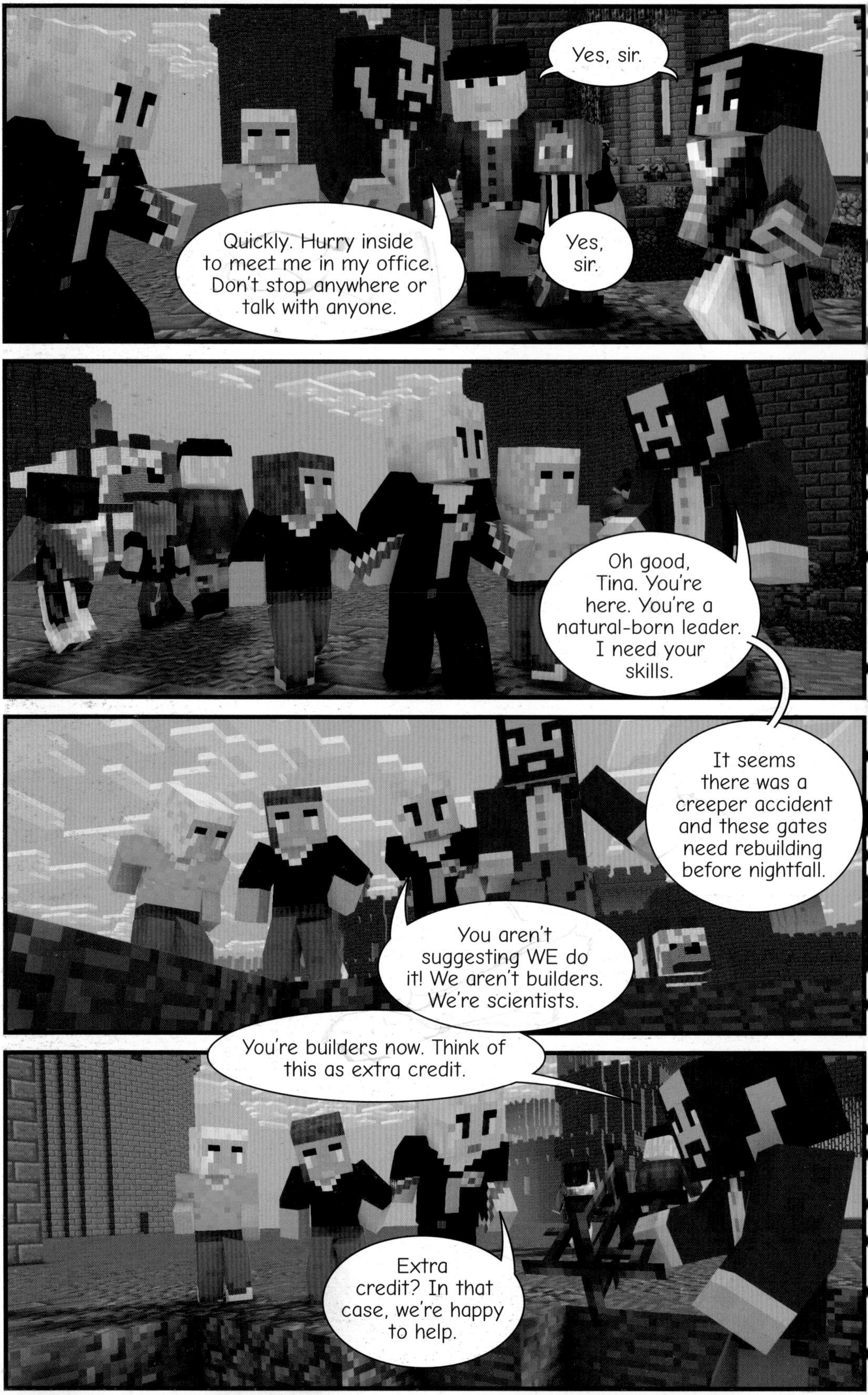
Yes, sir.
Quickly. Hurry inside to meet me in my office. Don't stop anywhere or talk with anyone.
Yes, sir.
Oh good, Tina. You're here. You're a natural-born leader. I need your skills.
It seems there was a creeper accident and these gates need rebuilding before nightfall.
You aren't suggesting WE do it! We aren't builders. We're scientists.
You're builders now. Think of this as extra credit.
Extra credit? In that case, we're happy to help.

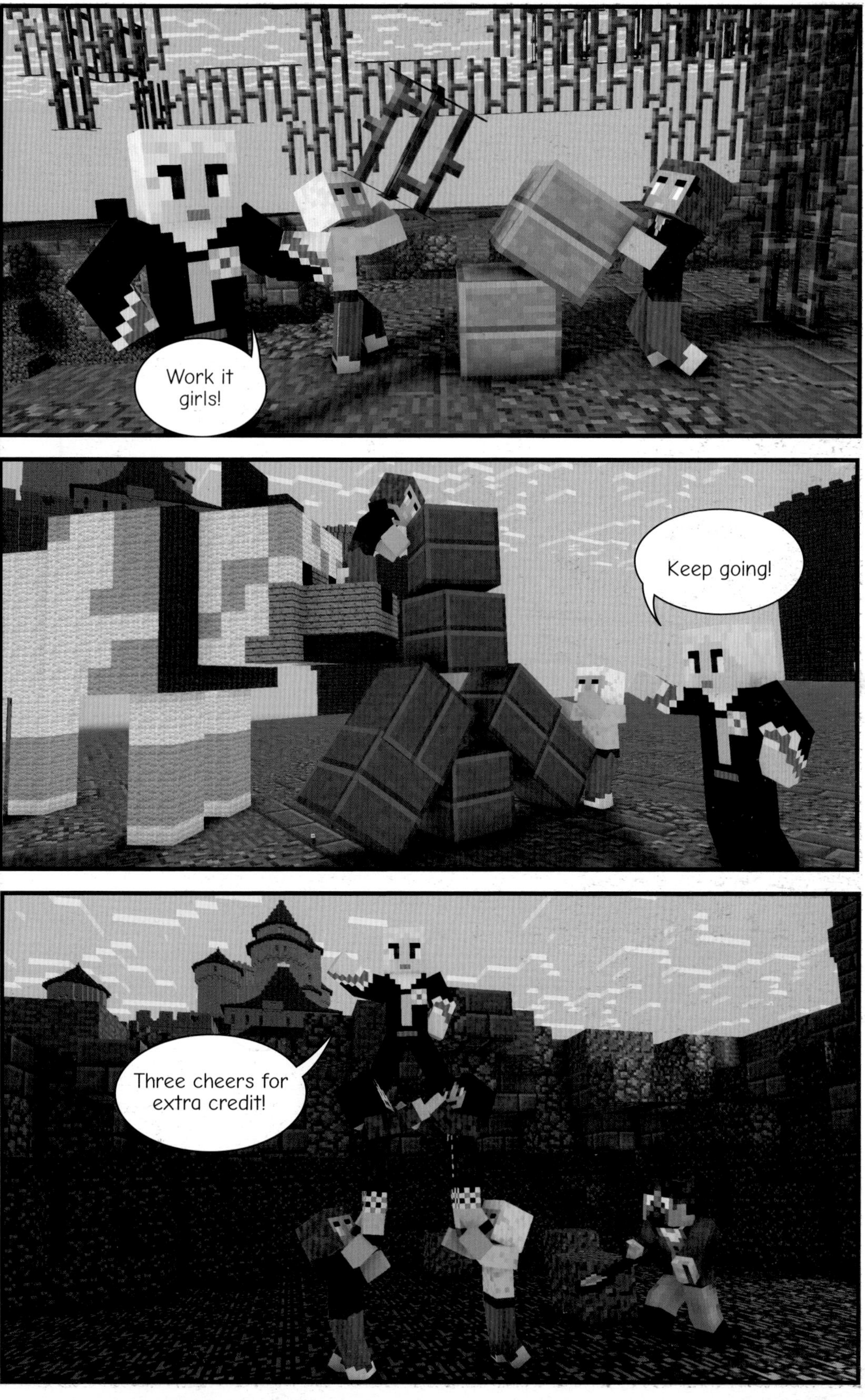
Work it girls!
Keep going!
Three cheers for extra credit!

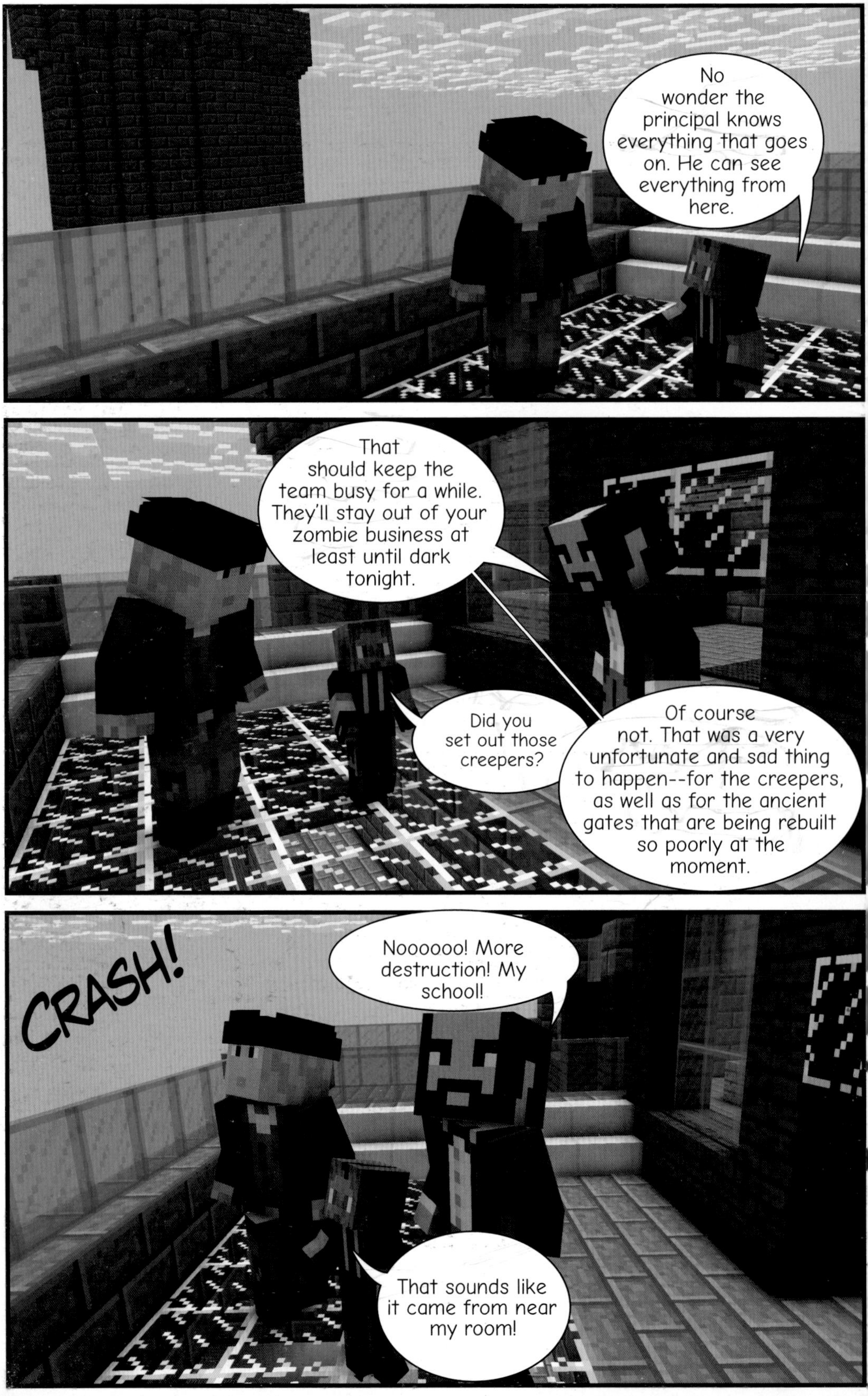
No wonder the principal knows everything that goes on. He can see everything from here.
That should keep the team busy for a while. They'll stay out of your zombie business at least until dark tonight.
Did you set out those creepers?
Of course not. That was a very unfortunate and sad thing to happen--for the creepers, as well as for the ancient gates that are being rebuilt so poorly at the moment.
CRASH!
Noooooo! More destruction! My school!
That sounds like it came from near my room!

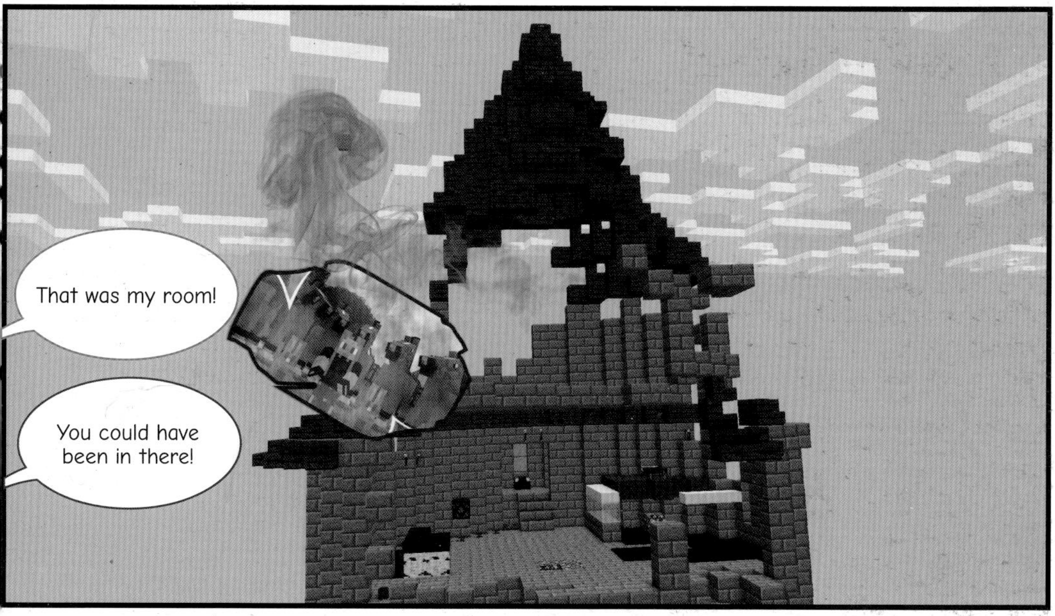
That was my room!
You could have been in there!

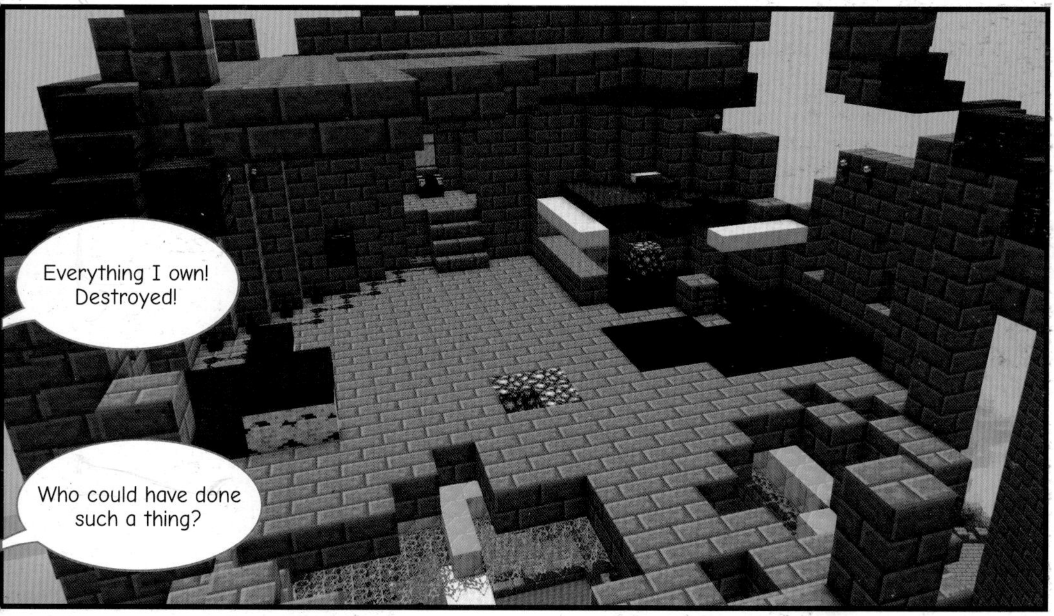
Everything I own! Destroyed!
Who could have done such a thing?

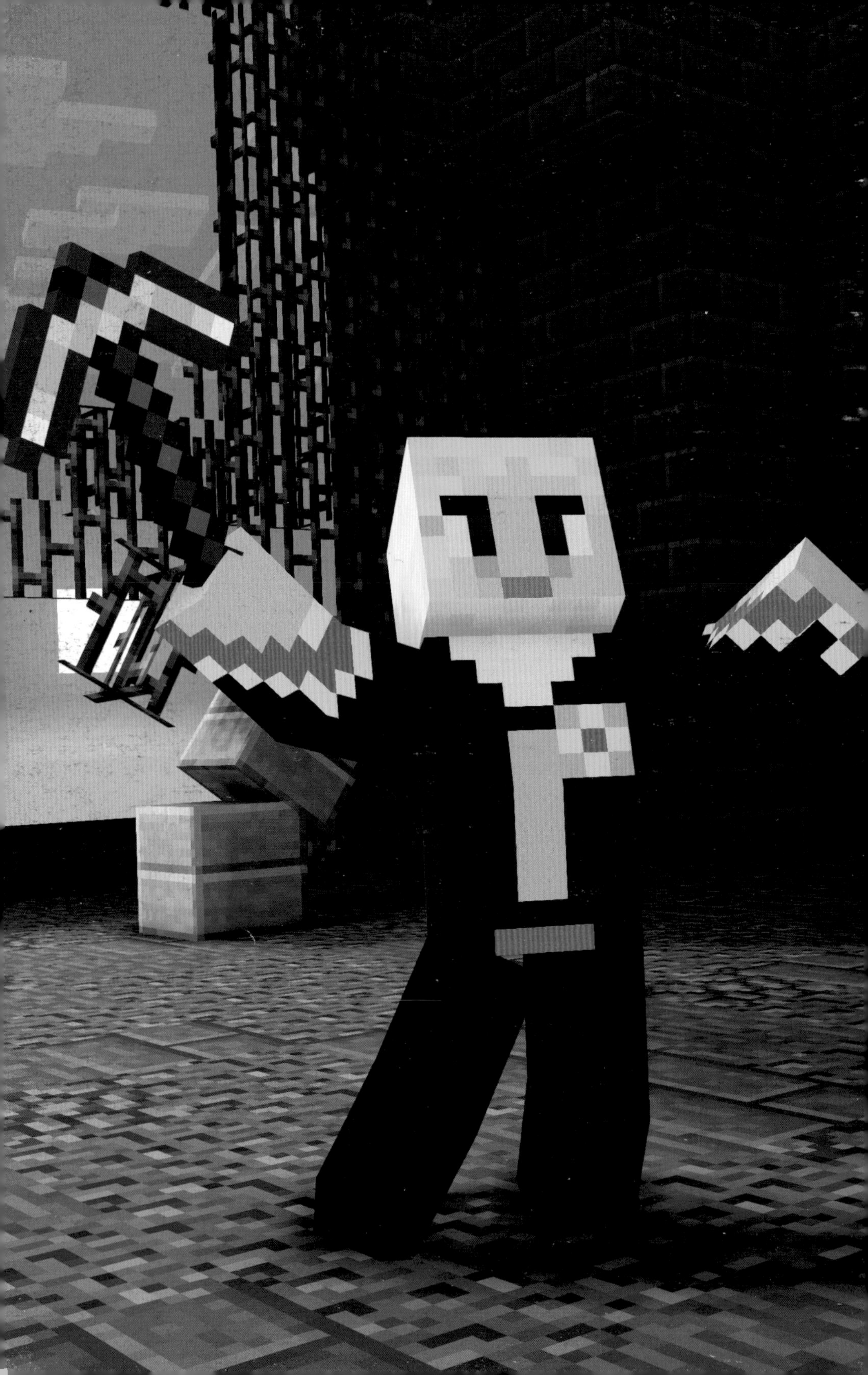

CHAPTER 9

BEST FRIENDS

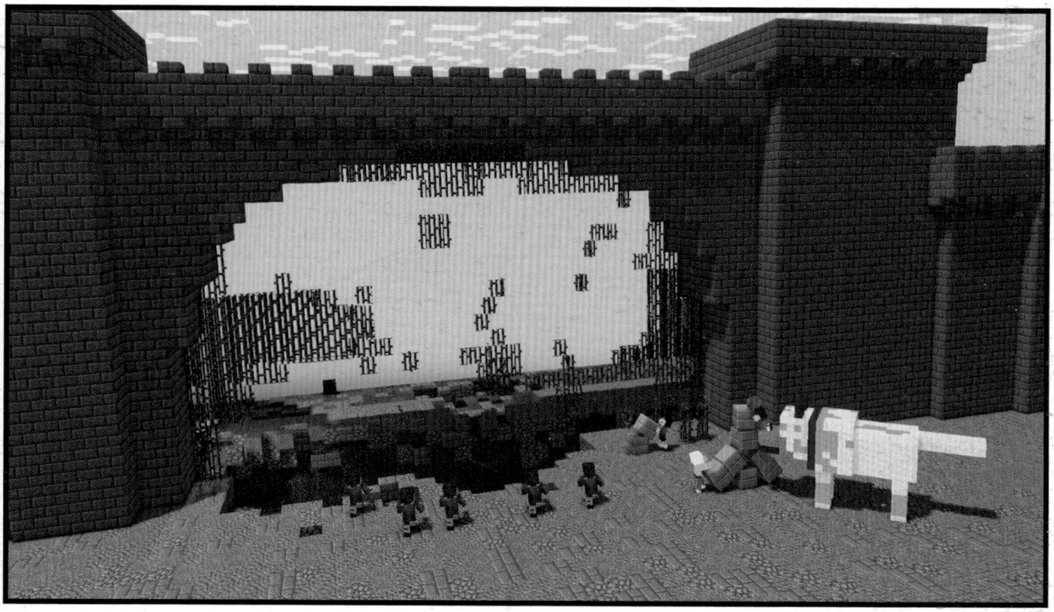

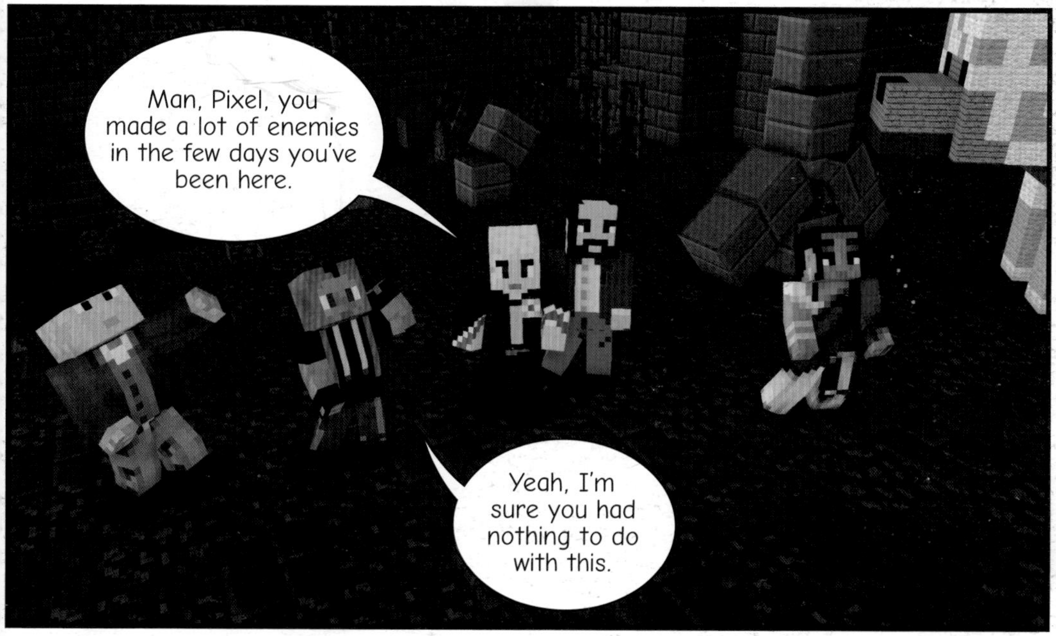
Man, Pixel, you made a lot of enemies in the few days you've been here.
Yeah, I'm sure you had nothing to do with this.

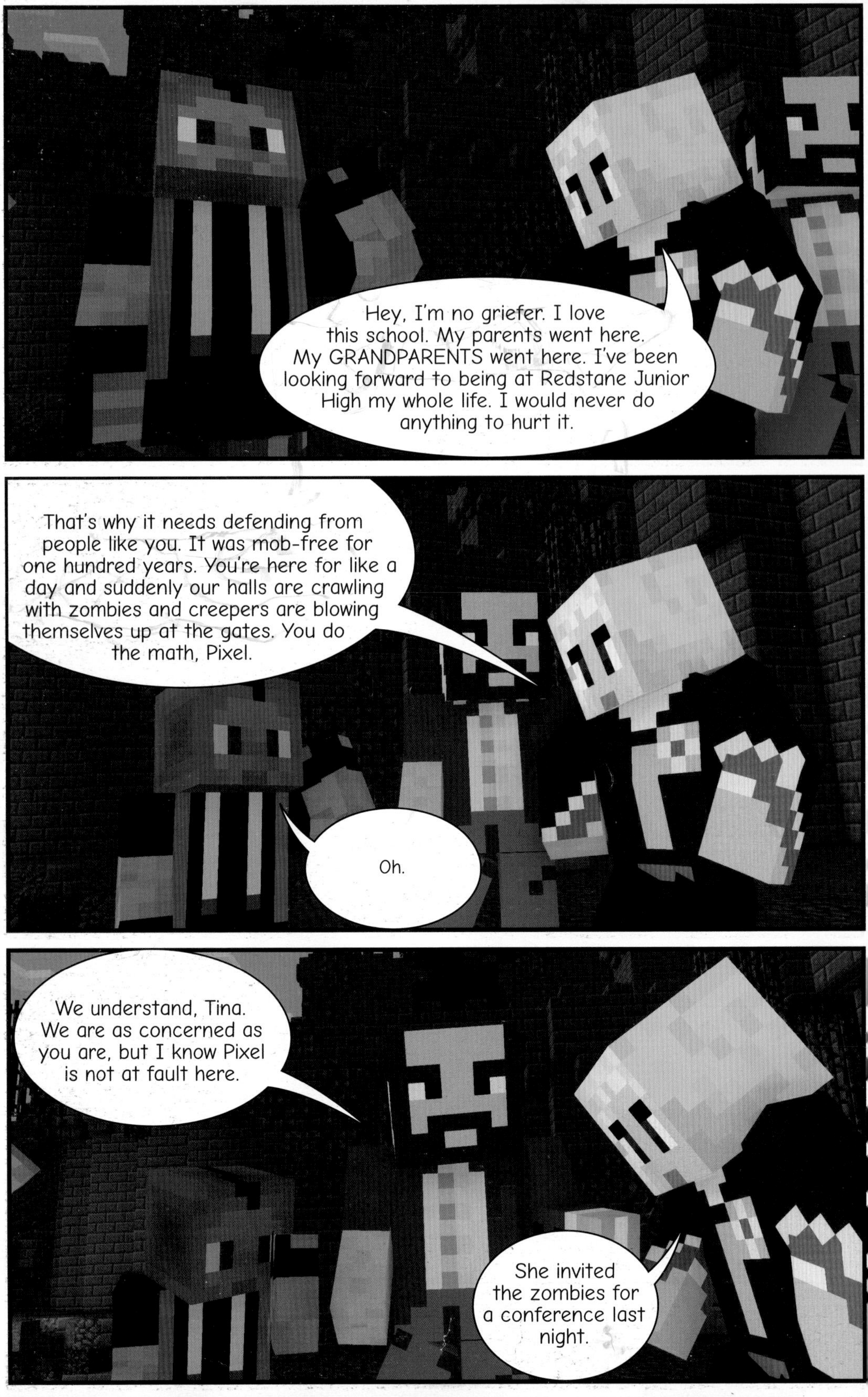
Hey, I'm no griefer. I love this school. My parents went here. My GRANDPARENTS went here. I've been looking forward to being at Redstane Junior High my whole life. I would never do anything to hurt it.
That's why it needs defending from people like you. It was mob-free for one hundred years. You're here for like a day and suddenly our halls are crawling with zombies and creepers are blowing themselves up at the gates. You do the math, Pixel.
Oh.
We understand, Tina. We are as concerned as you are, but I know Pixel is not at fault here.
She invited the zombies for a conference last night.

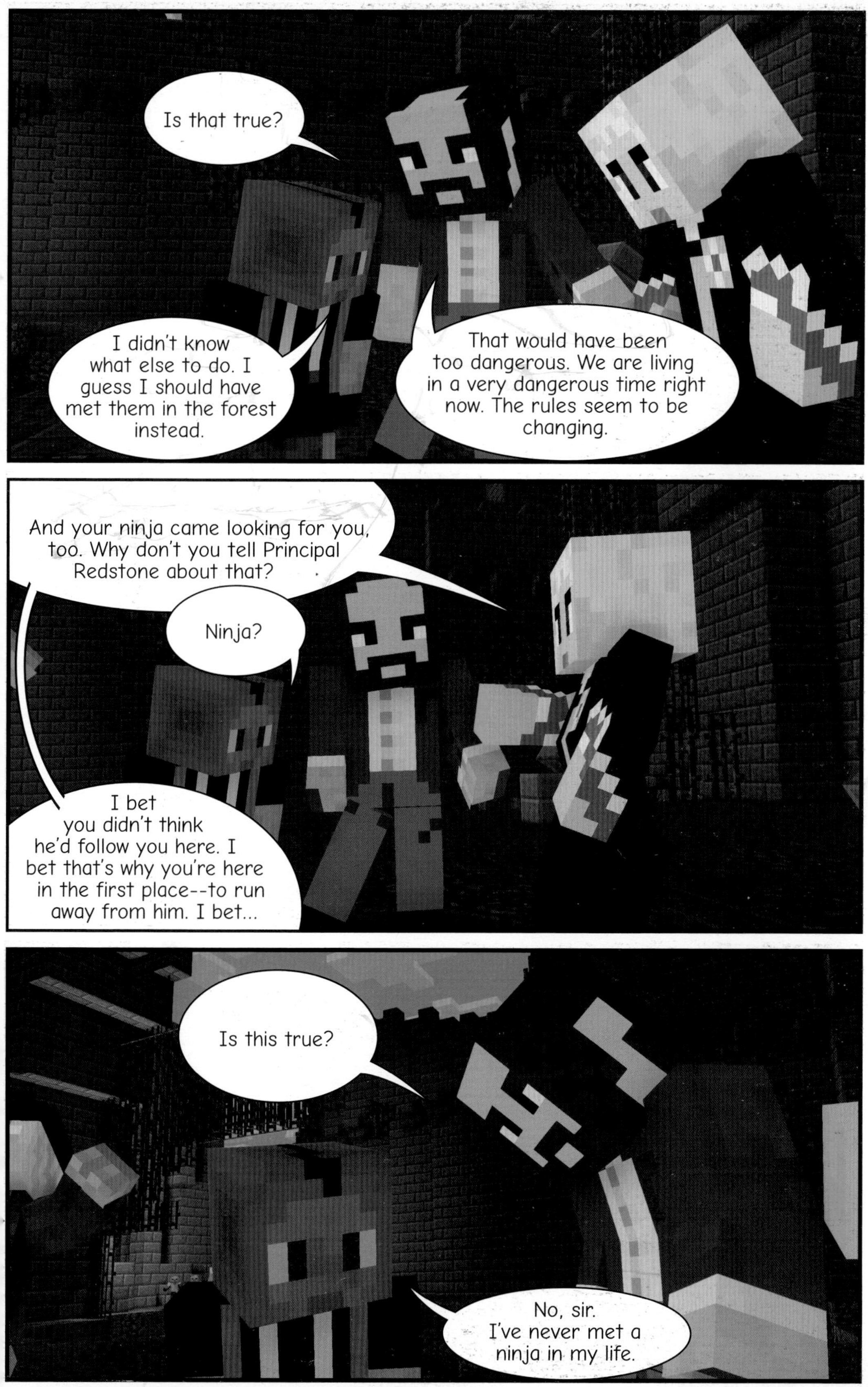
Is that true?
I didn't know what else to do. I guess I should have met them in the forest instead.
That would have been too dangerous. We are living in a very dangerous time right now. The rules seem to be changing.
And your ninja came looking for you, too. Why don't you tell Principal Redstone about that?
Ninja?
I bet you didn't think he'd follow you here. I bet that's why you're here in the first place--to run away from him. I bet...
Is this true?
No, sir. I've never met a ninja in my life.

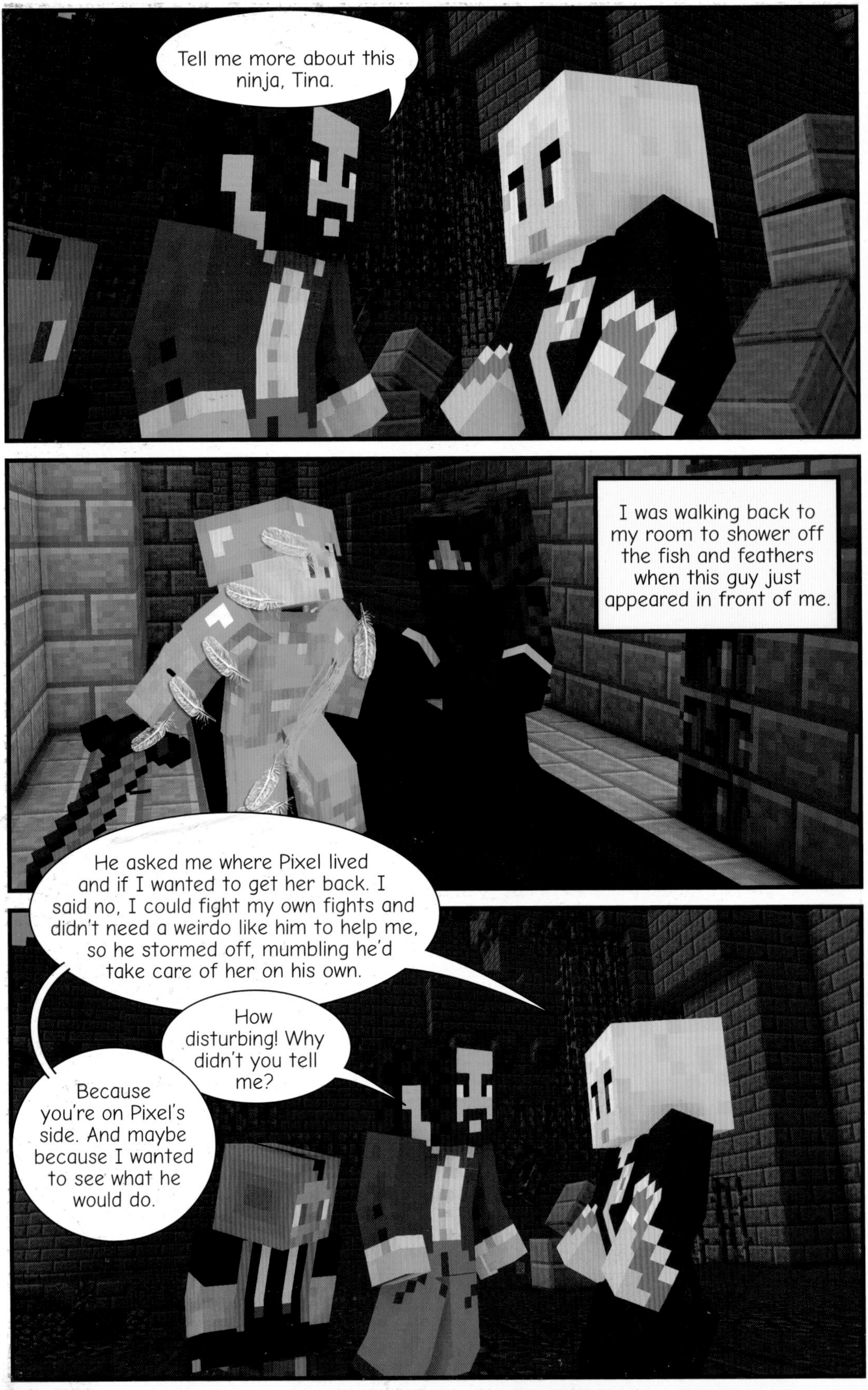

Tell me more about this ninja, Tina.
I was walking back to my room to shower off the fish and feathers when this guy just appeared in front of me.
He asked me where Pixel lived and if I wanted to get her back. I said no, I could fight my own fights and didn't need a weirdo like him to help me, so he stormed off, mumbling he'd take care of her on his own.
How disturbing! Why didn't you tell me?
Because you're on Pixel's side. And maybe because I wanted to see what he would do.

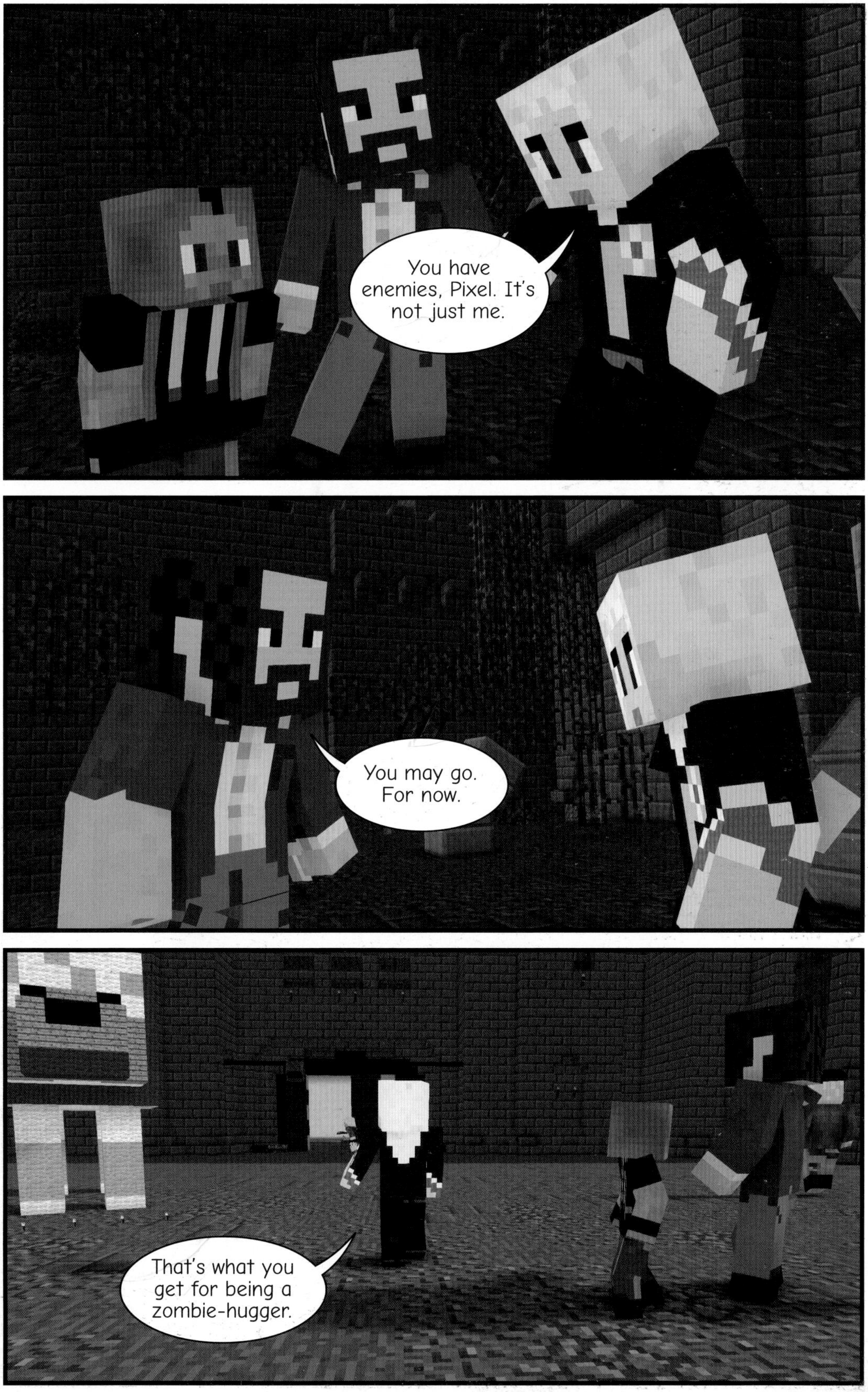
You have enemies, Pixel. It's not just me.
You may go. For now.
That's what you get for being a zombie-hugger.

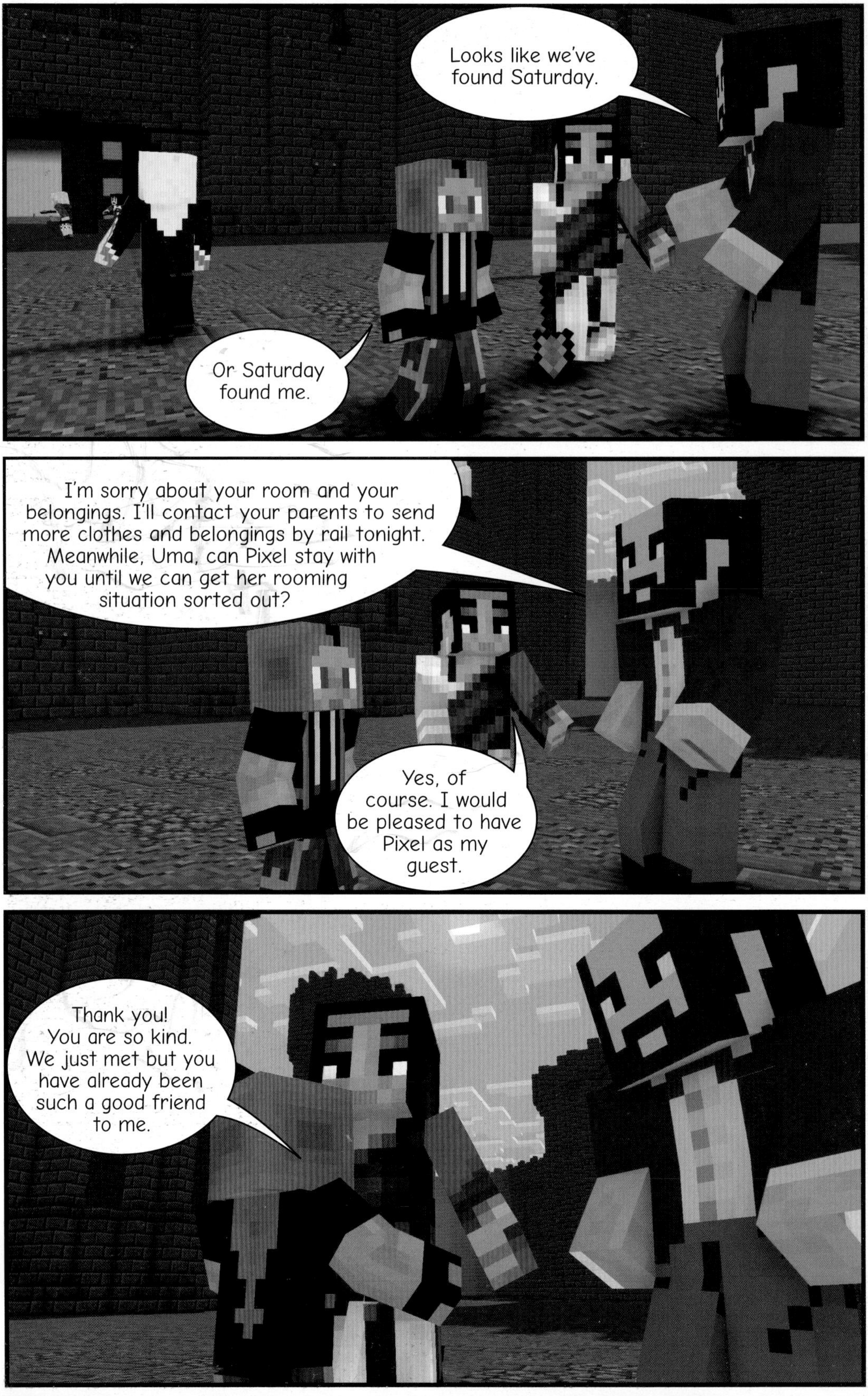
Looks like we've found Saturday.
Or Saturday found me.
I'm sorry about your room and your belongings. I'll contact your parents to send more clothes and belongings by rail tonight. Meanwhile, Uma, can Pixel stay with you until we can get her rooming situation sorted out?
Yes, of course. I would be pleased to have Pixel as my guest.
Thank you! You are so kind. We just met but you have already been such a good friend to me.

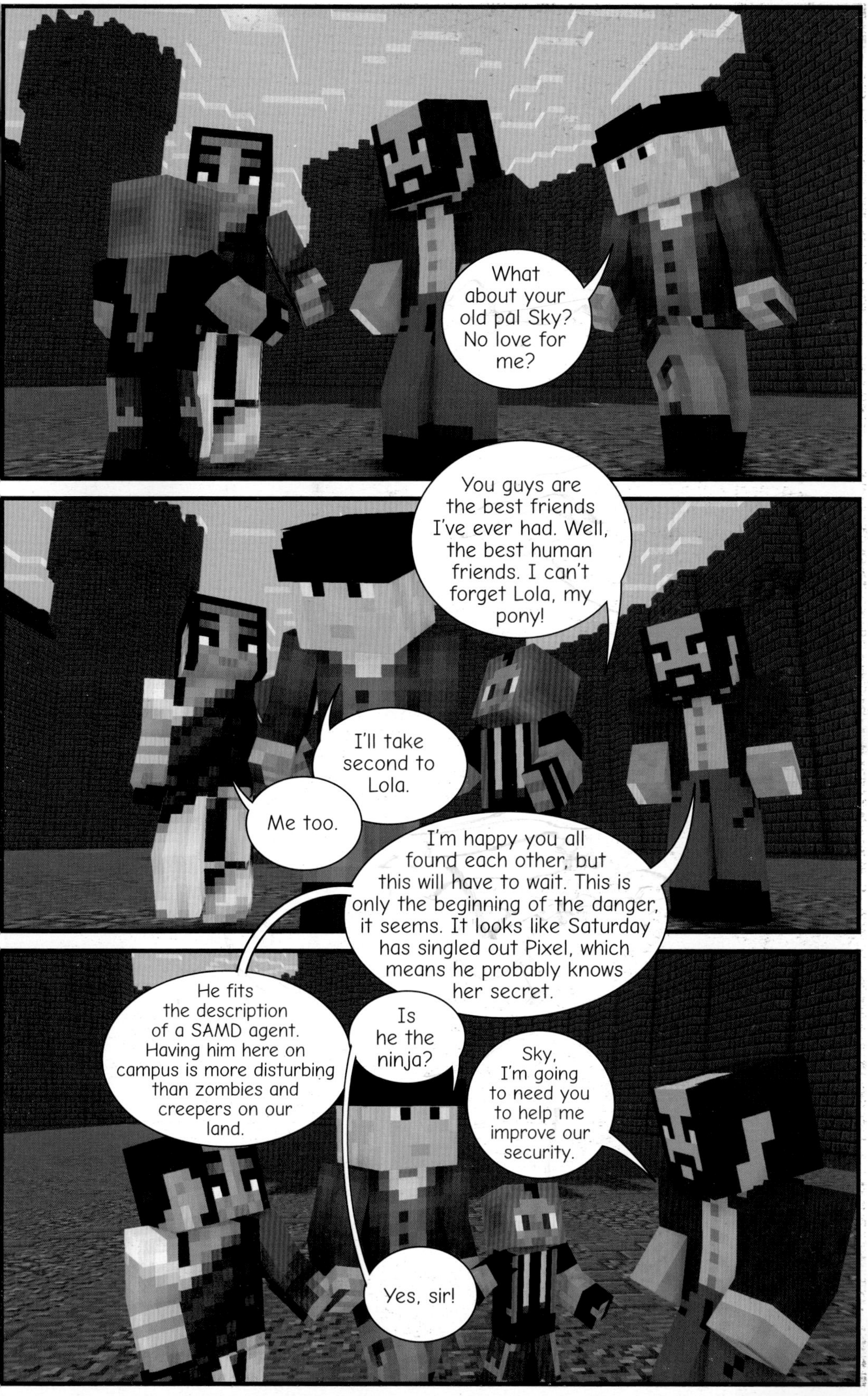
What about your old pal Sky? No love for me?
You guys are the best friends I've ever had. Well, the best human friends. I can't forget Lola, my pony!
I'll take second to Lola.
Me too.
I'm happy you all found each other, but this will have to wait. This is only the beginning of the danger, it seems. It looks like Saturday has singled out Pixel, which means he probably knows her secret.
He fits the description of a SAMD agent. Having him here on campus is more disturbing than zombies and creepers on our land.
Is he the ninja?
Sky, I'm going to need you to help me improve our security.
Yes, sir!

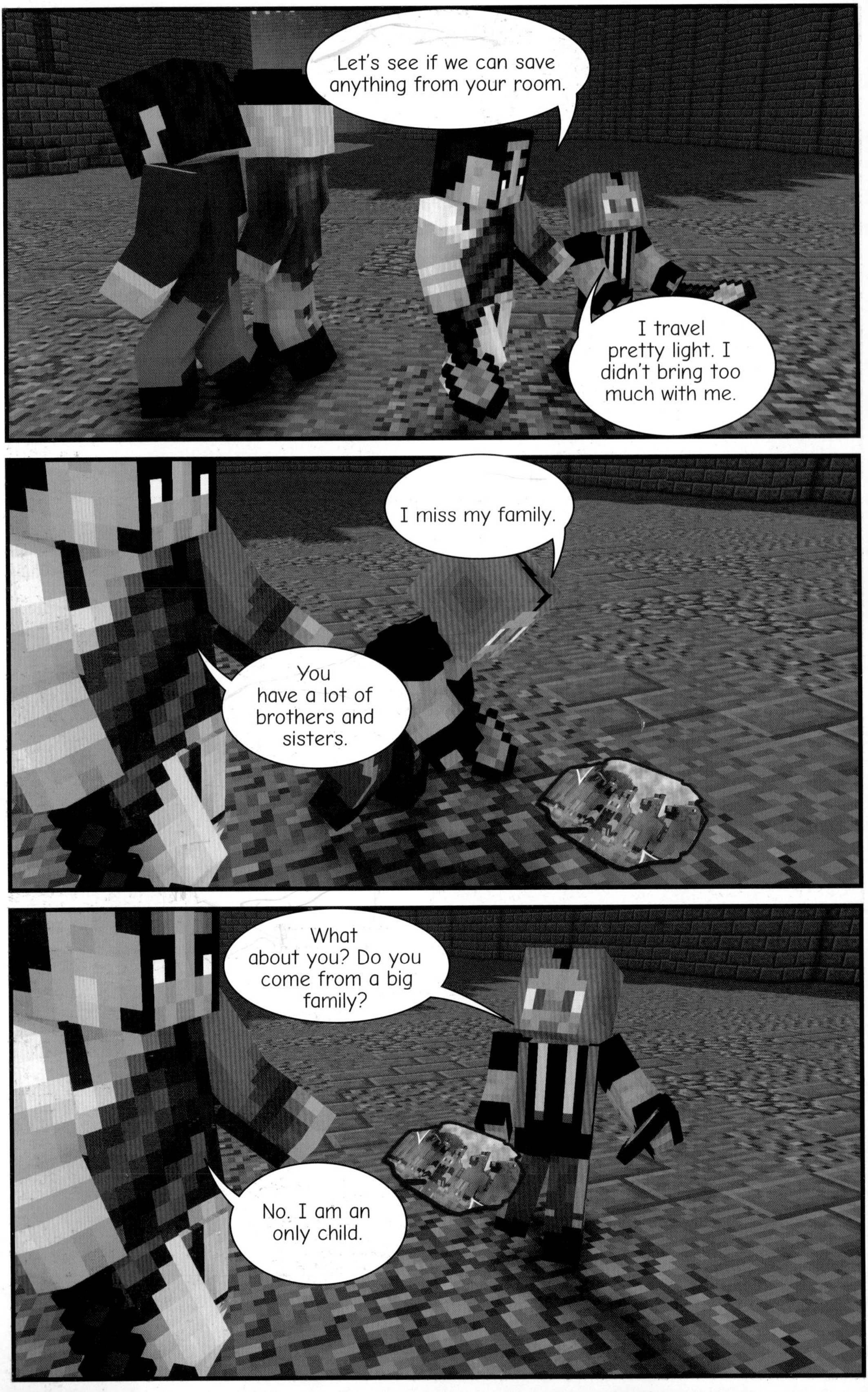
Let's see if we can save anything from your room.
I travel pretty light. I didn't bring too much with me.
I miss my family.
You have a lot of brothers and sisters.
What about you? Do you come from a big family?
No. I am an only child.

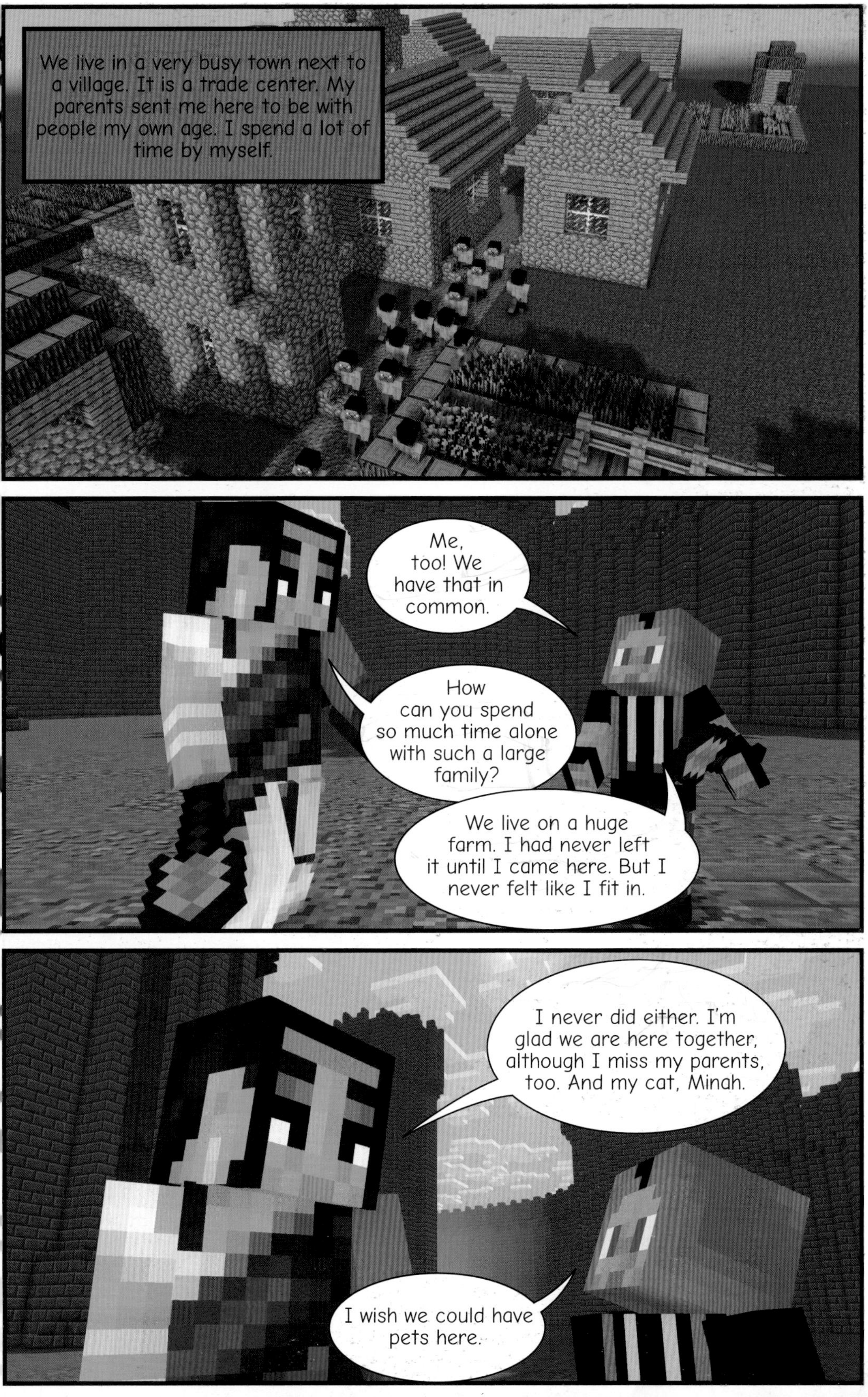
We live in a very busy town next to a village. It is a trade center. My parents sent me here to be with people my own age. I spend a lot of time by myself.
Me, too! We have that in common.
How can you spend so much time alone with such a large family?
We live on a huge farm. I had never left it until I came here. But I never felt like I fit in.
I never did either. I'm glad we are here together, although I miss my parents, too. And my cat, Minah.
I wish we could have pets here.

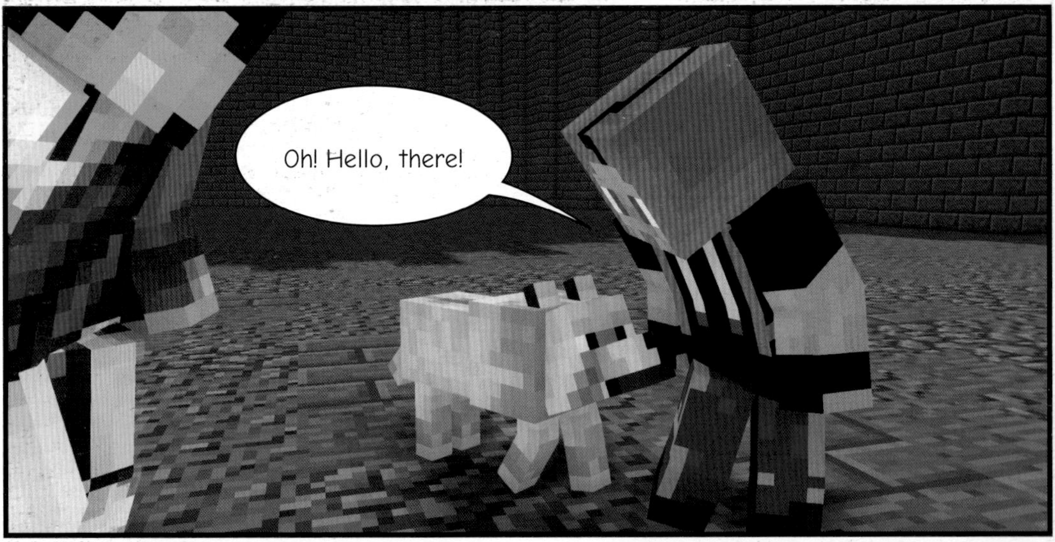
Oh! Hello, there!

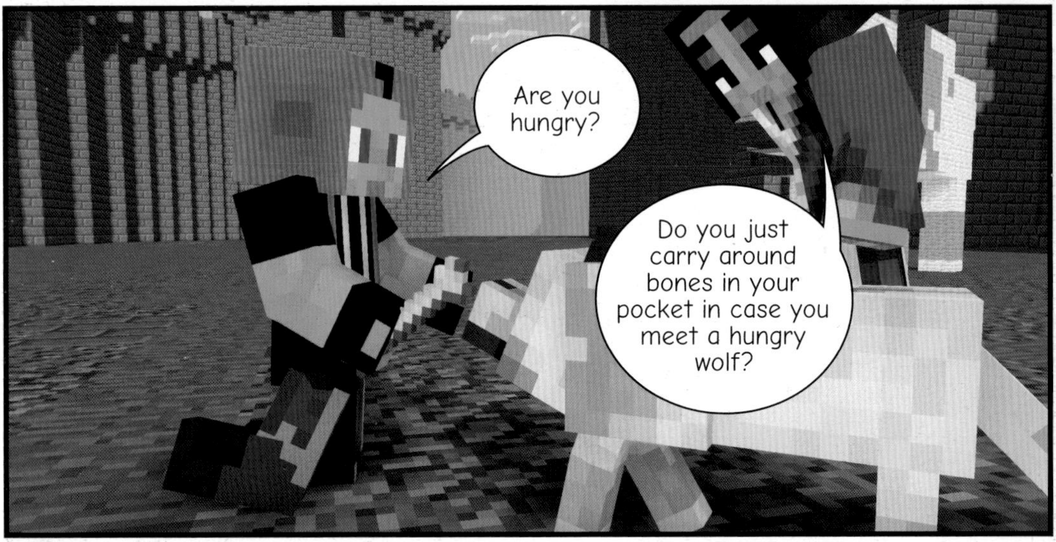
Are you hungry?
Do you just carry around bones in your pocket in case you meet a hungry wolf?

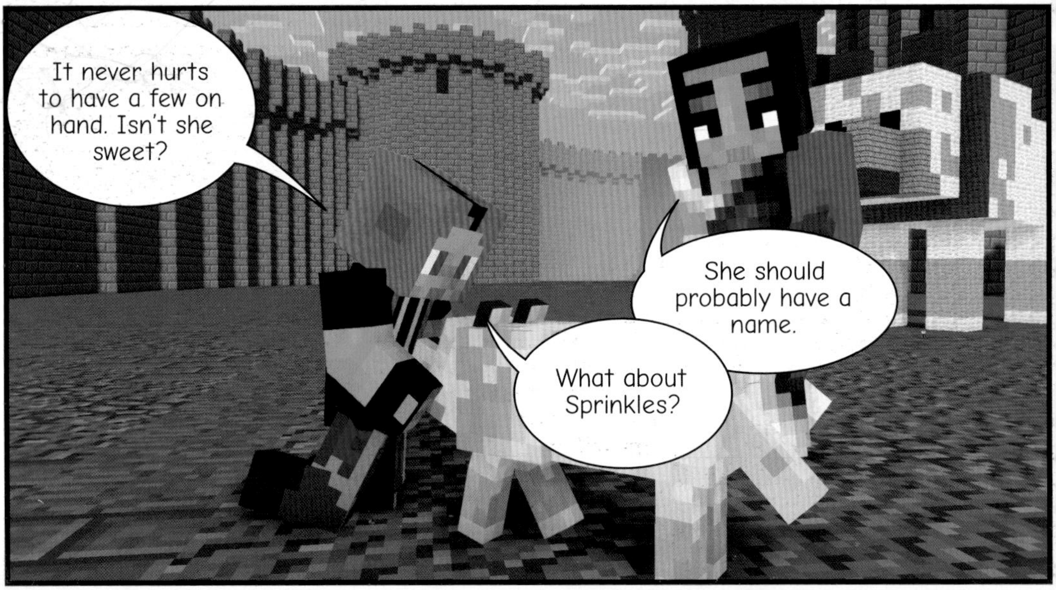
It never hurts to have a few on hand. Isn't she sweet?
She should probably have a name.
What about Sprinkles?

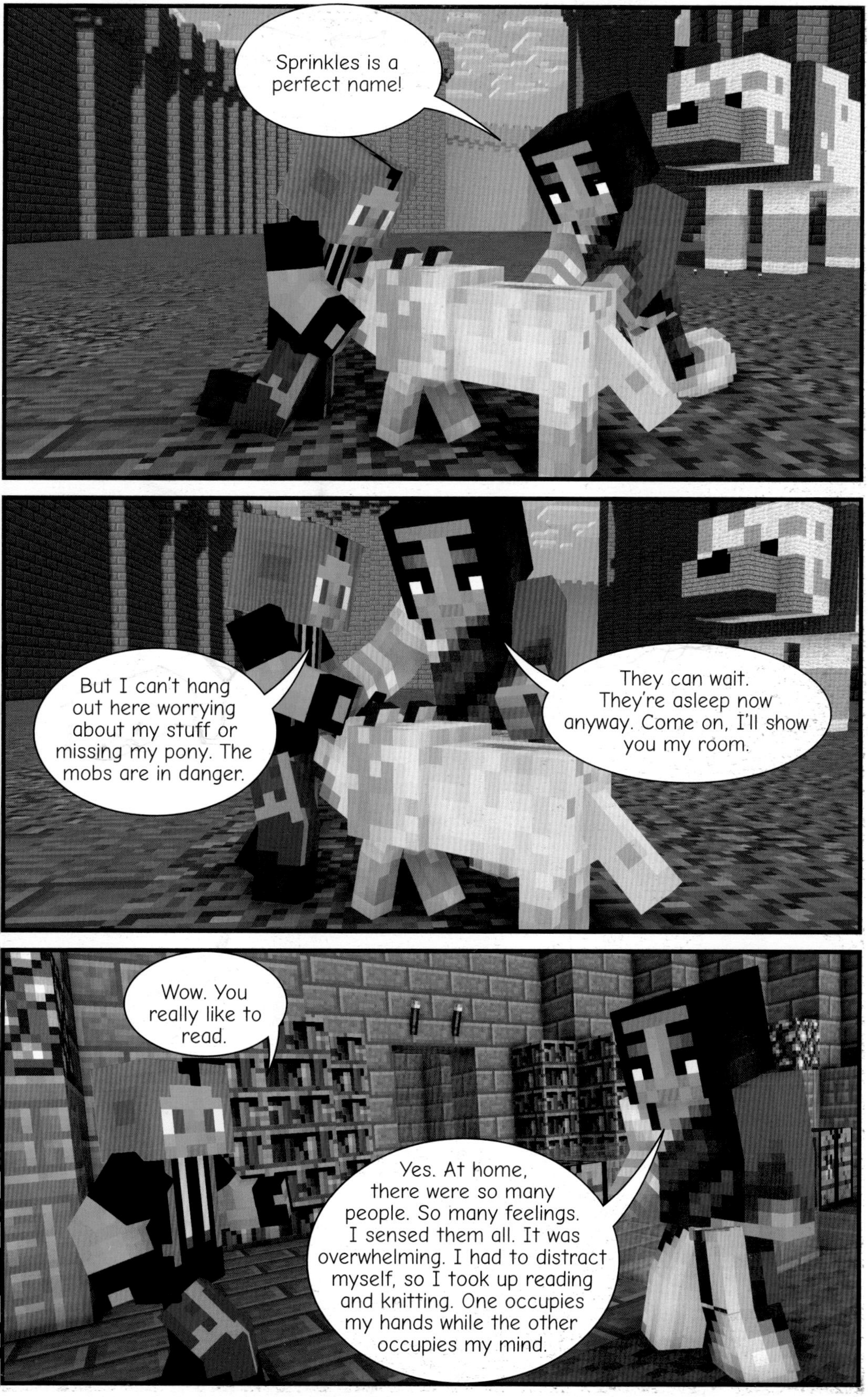
Sprinkles is a perfect name!
But I can't hang out here worrying about my stuff or missing my pony. The mobs are in danger.
They can wait. They're asleep now anyway. Come on, I'll show you my room.
Wow. You really like to read.
Yes. At home, there were so many people. So many feelings. I sensed them all. It was overwhelming. I had to distract myself, so I took up reading and knitting. One occupies my hands while the other occupies my mind.

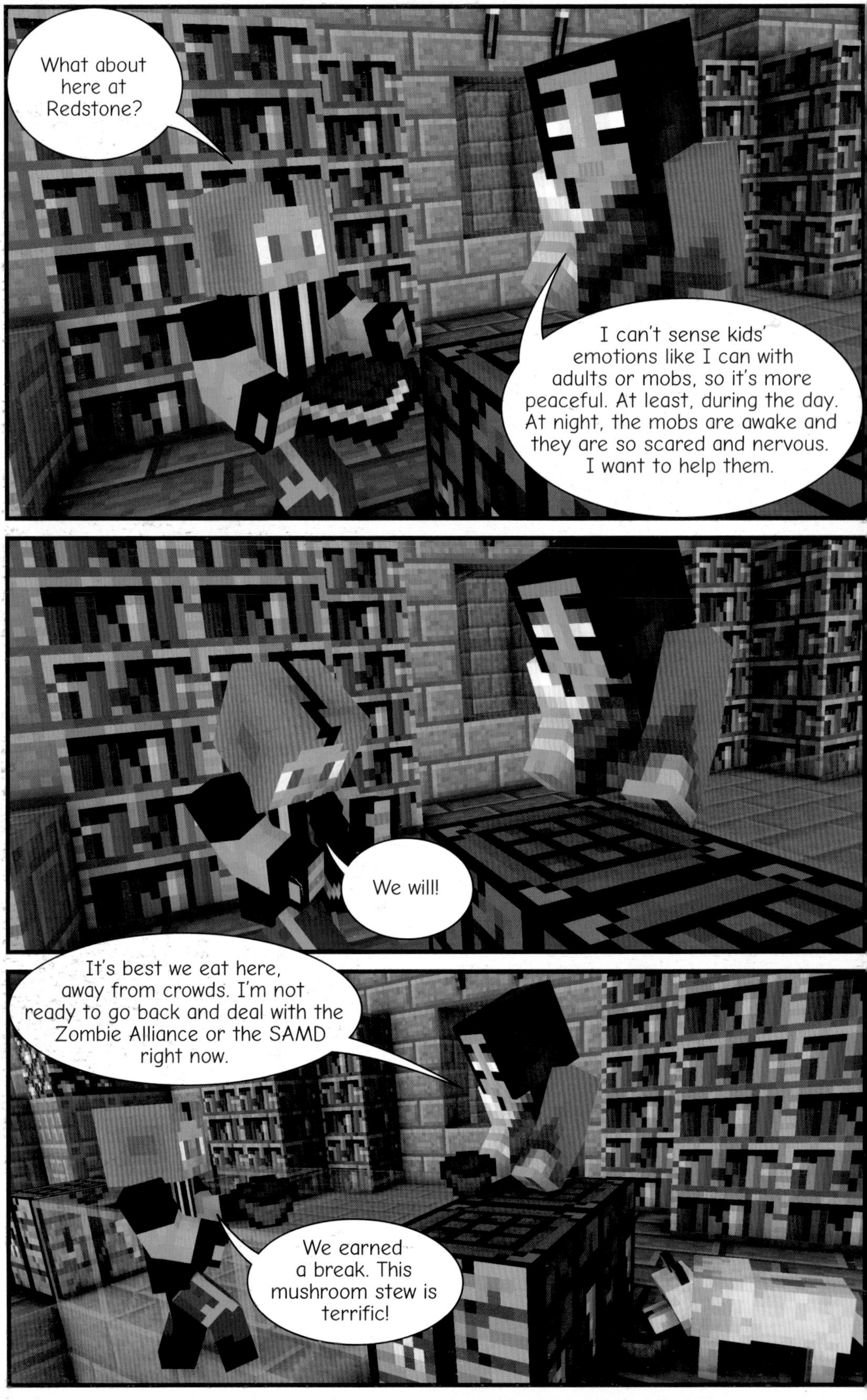
What about here at Redstone?
I can't sense kids' emotions like I can with adults or mobs, so it's more peaceful. At least, during the day. At night, the mobs are awake and they are so scared and nervous. I want to help them.
We will!
It's best we eat here, away from crowds. I'm not ready to go back and deal with the Zombie Alliance or the SAMD right now.
We earned a break. This mushroom stew is terrific!

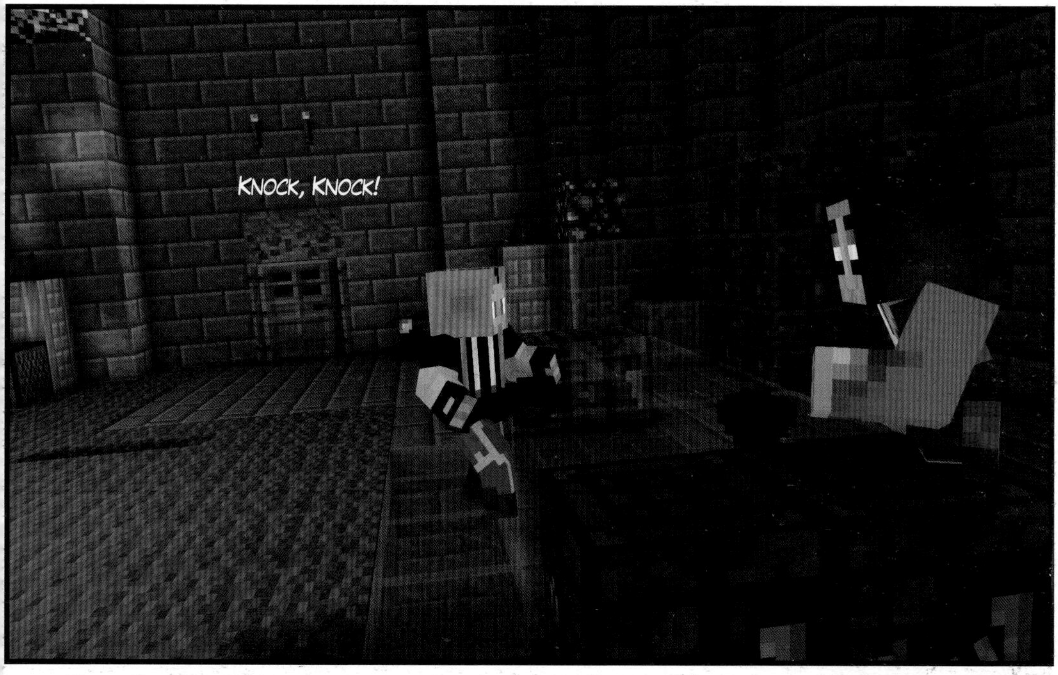
KNOCK, KNOCK!

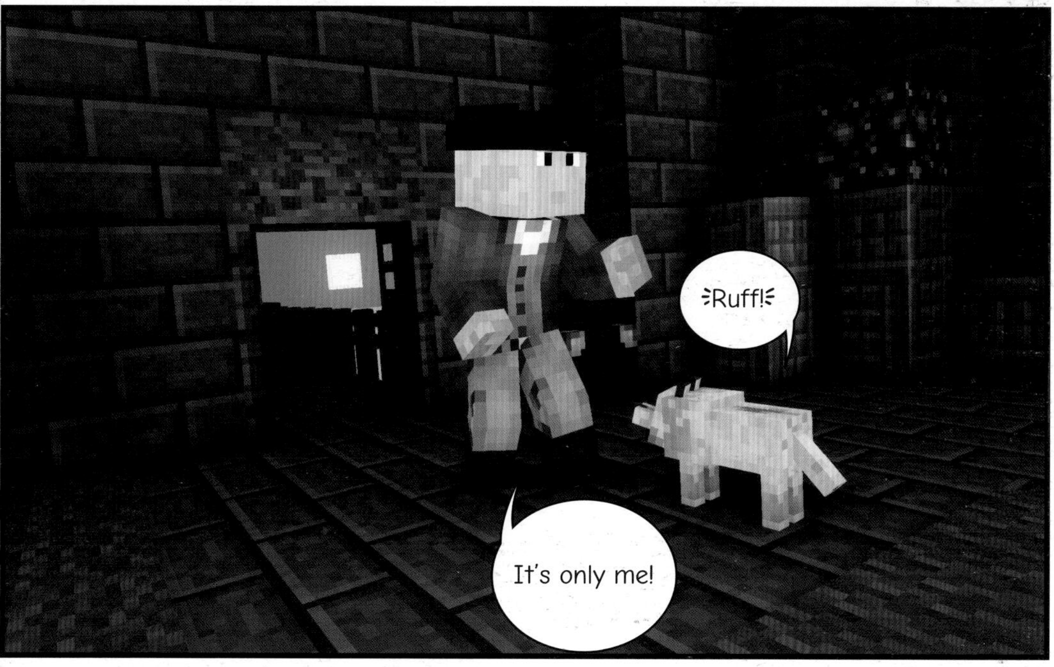
Ruff!
It's only me!

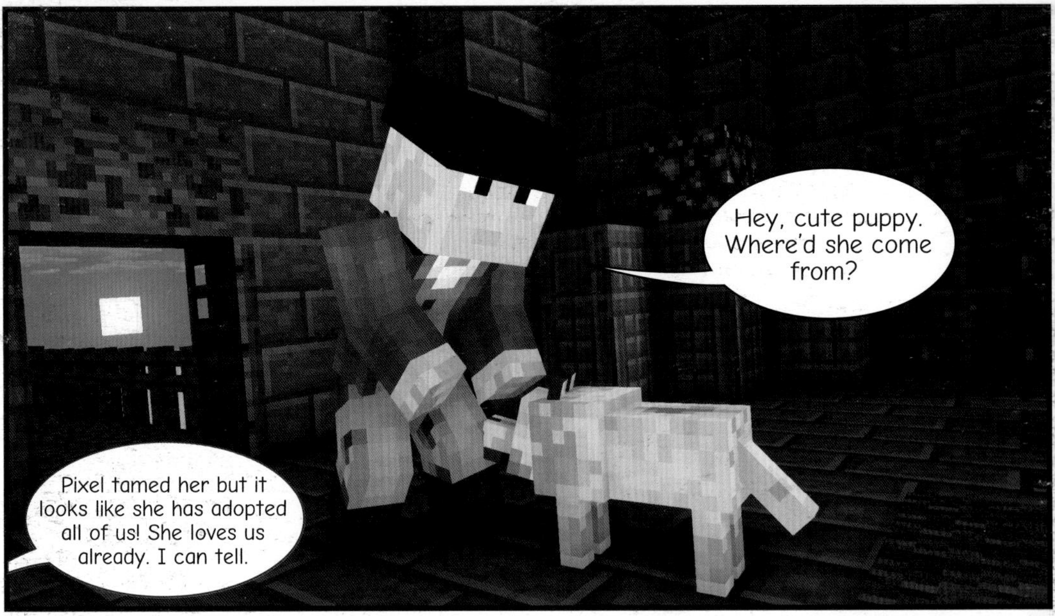
Hey, cute puppy. Where'd she come from?
Pixel tamed her but it looks like she has adopted all of us! She loves us already. I can tell.

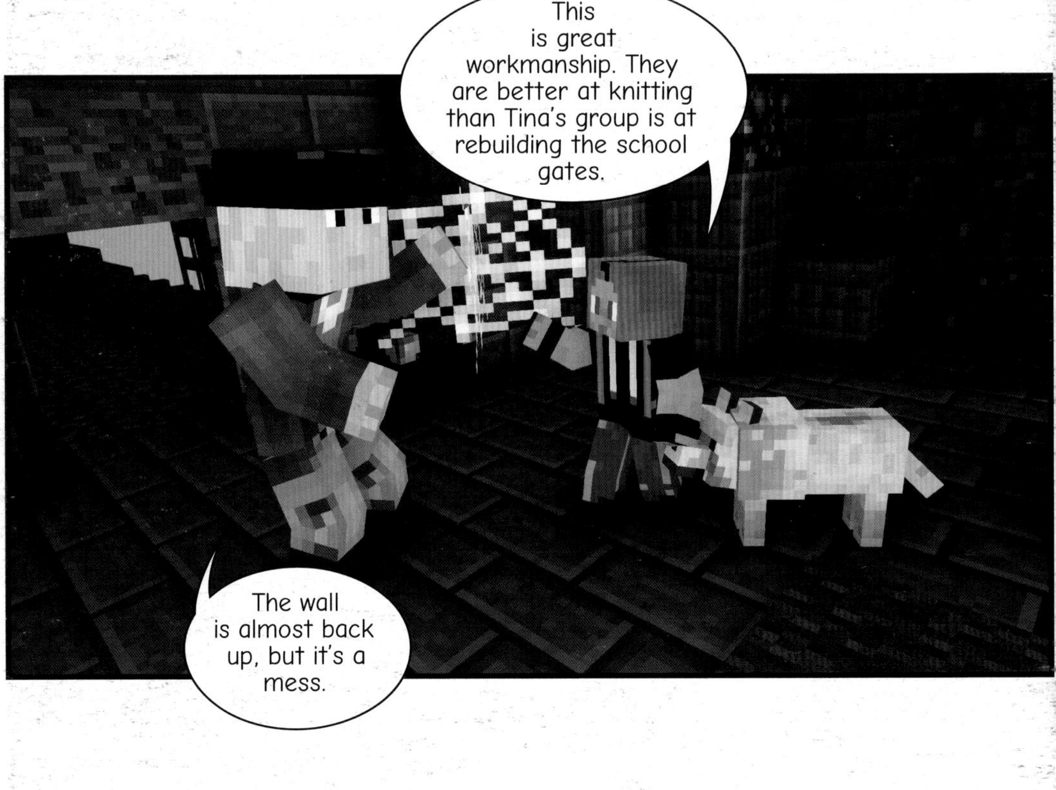
This is great workmanship. They are better at knitting than Tina's group is at rebuilding the school gates.
The wall is almost back up, but it's a mess.

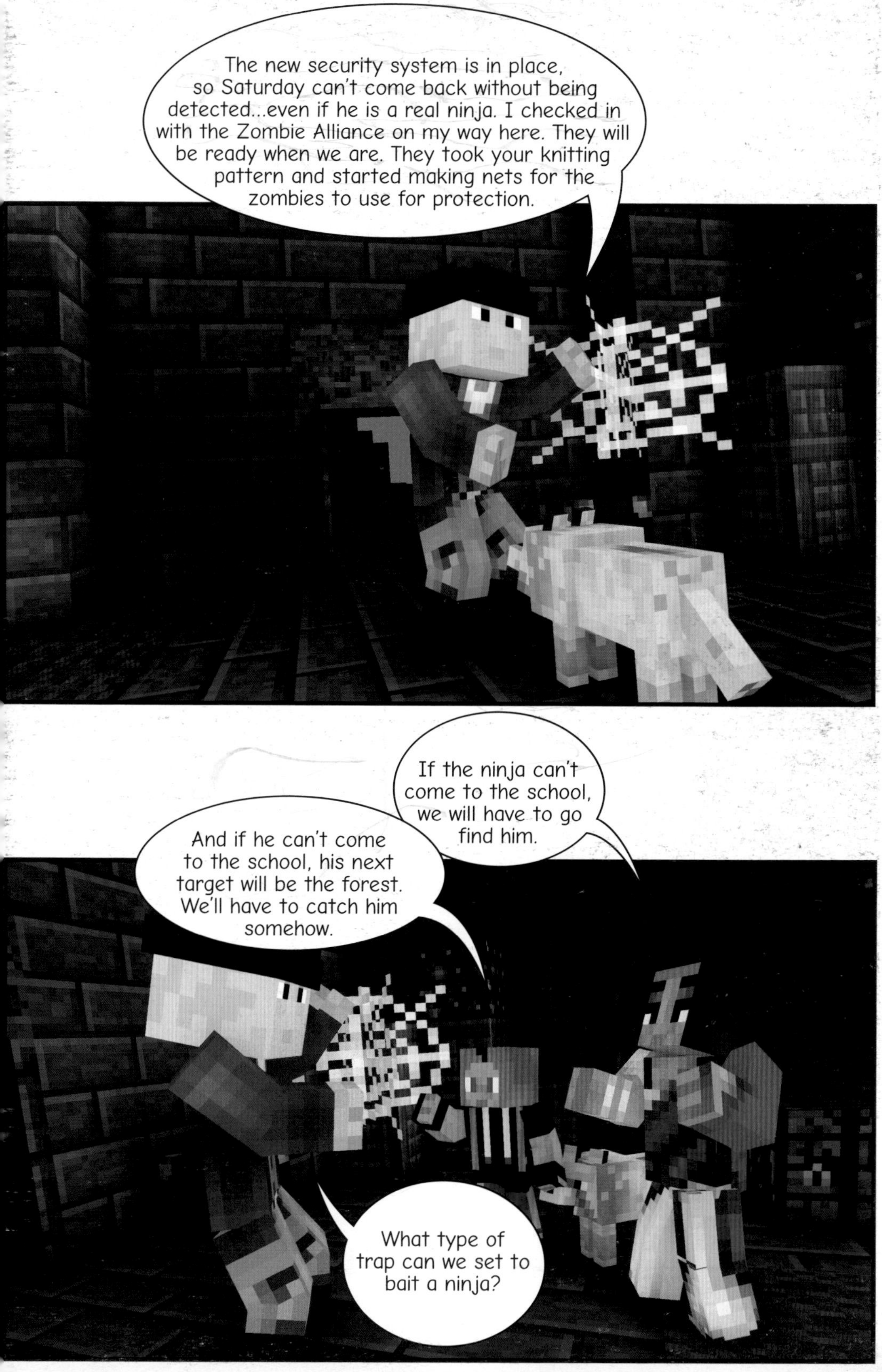
The new security system is in place, so Saturday can't come back without being detected...even if he is a real ninja. I checked in with the Zombie Alliance on my way here. They will be ready when we are. They took your knitting pattern and started making nets for the zombies to use for protection.
If the ninja can't come to the school, we will have to go find him.
And if he can't come to the school, his next target will be the forest. We'll have to catch him somehow.
What type of trap can we set to bait a ninja?

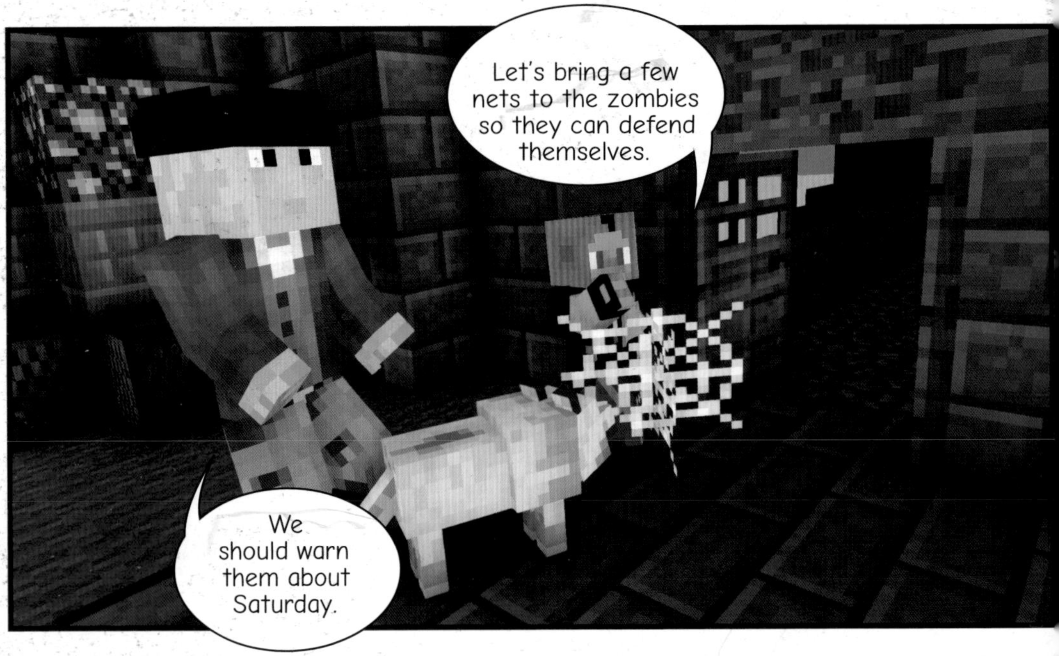
Let's bring a few nets to the zombies so they can defend themselves.
We should warn them about Saturday.

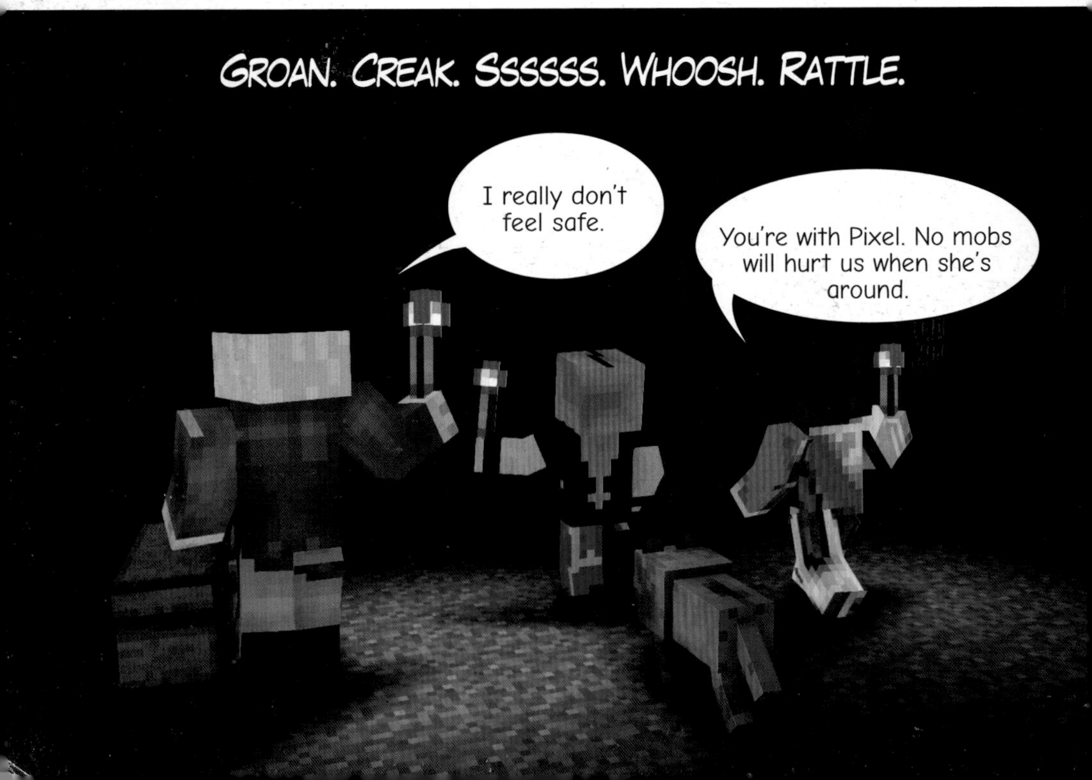
GROAN. CREAK. SSSSSS. WHOOSH. RATTLE.
I really don't feel safe.
You're with Pixel. No mobs will hurt us when she's around.

CHAPTER 10

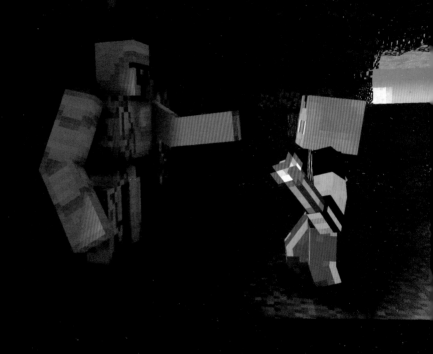

ATTACK OF
THE GOLEM

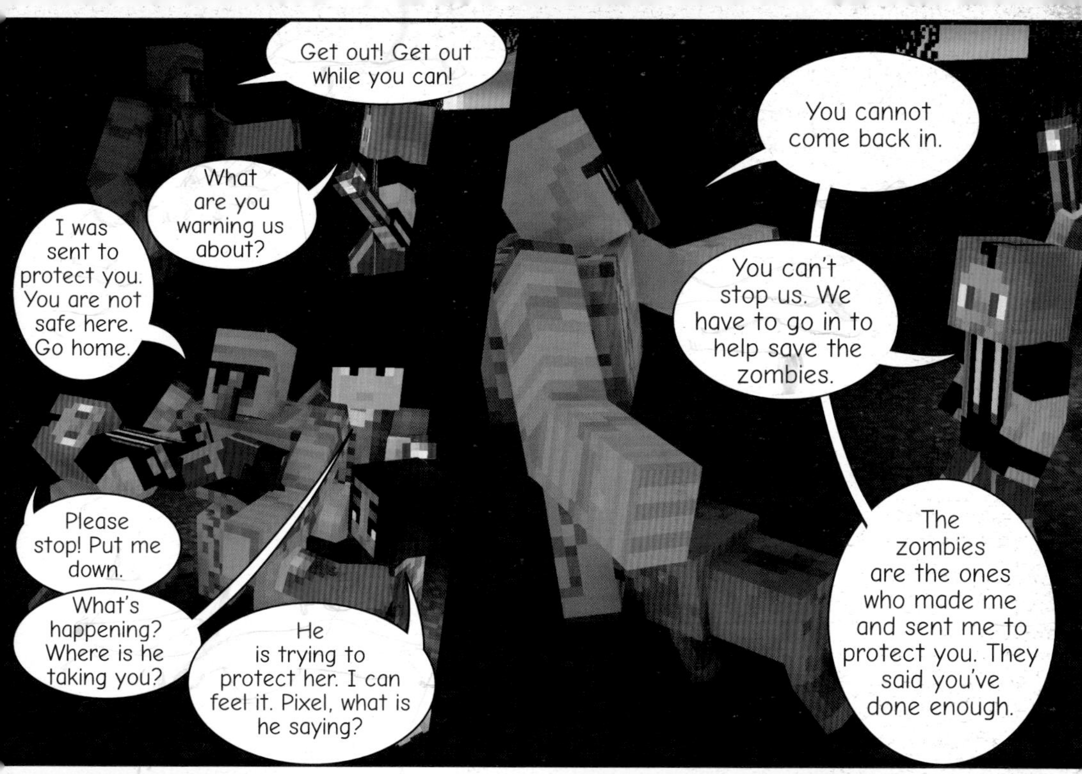
Get out! Get out while you can!
What are you warning us about?
I was sent to protect you. You are not safe here. Go home.
You cannot come back in.
You can't stop us. We have to go in to help save the zombies.
Please stop! Put me down.
What's happening? Where is he taking you?
He is trying to protect her. I can feel it. Pixel, what is he saying?
The zombies are the ones who made me and sent me to protect you. They said you've done enough.

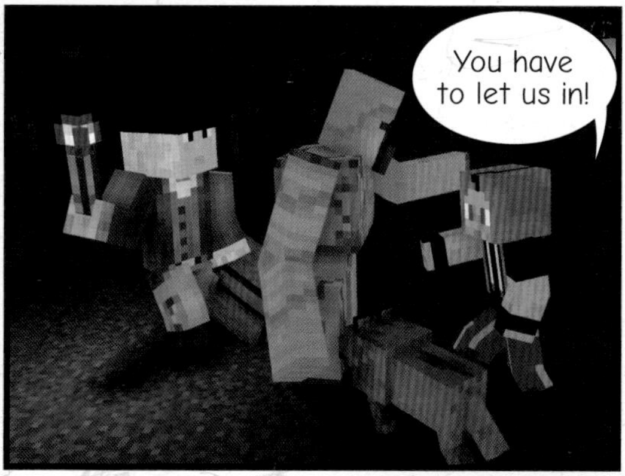
You have to let us in!

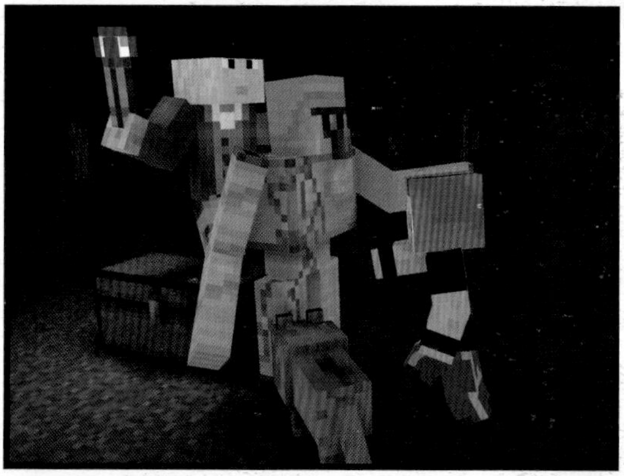

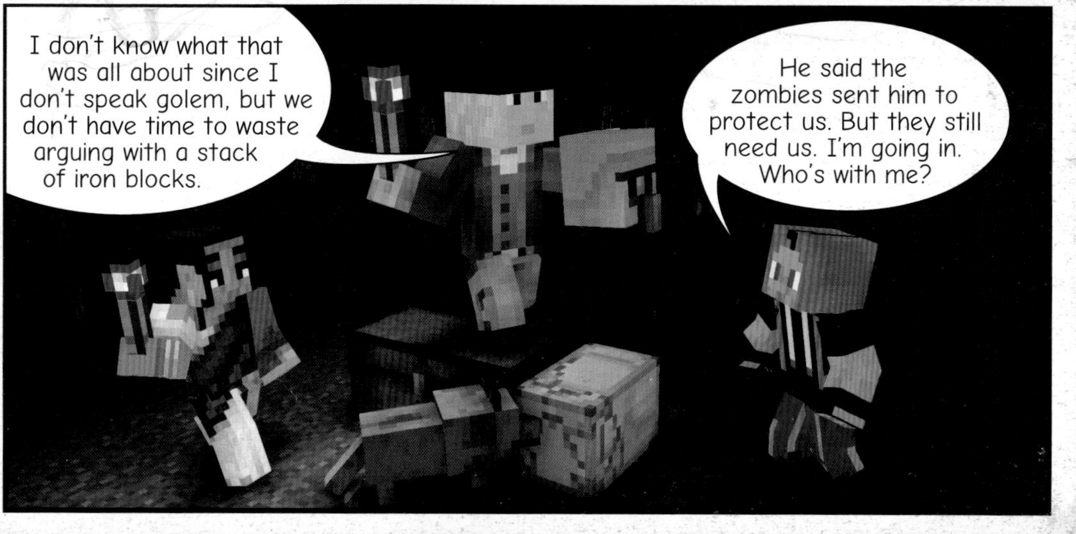
I don't know what that was all about since I don't speak golem, but we don't have time to waste arguing with a stack of iron blocks.
He said the zombies sent him to protect us. But they still need us. I'm going in. Who's with me?

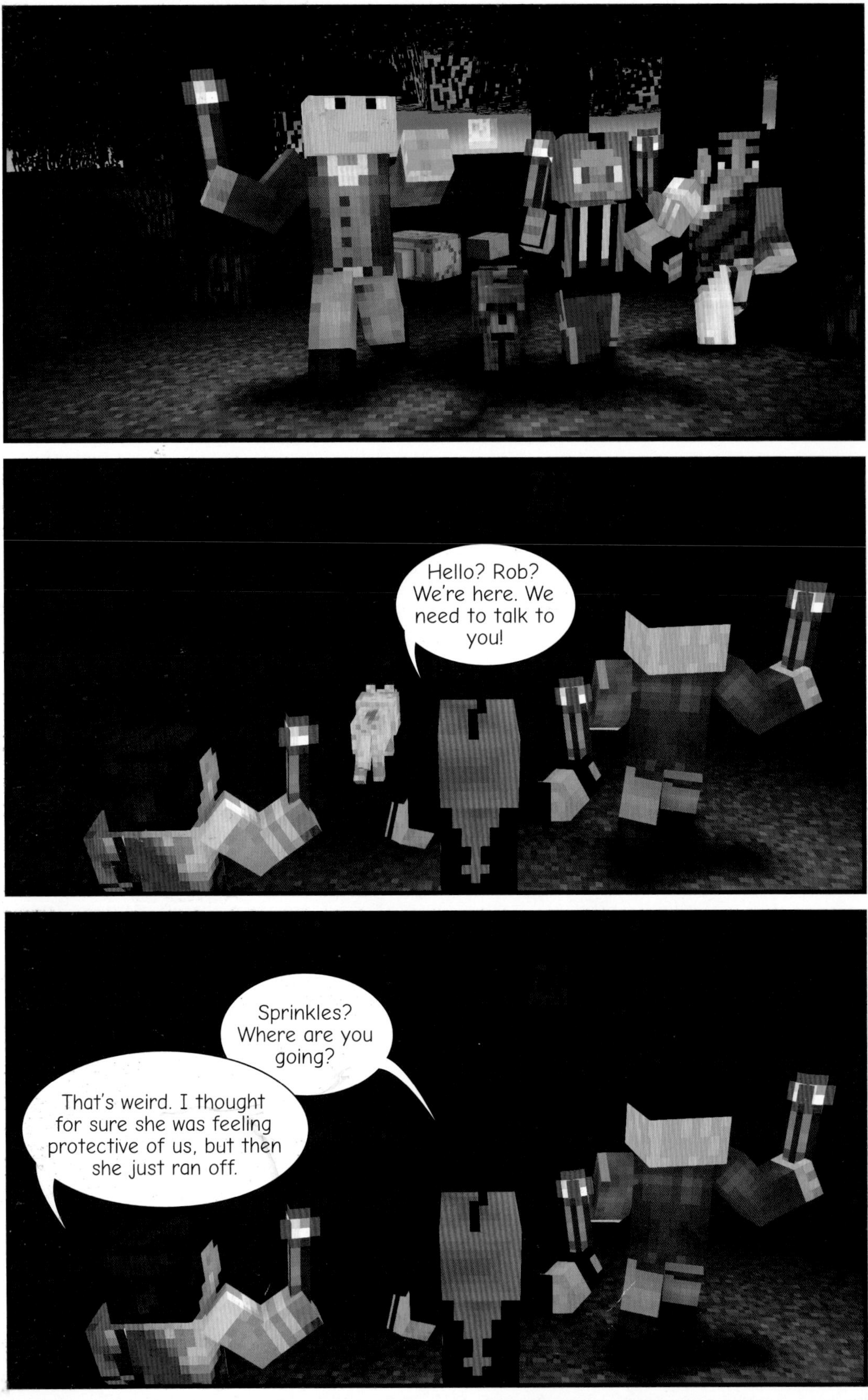

Hello? Rob? We're here. We need to talk to you!
Sprinkles? Where are you going?
That's weird. I thought for sure she was feeling protective of us, but then she just ran off.

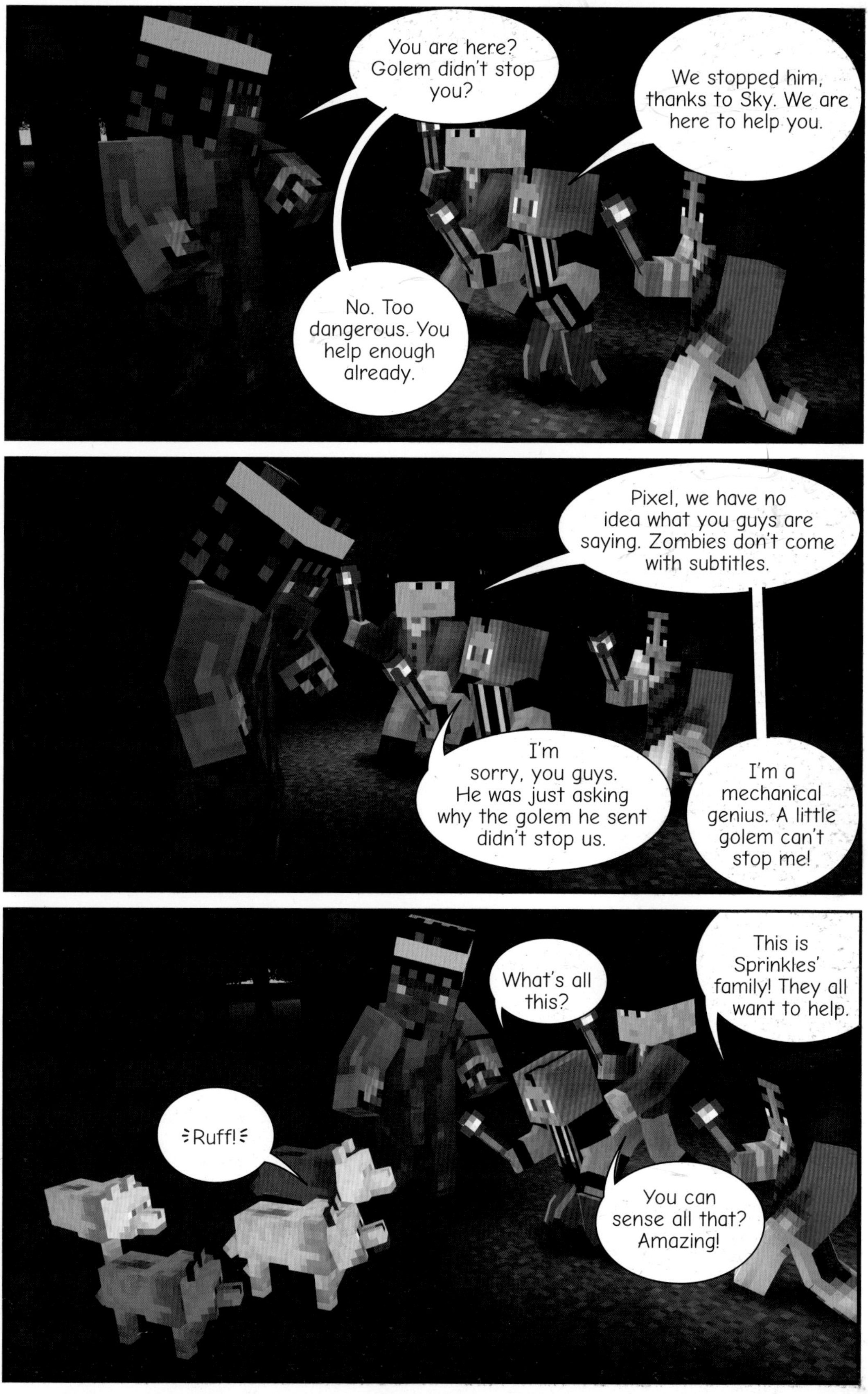
You are here? Golem didn't stop you?
We stopped him, thanks to Sky. We are here to help you.
No. Too dangerous. You help enough already.
Pixel, we have no idea what you guys are saying. Zombies don't come with subtitles.
I'm sorry, you guys. He was just asking why the golem he sent didn't stop us.
I'm a mechanical genius. A little golem can't stop me!
What's all this?
This is Sprinkles' family! They all want to help.
Ruff!
You can sense all that? Amazing!

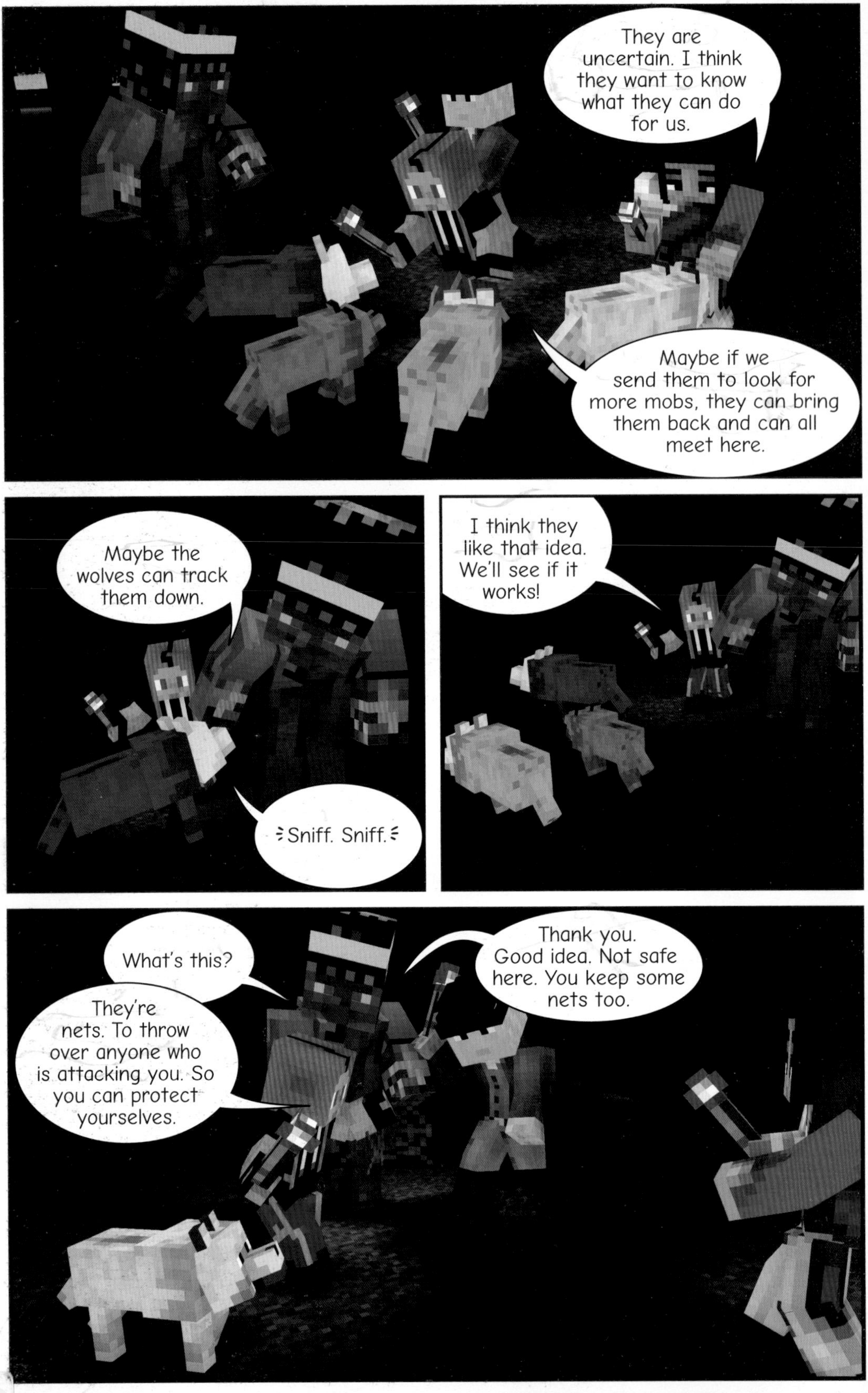
They are uncertain. I think they want to know what they can do for us.
Maybe if we send them to look for more mobs, they can bring them back and can all meet here.
Maybe the wolves can track them down.
Sniff. Sniff.
I think they like that idea. We'll see if it works!
What's this?
They're nets. To throw over anyone who is attacking you. So you can protect yourselves.
Thank you. Good idea. Not safe here. You keep some nets too.

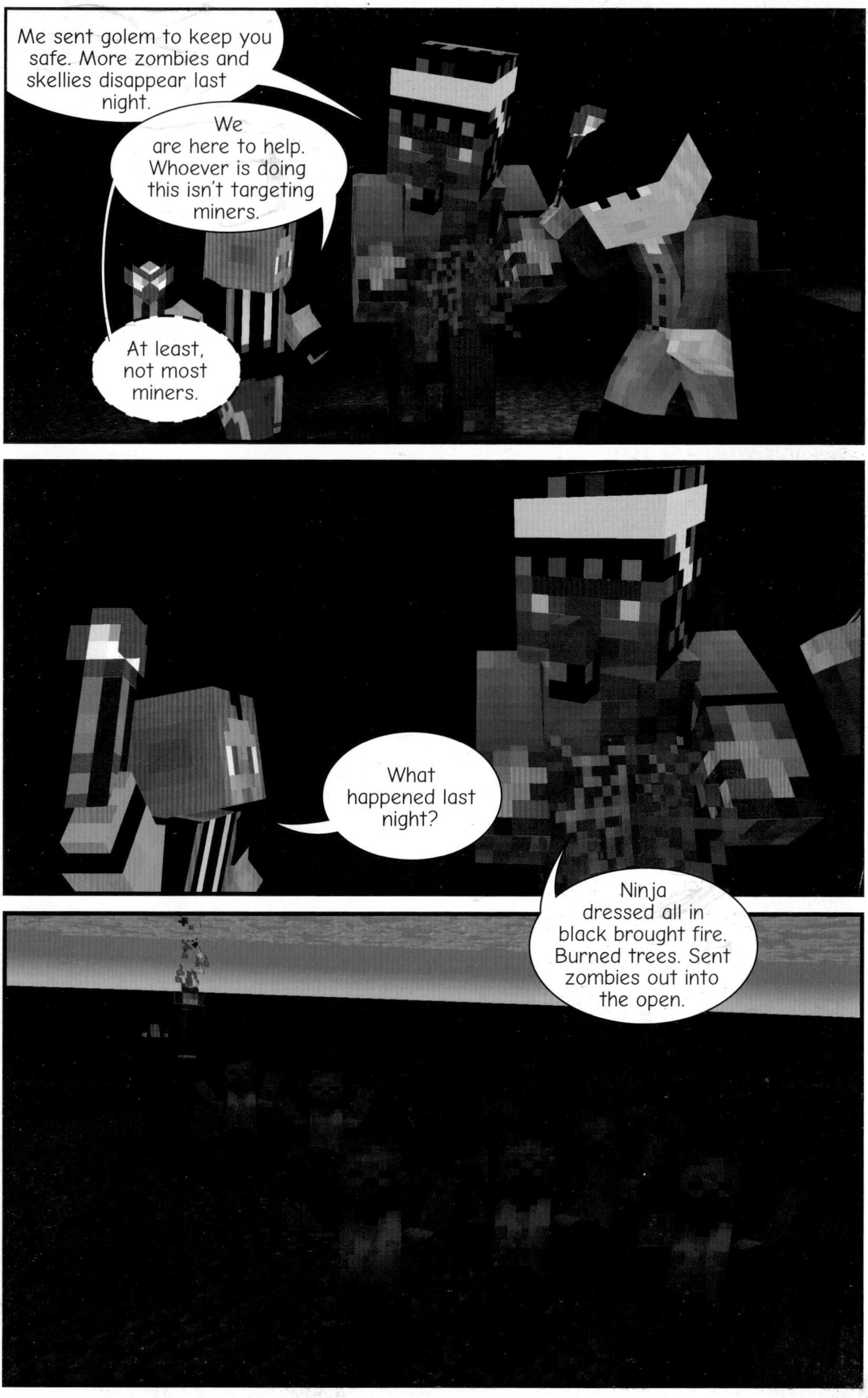
Me sent golem to keep you safe. More zombies and skellies disappear last night.
We are here to help. Whoever is doing this isn't targeting miners.
At least, not most miners.
What happened last night?
Ninja dressed all in black brought fire. Burned trees. Sent zombies out into the open.

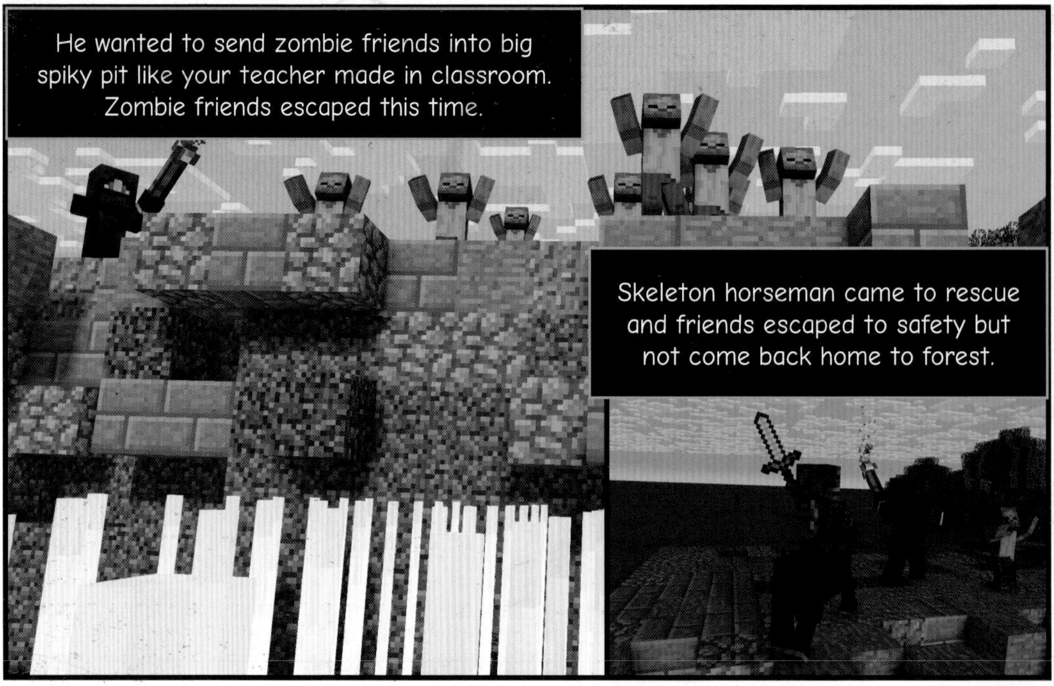
He wanted to send zombie friends into big spiky pit like your teacher made in classroom. Zombie friends escaped this time.
Skeleton horseman came to rescue and friends escaped to safety but not come back home to forest.

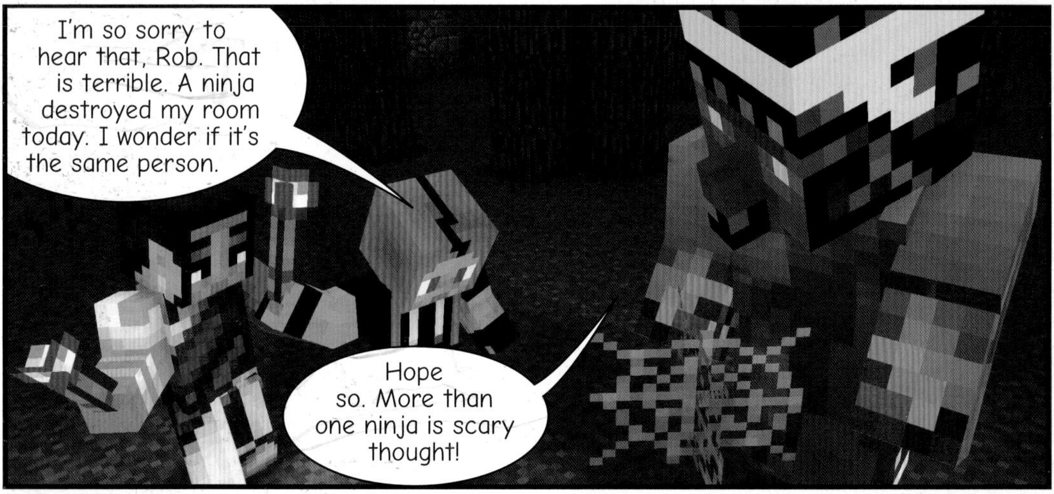
I'm so sorry to hear that, Rob. That is terrible. A ninja destroyed my room today. I wonder if it's the same person.
Hope so. More than one ninja is scary thought!

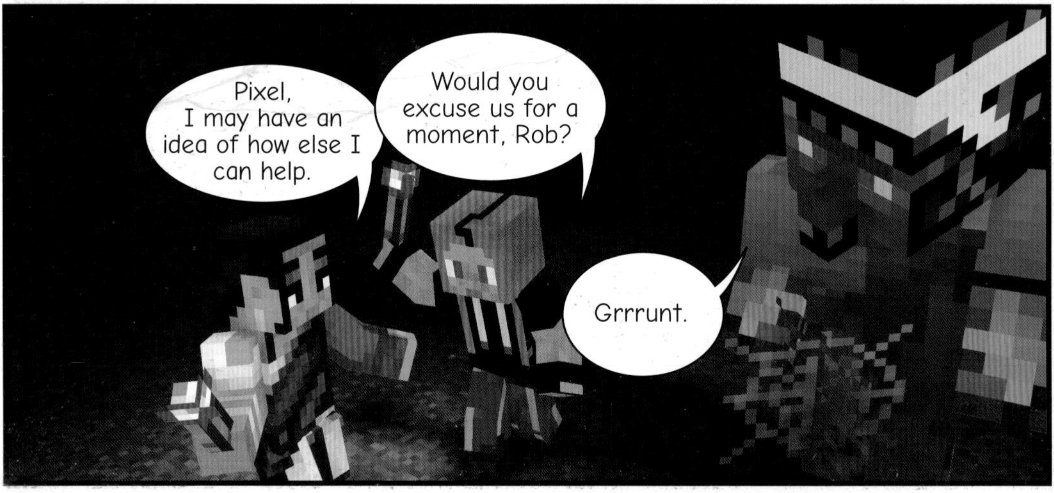
Pixel, I may have an idea of how else I can help.
Would you excuse us for a moment, Rob?
Grrrunt.

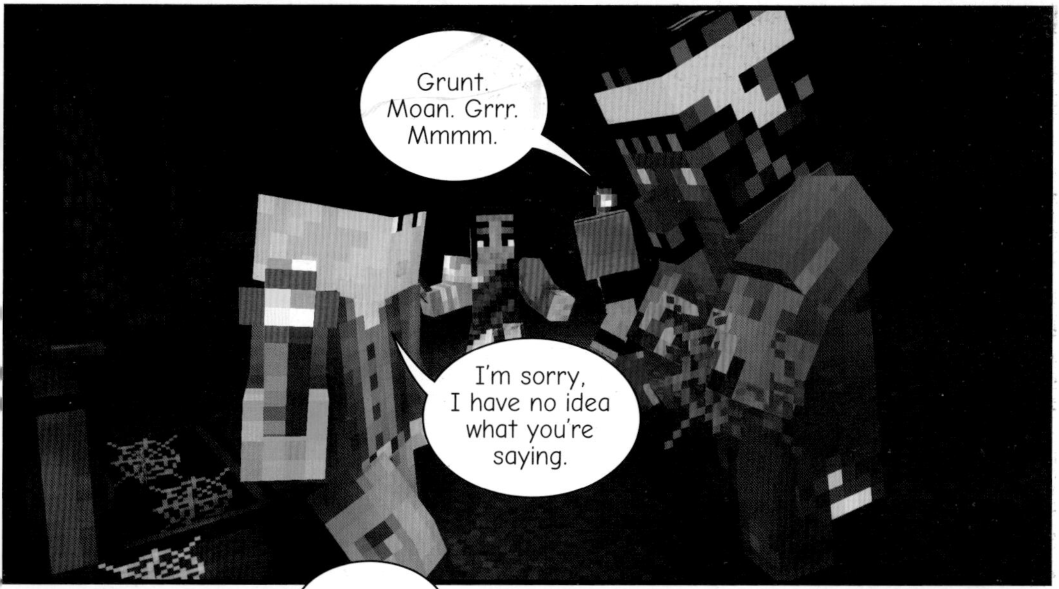
Grunt. Moan. Grrr. Mmmm.
I'm sorry, I have no idea what you're saying.

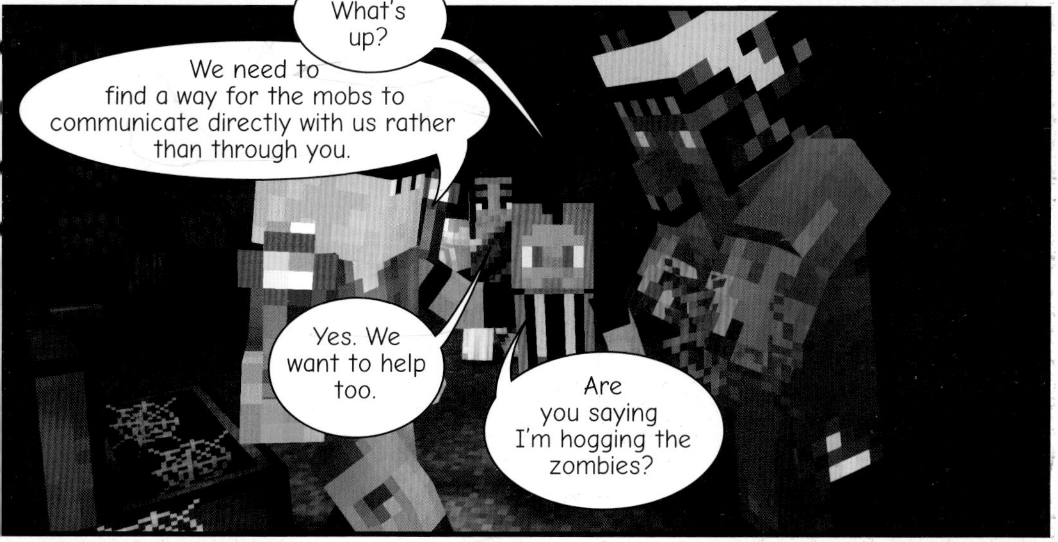
What's up?
We need to find a way for the mobs to communicate directly with us rather than through you.
Yes. We want to help too.
Are you saying I'm hogging the zombies?

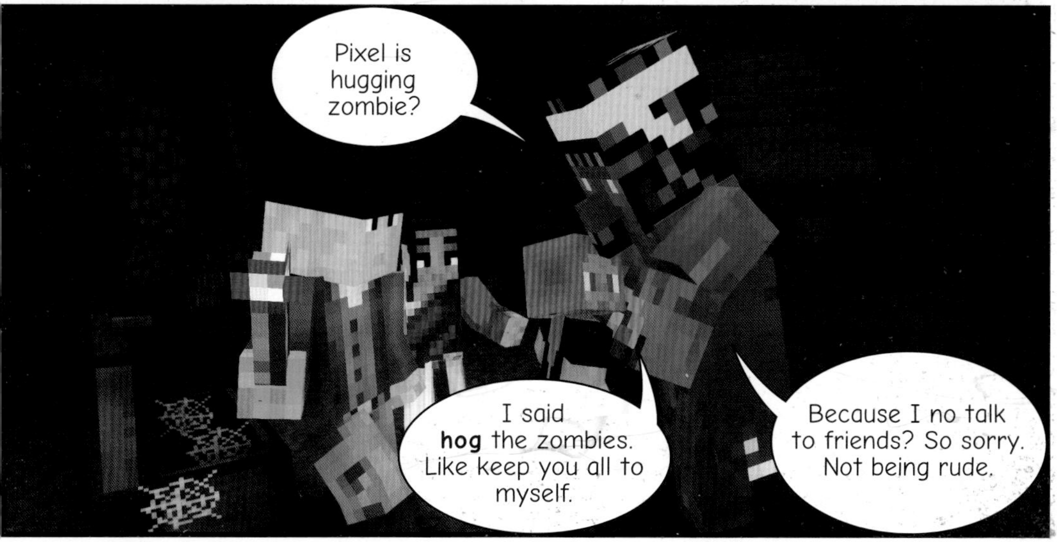
Pixel is hugging zombie?
I said **hog** the zombies. Like keep you all to myself.
Because I no talk to friends? So sorry. Not being rude.

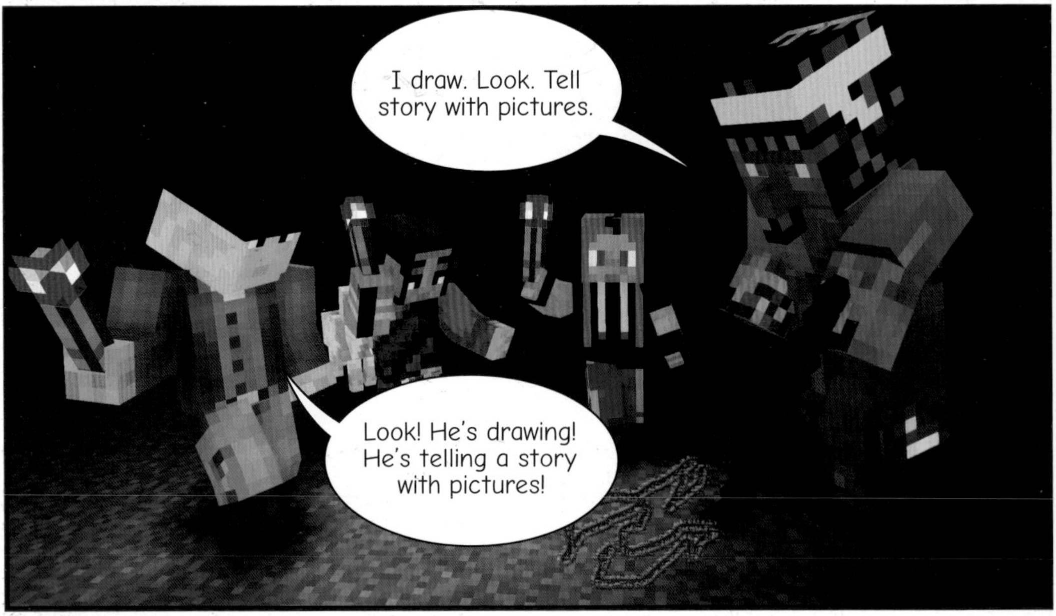
I draw. Look. Tell story with pictures.
Look! He's drawing! He's telling a story with pictures!

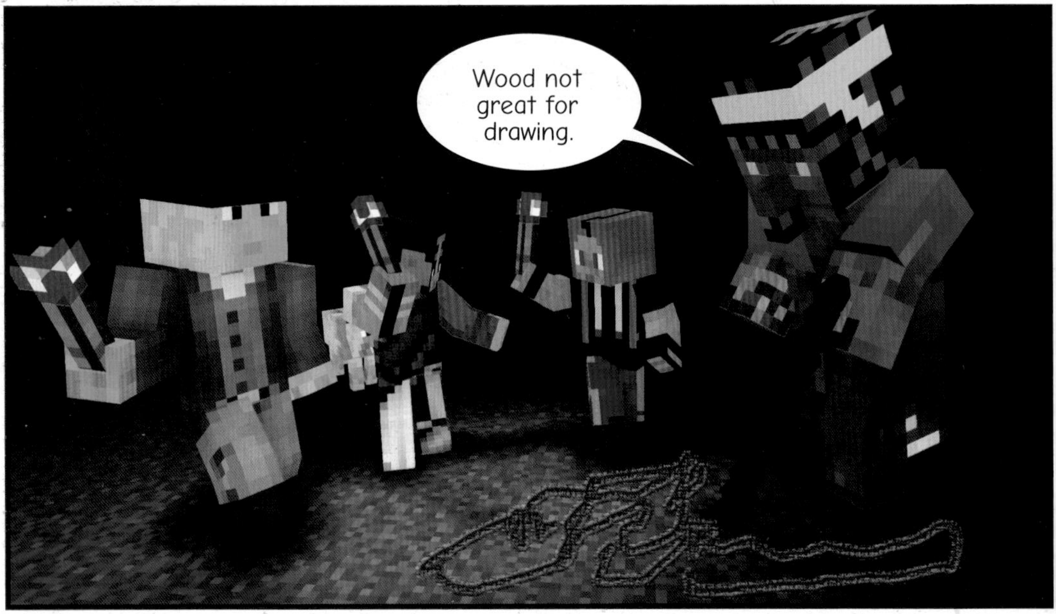
Wood not great for drawing.

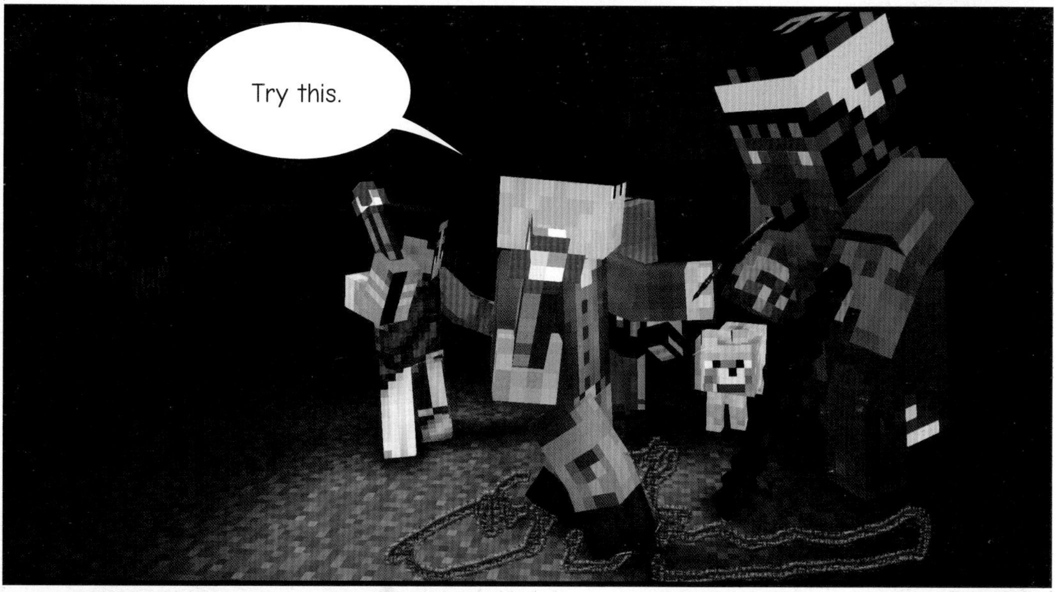
Try this.

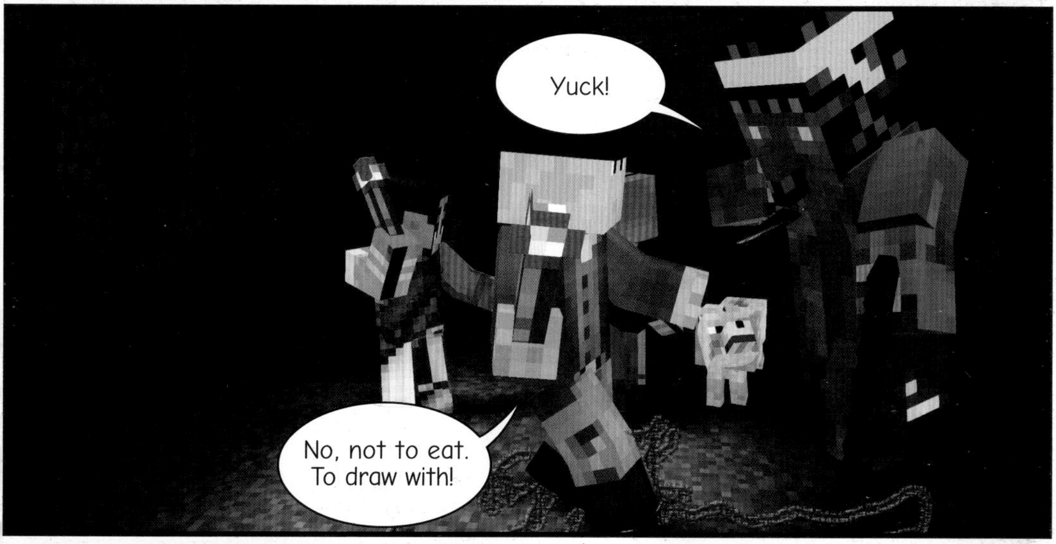
Yuck!
No, not to eat. To draw with!

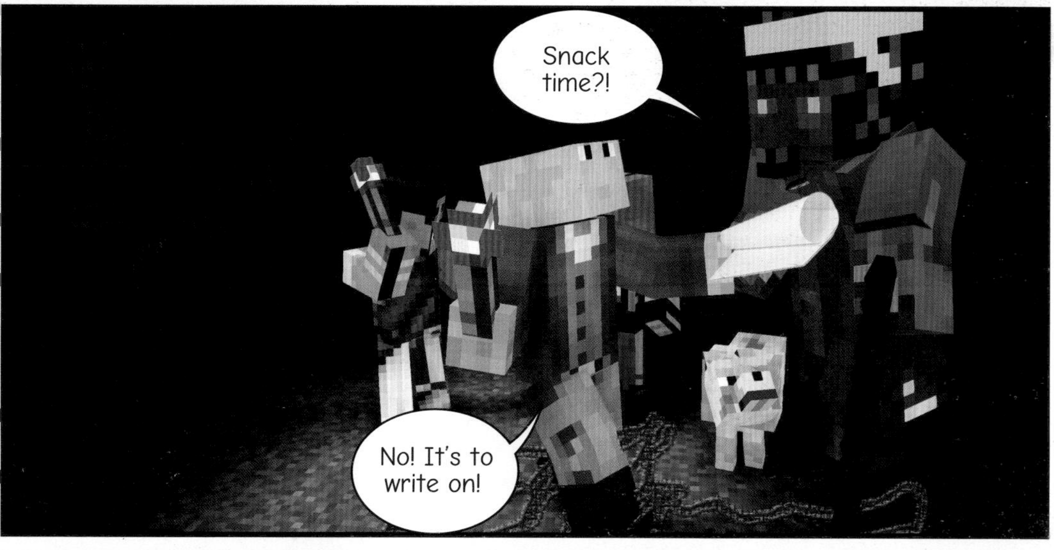
Snack time?!
No! It's to write on!

I was thinking we could create a trap like this...

Grunt! Ha ha!

You like it!

I don't. For one thing, it's violent. For another, if the ninja falls onto those spikes, we won't get to find out who sent him or what they're planning next.

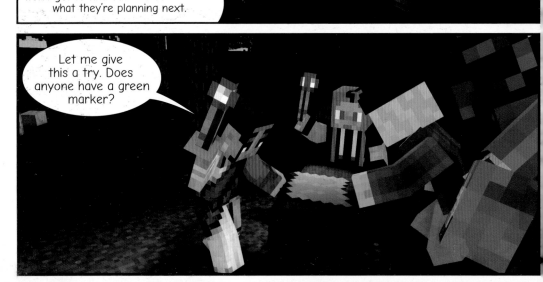

Let me give this a try. Does anyone have a green marker?

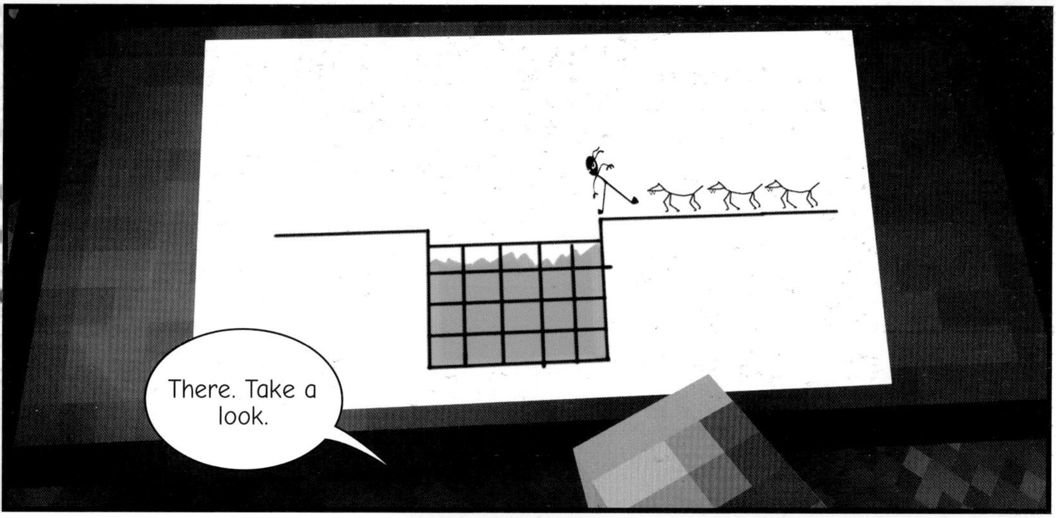
There. Take a look.

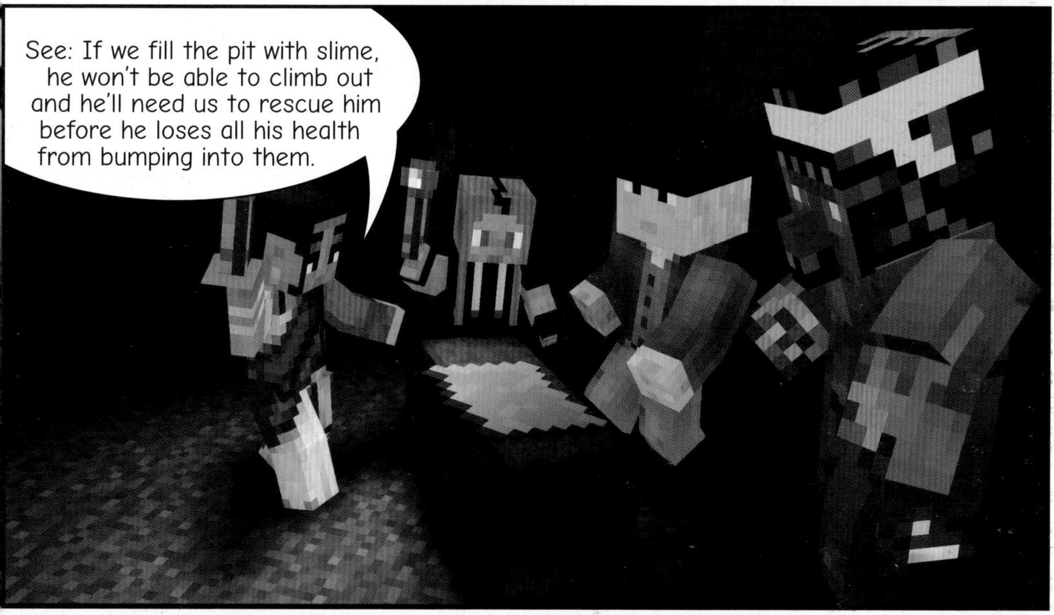
See: If we fill the pit with slime, he won't be able to climb out and he'll need us to rescue him before he loses all his health from bumping into them.

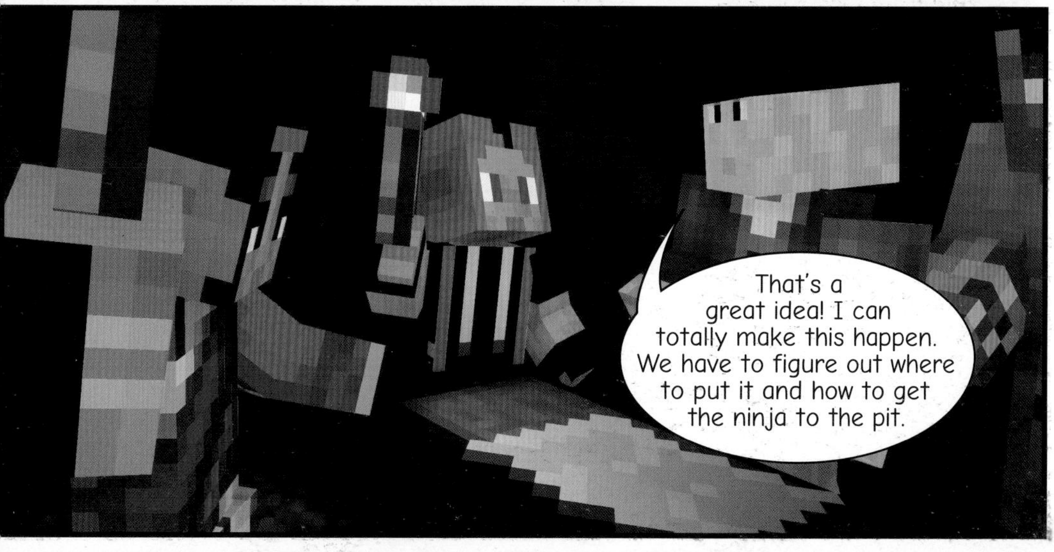
That's a great idea! I can totally make this happen. We have to figure out where to put it and how to get the ninja to the pit.

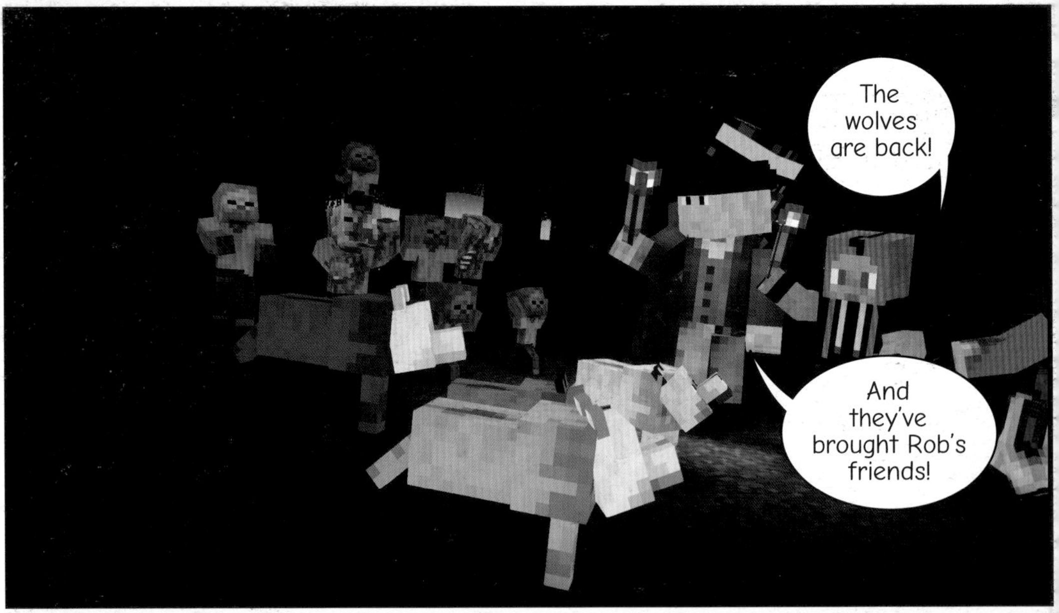
The wolves are back!
And they've brought Rob's friends!

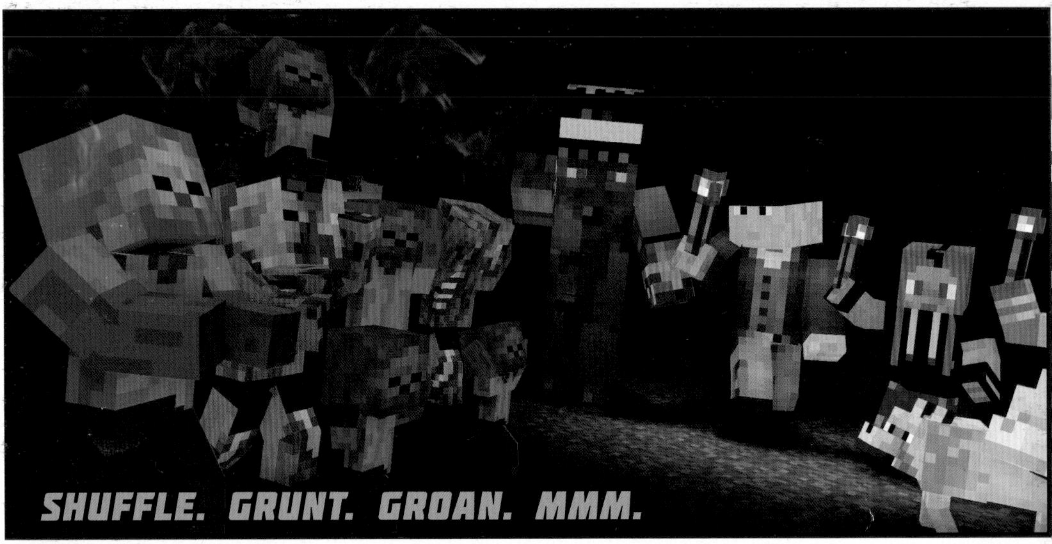
SHUFFLE. GRUNT. GROAN. MMM.

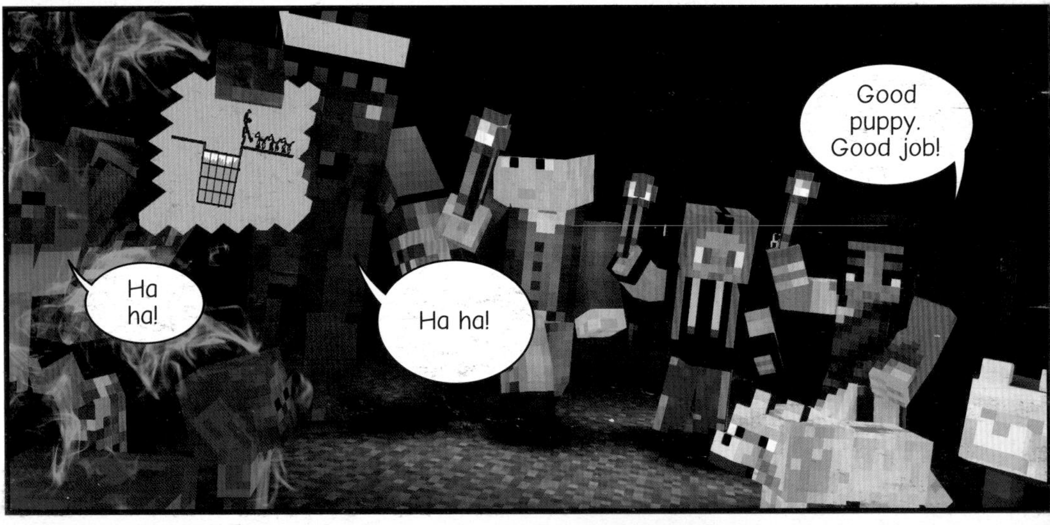
Good puppy. Good job!
Ha ha!
Ha ha!

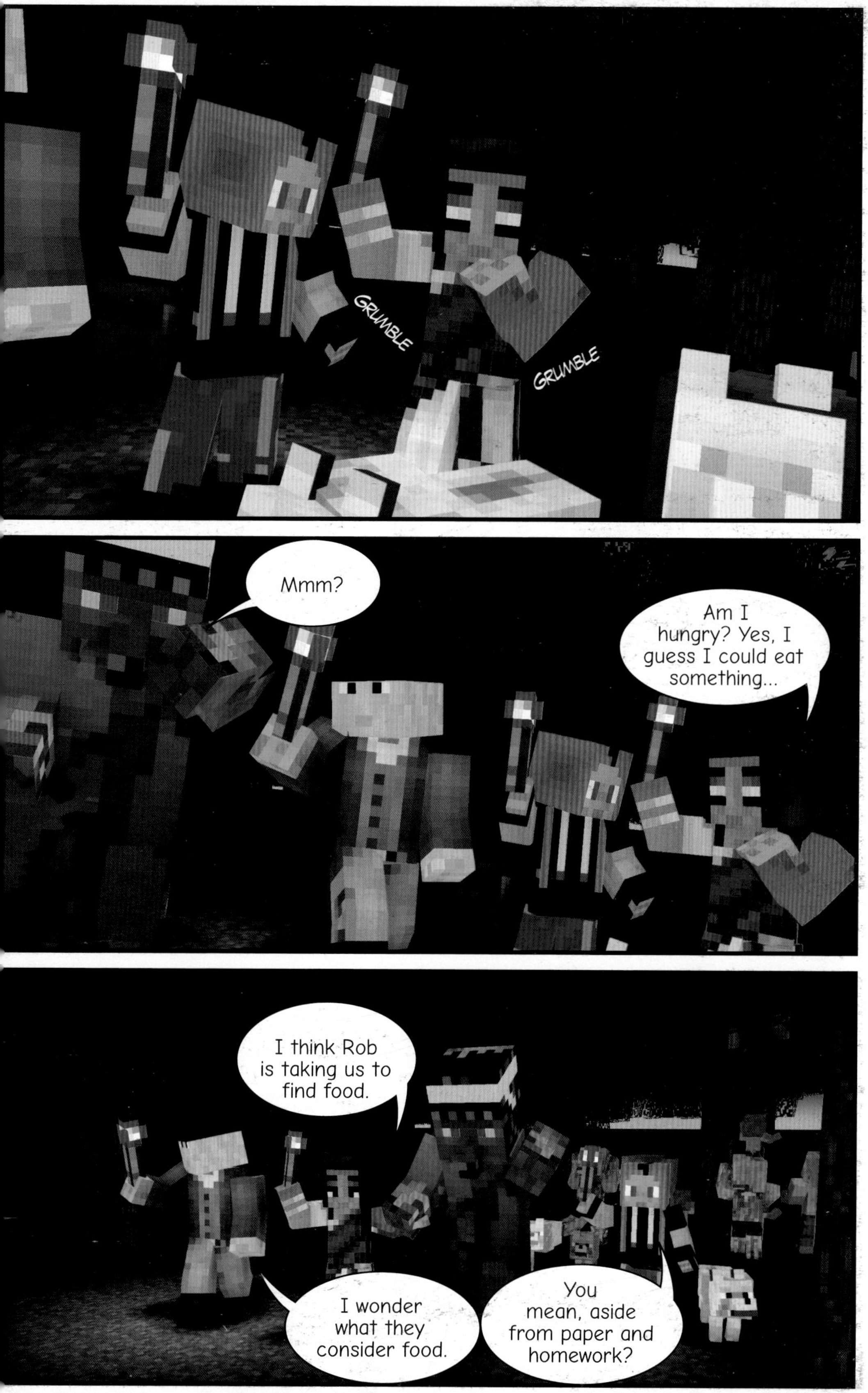
GRUMBLE
GRUMBLE
Mmm?
Am I hungry? Yes, I guess I could eat something...
I think Rob is taking us to find food.
I wonder what they consider food.
You mean, aside from paper and homework?

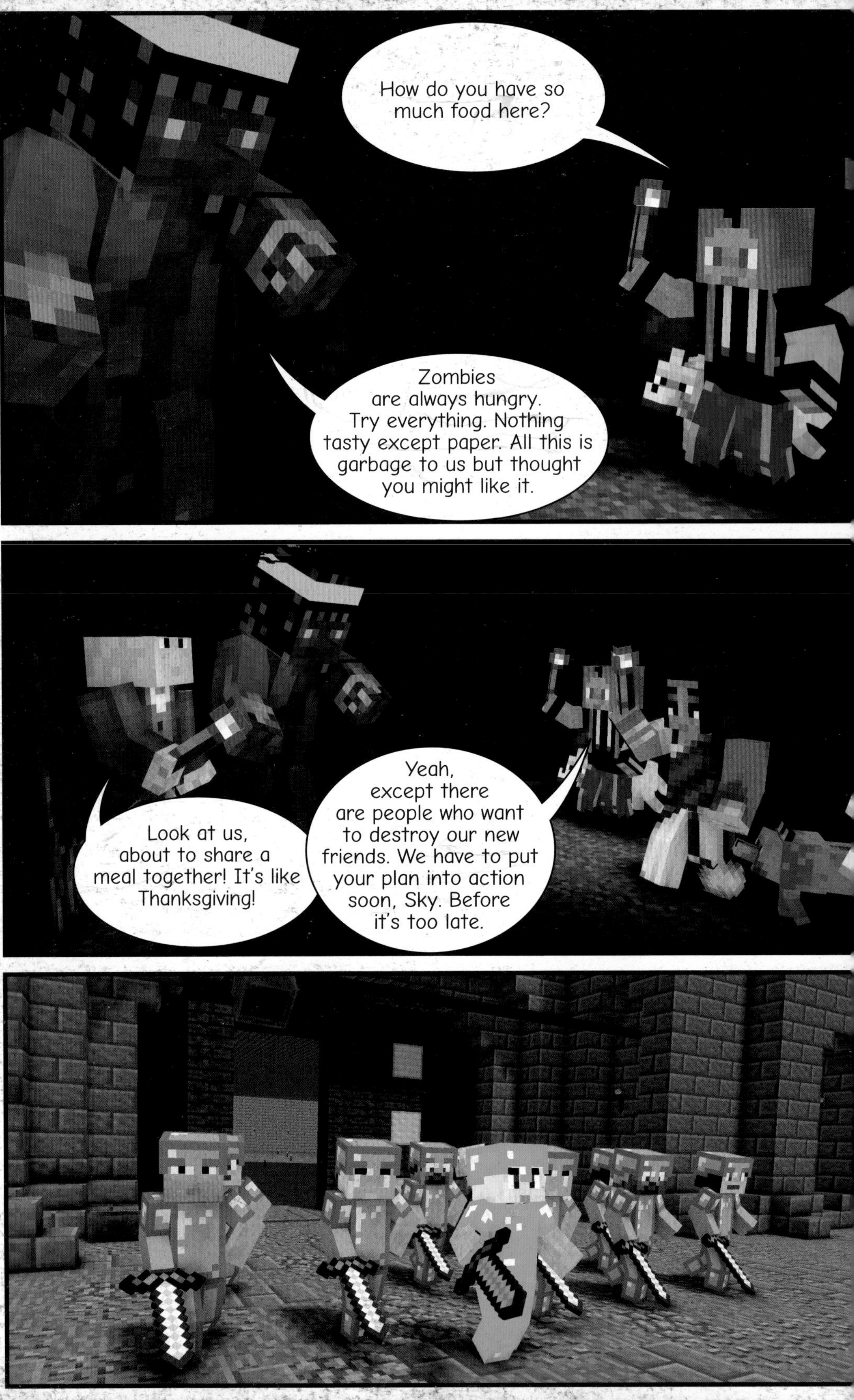
How do you have so much food here?
Zombies are always hungry. Try everything. Nothing tasty except paper. All this is garbage to us but thought you might like it.
Look at us, about to share a meal together! It's like Thanksgiving!
Yeah, except there are people who want to destroy our new friends. We have to put your plan into action soon, Sky. Before it's too late.

CHAPTER 11

NINJA
NO MORE

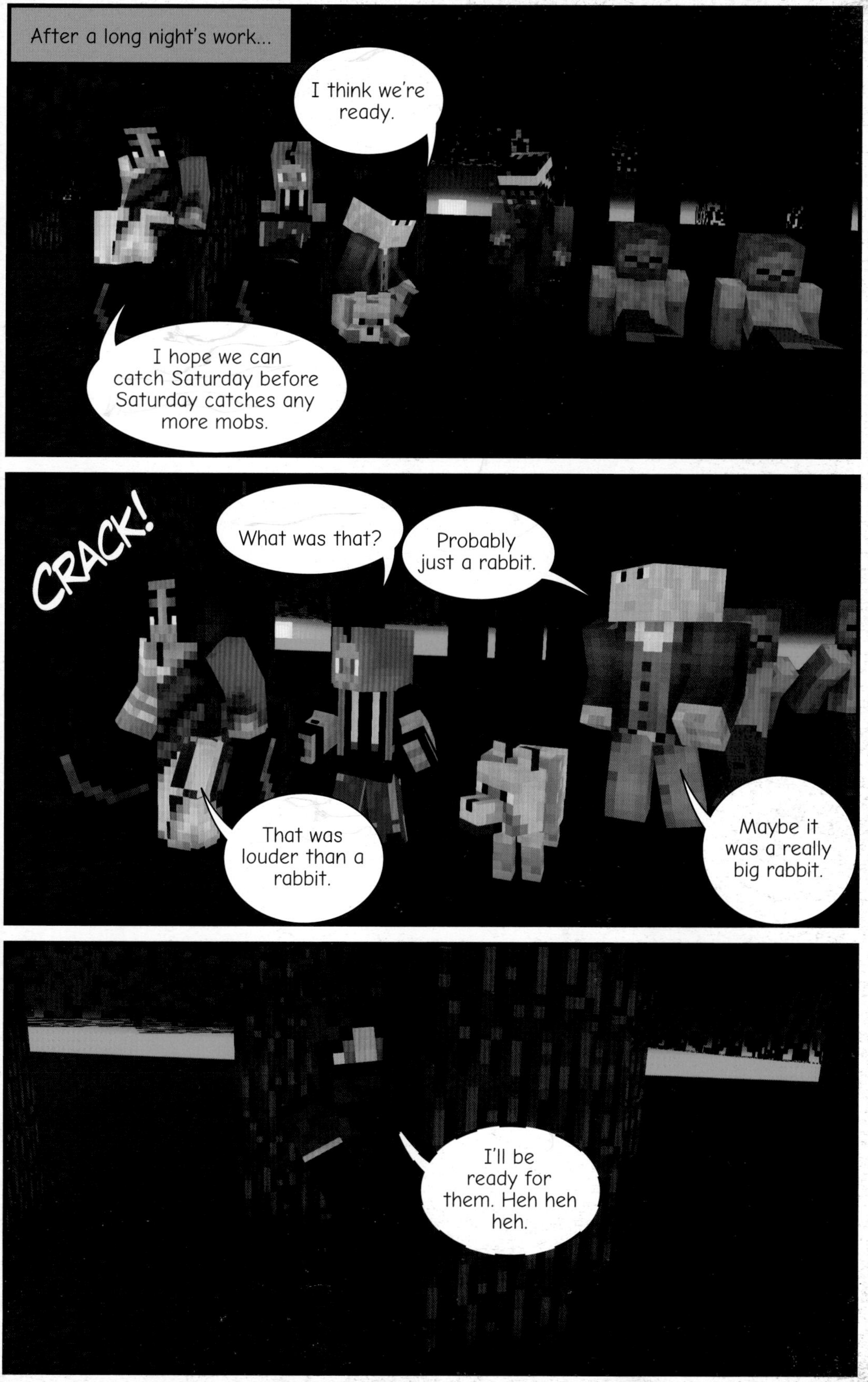
After a long night's work...
I think we're ready.
I hope we can catch Saturday before Saturday catches any more mobs.
CRACK!
What was that?
Probably just a rabbit.
That was louder than a rabbit.
Maybe it was a really big rabbit.
I'll be ready for them. Heh heh heh.

We're ready for your zombies. They'll never get through the gates again.

You bet they won't!

I told you, they aren't invading. They were just looking for shelter. Don't worry. They won't be coming back.

You mean those gates? A good rainstorm could knock those things down. Never mind zombies...they couldn't even hold back a chicken invasion!

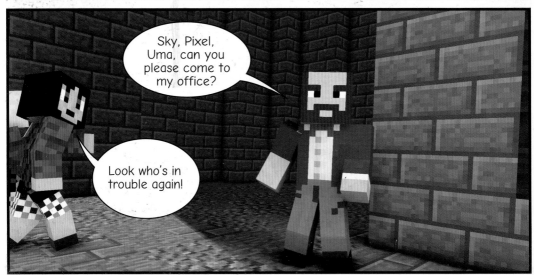

Sky, Pixel, Uma, can you please come to my office?

Look who's in trouble again!

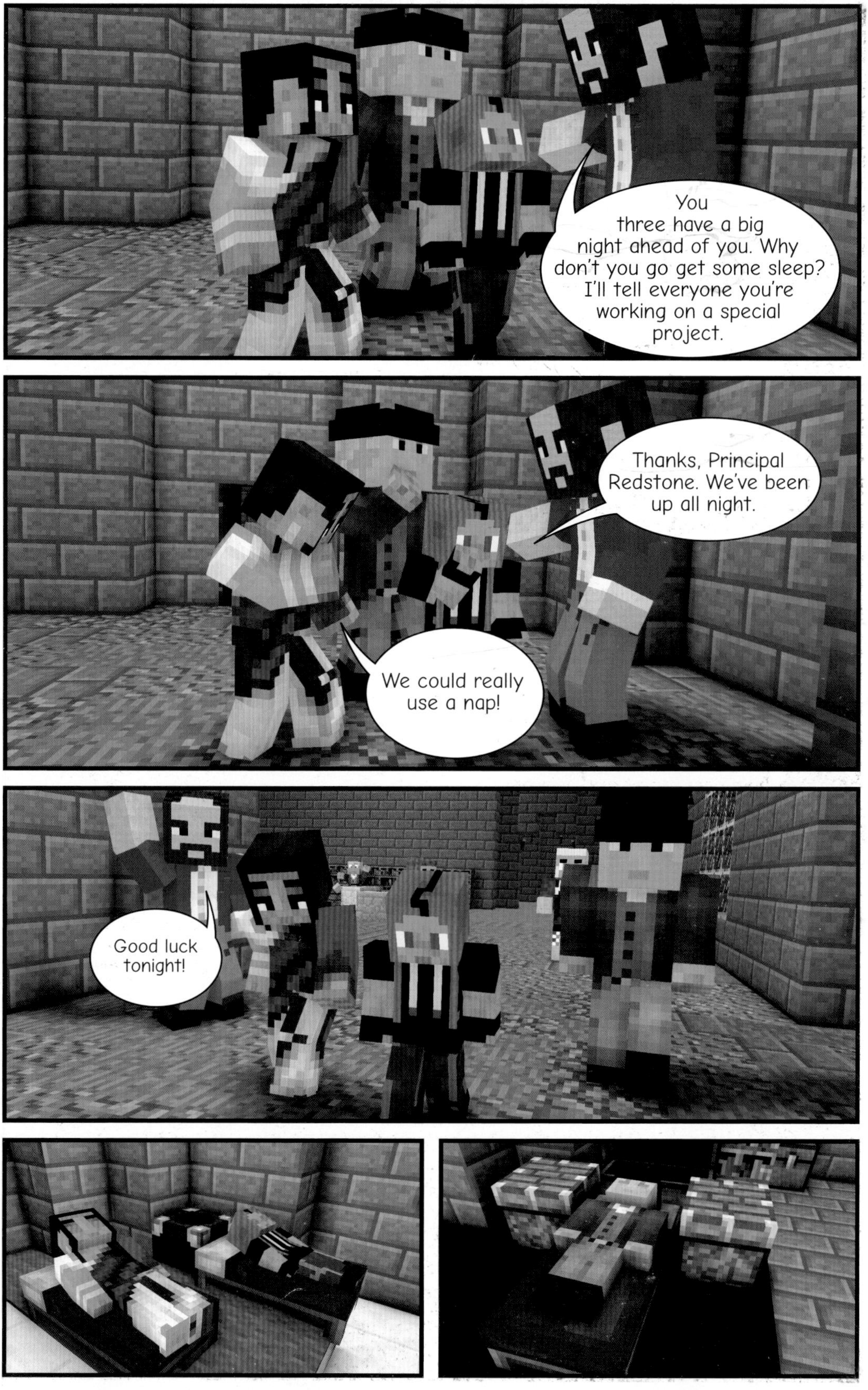
You three have a big night ahead of you. Why don't you go get some sleep? I'll tell everyone you're working on a special project.
Thanks, Principal Redstone. We've been up all night.
We could really use a nap!
Good luck tonight!

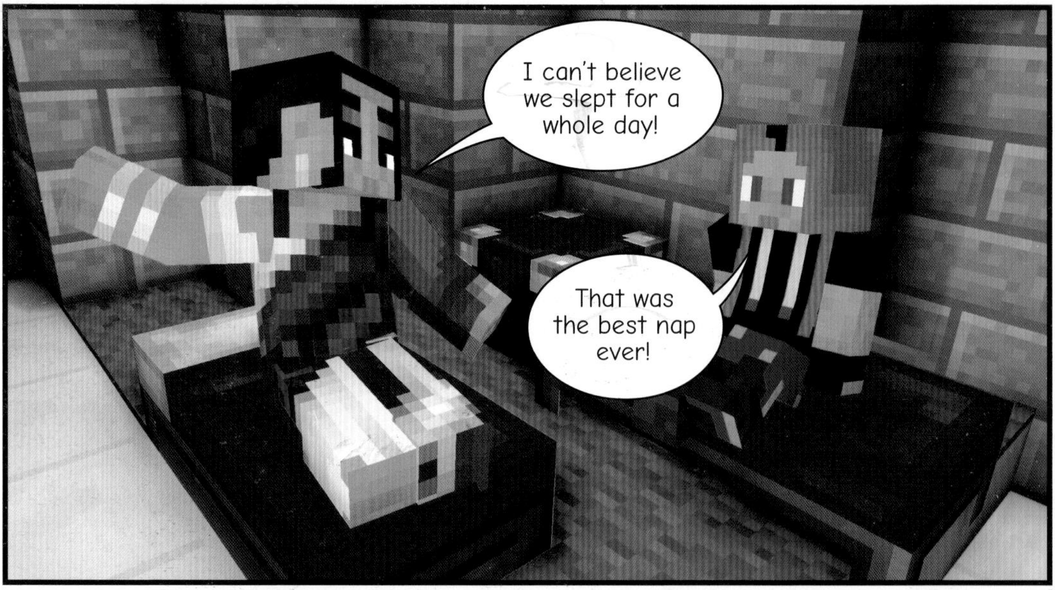
I can't believe we slept for a whole day!
That was the best nap ever!

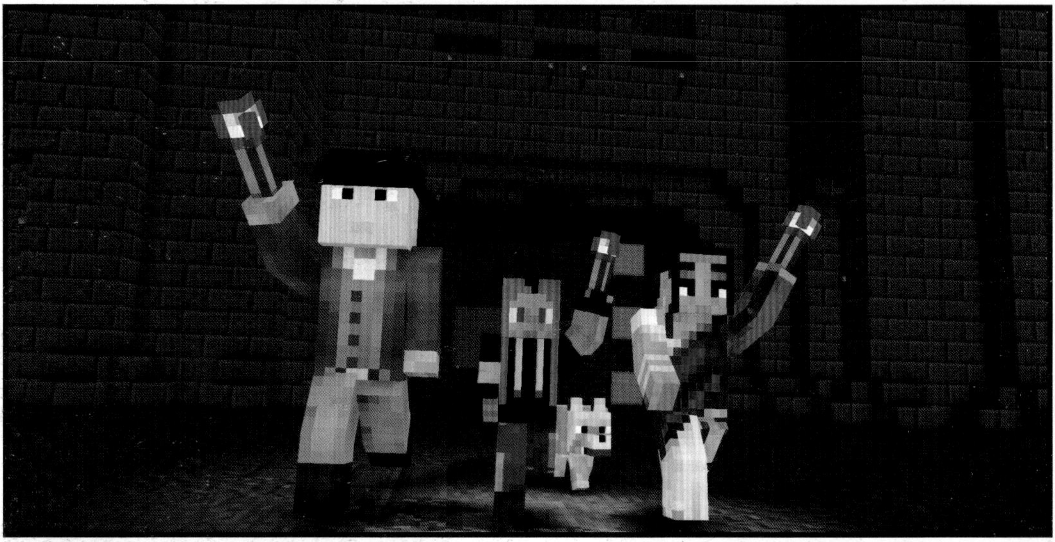

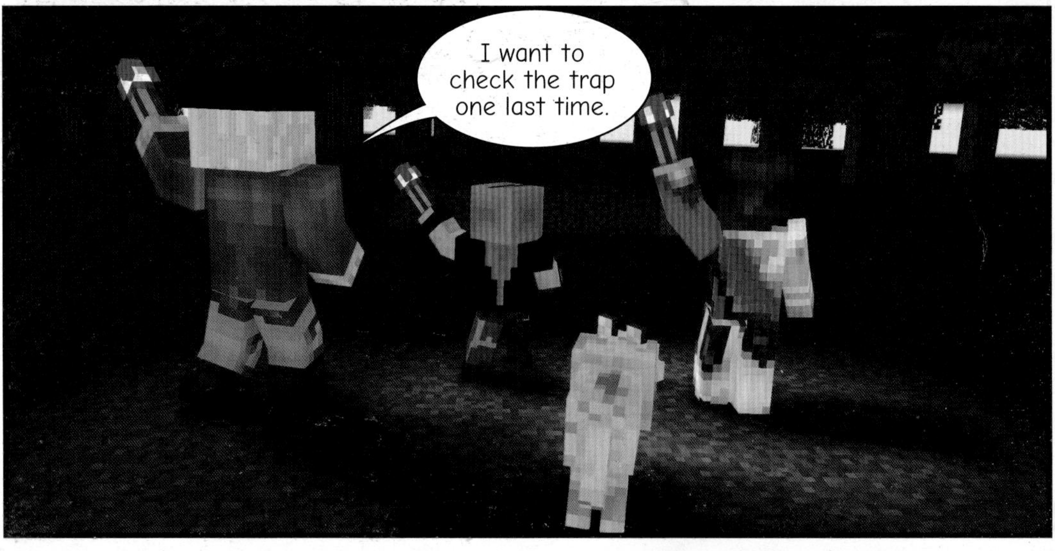
I want to check the trap one last time.

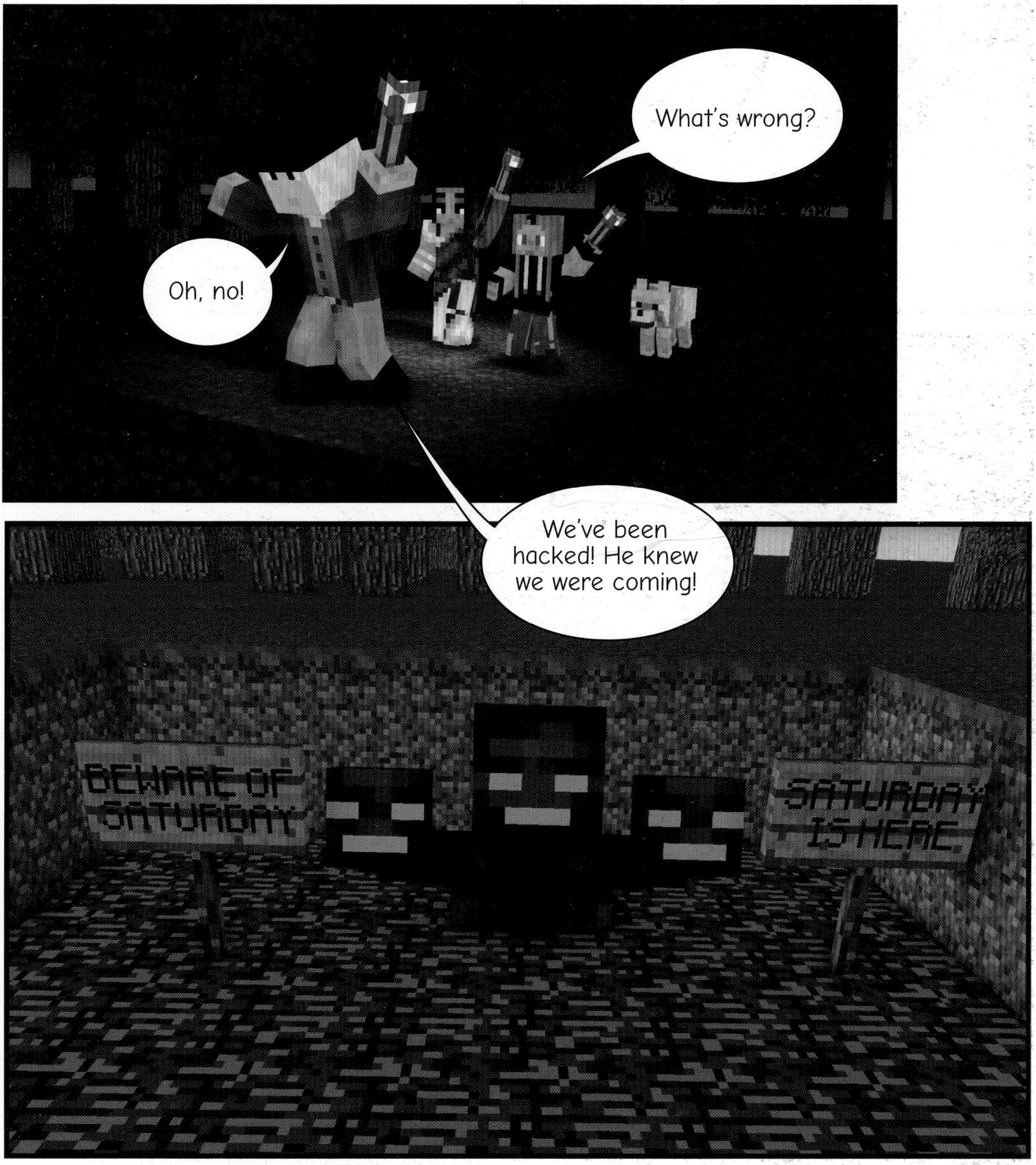
Oh, no!
What's wrong?
We've been hacked! He knew we were coming!
BEWARE OF SATURDAY
SATURDAY IS HERE

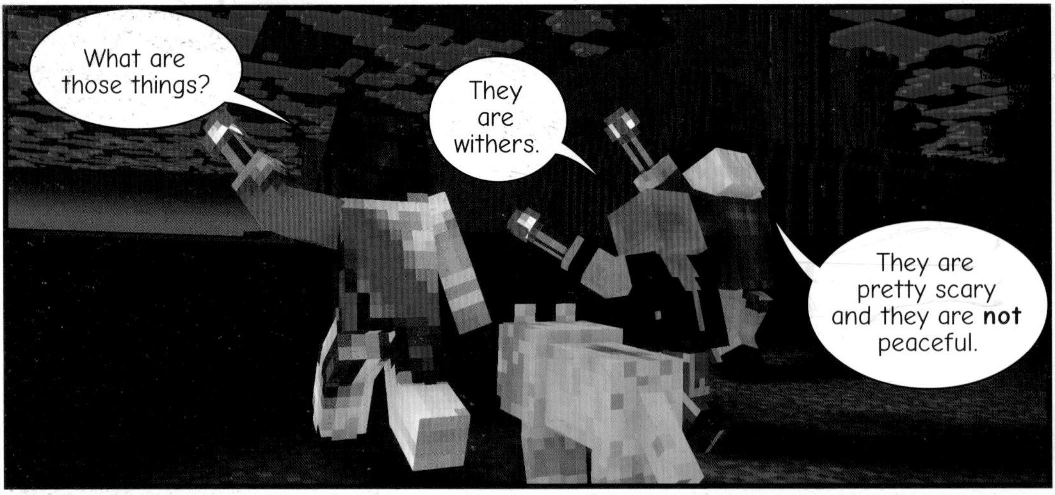
What are those things?
They are withers.
They are pretty scary and they are **not** peaceful.

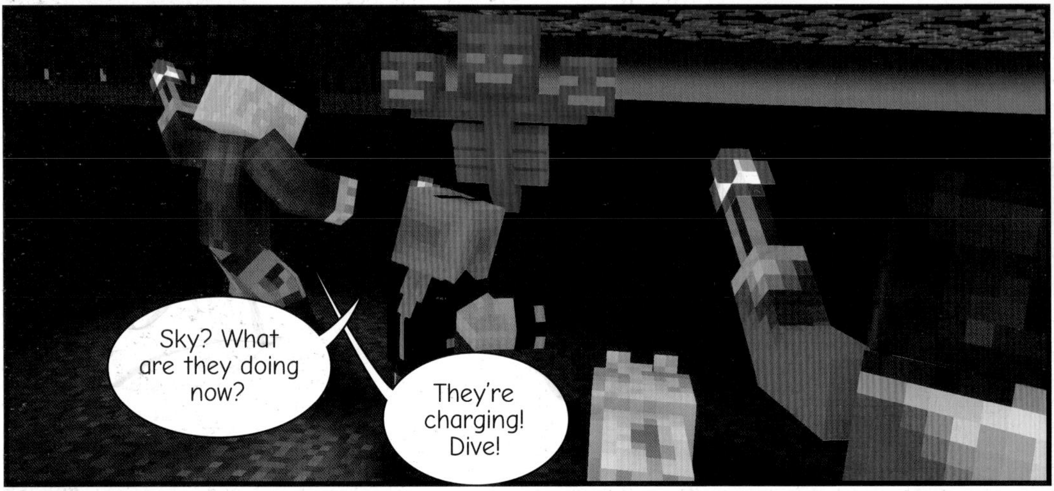
Sky? What are they doing now?
They're charging! Dive!

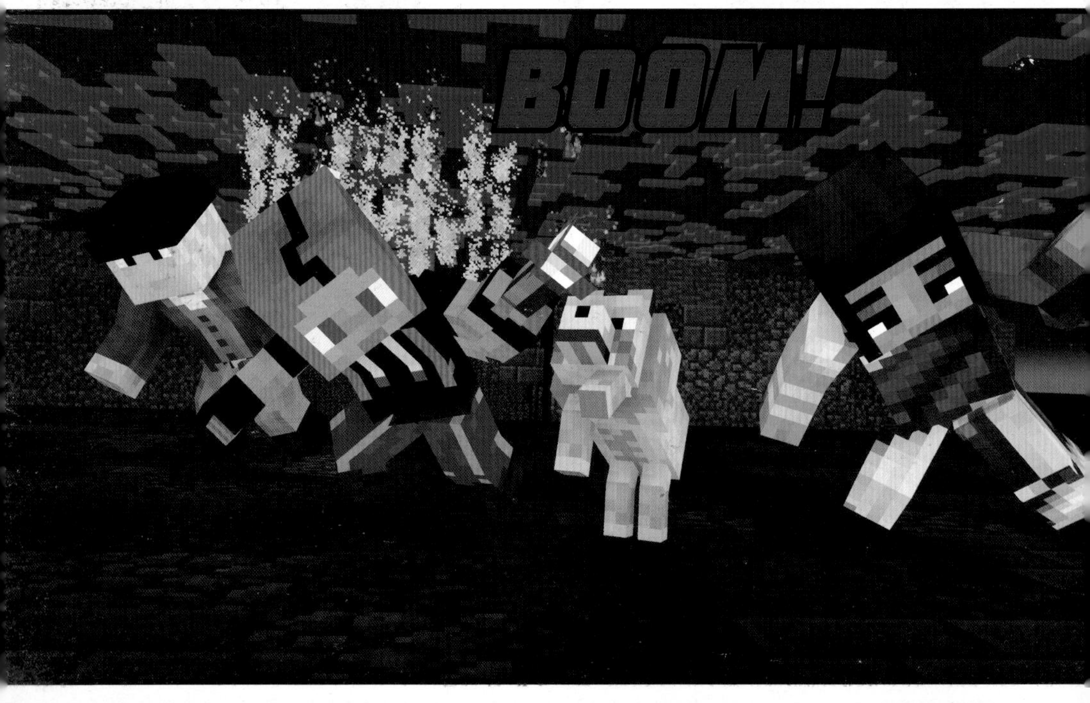
BOOM!

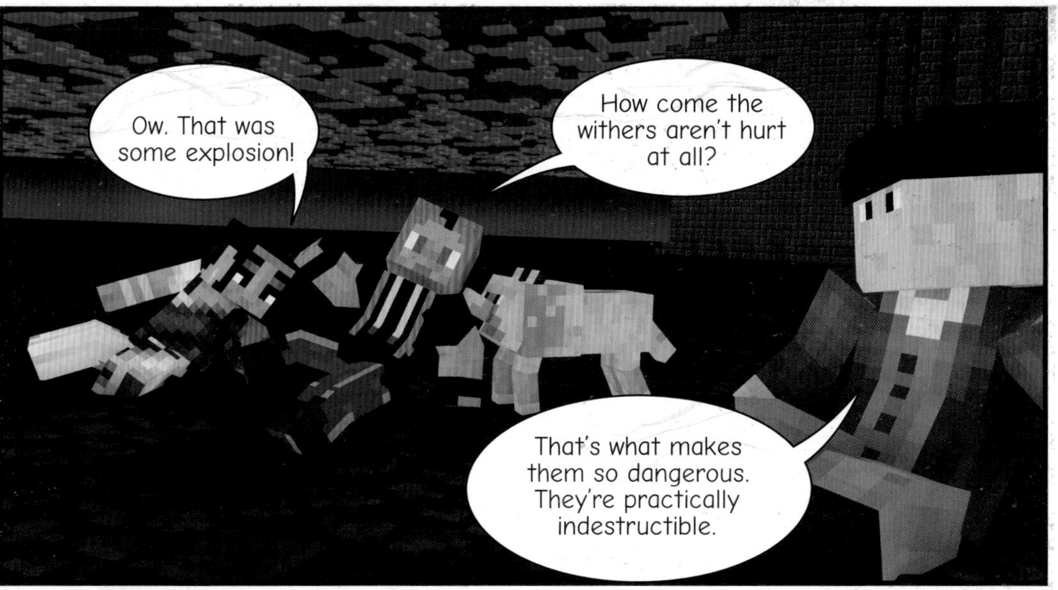
Ow. That was some explosion!
How come the withers aren't hurt at all?
That's what makes them so dangerous. They're practically indestructible.

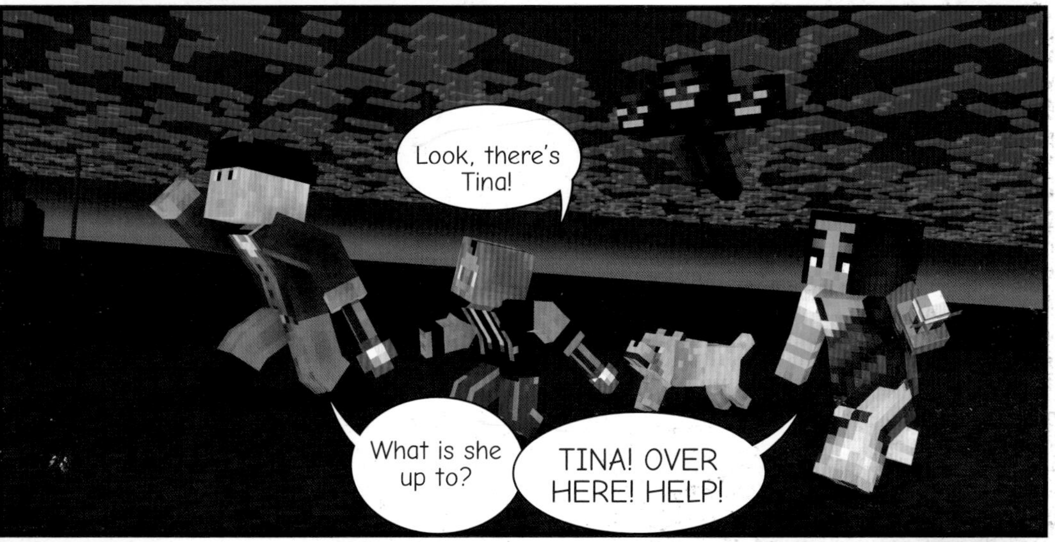
Look, there's Tina!
What is she up to?
TINA! OVER HERE! HELP!

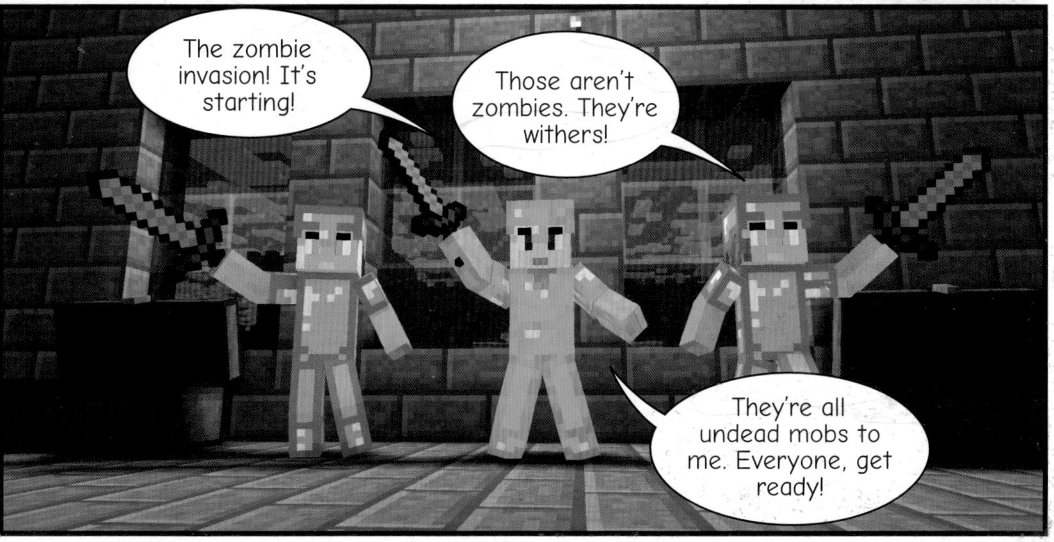
The zombie invasion! It's starting!
Those aren't zombies. They're withers!
They're all undead mobs to me. Everyone, get ready!

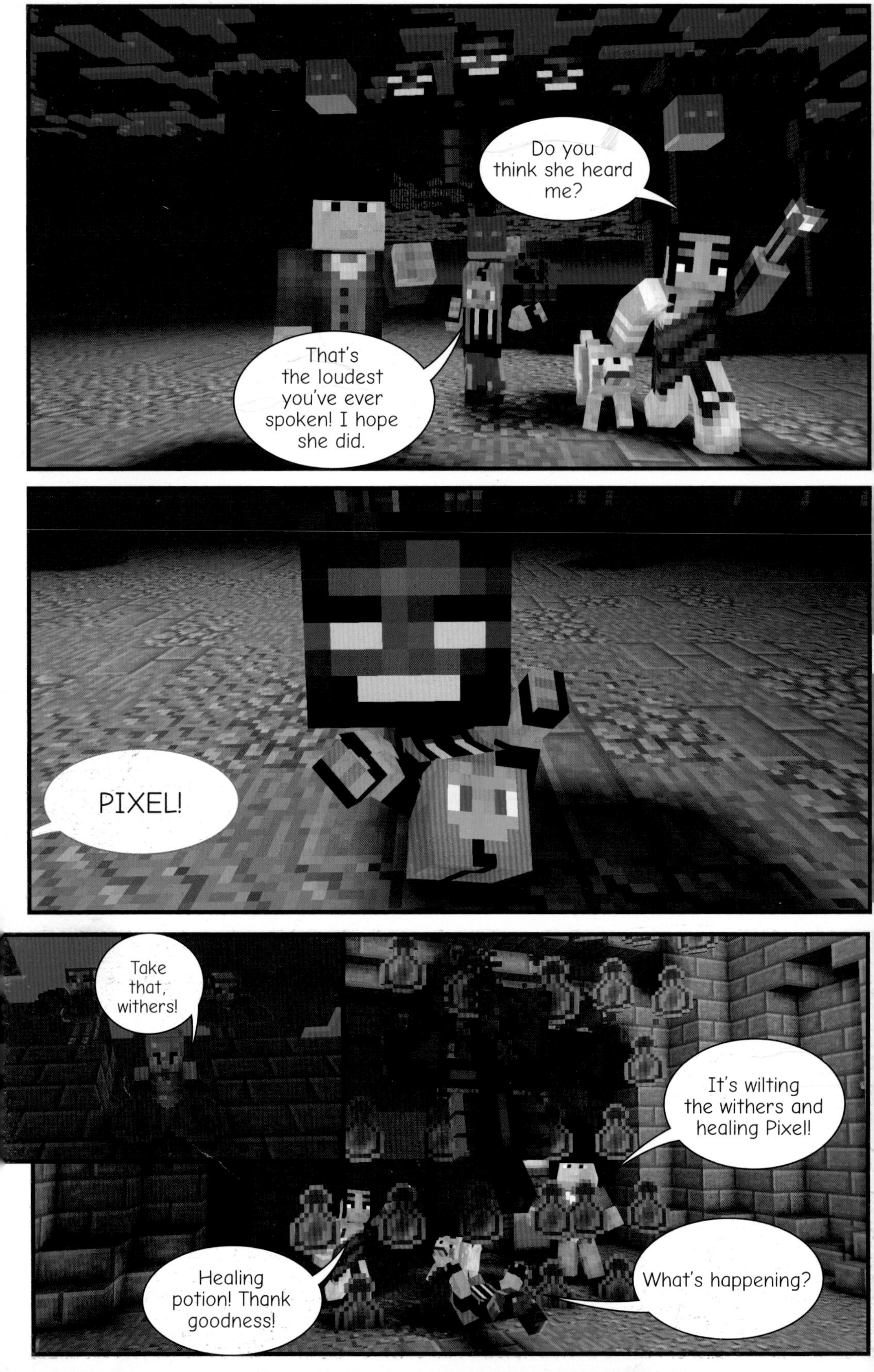
Do you think she heard me?
That's the loudest you've ever spoken! I hope she did.
PIXEL!
Take that, withers!
It's wilting the withers and healing Pixel!
What's happening?
Healing potion! Thank goodness!

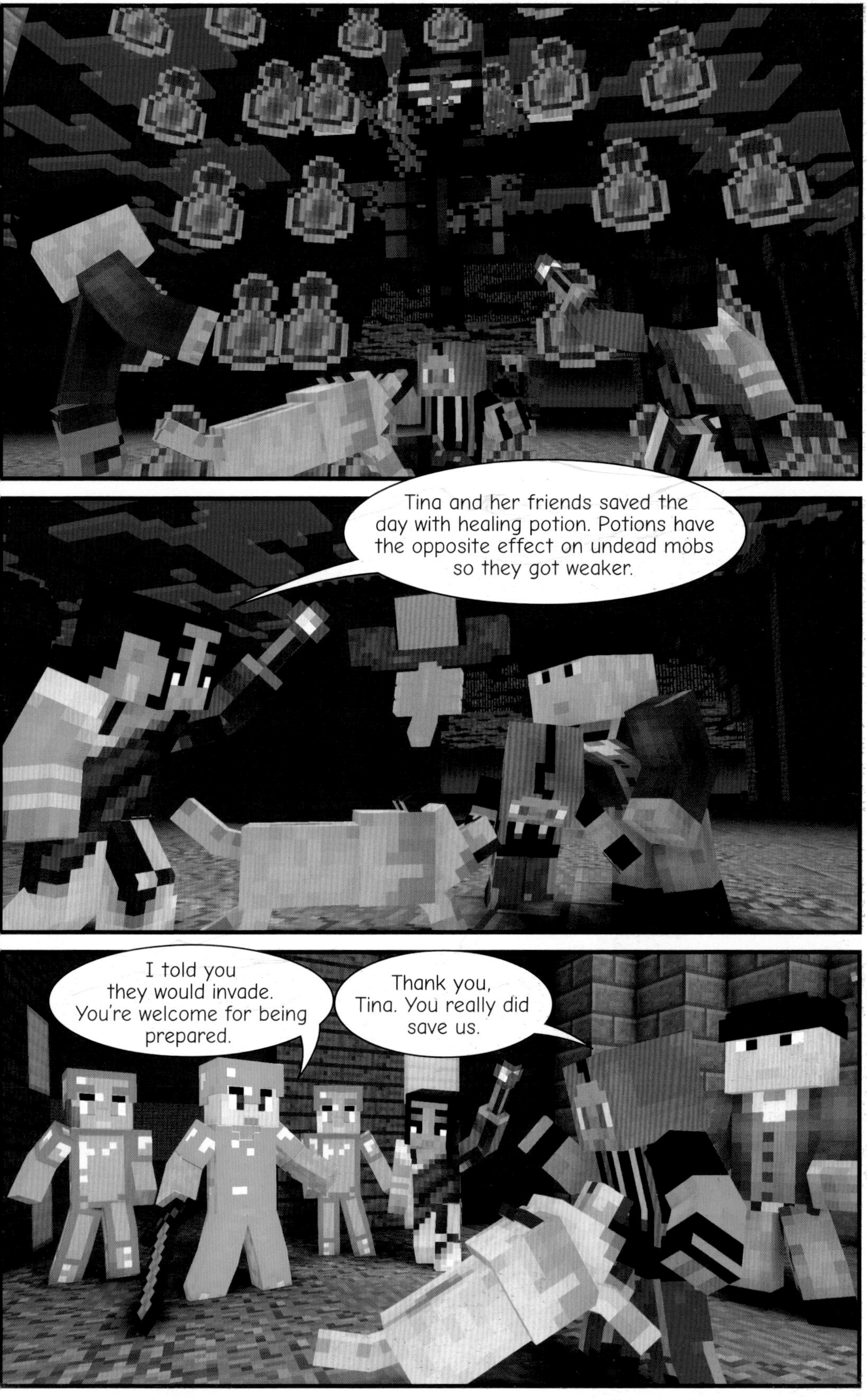
Tina and her friends saved the day with healing potion. Potions have the opposite effect on undead mobs so they got weaker.
I told you they would invade. You're welcome for being prepared.
Thank you, Tina. You really did save us.

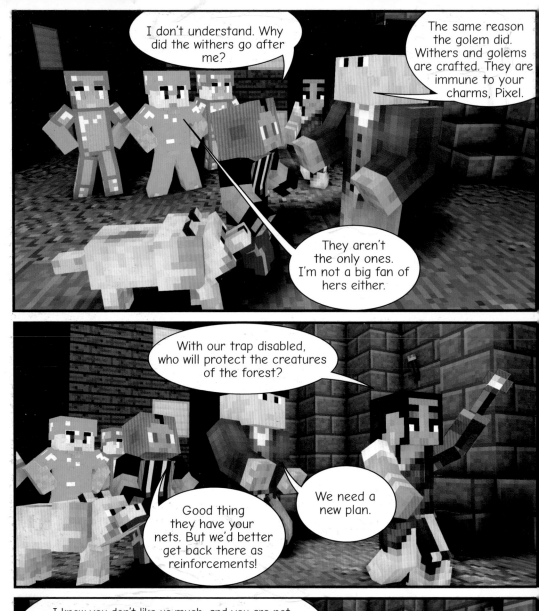

I don't understand. Why did the withers go after me?

The same reason the golem did. Withers and golems are crafted. They are immune to your charms, Pixel.

They aren't the only ones. I'm not a big fan of hers either.

With our trap disabled, who will protect the creatures of the forest?

We need a new plan.

Good thing they have your nets. But we'd better get back there as reinforcements!

I know you don't like us much, and you are not a fan of zombies either, but that ninja you met is destroying the forest and everything in it. Without a place to live, those creatures are going to come to Redstone Junior High. You wouldn't want that, would you?

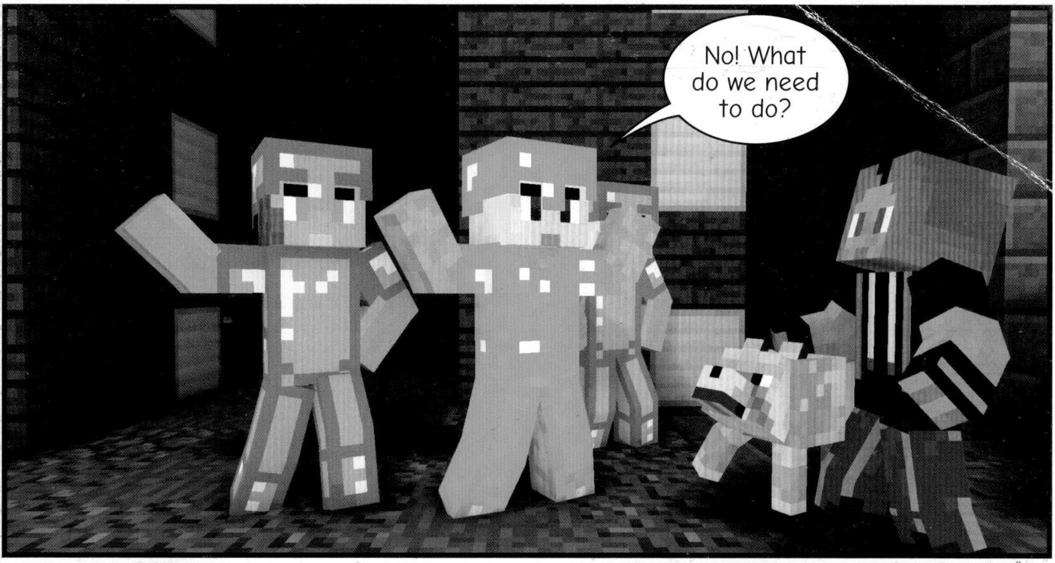
No! What do we need to do?

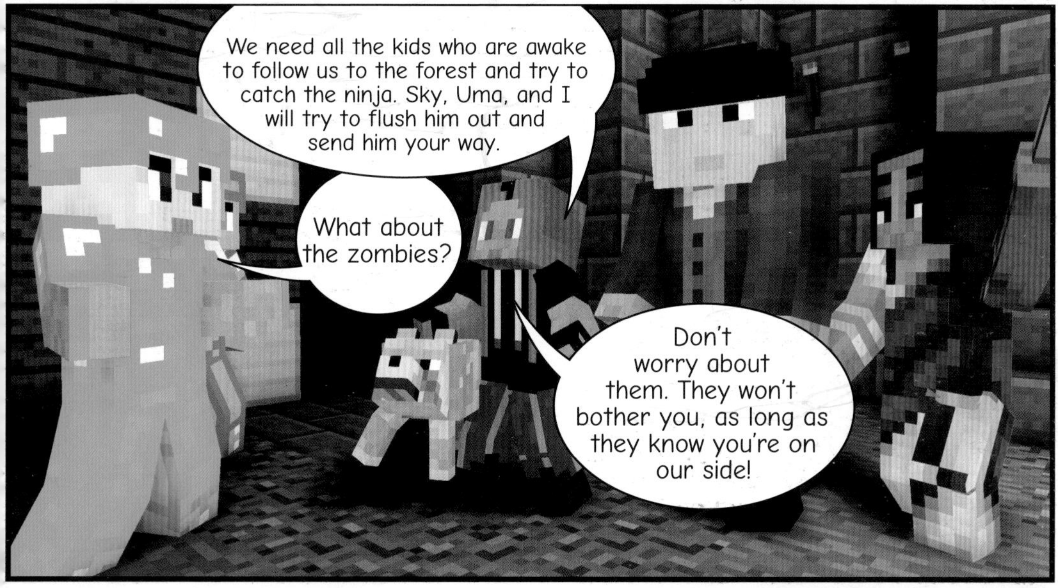
We need all the kids who are awake to follow us to the forest and try to catch the ninja. Sky, Uma, and I will try to flush him out and send him your way.
What about the zombies?
Don't worry about them. They won't bother you, as long as they know you're on our side!

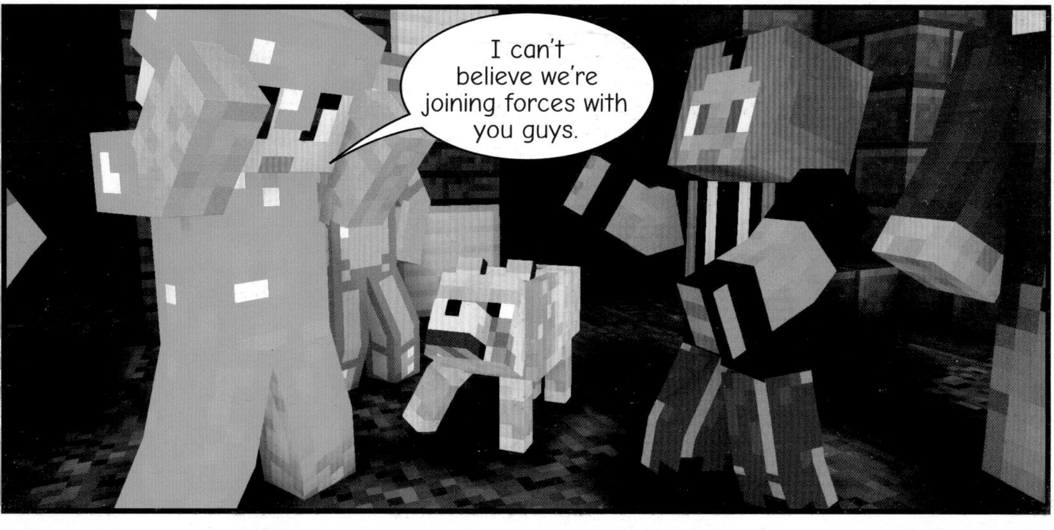
I can't believe we're joining forces with you guys.

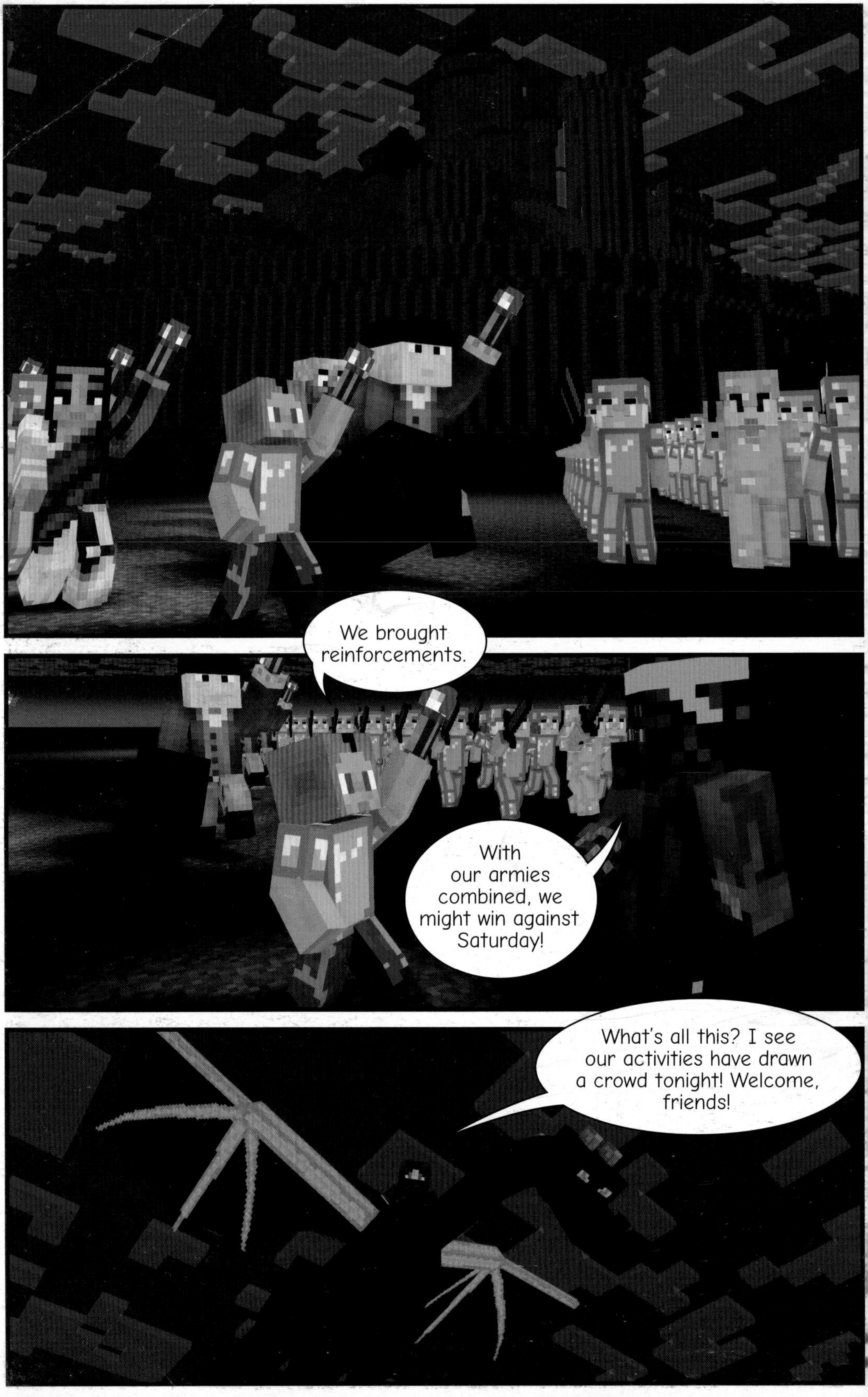
We brought reinforcements.
With our armies combined, we might win against Saturday!
What's all this? I see our activities have drawn a crowd tonight! Welcome, friends!

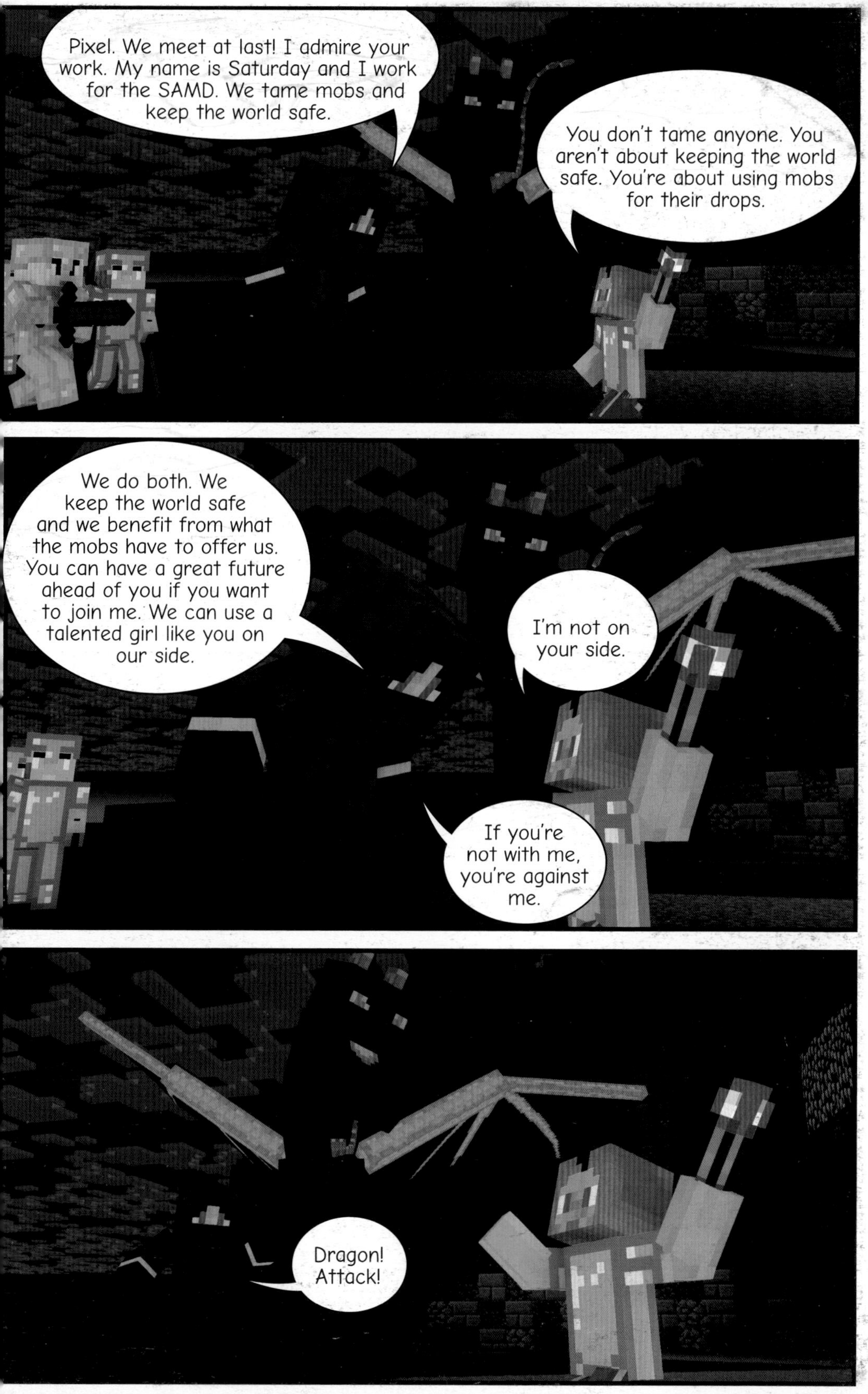
Pixel. We meet at last! I admire your work. My name is Saturday and I work for the SAMD. We tame mobs and keep the world safe.
You don't tame anyone. You aren't about keeping the world safe. You're about using mobs for their drops.
We do both. We keep the world safe and we benefit from what the mobs have to offer us. You can have a great future ahead of you if you want to join me. We can use a talented girl like you on our side.
I'm not on your side.
If you're not with me, you're against me.
Dragon! Attack!

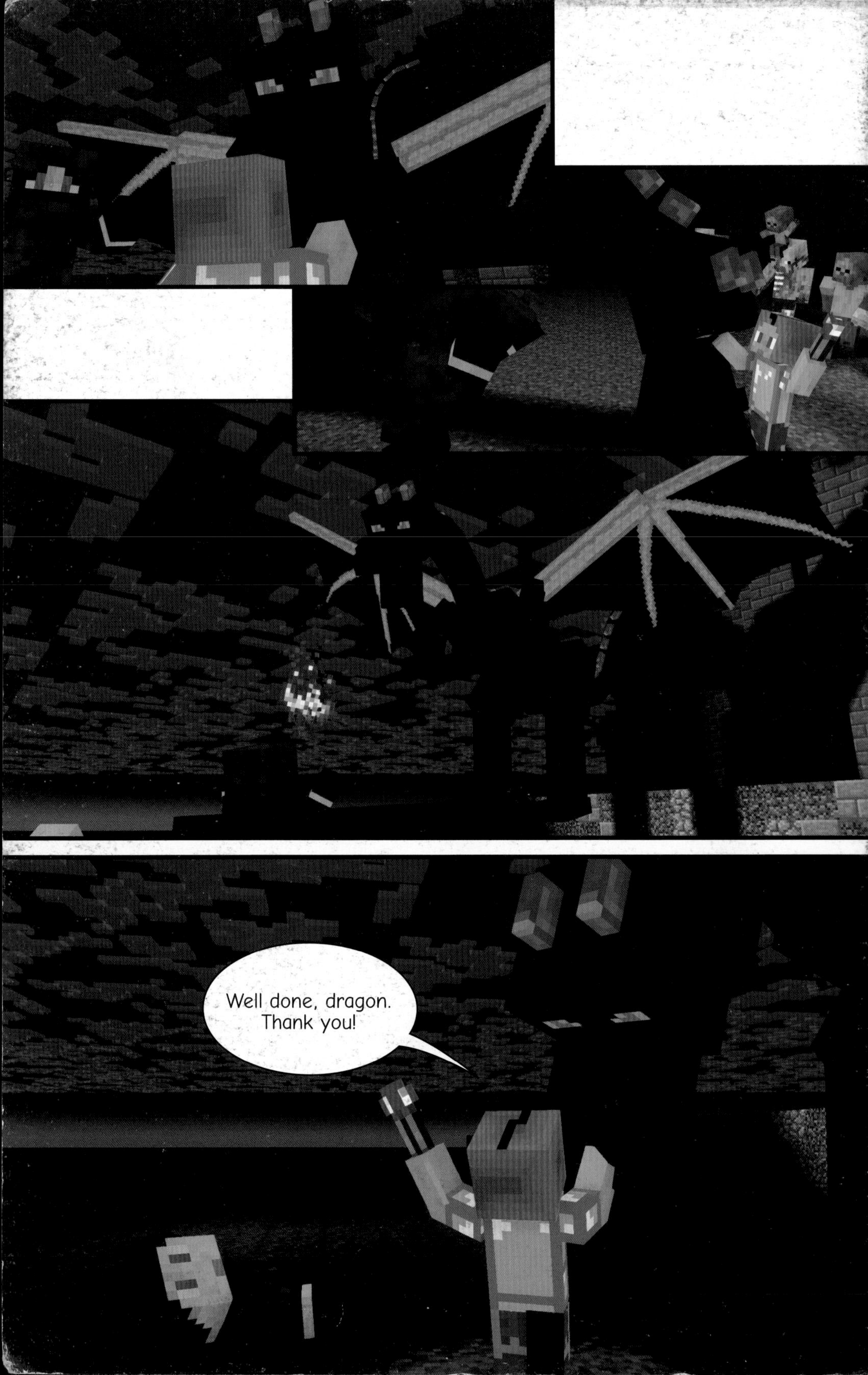
Well done, dragon. Thank you!

CHAPTER 12

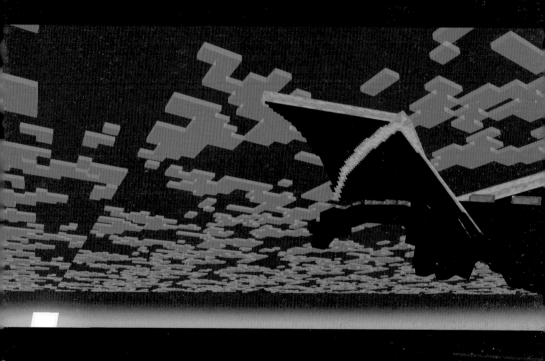

JUST THE BEGINNING

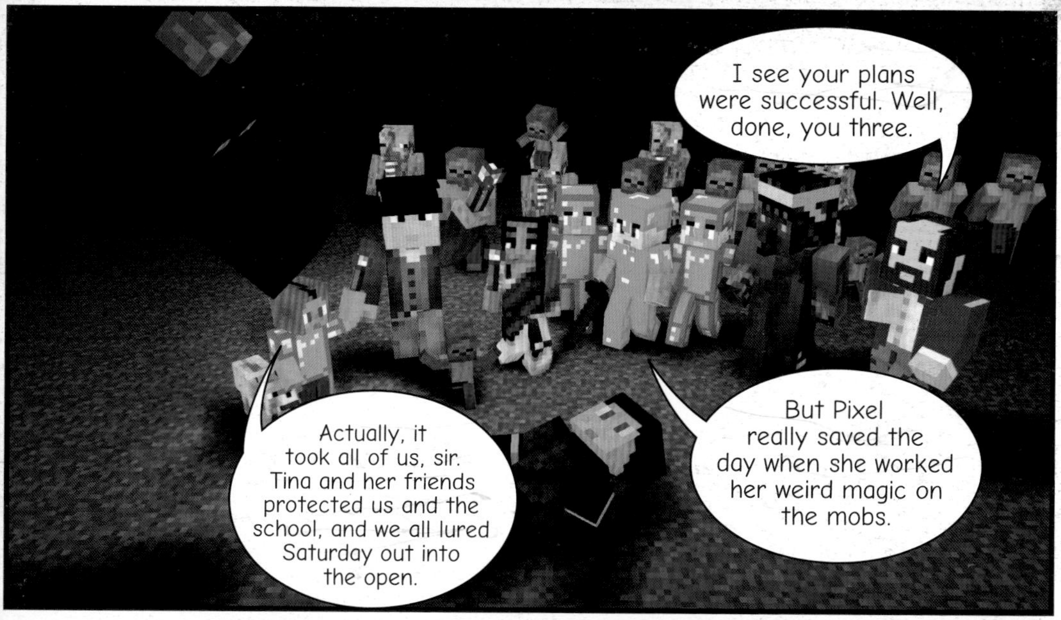
I see your plans were successful. Well, done, you three.
Actually, it took all of us, sir. Tina and her friends protected us and the school, and we all lured Saturday out into the open.
But Pixel really saved the day when she worked her weird magic on the mobs.

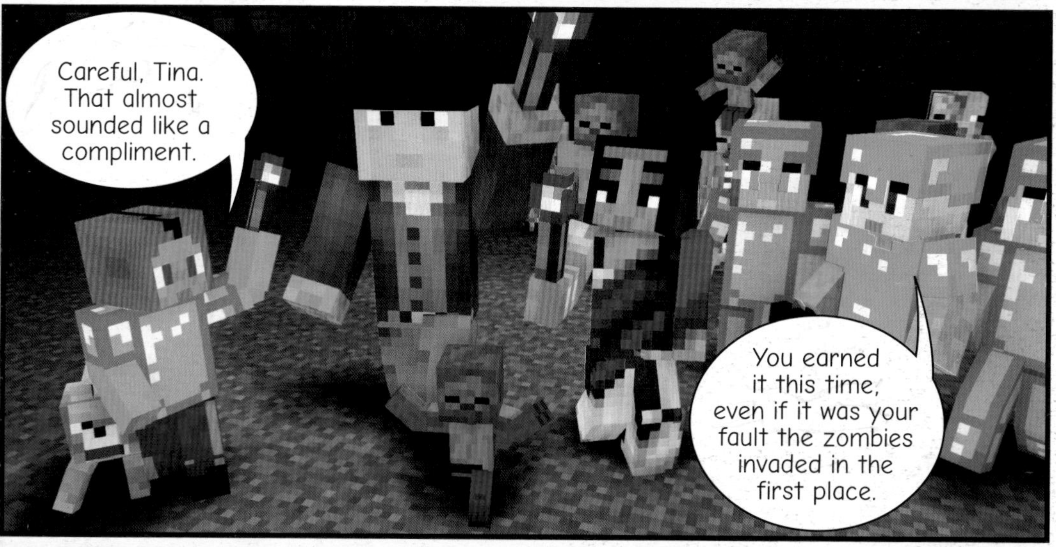
Careful, Tina. That almost sounded like a compliment.
You earned it this time, even if it was your fault the zombies invaded in the first place.

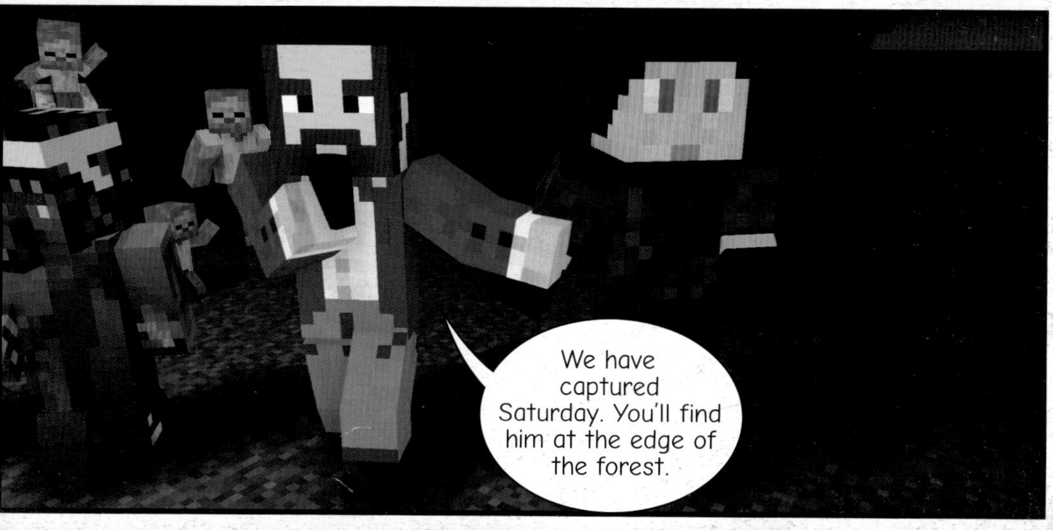
We have captured Saturday. You'll find him at the edge of the forest.

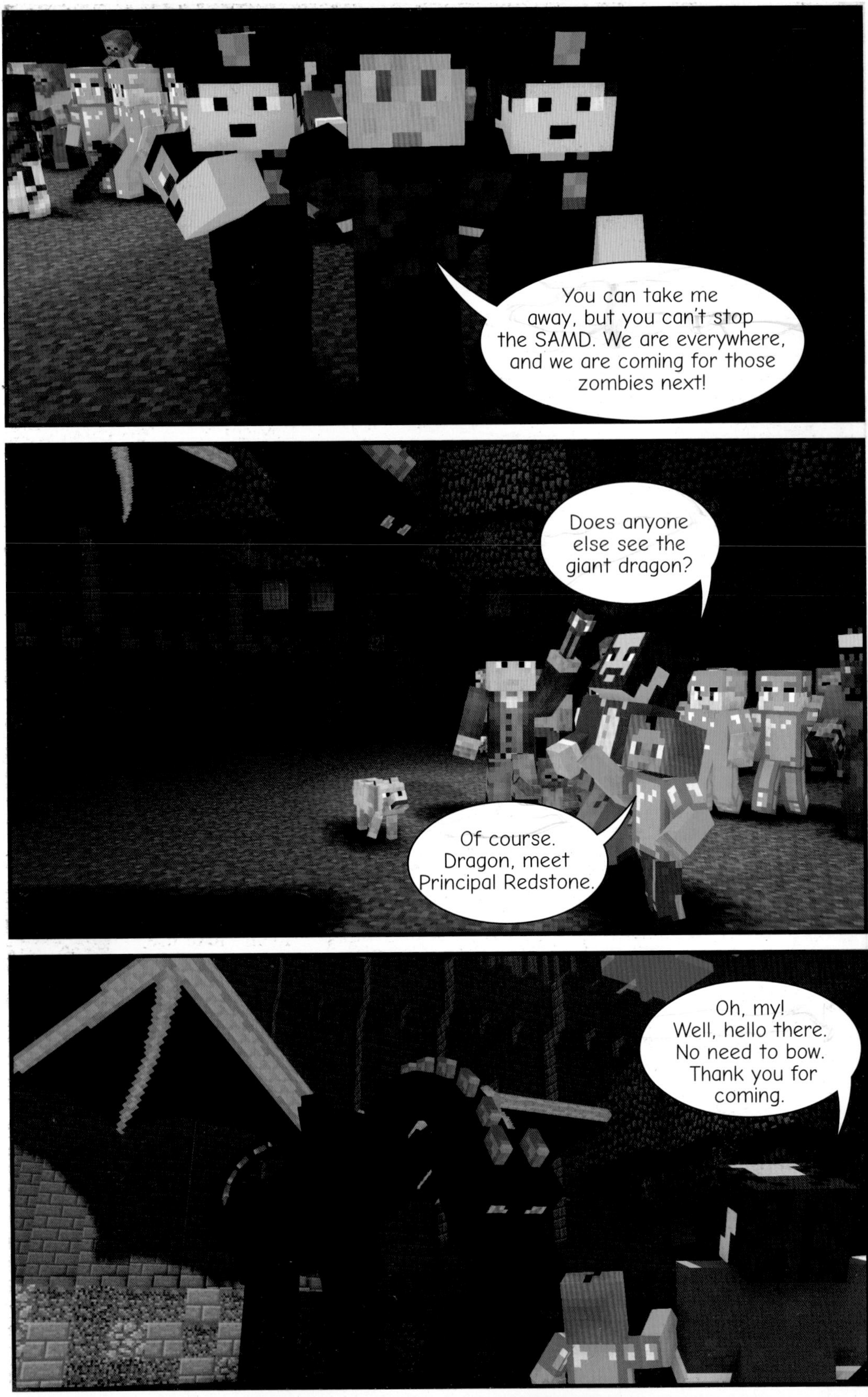
You can take me away, but you can't stop the SAMD. We are everywhere, and we are coming for those zombies next!
Does anyone else see the giant dragon?
Of course. Dragon, meet Principal Redstone.
Oh, my! Well, hello there. No need to bow. Thank you for coming.

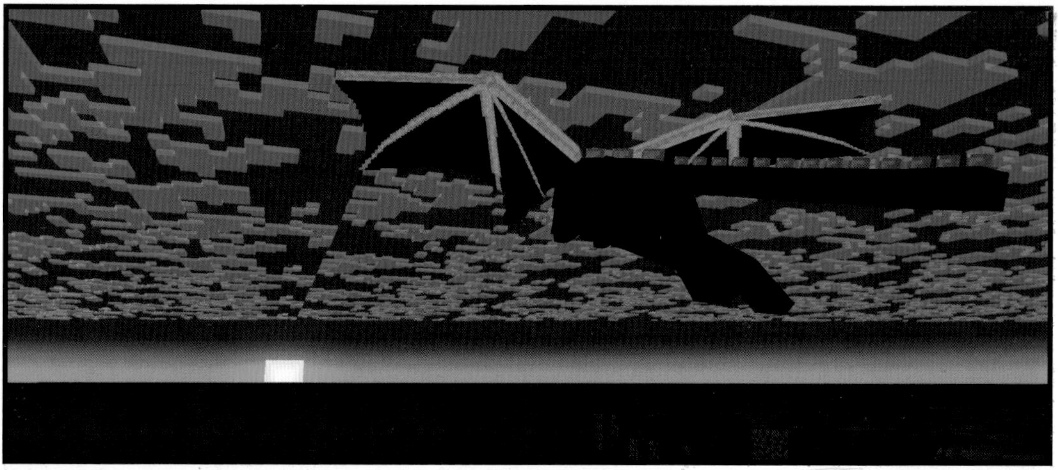

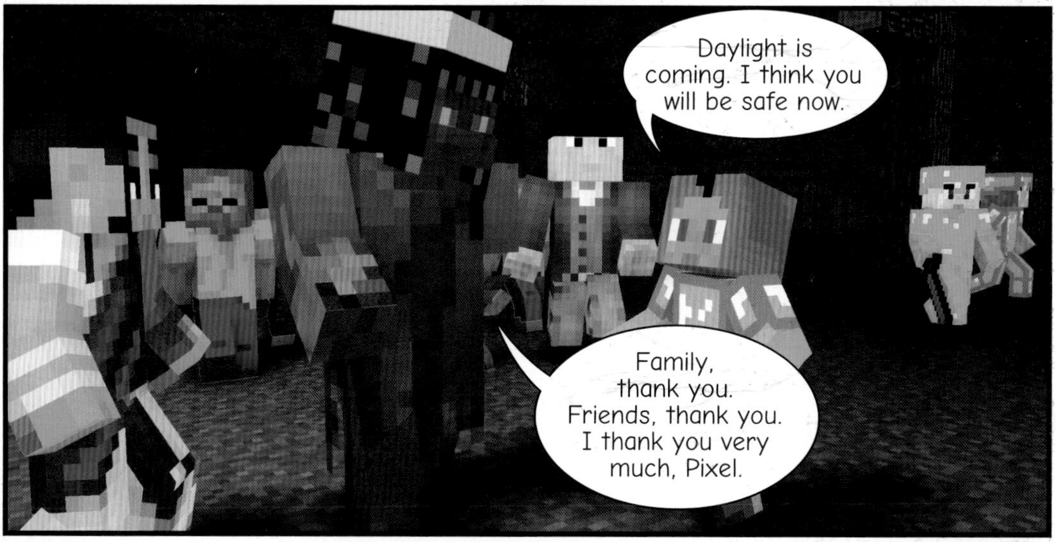
Daylight is coming. I think you will be safe now.
Family, thank you. Friends, thank you. I thank you very much, Pixel.

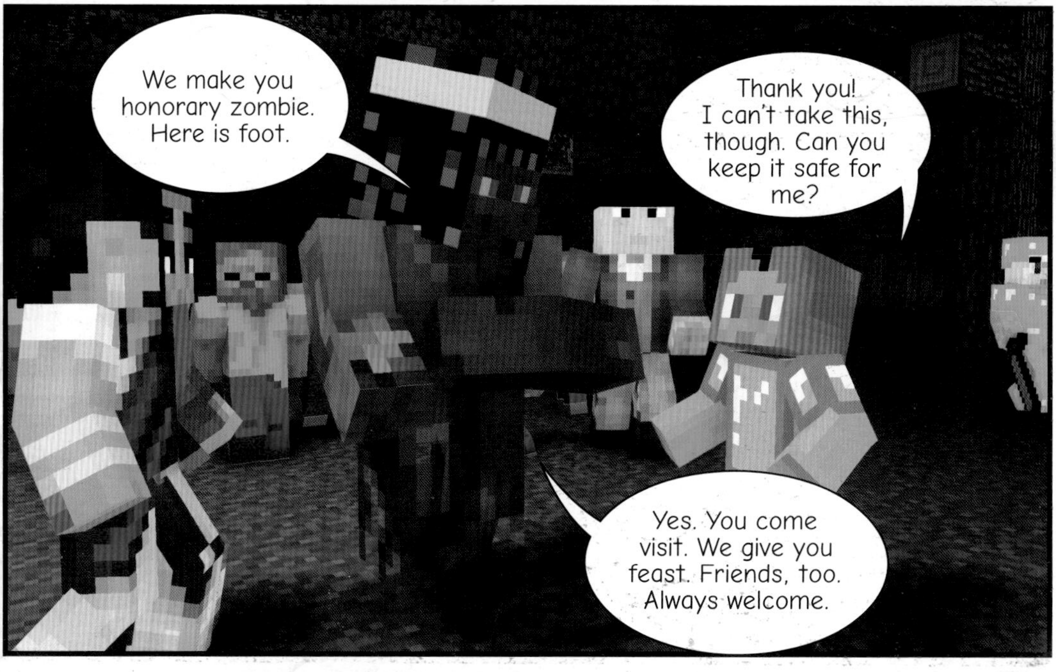
We make you honorary zombie. Here is foot.
Thank you! I can't take this, though. Can you keep it safe for me?
Yes. You come visit. We give you feast. Friends, too. Always welcome.

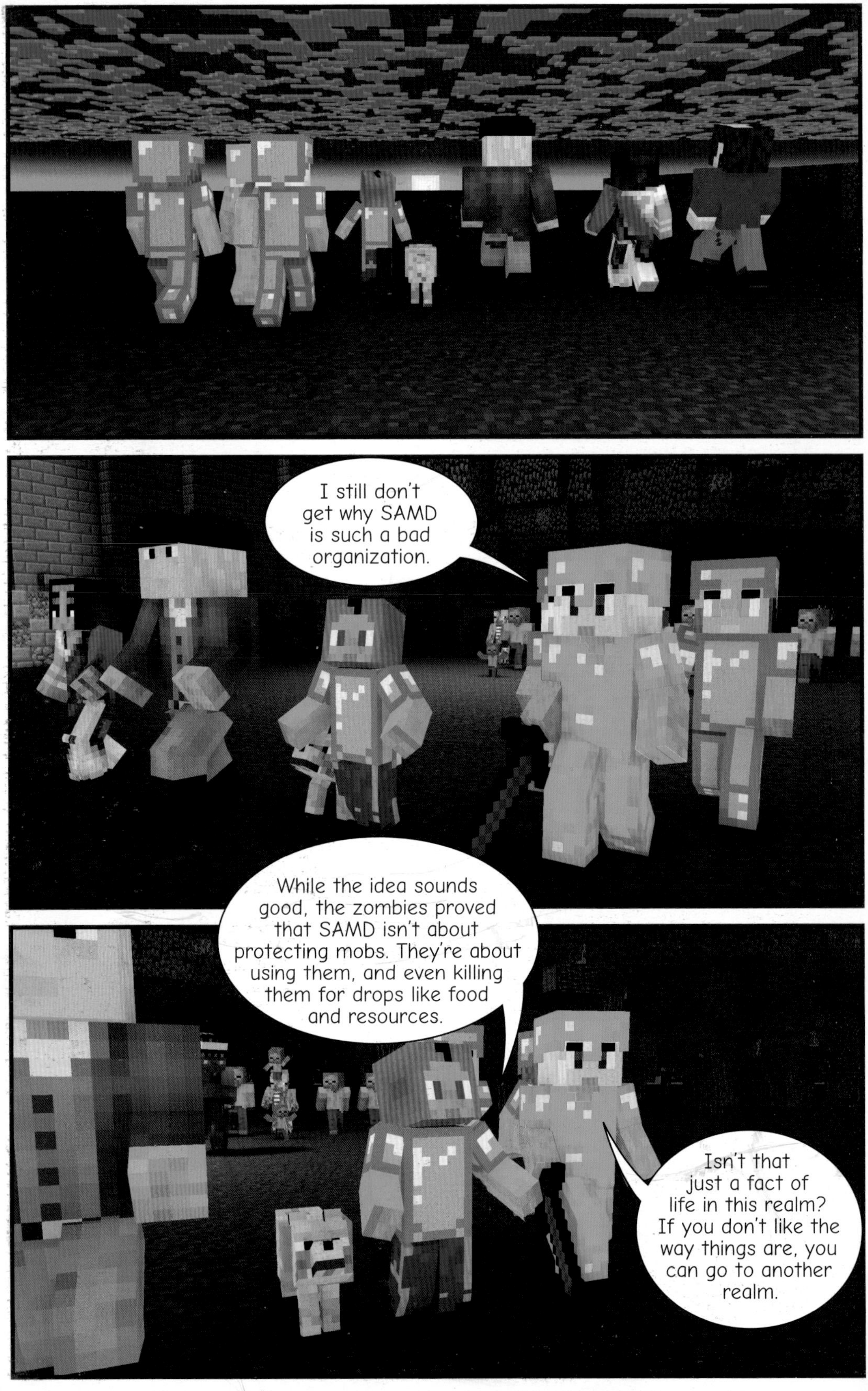
I still don't get why SAMD is such a bad organization.
While the idea sounds good, the zombies proved that SAMD isn't about protecting mobs. They're about using them, and even killing them for drops like food and resources.
Isn't that just a fact of life in this realm? If you don't like the way things are, you can go to another realm.

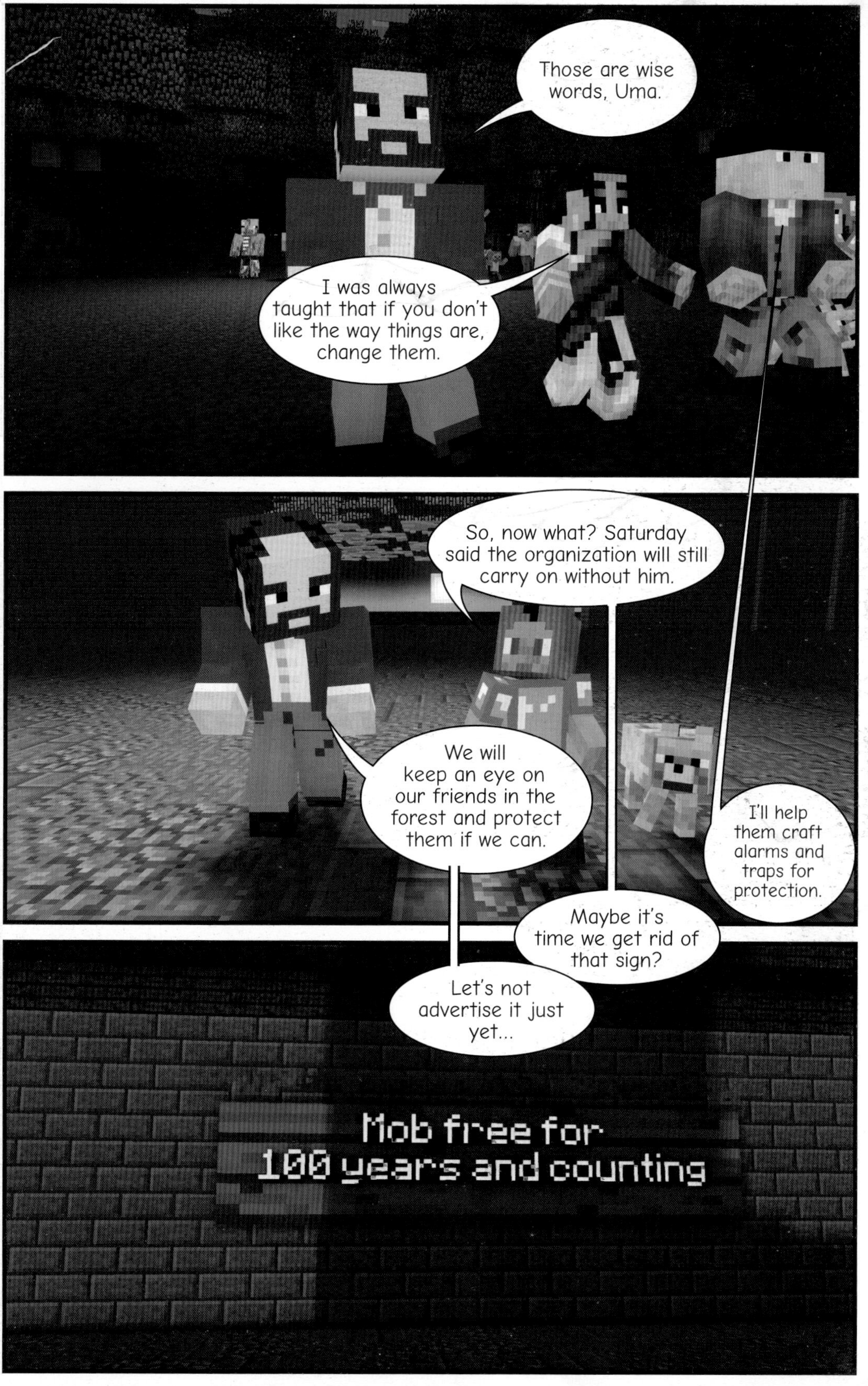
Those are wise words, Uma.
I was always taught that if you don't like the way things are, change them.
So, now what? Saturday said the organization will still carry on without him.
We will keep an eye on our friends in the forest and protect them if we can.
I'll help them craft alarms and traps for protection.
Maybe it's time we get rid of that sign?
Let's not advertise it just yet...
Mob free for
100 years and counting

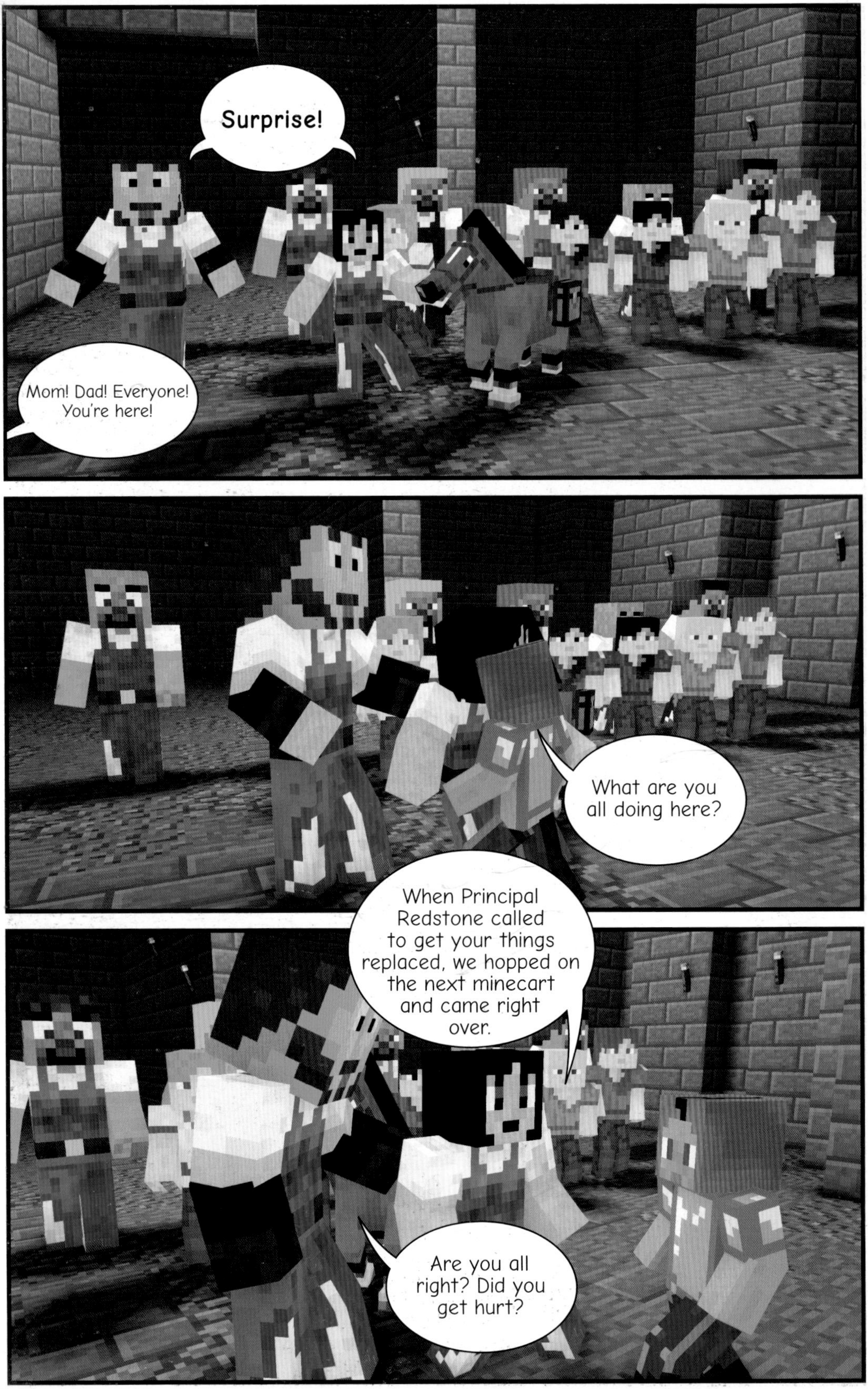
Surprise!
Mom! Dad! Everyone! You're here!
What are you all doing here?
When Principal Redstone called to get your things replaced, we hopped on the next minecart and came right over.
Are you all right? Did you get hurt?

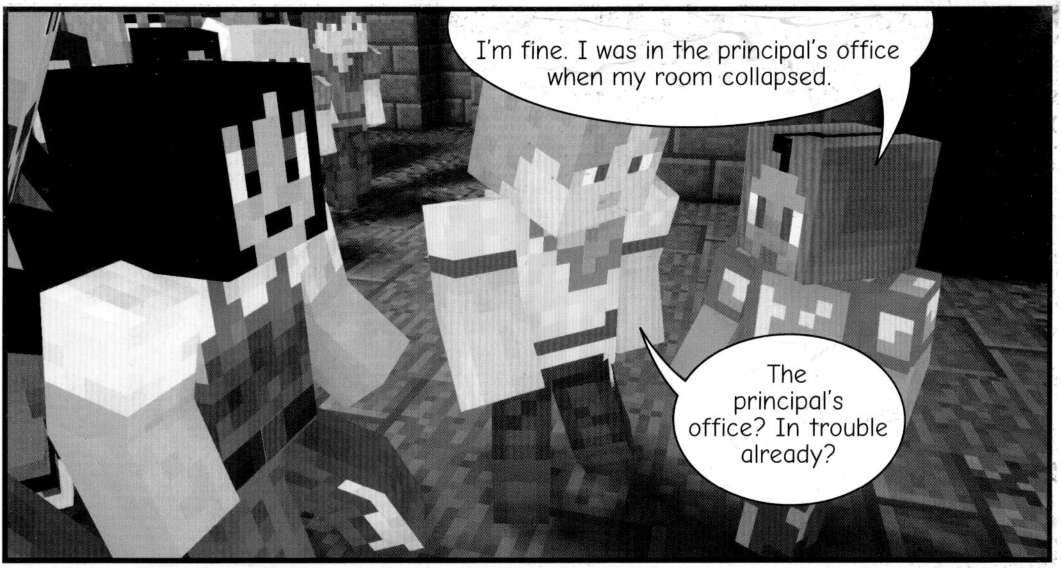
I'm fine. I was in the principal's office when my room collapsed.
The principal's office? In trouble already?

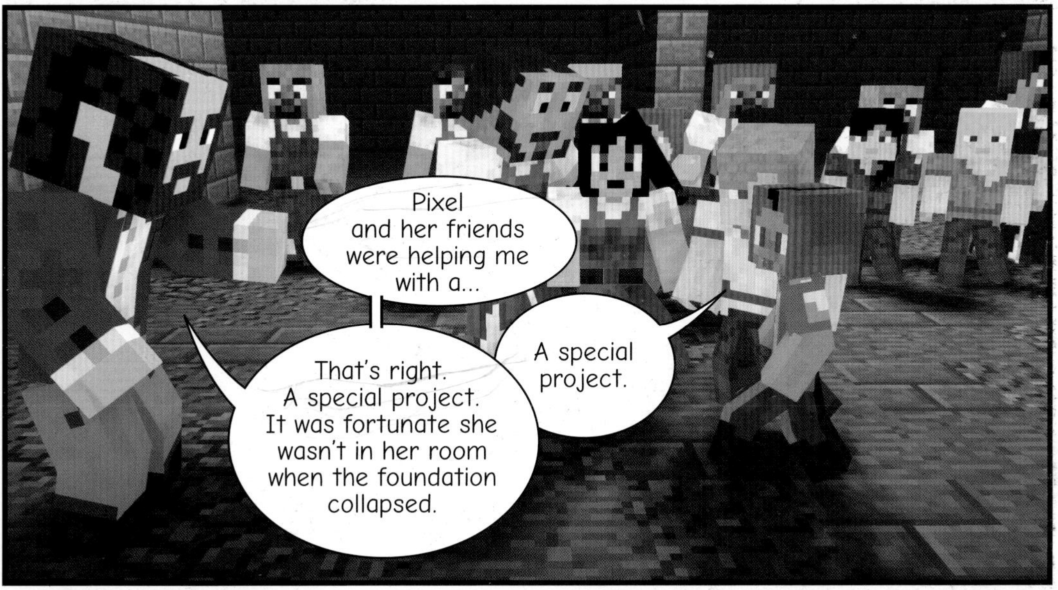
Pixel and her friends were helping me with a...
That's right. A special project. It was fortunate she wasn't in her room when the foundation collapsed.
A special project.

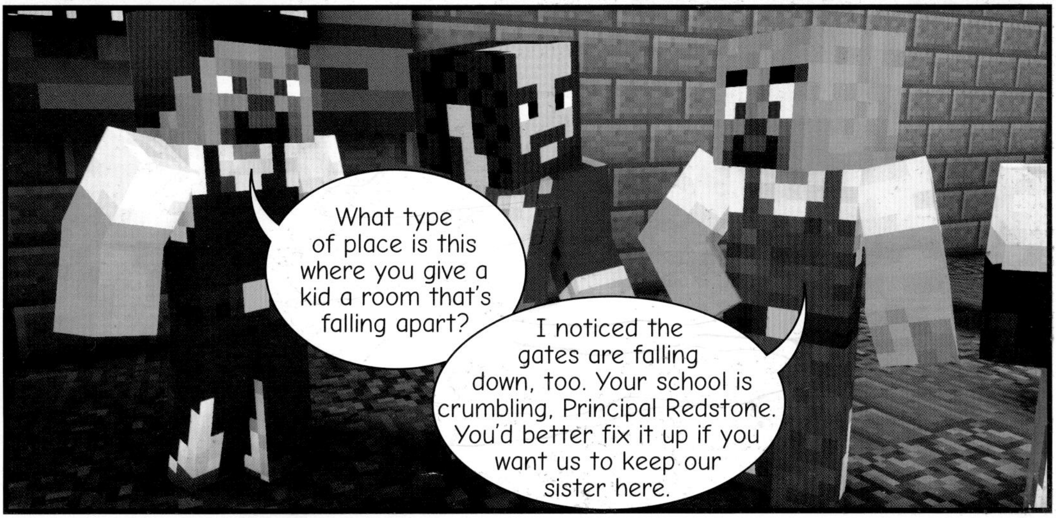
What type of place is this where you give a kid a room that's falling apart?
I noticed the gates are falling down, too. Your school is crumbling, Principal Redstone. You'd better fix it up if you want us to keep our sister here.

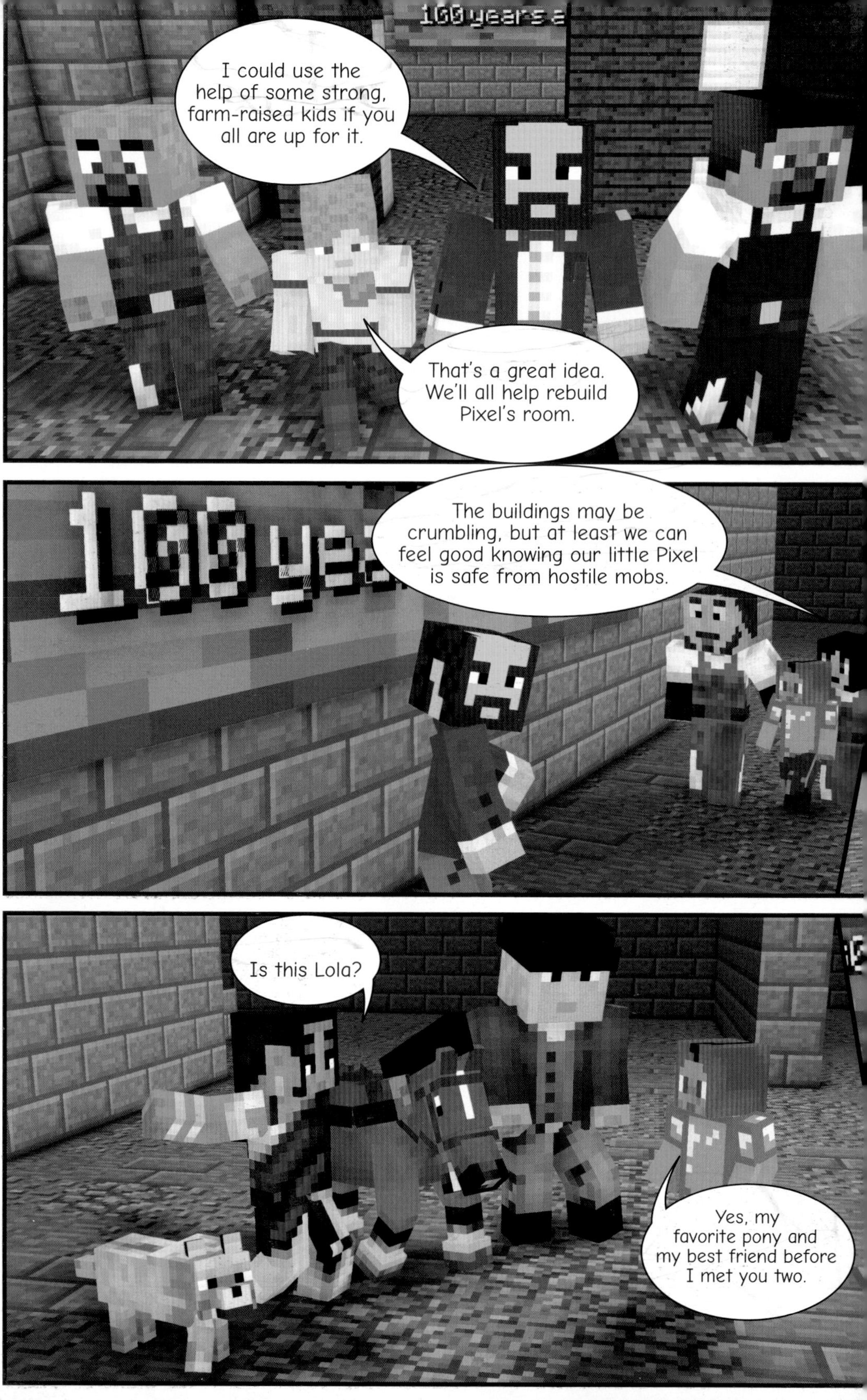

I could use the help of some strong, farm-raised kids if you all are up for it.
That's a great idea. We'll all help rebuild Pixel's room.
The buildings may be crumbling, but at least we can feel good knowing our little Pixel is safe from hostile mobs.
Is this Lola?
Yes, my favorite pony and my best friend before I met you two.

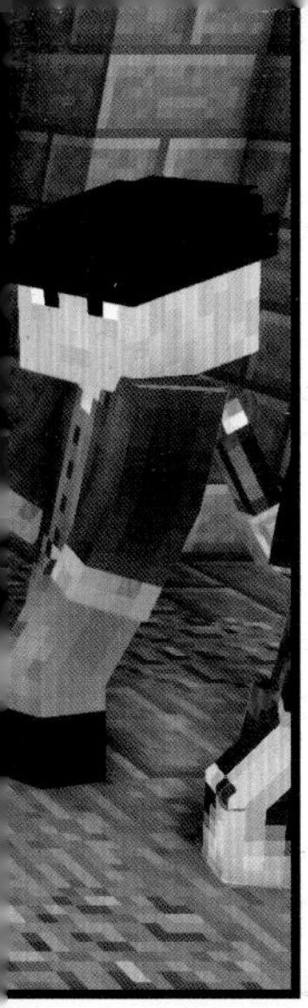

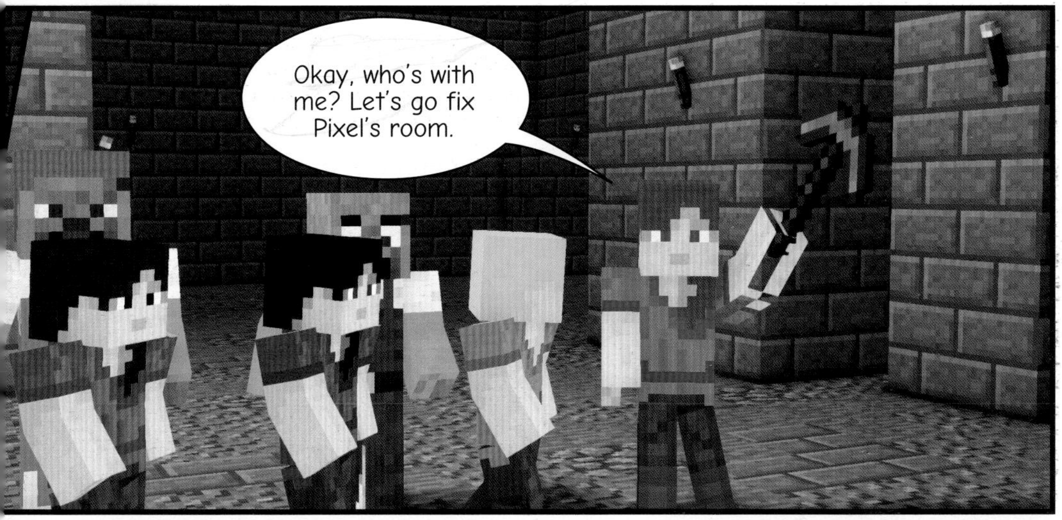

Okay, who's with me? Let's go fix Pixel's room.

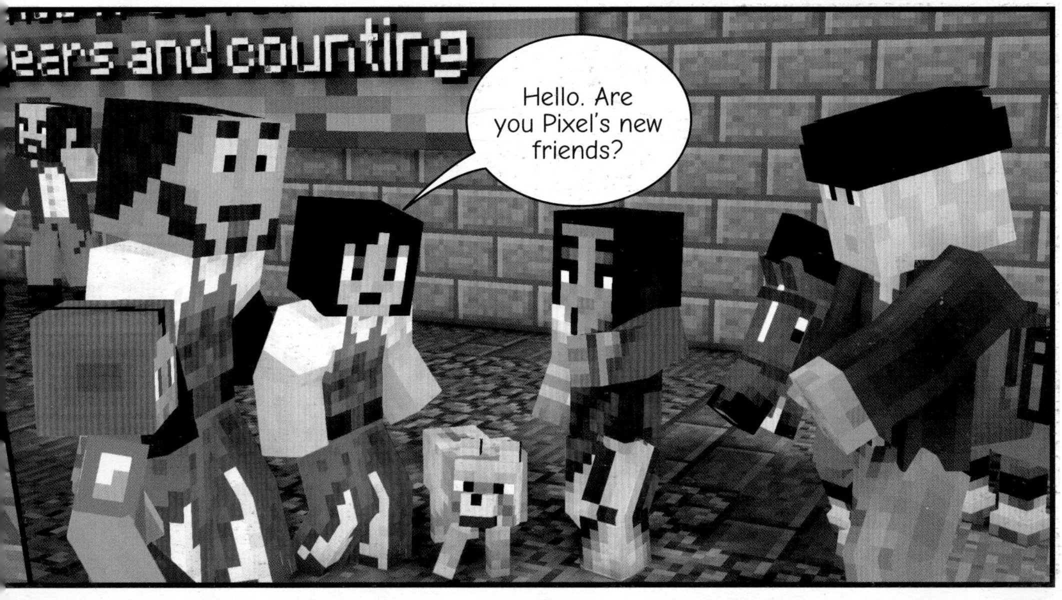

ears and counting
Hello. Are you Pixel's new friends?

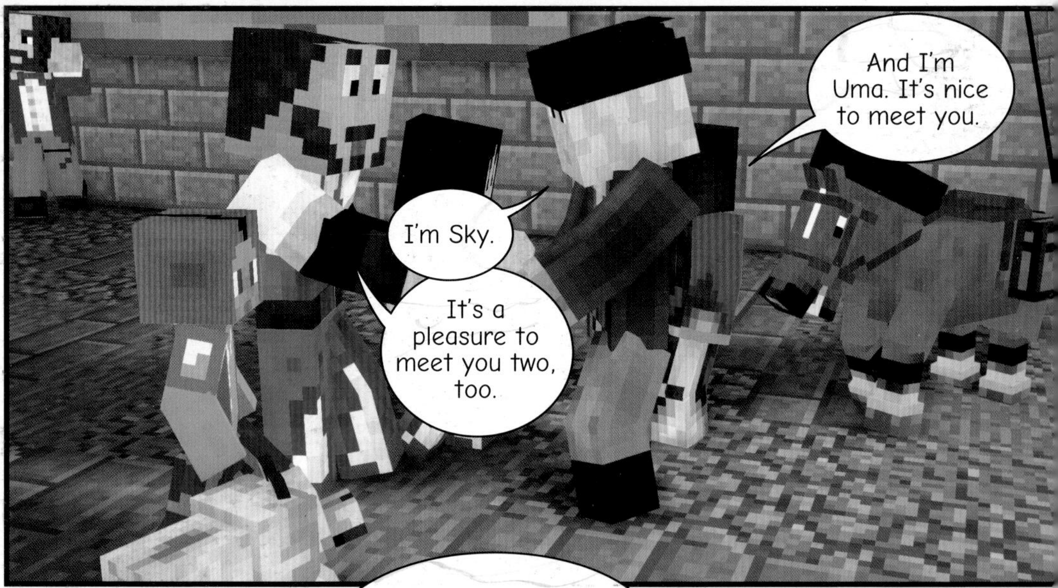
I'm Sky.
And I'm Uma. It's nice to meet you.
It's a pleasure to meet you two, too.

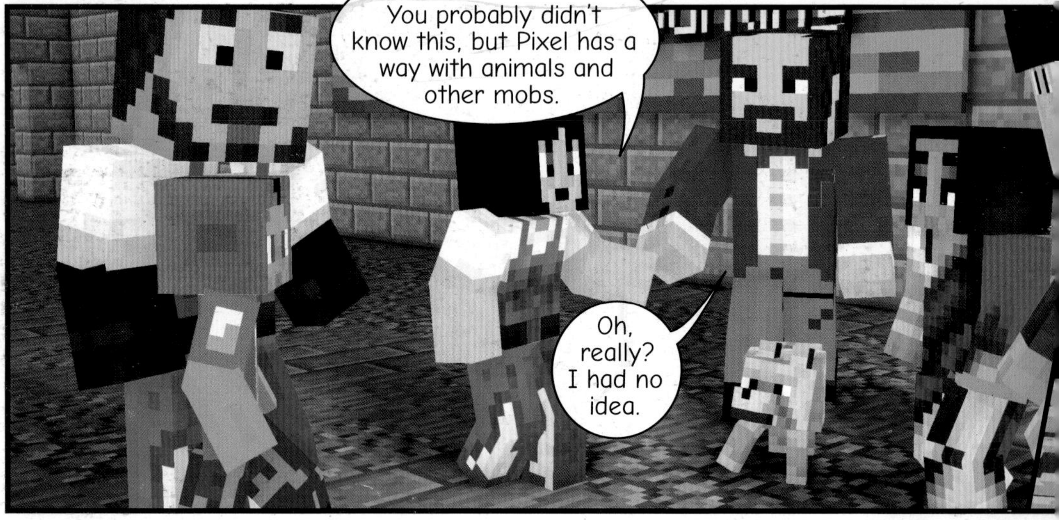
You probably didn't know this, but Pixel has a way with animals and other mobs.
Oh, really? I had no idea.

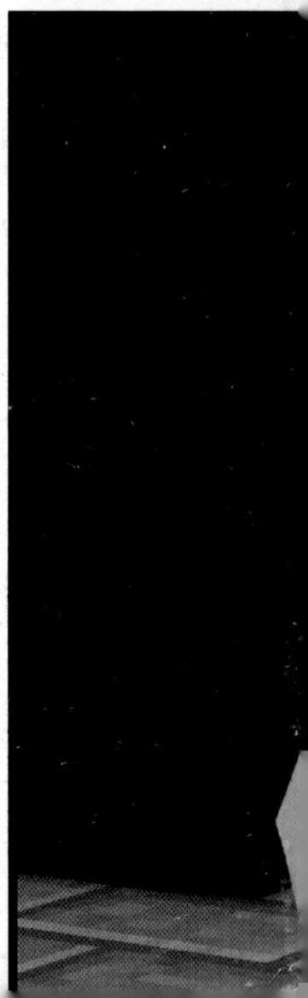

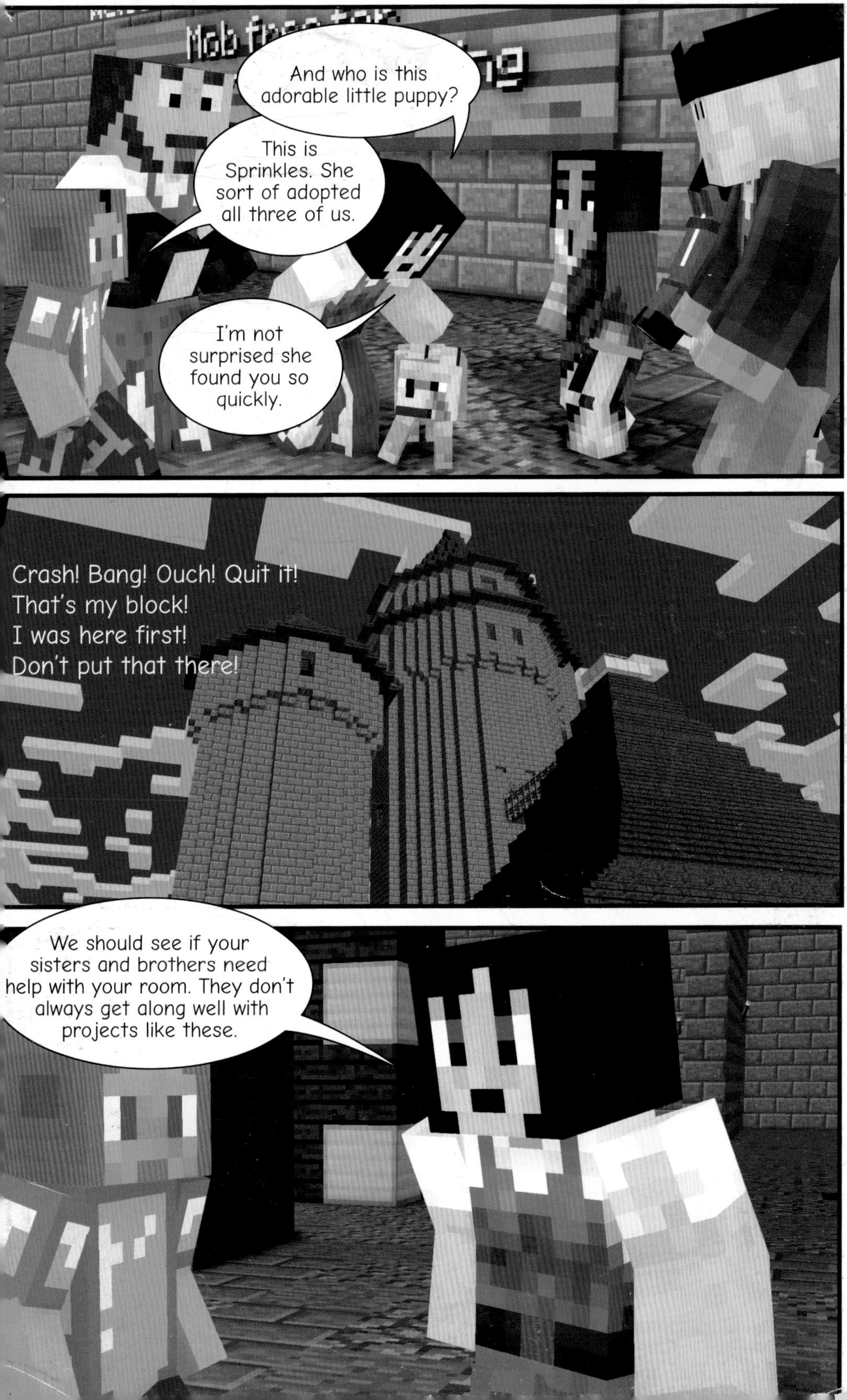
And who is this adorable little puppy?
This is Sprinkles. She sort of adopted all three of us.
I'm not surprised she found you so quickly.
Crash! Bang! Ouch! Quit it! That's my block! I was here first! Don't put that there!
We should see if your sisters and brothers need help with your room. They don't always get along well with projects like these.

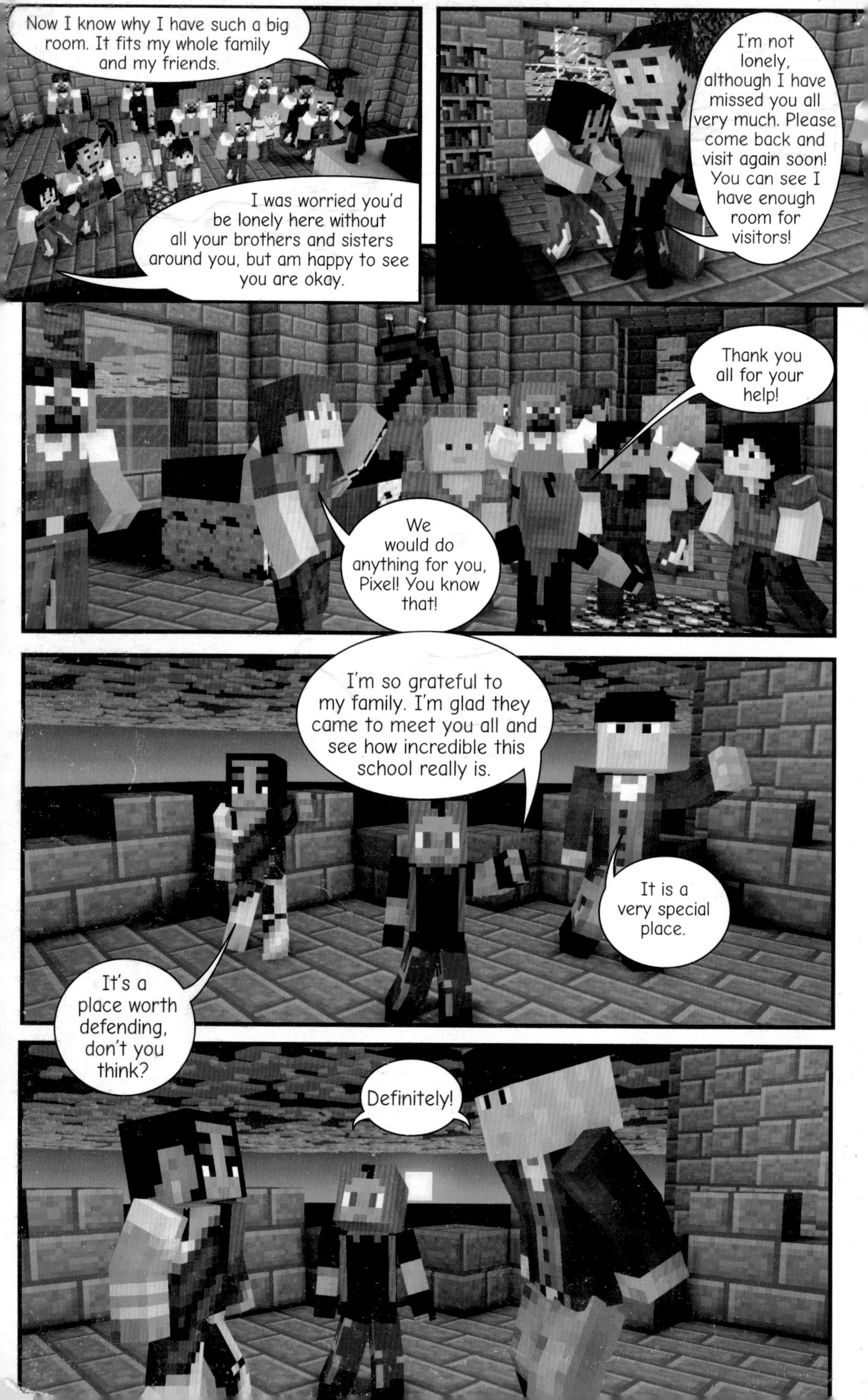
Now I know why I have such a big room. It fits my whole family and my friends.
I was worried you'd be lonely here without all your brothers and sisters around you, but am happy to see you are okay.
I'm not lonely, although I have missed you all very much. Please come back and visit again soon! You can see I have enough room for visitors!
Thank you all for your help!
We would do anything for you, Pixel! You know that!
I'm so grateful to my family. I'm glad they came to meet you all and see how incredible this school really is.
It is a very special place.
It's a place worth defending, don't you think?
Definitely!